Cursed Fate

Kassidy VanGundy

Ukiyoto Publishing

All global publishing rights are held by

Ukiyoto Publishing

Published in 2021

ISBN 9789354900099

Edition 1

www.ukiyoto.com

(Because I can't choose just one)

To my 18 year old self, who manifested this in her high school yearbook.

To my husband, Douglas. Thank you for rolling with the punches this past year. I wouldn't have finished this without your constant love and support.

To my family, who, combined with a plethora of anime, has provided plenty of inspiration for this book.

To my grandfather, who always responds to all of my good news with 'Holy F*ck!'

To anyone else who will attempt to psychoanalyze me after reading this: Leave it alone.

CONTENTS

Chapter 1

Black Leather

For the majority of his life, Vincent was more than accustomed to staring at the back of his mother's black leather car seat. Slowly, the black leather backside turned into the headrest in his aunt's car, next his grandmother's car, and then his neighbor's car until finally, he couldn't see the backside of any black leather headrest. It was replaced by a black tinted screen that could be rolled down if he had a question about where he was going. Most of the time, an old man with a barely functional voice guided him to where he needed to be. Today, however, should have been the singular day that he was able to stare at his mother's black leather headrest one last time before going off on his own, but unfortunately, he was trapped behind the black tinted glass once again, with Rosa who was checking his robes one last time to see if there were any overlooked spots.

"Don't worry, Mr. Vincent! You are going to be the best looking graduate there, I'll make sure of it. You've always been the most handsome child I have ever seen. I'm so proud of you!"

"Thanks Rosa, but you really don't have to make such a fuss -"

"Oh Mr. Vincent, please try to keep that cap on straight! Here take my bobby pin -"

"Rosa aren't those for girls?!"

"Shush!! You have the curly hair of a cherub and sometimes being an angel comes with a price. Now sit still! We are almost there Mr. Vincent.

Vincent spends some time finicking with his hair before sheepishly asking Rosa the question that's been on his mind since they both entered the car.

"Rosa, did mother send you to come watch?"

"No… Honey no, I'm sorry. I have to go back and take care of the house, but I am here now and I will hoard all the precious pictures for myself, I promise. Go ahead my sweet, you are doing a tremendous thing today. Don't be nervous."

With that, the decrepit gatekeeper of a driver opens the door for Vincent and leads him to the front of the school. Once again, nearly every single student gawks at Vincent for arriving in his stretch limo, even though he did this almost every single day. What makes matters worse are the looks he receives when they realize that not a single soul follows him out of the vehicle. Again, the boy is made to be a pitiful spectacle, elite but without family. From this day on, Vincent vows to never again be placed behind black glass.

After the guest speaker and other such formalities, Vincent and the rest of his peers only have to listen to one final speech before they can begin the procession to receive their diplomas: the valedictorian's. She rises and glides to the podium, her figure as lanky as can be. Her entire limited body weight is necessary in order to support such an unruly mess of hair. After a pompous cough to clear her throat, she fakes charming nervousness to begin her monologue.

"Good afternoon parents, teachers, and the class of 2019. Today marks the first day of the rest of our lives and the next chapter in our story. Will I continue to be a supporting character in your future stories? A protagonist? An antagonist? Who knows for sure? We all write our own futures and must always look ahead towards brighter things, unless you are planning to write another *Crime and Punishment*."

A few 'educated' laughs ring from the crowd.

"Some stories rely on a network of talented heroes to save the world, like *The Lord of the Rings,* while others focus more on a lone wolf or the singular struggles of a warrior like the *Odyssey*. We must choose for ourselves where we fit into the narrative of society and who we want to accompany us in all of our battles. I really hope to continue to play a small part in the plots in the rest of your lives, because I honestly could not have gotten where I am today without the support system of my friends and my peers. Thank you!"

While everyone else claps after her speech, Vincent snickers loudly under his breath at her last sentence, as if discretion didn't apply to the situation anymore. The sound causes a blonde vixen from previous math classes to lock eyes with Vincent and let out an equally condescending giggle.

"Oh Vinny, you are so funny, picking on the poor girl. You know she hasn't had the same sort of privileges that you and I had growing up. You could at least pretend to be nice for one speech."

"Oh you know what else is funny? I didn't know that we're so similar. Thank you for making me realize what good friends we really are."

She scoffs at him, but can't suppress her interest.

"Vinny, you don't need to be so cold and tough all the time. It's okay to have people who care about you by your side when you can't do things by yourself."

She rests her snow white hand on Vincent's knee.

"If you need to, you can put some of that weight on me."

After a pause, the blonde blushes and can no longer make eye contact with him. He was disappointed that once again, a conversation that had the potential to actually mean something turned into another ploy.

"I have no idea what you are talking about! I have plenty of guys to call on if I need help and I'm sure you do as well, or girls. Whatever, but trust me, a girl like that doesn't have a lot of friends."

Vincent mutters the rest of his thoughts underneath his breath, but it's not like the blonde really had any interest in it anyway.

"The more you try to climb straight to the top, the faster you forget about the people trapped below..."

At this moment, Vincent scans the crowd of parents out of the corner of his eye, searching for her. Dissatisfied, he returns to the golden distraction dangling off of his cap and after her failed attempt at flirtation, the blonde turns promptly back around in order to avoid any further embarrassment. Another plump girl near the scene giggles at this interaction, but Vincent hardly notices. He's too busy pondering over how the hell he can casually sneak out of the rest of the ceremony after receiving his diploma while wearing such a gaudy crimson robe.

Eventually, Vincent makes it out to the front lawn of the school only to be bombarded with other brand new alumni begging for pictures to document their friendship. He is obligated to pose with his team mates from track, seeing how he was the captain that lead them to state and ended up breaking a national conference record, but he's also desperate to get out of there before he is forced to spew some motivational quotes stolen from numerous films in order to get the others to be fired up about their own individual futures.

However, the girls are even worse.

Several cheerleaders, female athletes, party girls, future women's rights activists, and many more of the like all flock around Vincent as if this is their last chance to be courted for the rest of their lives. It's as if no woman in that building could resist tight black curls paired with smoldering eyes and an apathetic face. He picks out a few of his favorites from each variety, gives them each their fifteen seconds of fame and a tiny forced smile, before sending them away to their families.

But it is their families that ultimately causes Vincent to absolutely lose it.

One of the fathers of the sprinters corners Vincent after the photo with his son and gives him the most disgusting bear hug anyone could imagine. When he sets Vincent back down, he draws him closer in and gently whispers.

"You know it's a shame that your mother couldn't be here tonight, but don't worry! I made extra sure to take plenty of pictures for her just in case - just like I did at every track meet too. If you ever need it, Vinny, you are always welcome in my home, especially after all you did for my boy!"

The man forcibly pats Vincent on the back, knocking Vincent off his balance a little bit. Vincent's face lets it be known that he is extremely displeased in this situation, which causes the man to awkwardly chuckle before putting his foot even further into his mouth.

"You can always count on your 'track dad'!"

Vincent loses it.

"You should be a little more careful about giving out that title so freely. You can't claim me just because my parents aren't around. Trust me, you wouldn't want me for a son and I sure as hell don't want you for a father! I might not know my father, but I know he wouldn't let anyone else call him dad. You actually have a relationship with your son and you are willing to throw it away! For what? Me? Why? Probably for the same grubby reason everyone else in this building wants to be associated with me. Well, I'm tired of it! You wouldn't even compare to my father so don't you dare try to take that title away from him!"

As Vincent is about to storm off, the sprinter attempts to step in and calm the opposing parties, but ends up getting a fist to the ear by Vincent, which ultimately leaves him out cold. A crowd begins to gather around the scene and babbles in disbelief that such a good boy did this to his friend. One woman pulls out her phone and tries to call the police, but Vincent snatches it out of her hand in a flash and hurls it up onto the roof of the school. Without hesitation, he sprints towards the nearest city bus stop, diploma in hand, before the rest of the audience comes to terms with what has happened.

Chapter 2

He stays motionless on a grimy turquoise bus for a few hours before he recalls that he should have gotten off on 5th avenue. With a sluggish step, Vincent rises, and with a tear in his eye, he pulls on the chord to be let off. His feet, like sandbags, seem to take hours to move. He is in a part of the city that he has never been to before. Tall industrial skyscrapers are replaced with cramped shanty apartments. A dialogue between graffiti artists exists on the numerous sides of these dwellings. The simplest solution would be to call home on his new phone and have someone come pick him up, but this would completely go against Vincent's vow to himself, so he keeps on trudging along in his bright crimson robes.

After walking through countless puddles and having his lungs exposed to as many toxic fumes as possible, Vincent stumbles across what appears to be the remnants of an abandoned bus stop and decides to wait. He sits down in an awkward position to avoid jagged pieces of rust and glass. Rain drops dribble down the golden tassel, at first slowly and steadily, but then they begin to pick up with a more ferocious speed. There is no sort of roof overhead to catch the rain, so the only thing protecting Vincent from the elements is the cap that Rosa pinned to his head.

Gentle splashes and footsteps reverberate all around Vincent, but there is a certain noise that captures his attention. While the majority of people move rhythmically and carry their own very distinctive beat, this new stranger sounds jagged and incomplete. Or wait, is it more hurried and hyperactive? Vincent finally decides that it sounds the closest to a crowd of people all running toward something. Just as soon as the ruckus rushes towards Vincent, it suddenly disappears and blends in with the tapping of the rain.

Out of nowhere, a man in a black trench coat leans up against a rusted pole that was previously supporting the nonexistent roof of a bus stop. Vincent immediately tightens up out of nervousness. The stranger's hat covers his face so well that he is completely indistinguishable. He is only able to make out tiny puffs of white hair. Despite his best efforts, Vincent couldn't resist staring at him.

They lock eyes.

After that moment, all sorts of oddities ensue. Vincent becomes catatonic. It is as if a collection of ghastly threads entered his body and anchored his entire self into that seat. A purple mist clouds his thoughts and blurs his vision. Even though all of his senses are beginning to fail, Vincent does not falter in maintaining eye contact with the stranger, because somehow this connection is the only thing keeping Vincent from falling into the darkness.

The stranger's eyes originally contained a deep brown pigment like fertile soil, but now they are quickly engulfed by a molten amber and with this amber a whole new wild persona takes over the spell. A rhythmic drum falls in line with his very own heartbeat. Vincent senses a richness circling around him, although he can not visibly see another person in the area. He hears light delicate footsteps dancing around him, feels a tiny breath on his neck, and detects some very texturized, nonexistent hair brush against his cheek.

A young woman's voice rings out amongst the madness.

"It's him! I'm sure of it! He looks just like his father!"

Vincent manages to mumble.

"My...my…father?"

The stranger responds to the disembodied girl.

"Understood, Lalaina."

A faint satisfied chuckle can be heard in the distance. Vincent is released.

With a heavy breath, Vincent frantically looks all about for the stranger, desperately trying to understand all that just took place. He is so distracted by the visions that he doesn't even notice that he has been transported to an entirely different neighborhood. Cars and buses zoomed by Vincent so quickly that they appear to blend together. People flood and move throughout the sidewalks like a never-ending stream. Vincent is the only stationary figure planted at that bus stop, or so he thinks. Through the tiny pauses in between moving vehicles, Vincent sees the cloaked stranger observing him in an alley directly across the street. At the sight of the dangerous intruder, Vincent leaps to his feet, clenches his fists, and shouts at the top of his lungs.

"Who are you?! What do you want?! Where is my father?!"

Vincent pauses, breathing heavily to steady himself. He whispers something more with a single tear dripping down his face, indistinguishable with the rest of the storm surrounding him.

"Please… I need to know."

A sudden gust of wind almost knocks Vincent back down onto the bench, but Vincent braces his body and takes the remaining impact. He sees glimpses of the stranger for milliseconds, weaving in and out of traffic effortlessly, his footsteps not even making a sound against the pavement. He reaches Vincent in a heartbeat and stands centimeters away from his face.

"You'll find out soon enough."

Without waiting for a reply, the stranger takes a sidestep and completely disappears. Mesmerized, Vincent stares off into the direction in which the stranger escapes. He is searching for not only this fearsome man, if he was even a man at all, but for answers to questions he thought he would never have to ask again. The thought of his father, or even someone knowing his father, causes a complete uproar throughout Vincent's body. He forces back enraged tears and attempts to compose himself for the busy masses of pedestrians who behave more like drones than people.

Chapter 3

It is now that Vincent recognizes the array of steel and chrome towers that decorated the area and replaced the broken shanties from before. He looks upward towards the sky and sees a dark cylindrical skyscraper that seems to reach the clouds. It has bulging glass windows that resemble rounded petals, and towards the very top of the building where the roof blends into the sky, a stalled, blinking red light can be seen seeping through a bundle of grey clouds. Vincent brings his gaze back down to ground level and walks towards the plaque label of this monstrous building. He grazes his hand against the marble. Not many people have their last name adorning one of the tallest skyscrapers in one of the world's largest metropolises, but he did. He somehow found his way back home.

A gentle cough breaks through Vincent's well deserved daze. He didn't realize how long he had been blatantly standing in front of the glass doors, preventing other pedestrians from entering the building. After what all had occurred, time started twisting and contorting in his mind, becoming an entirely different concept altogether.

"Excuse me sir, would you like to come inside? You don't look so well. We can have someone escort you to your flat, sir, if you need it."

"No… I don't need that, thanks."

Vincent begrudgingly walks past the delightful doorman and his chipper smile. Every summer he occasionally brings in a little blonde girl with perfect pin straight hair and takes her on a tour of every single floor of the enormous building. She is always so impressed that he knows so many lavish people who would walk around his building daily. She looks at him like he is the most important man in the entire universe. Vincent can't remember any time in his life where he looked at any adult with this sort of fascination.

He makes his way across the lobby and through the routine mass of intimidated stares and awkward attempts of avoidance from the employees. Vincent charges towards the elevator, and once he is inside the poor young maid is completely flabbergasted.

"Oh Sir! I… I'm…"

Vincent turns and disappointingly looks at the stammering lady. Her face sinks into a pool of blush, presses the button for the closest floor, and flees as quickly as she can.

Vincent thinks to himself.

"Oh well, at least she tried."

The elevator ding goes off when he finally reaches the very top floor. His mother owns the entire top three floors, but Vincent enjoys exiling himself to the very top. A key code is needed to actually get into these floors. It's actually very simple. His mother's birthday allows someone to get to the bottom two, but his birthday gives him access to his own space. Only one other person knew his personal key code. Rosa needed it to give him grilled cheese sandwiches and then later help him get grease stains out of the leather couch before his mother would see.

The walls of his flat are all a pure lab coat white, lacking in any sort of teenage personality, but keeping up a modern flare. Every single aspect of this floor is crisp and geometric. It contains different rooms, but not a single one is completely closed off from the other. Glass divides some of these living spaces, whereas stylish differences in elevation also contribute to these loose boundaries. However, one wall actually consists entirely of glass and bubbles out like a fish bowl. This is Vincent's favorite part of his entire room. This is where he often spends his nights sleeping on the gentle curve of the window instead of his mattress. He finds comfort in submerging into a gradual swirling vortex of polluted clouds that are somehow still able to periodically glisten in the light of the sun. It's here that he feels the least alone.

Rosa discovers him once again clinging to the glass in his sleep. She pulls back the thin sheet and starts shaking him violently while weeping.

"Mr. Vincent!! How dare you play these games with me?!! No one picked you up from the school and no one knew where you were!"

Vincent somehow works up a response in between shakes.

"Rosa, don't worry. I was only gone for about two hours, I think."

"You think? Well think again Mr. Vincent! It is 8 in the morning right now, don't you see the sunrise?"

Vincent tries to recall when exactly he stumbled home yesterday. He didn't think it was too dark but his memory is fading now. Rosa continues, but Vincent finds it hard to pay attention to her.

"I was waiting here as long as I could yesterday, but I had to come back to my son Mr. Vincent, so I left at 9… "

There is no way he could have arrived home that late last night. The graduation ceremony ended in the early afternoon and he only stumbled around for what seemed like an hour or two. It was still daylight when he talked to the doorman and the maid, but if everything he believed was correct, that would mean hours of his life completely disappeared.

This had to be the work of the stranger. Vincent urgently needs answers, but it would break his heart if he makes Rosa more upset than she is right now.

"I'm sorry Rosa, really I am..."

She swoops him up into a giant embrace. Vincent rests his head on her plump chest and Rosa rocks him back and forth.

"Just promise me that you will never do something like this again. It is so unlike you! You are always such a good, sweet boy Mr. Vincent. Don't worry, I won't tell your mother that Mrs. Weaver called earlier about her cell phone."

Vincent chuckles under his breath.

"Oh Rosa no, it was very wrong of me to do that. That woman needs to be reimbursed in some sort of way -"

"Shush shush shush!! Mr. Vincent. I handle your mother's checkbook. It's taken care of. You wrote her a very beautiful apology by the way."

Vincent looks up at her in shock and she in return winks at him.

"I really wish you didn't do that..."

Vincent looks back down, disgusted with himself.

"I don't deserve any sort of special treatment."

Rosa is quick to comfort him.

"Yes you do Mr. Vincent, of course you do!"

Vincent snaps back.

"And why the hell is that? Most people could go to jail for destruction of property and here I am prancing around out in the open because I can write them off! The world is a terrible place for everyone else. I see it every single day, so why am I exempt? Why can't everyone else catch a break once in a while? It's like I've had more opportunities and riches than half of the people in this city!"

He pauses for a brief moment.

"I took it away from them."

"Mr. Vincent, you know very well the world doesn't work like that, and everyone has their own sadness. You suffer just like everyone else, Mr. Vincent."

She takes a very deep breath.

"We just want you to forget it for a while."

This phrase from Rosa sounds cryptic in a way, and completely unlike her normal tone of voice. Vincent breaks away from her hold and looks puzzled.

"Why? And what do you mean by 'we', Rosa?"

She is frazzled. Rosa realizes she let something slip.

"Oh, uh, nothing Mr. Vincent! I mean, I mean your mother and I of course Mr. Vincent! And well we just want you to be happy because she works so hard, and you know she can't come see you at school all the time -"

Vincent interrupts her.

"You know that doesn't bother me Rosa. I'm smart enough to know that she chose a time consuming career."

She has to play catch up now.

"Yes, but that can be hard on any boy really!"

Suddenly, Vincent starts to get flashbacks of his encounter with the stranger at the bus stop and the musical voice of the young woman. They knew about his father. Vincent never asked anyone about his father before. Doesn't that seem unnatural for a young boy to not be curious about a lack of a father figure in his life? Vincent wonders now what has been mentally wrong with him all these years for not at all being compelled to even think about his own father. For years, he just simply watched others. The little girl and the doorman, his team mate and his pushy dad, and countless other families. Every single instance he had a strange feeling in the pit of his stomach like something was missing. Not only that, he felt an overwhelming sense of joy to see these pairs really interacting with each other. Interacting isn't exactly the right word. Was it playing? No, this word seems too juvenile. He couldn't decide. In any case, this joy was immediately replaced by a selfish remorse that always left Vincent feeling guilty. How dare he feel envious of these people struggling to survive, when he was living so successfully? Any one of them would have traded lives with him in a heartbeat, wouldn't they?

"Rosa, do you happen to know anything at all about my father? Has mother ever mentioned anything to you before?"

"Oh well, you never asked about him before! Why the sudden interest, dear Vinny?"

Again she makes the choice to use this completely new tone. This doesn't sit well in Vincent's stomach. He cringes at the fact that she actually called him by that abbreviated sickening pet name. Vincent feels as if he is treading dangerous waters.

As if on cue, the tiny footsteps from before leak into the room and swirl themselves around Vincent. He becomes anxious and searches for the same paralyzing darkness from earlier, waiting for it to strike, but it never comes. Vincent is able to move as he pleases, but he still chooses to remain stationary and becomes encompassed by the familiar rhythm. Rosa behaves as though she can not hear it at all.

"Be careful Vincent!"

The young woman's voice breaks through the tension once again. At this moment, his paranoia is completely eradicated. Although it is cautionary, there is a comforting presence about her. A genuineness that he has never felt on any other person before.

"Lalaina?"

He thinks to himself. She responds to her name.

"Be careful. She's clever. Think about what you say."

Vincent felt a brush against his shoulder, a sign that he isn't alone.

"Well I guess you were right, Rosa. Now that I think about it, it is very difficult not having parents around, especially during your developmental years."

He stops to check Rosa's expression. She is obviously taken back, but keeps her cool. Vincent realizes that they are caught in a trap of verbatim.

"I just think that, maybe, knowing more about my father may help me reconcile any confusing emotions that I have now, not only about his absence, but my mother's as well."

A tightening grip of approval applies pressure to his shoulder. It is Rosa's turn now.

"In that case..."

She starts out in this new tone, but quickly transitions back into her old self.

"Of course, Mr. Vincent! Of course, of course. Well it's quite sad actually, that's why I never mentioned it to you before. You've always been such a fragile boy and all. I didn't want it to shock you."

A staged melancholy pause ensues.

"Your father was a well known anthropologist, and some of his work is still relevant today -"

Vincent interrupts.

"You almost make it sound like he is a thing of the past."

Rosa cunningly replies.

"Well Vinny, that's because he is. He died while your mother was pregnant with you. A tragic overdose, unfortunately. You see, he had been going through a rough patch with his research. He wasn't financially or emotionally ready for a son anyway. So really, in a way, maybe it is better for you. The money from his research and publicity after his death really helped fund your mother's career and now I get to take care of you, my boy!"

The lack of empathy in her words is more than Vincent can bear. Her words, whether or not they had any truth to them, are like tiny needles that had pricked through every single cell in his body. He clenches his fists and struggles to fight back tears. Vincent would have lunged forward at her after saying something that horrible, even if she was his guardian, but Lalaina's presence protects him from giving himself away.

"No, don't, Vincent! Those are all lies!"

Vincent now can see a dark silhouette appear in front of him, separating him from Rosa. It is transparent enough that he can make out Rosa's poker face, but distracting enough to prevent him from attacking. He sees the figure of a young woman, petite but powerful. Despite her size, the shadows radiating from her burst out in waves, magically keeping in time with his own heartbeat. This magnificent sight regains Vincent's confidence and he is able to continue on with such an unforgiving conversation.

He consciously contorts his anger into a false sadness.

"But, why Rosa? If he was really as brilliant as you say he was, he would have known how harmful those things would be, for himself and… for me."

He manages to let one angry tear escape so that his sob story would seem slightly more convincing. It works.

"Oh honey! You know sometimes there are things in this world that's better off left unanswered."

She walks over towards him, arms outstretched for a hug.

"I guess you are right, Rosa. There are things that I am never supposed to know about. That's why you have kept me in the dark so long about my father and you keep me completely separated from my mother at all times!"

He has her trapped now.

She struggles to keep her composure. Her entire identity is under speculation now that Vincent is able to understand that she might have been the reason he had trouble connecting with others after all. All the write offs, special treatment, fulfilling his every single wish, was this actually done out of love? Or was it a ploy to keep him stable and out of the public eye?

"How dare you say that?"

She expels a puff of anger.

"I've just been following your mother's orders! She's the one to blame! I've been more of a mother to you than she has ever been!"

The tiny silhouette lets out a command.

"Press her for more!"

Vincent takes one step towards Rosa.

"But why Rosa? Why would any mother be so out of touch with her own son to the point that she didn't even show up for his birthday once in the past six years? Or completely miss his high school graduation?"

Before she could answer, Vincent understood.

"I'm not supposed to talk to her, am I?"

Chapter 4

A huge commotion ensues at the top of the building after Vincent's sudden realization. Helicopters and all sorts of spinning propellers take up all the air space and cut through Vincent's precious swirling smog. Bright searchlights pierce through the glass windows of the room and leave him temporarily blind. Rosa attempts to sneak upstairs and exit through the hatch to the roof, but Lalaina's figure uses her pulsing shadows to anchor Rosa to the steps. They cling to her feet like a network of roots, but soon travel up her legs like vines. Her roots finally reach Rosa's vital organs, where they expand far too rapidly for her physical body to handle. Instantly she dies from multiple excruciating ruptures and aneurysms. Lalaina releases Rosa from her bond and she tumbles down the stairs.

It is at this moment that Vincent finally regains his sight. He sees the woman who he once thought to be his only source of parental care mangled on the fresh white carpet that she cleaned every day. If it hadn't been for the conversation that just transpired, Vincent would have leapt towards her in an instant and rocked her in his arms while sobbing. However, he wasn't even sure who this woman was anymore. Out of reverence, he carries the fresh corpse over to his glass bubble canopy to check for any sort of wound. He could tell that she is suffering from massive internal bleeding for some reason, but he needed a closer look to figure out why.

One of the more sizable black helicopters spots Vincent as he is setting Rosa down on the glass bubble and immediately opens fire. Numerous bullets strike the powerful glass until it finally gives out and shatters into billions of ragged pieces. Vincent is able to lunge away safely and hide behind an industrial kitchen island, but the same cannot be said for the recently deceased Rosa. Once the glass shatters, her body is immediately punctured by hundreds of tiny bullets. The floating glass around her cuts her and exposes layers upon layers of flesh, blood, tissue, and bone. She is absolutely indistinguishable now. Vincent watches as her body seemingly takes an eternity to obey the laws of gravity. She floats down towards the ground until she is no longer within sight.

Satisfied with their work, the helicopters cease their attack and head towards the ground to retrieve something that was once precious to them. Several moments pass until Vincent works up the courage to get out of his hiding spot. Every glass structure within the flat is reduced to tiny crystal beads. Because the glass walls are no longer supporting some of the other structures, the elevated bedroom completely crashes down towards the living room. The bed itself slides down the bedroom floor and flops into the living room below. It knocks off the mounted plasma television, which snaps in half between the weight of the bed and its contact with the living room floor.

Vincent now becomes aware that everything in his flat is about to collapse on itself. Before he can even process his next move, he notices a swift wind blowing in his direction. A blurry figure rushes towards him, grabs his waist with a huge force that almost squeezes all the air out of Vincent's lungs, and continues sprinting down the side of the building at an unbelievable speed.

Out of the corner of his eye he sees the same puffs of wiry white hair belonging to the stranger, but this time he is able to see his entire profile. He has a very flat, wide rimmed nose, distinctive cheekbones with flattering dimples. His skin is dark and leathery with the occasional freckle popping up here and there. The same wiry white hair decorates the top of his earthy eyes in the form of bushy eyebrows and unruly facial hair. He notices Vincent's stare and replies with a glare of his very own.

"Hery!"

Lalaina shouts.

"I'm sorry! It happened again!"

He is very stern and abrupt with his reply.

"We will discuss this later. Not now."

Lalaina's apparition is struggling to keep up with the stranger's speed. She's constantly appearing, disappearing, and then reappearing again, as if her energy is fading. Her dark pigmentation is now constantly fading from a dark shadowy tone into a beaming amber, a similar shade to the eyes Vincent saw when he first met her. At this point, she is practically a ball of burning light.

The stranger shouts at her.

"I need an opening, now!"

"Got it Hery!"

She then shoots straight ahead and veers quickly to the left. Her light contorts the glass window and turns it into a soft malleable liquid.

"Hang on!"

He commands Vincent.

The stranger makes the same abrupt left turn and leaps through the melted glass. Surprisingly, once Vincent passes through it, the liquid doesn't even touch his skin. It's as if there's an invisible impermeable membrane shielding Vincent and the stranger from the rest of the outside world. They crash into one of his mother's various office floors and knock over a few collapsible cubicles and cheaply made chairs. Vincent is thrown to the ground and hits a copy machine with a loud thud. A huge jolt of pain goes up Vincent's spine and reaches his head. While Vincent rubs the back of his head, he notices the melted glass slowly contorting itself back to its original form. The damaged office supplies and cubicles also mend themselves effortlessly to look as though the three, or technically speaking, two of them haven't been there at all.

Vincent looks up at the man that brought him here. It's impossible for Vincent to suppress any sort of emotion now. He begins sobbing uncontrollably, and then raises his voice.

"Okay, what the hell was all of that?!"

There is a brief pause. The stranger takes too long to answer. He just stands there with insensitive eyes. Vincent continues.

"What happened to her?! To Rosa, or whatever her name really is?! And why in the world were those people trying to kill me?! What the hell have I ever done to any of these people?! And the building! Oh my god, my mom is going to kill me!"

Vincent begins to take long angry strides toward the stranger, fists at the ready.

He cuts Vincent off, his palms stretched out facing Vincent.

"Enough!"

Vincent's body freezes, waiting for the stranger to respond.

"That is where I am going to take you -"

"Oh no!"

The flickering amber light gasps in shock.

"Please no Hery, he isn't ready for that!"

"It's too late!"

He chastises the glowing girl even further.

"Because of your mishap, he is completely exposed. It's not safe here and the boy is going to need answers now that you've thrown him into this!"

She stands up for herself.

"Then let me help! You're right, I've caused all of this."

Vincent grows tired of being a helpless third party.

"What's going on?!"

After a quick glance at the flickering girl, the stranger walks towards Vincent and puts out his hand.

"Call me Hery. I believe we have some business to discuss, but not here. We need to go somewhere quiet... Lalaina, please."

She then, too, also appears next to Vincent's side.

"Sure thing!"

It feels as though she turns and faces Vincent directly. He feels a gentle squeeze on his hand.

"I know a lot has happened today, and I'm very sorry for causing you pain, but now you are about to face even more today than most people have had to face their entire lives."

She pauses before she acts.

"Don't be scared."

A moment later, Vincent hears the same drums beating in the continuous rhythm from their first meeting. The silhouette takes his hand and sends pulsating waves of amber light up his arm. Even though they behave like fire, the waves are cool to the touch. They keep a steady beat until they reach his head. On contact, Vincent becomes drowsier and drowsier. Finally, he is lulled to sleep by Lalaina's essence. The last thing he feels before his slumber are Hery's muscular arms carrying him and Lalaina's gentle invisible touch stroking his curls.

Vincent starts regaining consciousness little by little. His blurry vision can barely make out his surroundings, but they seem vaguely familiar. Vincent is able to spot the same worn down shanties from the scene where he first met Hery and Lalaina. However, Vincent doesn't have the slightest clue why any important information about his parents would bc in the slums. This is the second time in his life that Vincent has been to this neighborhood. Was Rosa trying to keep him out of here for a reason?

Hery moves carefully at a gentle stroll instead of his usual superhuman sprint in an attempt to keep Vincent asleep. Vincent decides to keep up this charade and immediately closes his eyes. He hears Lalaina's voice again, but this time her reassuring nature vanishes and is replaced by unexplainable nervousness.

"Hery, I…I can't keep this up much longer…"

This concerns Vincent dearly. He attempts to discreetly locate Lalaina out of the corner of his eye. Her golden flickering light grows weaker and weaker. She is now gradually fading and glowing in small bursts, like the glow of a lighthouse in the distance. Vincent wants to stare longer and figure out what exactly he can do to help Lalaina, but he must shut his eyes again so that they won't notice his eavesdropping. He slows his breathing down to make his phony slumber more believable and listens.

"Are you sure? I'm going to need you for the explanation. I am unable to do this by myself."

"I know, but it's either I help you get there or I help you explain. I can't do both Hery. I've used so much energy already! I need to rest -"

"But you'll be exposed, Lalaina! And I cannot protect you while he is here."

"I know Hery, but we need him. We need him now more than ever and he needs you more than he needs me at this point. Trust me."

"No! I won't let you do this!-"

"It's my choice Hery! You are almost where you need to be. It's going to be okay! I am going to rest now for a short while. Call me back when you need my help with the explanation. I promise I'll return to you, Hery."

There is a short pause and a tender moment of what appears to be intimacy. Vincent thinks he detects a gentle, loving pressure being applied to the strong arms that are cradling him.

"But after that, you know what you have to do."

Vincent hears light sniffles above him. It is obvious that Hery is trying to suppress his grief, but a few small tears manage to escape. Tears trickle down his aged cheeks and eventually land on Vincent's forehead. Hery laughs despite the emotional pain.

"Alright Lalaina, just don't be gone for too long, and please don't go looking for any trouble this time."

She cheers in return.

"Don't worry about it, Captain!"

Vincent feels a warm sensation surrounding him and Hery, embracing them tightly and melting into their own body heat. Slowly this warmth fades away, until finally Vincent and Hery are left completely in the cold. Vincent opens his eyes just a tad to take in everything that's happening.

Without another word uttered, Lalaina's light goes out.

Chapter 5

Minutes pass by for what seem like decades. Without Lalaina's presence to guide them, Hery behaves as if he is fumbling around in the dark. Vincent eventually falls back asleep in Hery's arms, but after a while he awakes to a falling sensation, a loud thud, and a sharp pain in his tailbone. Vincent lands on solid cement.

After the initial shock fades, Vincent springs to his feet, fully alert. He looks up at his muscular elderly escort with frustration.

"What on earth was that for?!"

Hery nods his head upwards.

"We are here now. Look."

Vincent obeys and turns towards the area. His assumption earlier proves to be correct. They are indeed back in that neighborhood on the outskirts of the city, but it's not the same. Vincent and Hery are submerged even deeper into slums. They stand in the middle of a road, which consists more of potholes and worn out gravel than actual pavement. All of the houses on the street are boarded up and pieced together with flimsy plywood. Some of the small houses that are fortunate enough to have lawns suffer from a complete lack of care, so much so that the vegetation has transformed them into miniature jungles. In some cases, vines engulf the siding and slowly consume the entire structure of the buildings from the outside in. After observing all of this, Vincent spots a dull red light fading and reappearing in the building to his right.

"Do you recognize it?"

Vincent turns around to look back at his guide.

"What do you mean?"

Hery seems frustrated at his response.

"Look a little bit longer."

Vincent stares back at the building with the glowing red light. It is unbelievably in the worst shape out of all the homes in sight. One would assume that the light would be able to be seen through some sort of cracked window or crack in the door, but no. Vincent sees the light through the giant gaping hole in the roof.

Vincent matches Hery's frustration.

"I have no idea what you are talking about!"

Hery replies with disappointment in his voice.

"That's very unfortunate… because this is your home."

Vincent continues to stare at Hery, dumbfounded. Hery continues on without noticing Vincent's reaction.

"This is where your mother and father lived. In fact, you were born and lived here as well for the first years of your life. They must have made you forget all of this."

"I don't understand, Hery. What's happened here?"

"Not here. Let's go inside"

Hery takes the first step towards the condemned house. Vincent carefully follows. Rusty, bent iron bars serve as the screen door, but they refuse to budge.

"Can you open it?"

Vincent looks back at Hery with an annoyed expression. He can't believe that this old man actually asked him to break open a door that is obviously locked and braced like a jail cell. However, in an attempt to entertain him anyway, Vincent grabs the bars and prays that he doesn't contract some disease.

He pulls, tugs, and yanks at the bars with all of his might and with some luck, he manages to jiggle one of them loose just a tad. Vincent then decides to glance back at Hery for some sort of approval, but immediately gets shut down with the same exact annoyed look from Hery.

"What? Well then, how about you try?"

With a small friendly huff, Hery pulls out a small contraption from his back pocket. It is sleek, metallic, and golden. With a flick of his finger, Hery removes the top cap off of the device. A small, powerful, bright flame dances from the inside of the tube shaped trinket. Hery uses it to heat the rusted iron bars to the point in which they are malleable. He then pushes them aside and makes a gap large enough for the two of them to walk through. Vincent grumbles under his breath.

Hery decides to turn this into a teaching moment, despite Vincent's obvious irritation.

"Vincent, you should learn to be more resourceful when trying to solve problems."

Vincent whispers to himself before internalizing the rest of his thoughts.

"How was I supposed to…?"

How hot is his enhanced lighter? Even with the amount of damage done to the bars, the flame has to be extremely hot in order to bend the metal. No common lighter can do this. However, Vincent realizes that arguing with a man who can move faster than a bullet probably isn't his best option right now. So he chooses to remain the silly fool in this scenario.

Hery chuckles and teases him once more.

"You have a lighter in your pocket don't you Vincent?"

"Yeah…yeah… sure I do… everyone does..."

Vincent reaches his arm through the newly created gap and grabs at the door knob. He twists, and it's locked.

"Well now what do we do?"

He asks Hery with one of the worst attitudes possible.

Hery then nudges Vincent out of the way. He reaches for the same door knob and tightens his grip drastically. His dark thick arms flex and turn into solid stumps of flesh. Veins emerge like snakes from his forearm down to his fingers. With a slight force, Hery pushes the door off of its worn out hinges and tosses it aside. The fragile wood cracks immediately once it makes contact with the wall.

"See? Easy."

Vincent shakes his head.

"What happened to resourcefulness?"

Hery chuckles and then responds.

"I figured that I would try things your way this time."

With that Hery slid through the gap and went inside the shanty house. Vincent pauses to blow off some steam and once he recovers, follows Hery into his former home.

Chapter 6

It is completely pitch black inside, except for the ominous stalled glowing red light. It is difficult to pinpoint where exactly the light is coming from, because it floods the entire space. Most of the space has been cleared out and anything valuable has already been claimed. Glass is scattered all across the cracked tile floor. Vincent takes a step forward and hears an eerie cracking noise. He looks down and notices that he broke a picture frame.

Vincent bends down and picks up the photograph that resided in the broken frame. It consists of a handsome young man, a beautiful young woman, and a small toddler in a little sailor suit.

The young man in the photograph is light skinned and has Vincent's same very distinctive jaw line. He has voluminous textured hair and very thoughtful eyes. The man is dressed very sharply in an inexpensive outfit consisting of khaki pants, a patterned dress shirt, a velvet coat, and a bow tie with an opposing pattern. He has one arm around the woman in the picture and the other facing out to catch the running little boy in the sailor suit.

The woman also has both arms outstretched towards the running boy. Her caramel skin makes her dark brown eyes and dark brown curly hair really stand out as her most beautiful features. She is very petite, but being near her lanky husband makes her look even smaller than she actually is. Her rose colored sweater and light airy floral dress match the color of her lips. Vincent can hear her soft giggle just by looking at her.

A similar giggle can be heard from the small boy in the photograph. There is no mistaking the resemblance between himself and the toddler. Vincent's massive dark curls swallow up the tiny white sailor hat that is bobby pinned to his head. His chubby legs and arms are in complete motion as he tries to escape from his parents chasing him.

A tiny tear begins to form in Vincent's left eye. He clings to the photograph even more tightly for a moment, folds it up, and then carefully tucks it into his pocket for safe keeping. Vincent takes one last deep breath, and looks around for Hery.

Vincent finds Hery leaning against the wall in the corner of the tiny room. He crosses his arms and remains perfectly still for a short while. His intimidating stature is only intensified by the tide of red light and its inconsistent nature. Vincent is taken back for a moment, but once Hery speaks, Vincent is comforted once again.

"Like I said, this is where your father and mother spent most of their lives, researching, discovering, and most incredibly, raising you."

Vincent swallows hard and slightly clenches his fists, bracing himself for the news that is yet to come.

"Unfortunately, when your parents left the neighborhood, the spirit of the environment left with them. No one wanted to be here if they weren't here. So they allowed nature to run its course. Bigger people with a lot more money, power, and influence decided that the neighborhood should be condemned and demolished soon in order to build a commercial plaza and create more revenue. That's why Lalaina and I were forced to barge into your life so abruptly. I am truly sorry Vincent. This is not how we had planned any of this, but you need to be here now. You must learn these things now before it is too late."

"But why did we have to leave? Where did they go? I don't understand!"

"Well your father was on the brink of something... powerful, something connected to his hidden ancestry."

Hery straightens up and takes a step toward Vincent.

"Something that I'd like to show you."

He turns around and gently knocks on several places on the wall adjacent to him. After a few missed guesses, both of them hear a drawn out creaking sound. They witness the previously conceived wall open up and become a doorway into another small secret room. The doorway is narrow, jagged, and uneven, but somehow Hery and Vincent both manage to walk through.

The low ceiling forces the two men to hunch over in a very unflattering fashion. With a stiff neck, Vincent looks around the room and notices that the entire tiny room is wallpapered with old oak bookcases and decorated papers poking out of every nook and cranny. The book cases are filled with varying spines arranged in various hues of gold, emerald, and burgundy. The only other pieces of furniture in the room are a grand desk and leather chair combination. Only one singular long scroll of parchment lies on top of the sturdy desk. Vincent takes a few steps toward the desk to get a better look. It is a hand drawn map of a large island with illegible notes covering most of the blank space available.

"Madagascar? But why?"

"Vincent, there are some forces in this world that most people are completely unaware of. Your father was one of the few people belonging to a lost lineage who could sense these irregularities in the world and use them for his own needs, much like myself."

At this moment Hery takes out his odd golden lighter once more. He pops the top off and on his command a gigantic roaring flame bursts out of the tiny opening. It steals all of the oxygen in the room in order to power itself and nearly scorches Vincent and all of his father's books. However, even though extensions of this massive flame occasionally touch Vincent's skin he feels no pain. Likewise the books never catch fire even though they are being grazed by the flame in the very same manner. After this spectacle Hery recalls the flame and tucks his lighter back into his pocket.

"Your father had his own favorite tricks as well, but he was always far more hesitant to use his abilities. Instead, he searched for answers. He wanted to know where all of this originated and why these gifts were given to a select few."

Hery pauses for a moment, lost in thought, but then he continues.

"That man was selfless until the day he disappeared. He had the most natural talent out of any one of us, but he chose to hide it away, especially from you. Your father wanted to research these things so that none of us would have to question who we truly are anymore. We could have a place in this world, but still belong to another."

Vincent has to interject.

"Hery I'm not quite following you…"

Hery sighs.

"No, that's why I need Lalaina for this part…"

Hery stops, looks about the room for a sign of his metaphysical companion, but then gives up.

"But she is resting."

Irked, Vincent continues.

"How does Madagascar tie into all of this? Is that where my father is?"

"That is where Lalaina and I last saw your father. You see, it was the beginning of your father's work. He believed that the lineage of our people began there, and he was correct, in a sense. Once he found us, we confirmed his research and agreed to take him back to our homeland, a series of concealed islands that can only be accessed through a concealed location in Madagascar. It's how we interact between the old world and the new. However, your father was hilariously unprepared to face the darkest aspects of our nature. Lalaina and I tried to warn him, but our adversity only motivated him further."

Hery takes another breath.

"We pushed him too far. That's why we are forced to ask you for help. We need you to complete the task that your father couldn't. I agree to train you until you are properly prepared to handle the dangerous situations that lie ahead, if you do choose to join us."

Vincent responds immediately.

"But Hery, I can't leave yet! What about my mother? I need to find her and tell her everything! I need to make sure that she's alright!"

Vincent then notices an obvious emotional shift in the atmosphere. Instead of being inspired and excited about carrying on his father's legacy, Vincent feels extremely morose. It's as if a newly discovered part of himself had been taken away from him permanently.

Hery hesitates before giving some sort of response. This deeply troubles Vincent and he starts becoming anxious. His heart beat intensifies and his palms become sweaty.

"We need to protect her, Hery!"

Vincent shouts, then begins to stammer.

"There could be more people like… like Rosa! Oh god she probably didn't even know about Rosa! We need to find her office quickly! You can keep her safe, can't you?"

Hery takes a huge sigh and turns away from Vincent and the conversation. He heads toward the exit of the room and stops in the doorway.

"I've been dreading this part."

Vincent raises his voice out of panic.

"Hery?!"

Hery replies very calmly, but sternly.

"Vincent, come with me. There is more you need to know."

Without another word, Vincent follows Hery out of the cramped study and back into the slightly larger main living room. They turn the opposite way from before and ascend down the rickety stairs that perfectly sum up why the building was to be demolished in the first place. Vincent holds his breath with every gentle tiptoed step to get to the bottom.

Chapter 7

At last, he can breathe again. Hery and Vincent finally make it to the basement where they are greeted by a cold concrete floor. In fact, the entire area was completely made of plain concrete, a giant long corridor of plain cold concrete. Down here, the captivating glowing red light burns even brighter. Its source seems to be located at the end of this hallway, right in the very same direction where the two of them are headed. It's as if the light beckons Vincent to come closer and discover all of its secrets.

"This way."

Hery commands and Vincent obediently follows. Time seems to stand still for a moment as the two of them draw closer and closer to the red light. All this time, an overwhelming anxiousness sinks deeper and deeper into Vincent's soul.

At last they make it to the end of the hallway. They discover a giant industrial bolted door with a tiny glass window. Hery grabs the large metal handle and barely has to use any strength to open it. Hery steps in the room first, and Vincent drags himself in after him.

They enter into what looks like an old abandoned laboratory. There isn't a single light on in the entire room except for the glowing red light. It warps Vincent's perception of the whole lab. The floor tile is a faded green and black and extremely cracked. There are white cupboards and cabinets with glass accents containing an array of instruments, tools, beakers, and the like. All the counters are the same shade of stained black as the tiles, but the most interesting feature of the room stands right in the center of it all.

In the middle of the lab stands a giant metallic casket with a glass lid. The red light comes from the top end of the industrialized test tube.

Vincent stares at Hery for a quick second and Hery nods in return. Vincent begins to walk over towards the large container with utmost caution, while Hery remains back in the door frame. Vincent trembles the entire journey.

He finally approaches the container and is able to see what exactly is inside. He presses his hands against the glass and clenches at the surface with all of his might. Vincent is so overwhelmed by the sight of what lies in the tube, that he can do nothing more but rest his forehead on the glass and sob in silence.

The tube is completely filled with a green galactic fluid, but what's more important is what the fluid is embracing. A woman's body, or what is left of a woman's body, floats motionless in an unnatural resting state inside the chemical mixture. Her most prominent wounds would be disturbing to even the most experienced surgeons.

Her slender right leg is completely severed at the knee, the damage looking so recent that the rigged flesh and oozing blood is still contaminating the green substance within the space. Further up, her entire chest and abdomen are ripped open. Her left breast is shredded to the point where it is almost nonexistent. Tiny pieces of her ribs can be seen poking through various points of her wound and some of her vital organs move in and out of her tortured corpse.

However, the worst infliction is applied to her gentle, beautiful face. There is a giant gash spread diagonally across her face, separating it in half. Luckily her bone structure remains intact, but her skin peels back slightly in a few places, showing muscular tissue underneath. Small drops of blood travel through her beautiful dark curly hair.

This woman naturally had such a gentle disposition in the photograph that Vincent finds it nearly impossible to believe that anyone on earth would be so vile as to do this to one of the world's most helpless creatures. At this point it is too much for Vincent to take in, and he must look away. He closes his eyes tightly, shakes uncontrollably, and drops down to the icy cold floor.

"How long?'

Vincent asks Hery without even looking at him. Hery seems thrown off at first.

"...excuse me?"

Vincent shouts, his voice echoes through the entire room.

"How long has she been like this?!"

The tears emerge once again after this emotional release. A rush of faded images, like a mixture of dreams and memories, fill the capacity of his head. Visions of the woman he now knows to be his mother over power his thoughts. He sees her curly chocolate hair emerging from behind the black leather seat of her car. She turns her head and looks back at him, smiling and laughing. She gently grabs his tiny foot, wrapped in an even tinier baby sneaker, and then shakes his chubby stumpy legs in time with the music playing. A baby giggles, and once she lets go and turns back around to drive, the baby keeps on kicking its little legs to the song, "The Girl from Ipanema".

Hery stirs Vincent away from his thoughts.

"She was in danger the minute your father decided to leave and search for answers, but she was fully aware of that and encouraged him to go with us anyway."

Confused, but understanding the importance of the conversation, Vincent finally works up the courage to look Hery right in the eye.

"Vincent, she was not of our bloodline. She did not have the abilities that we possess. However, when she met your father, she was far more than understanding and intrigued by our world and devoted the rest of her life to helping us in our comprehension of our own nature. She loved your father for the person he was, everything that he was, and she hoped that one day, when you realize who you are, and everything you are, the world would be a far safer place for you than it was for them."

Vincent forces himself to look away for a slight moment. He has already been far too emotional in front of Hery for his own personal liking, and did not want to appear weak. With a slight sniffle to compose himself, Vincent turns back and faces Hery dead on.

"Adrianna, your mother, was one of the most brilliant minds to ever grace this world. She worked and studied as a biochemist up until she met your father. Once she learned of his condition, she started tampering into the world of quantum biology. She believed that if we understood how exactly our skills worked on an atomic level, then we would not only be able to enhance them, but we could mask them from other people that were out to hurt us."

"No offense Hery, but I don't really care how my mother helped you out with your abilities… powers, …whatever. I just want to know who and why the hell would anyone want to hurt her?!"

Hery raises his voice.

"Because she was right! Because she knew everything! Do you honestly think that we are the only people like this? Or who knows people like us? Your mother was on the verge of discovering the reality behind forces that people believed were simply fabled magic!"

Vincent continues to stare blankly at Hery, stunned. Hery continues on with his speech at the same overwhelming volume and then slowly quiets down.

"Those forces never wanted simple human beings to completely comprehend how they truly operated, in their world and ours. No matter how brilliant she was, your mother was still never meant to know. Although, I must admit, she discovered aspects about them that I had never even considered…"

Annoyed, Vincent is forced to ask once more.

"What happened to her? Tell me!"

"Vincent, you must understand, these forces can act on people, not on you or I, but on other people. They make them do things, or behave a certain way..."

Hery pauses. He's completely uncomfortable with this discussion and does not know how exactly to go about this in a compassionate way. Hery searches about the room for a slight moment for any other twinkling light besides the ominous red beacon on the metallic casket. Lalaina is visually nowhere to be found. He can't even sense her presence metaphysically. Hery notices the red light glowing and dimming at an even faster rate. Worried, he glances at Vincent and confirms his fears. The rhythm of the light escalates with Vincent's increasing anger over his mother's injuries. If he does not calm himself soon, Vincent will set off the reaction before he is fully prepared.

Hery mutters under his breath.

"Lalaina, help me."

There is no response.

Vincent shouts.

"Hery!"

The light begins to blink faster and faster. Without wasting any more time, Hery makes his way over to the cabinets and searches feverishly. These movements distract Vincent and the oozing red light bleeds once again at a steady pace.

Hery mutters under his breath.

"It's no use."

Whatever he has been searching for is absolutely nowhere to be found. Hery digs through mounds of paperwork, scuffles through vials of unmentionable material, and overturns every instrument in the room without even a hint of the items he needs. Hery looks back towards the red light on top of the metallic sarcophagus for a moment and then struggles to look Vincent in the eye.

"I am searching for your mother's journals. She wrote in them every night. Not only do they contain a vast amount of notes on her research into our lives, they may have information that you need as well."

Vincent begins to look hopeful and gets up slowly from his anchored position.

"However, they are no longer here. I believe that the people who did this..."

Hery stretches his hand out towards Adrianna's remains.

"...the people who hurt her, who tried to keep her quiet, must have taken her journals after this incident."

Vincent's optimism diminishes after hearing this, but before he can be miserable, Hery speaks once again.

"We can search for them together, but I'm afraid we can't leave yet."

"What do you mean? Why not?"

Hery lets out an exhausted sigh.

"I brought you here because we need something. It is essential in finding your father and keeping everyone safe, but it will require you to make a very, very difficult choice. You see... we need that."

Hery points over towards the red light. Vincent never really noticed the light while all of this was transpiring, but now the light burns through Vincent's eye sockets and etches itself permanently into his memory. The light comes from a bright red stone, less like a gem or a ruby. It resembles more of a large glass orb completely filled with a thick liquid. Vincent doesn't want to even consider the possibility of human blood being encompassed in the glass, but his observations would make it impossible to argue against it. It is locked into the machine keeping Adrianna alive by rusty golden chains with tiny spikes evenly spread out on every other link, like the stem of a rose.

Vincent takes one more look towards his mother in her gruesome resting state, recollecting all of the fairy tales and stories of princesses sleeping until they are awakened by true love's kiss. Never were they enraptured in the same amount of peril. Never did they have their lives in any sort of extreme danger to the point where their last breath could come at any moment. Her true love is missing somewhere on an island on the other side of the world and here she is, alone.

Vincent places his hand on the glass.

Her life was the furthest thing away from a fairytale.

Hery speaks up once again.

"We need that, but Vincent, you must understand that the machine cannot work without that stone. It is what powers the vessel. It is from our world, not your mother's, but she understood some of its many powers. She was able to create something to heighten its regenerative properties without using our abilities…"

Vincent interrupts.

"So if we take the stone off of the machine, my mom, is she going to die?"

Hery takes a while once again to reply to Vincent.

"Yes."

Vincent passionately rebuts.

"Then why in the world would I take it?!"

"Because it cannot cure her, Vincent. This relic needs our abilities to fully function. She is stuck in a limbo, somewhere between life and death. Can't you see, she is suffering?"

Vincent looks back towards his mother's face. Her gash still seems oh so fresh upon her dainty face. Tiny shreds of skin dance about in the gelatinous mixture.

"Can't I use my powers, I mean abilities, to save her then? What do I have to do, Hery?"

Hery's heart begins to race. He clenches his fists slightly, desperately trying to mask his anxiousness and fear. Vincent is far too focused on how he can avoid this situation in order to notice Hery's change in demeanor.

"Vincent, no. That type of magic hasn't been used for ages because it is far too dangerous. Too many people have suffered trying to meddle with the natural order through their abilities. It is not to be repeated ever again."

Vincent goes pale at the realization that there is absolutely nothing he can do to save his mother. His mind, body, and soul sulk in a defeated state. Hery notices and quickly tries to salvage the mission.

He moves closer towards Vincent to show a moment of compassion.

"However, Vincent, this relic is the key to finding your father. With any luck, he is still alive, but we need to act quickly before something could happen to him. Even the strongest of people cannot survive completely on their own."

"Hery..."

A small tear streams down Vincent's face.

"You have to do it. I… I… can't. I can't do this to her."

"I cannot, Vincent."

"But, why?"

Two more tears emerge from Vincent's eyes.

"Look at the relic, Vincent. Its pattern matches your heartbeat. It's been responding to you this whole time."

Out of disbelief, Vincent hurryingly turns his head back towards the glowing red light. As his pulse rises out of fear, the blood red beacon fluctuates faster. Vincent becomes even more frightened and now the fluctuation of light changes so quickly that it appears to be constant.

"Your bloodline is especially unique to our people. Your ancestors are the ones who created this object, so naturally it responds to you. Your blood, your family's blood, powers the Blood Stone."

Vincent moves away from Henry and walks towards the relic on his mother's industrial coffin. The rhythm of the glow has slowed down to a normal pace as Vincent prepares to embrace his reality. He places his hands on the chains. The tiny rusted spikes pierce his skin, but this does not bother Vincent. A few drops of blood travel from the small incision into the spikes, where they are absorbed through the metal like molecules of water through a cell membrane. With this addition, the glowing pattern stops, and the red light shines so insanely bright that it encompasses every free space in the room. It became more powerful than ever before.

Vincent looks down at his mother's face and gently whispers.

"I'm so sorry..."

He closes his eyes tight, and yanks down on the chains with the force of a steam engine at full speed. Right before the relic breaks away from the machine, something strange occurs to Adrianna's body inside of the tube.

Her eyes open.

Her beautiful soft chocolate eyes meet Vincent's and overflow with the purest form of love that a mother can have for her child. Despite the cut on her face, her gentle smile radiates happiness and she presses her perfectly feminine hand against the glass.

"Vincent, my baby, is that you?"

Vincent flings himself against the glass with all his might and wraps his long arms around the tube. His heart flutters and Vincent is overwhelmed with an emotion that he has never felt before in his life. His hands grasp the glass even tighter in an attempt to keep her here with him forever.

However, Vincent hears a mind numbing rattle as all the gold chains and the ever important Blood Stone hit the floor. He panics and jumps back a little from the glass tube. Vincent looks down at his mother to make sure she is still okay, but nothing could be further from the truth.

Suddenly, the lovely expression on her face contorts itself into a shockingly painful cry. She begins twisting, turning, and sobbing from the pain. The green gelatin preserve becomes tainted with her blood and turns into a deeper and deeper red. It fills the tube continuously until Adrianna stops moving altogether. She lets out one final loud shriek of pain and then finally relaxes. Her face transforms back into its gentle state as she is accepted into death's comforting arms.

Chapter 8

Vincent's arms remain transfixed to the glass as if they had been petrified from the encounter. In a complete state of shock, Vincent continually stares down at his mother's fresh corpse without conjuring up a single sniffle. He unconsciously begins to apply more and more pressure onto the glass. This worries Hery as he notices that Vincent is putting all of his enhanced bodily muscle mass to use. Cracks appear and multiply on the tube rapidly and Hery is forced to stop him.

"Vincent! Don't!"

He pushes Vincent down onto the ground once more, but Vincent behaves as though life has left his body. Once his body meets the solid tile floor, he flops about like a rag doll.

"Why?"

Vincent asks in a weak whisper.

"I thought you said I couldn't do it. You said I couldn't save her."

Before Hery can think of an explanation, heavy vibrations knock him off of his feet and he joins Vincent on the ground. Something resembling an earthquake parades throughout the tiny dilapidated house, causing innumerable objects to abandon their posts and violently crash onto the floor. Vincent hardly seems to be able to focus or notice anything that's happening around him.

A singular voice rings out over the chaos.

"Hery! They're coming! Quickly, this way!"

Hery's eyes travel to find her silhouette.

He feels her presence coming from somewhere in the back corner of the room, as far away as possible from himself and Vincent. Her usual golden airy figure has been contorted into a dark ghoulish image. Those metaphysical infernal vines wrap around her frame and anchor themselves into the cabinets and tile of the laboratory as if they are searching for something.

Lalaina works up enough strength to free her arm from the ensnaring mesh of dark restraints. Once it is loose, her arm returns to its airy gold pigment, while the rest of her body remains lost in the shadows. She points directly upward.

"Hurry! It's the only way. Just don't get too close to me!"

Hery nods in agreement. He scoops up Vincent and the Blood Stone in one swift motion, makes a fist, and creates an escape route through the ceiling. They pass through the father's study once more, but before exiting the building altogether, Hery stops, and looks back down to check on Lalaina.

"What on earth are you doing Hery? You need to leave now!"

Hery refuses to budge, even with all the rubble collapsing around him.

"Lalaina, it has never been this bad before. You're in danger!"

"Well so are you! You know exactly what it wants. We've talked about this before. Please just go. I can stop them for a bit and then I'll go back into hiding like before. Everyone will be safe this way -"

Hery interrupts her.

"We can't do this without you! He needs you.... I need you."

At this moment, the movement of the darkness becomes erratic and berserk. It ceases its search and becomes more interested in threatening its hostage. The vengeful shadows jab at Lalaina's translucent body over and over again, causing her to shriek in pain. In an attempt to muffle her voice, the sinister vines wrap themselves around her neck and head.

Before they reach complete coverage, Lalaina herself begins to vibrate on the same level as the rest of the house. Gradually her vibrations become more intense and rhythmical compared to the frantic shaking around the rest of the house. Her rhythm overpowers the chaos. Lalaina's body begins to glow slightly brighter despite her chains, and she is able to wiggle out of about half of her bondages.

"I said go! Now!"

Fighting his instincts, Hery decides to obey Lalaina. Carrying Vincent and the stone, he bursts through the roof of the shanty and sprints off into the opposite direction.

Vincent finally begins to emerge from his emotionally induced coma and looks over Hery's shoulder towards the house. His vision is extremely blurred, but Vincent is still able to make out the raging trembles of his home. In an instant, the vibrations cause the house to come apart at the seams. Pieces of lumber and hardware unravel like thread until his parent's home is entirely demolished.

Even though this sight breaks his heart, Vincent can no longer outwardly express his sadness. He is completely numb from all of the pain that he has endured throughout this short time. Despite an overwhelming desire to look away, his body remains frozen in this position. Vincent is forced to remain fixated on the spot where he should have spent his childhood and to watch it grow further and further out of sight until it absolutely disappears.

Chapter 9

They arrive at the same shattered bus stop. Hery sets Vincent down on the rickety bench and lets him rest his head against his shoulder. Vincent still hasn't quite calmed down yet and his only other option was to rest against the jagged rusted poles. While Vincent gathers his strength, Hery grasps the Blood Stone tightly in his hands, occasionally turning it over. When he does this, the metallic spikes rub against each other and make a highly unpleasant noise. The previous eerie red glow is no longer present. It began to fade as soon as they had left the house and now it resembles more of a solid pool of deep red ink.

Vincent manages to ask Hery a question in his weakened condition.

"Hery, where did my house go?"

Hery lets out a large sigh.

"It was condemned, Vincent, don't you remember?"

"Does that mean the bulldozers and big machines knocked it down?"

Hery contemplates for a moment and finally makes a decision.

"Yes, a very big machine knocked it down."

Vincent pauses but then looks back up at Hery.

"Well… where am I going to live now?"

Hery shifts his weight slightly so that he can put his arm around Vincent's shoulder. He then proceeds to try and lift Vincent's spirits.

"Now that's a question, isn't it?"

Hery begins to laugh awkwardly, avoiding the need to address what really happened as much as he possibly could. Vincent stares up at him and his facial expression reminds Hery of his inappropriateness. Hery chooses to cut the act and be as deliberate as he must be with Vincent.

"I cannot answer that question, Vincent. I do not have the sort of information that you need.... not quite yet."

The word 'yet' gives him hope. Vincent perks up a little when he hears this possibility of moving forward. He sits up on his own and listens more.

"You can stay with me if you choose, but we can't leave here quite yet. We need your mother's journals, Vincent. They're of vital importance now."

That hope is pretty short lived. Vincent now feels a slight pang of betrayal from the only person he could literally and figuratively lean on in this moment.

"Why is that? I don't really appreciate you trying to snatch up all of my mother's belongings right after she just... she..."

He is behaving more like himself now.

"No, I understand."

Hery takes a moment to gather his thoughts.

"But those journals will serve a purpose to you as well. She would have wanted you to have them. You are her son and right now the people who currently own them are the very same people who put her in that unnatural state."

Visions of all of the recent events shroud his head, distracting him from all of his thoughts and feelings. This causes Vincent to react just as Hery had predicted. He is unstable. Consumed by the storm of emotions, Vincent's grief quickly converts into anger.

"You're right! You've been right about everything else this whole time, Hery. Those journals do belong to me!"

He rises to his feet.

"Where are they?"

"Well -"

But before Hery could finish, Vincent already begins walking away from the bus stop. He trudges along in a daze, not realizing where exactly he is headed. His footsteps pound against the pavement as if he is enabling them to satisfy his desire for vengeance. Not once does he look back at Hery. In return, Hery does not leave from his spot.

Vincent's head fills with a conglomeration of whispers that when combined, echo through his head like television static. This causes him to feel some mild pain, which he shakes off immediately. His vision blurs, but Vincent moves along anyway, despite this disability.

He regains his sight after a time lapse of about an hour and finds himself in front of a familiar large industrial building. He pushes past the friendly doorman before he can utter any sort of greeting and rushes through the lobby filled with gawking workers. Other strangers, or guests that would occasionally come around for rest or business transactions are nowhere to be seen. Their positions are filled by a drone of construction workers making repairs to various parts of the tower.

Vincent follows a small gaggle of muscular men into the elevator. They continue on with their conversation as if they didn't know he was even there. A tiny thought manages to escape from the unnatural static. He realizes that he probably would have enjoyed this type of moment before graduation and before everything that has just taken place.

The men ride with Vincent to the very top floor. They then fan out in front of him in order to tackle the ordeal ahead, one that Vincent, once again, fails to comprehend. What used to be Vincent's room is completely trashed. Tarp covers all the places where glass stood previously and all of the damaged furniture huddles together in a disorderly fashion.

The construction workers are occupied in rebuilding the wall that was not there before the accident. Instead of the stylized glass adding a unique flare to the space, the workers manipulate different forms of concrete, iron, wire, wood and plaster to create walls that match the layout of every other floor of the building. This would have saddened Vincent in a normal state of mind, but as it stands, Vincent is incapable of formulating his own thoughts right now.

A stout employee tosses Vincent's torn up mattress into the pile of rubbish. Patches of foam grow out of incisions like mold out of old tree bark, and patches of stains discolor what remains of the sheets. He walks up towards the pile, and with every step he takes the static noise grows louder and louder. The pain he attempted to ignore escalates, forcing him to collapse on to his knees. His vision blurs to the point where all he can see now is a deep sea of black. Vincent falls over onto the mattress and is put into a forced slumber.

He hears a woman's voice in his sleep. She's frantic and distressed.

"No! Please! Stay away!"

Vincent now hears hurried footsteps. At first they sound clunky, random, and heavy, but then he hears a different pair of footsteps. This time they are light, quick, and sound as though this person is running through shallow puddles on an asphalt road.

Then silence.

The woman gasps when she sees him lying on the ground.

"Vincent!!!!"

Her cry fades into the sound of a deeper familiar voice.

"Vincent. Vincent. Wake up!"

Something shakes Vincent softly, but after the first failed attempt, the shaking becomes rougher and more violent.

"Vincent, you need to wake up now! Listen to me!"

Vincent knows that it's Hery trying to wake him up, but for some reason he is unable to speak or move. His vision is starting to return, but everything is still as fuzzy as it was while he was traveling to his room. He can barely make out Hery's face.

Hery's gentle nudges have completely transformed into terrifying waves that make Vincent's limp appendages fling about swiftly. He moves Vincent so rapidly, that it seems as though Vincent is vibrating.

Vincent's vision slowly comes back into focus, but all of this extreme rattling damages Vincent's body and he becomes ill.

He manages to spit out:

"Hery… Please… Stop..."

Vincent surprises Hery with his ability to speak. Frightened, Hery lets go and Vincent drops down to the ground. He lands with a thud, rolls over to the side, and vomits onto the wood pile.

Hery interrupts Vincent's heaving.

"What happened? How did you get here? You disappeared from me!"

Vincent struggles to utter a response due to a huge coughing fit. Hery becomes impatient.

"You must tell me now Vincent, did you see anyone? Did anyone see you or talk to you as well?"

Vincent yells back at Hery.

"No! Stop it! I didn't talk to anyone! Leave me alone and stop acting so weird, Hery."

Hery takes a few steps back and tries to control himself. He allows Vincent a few minutes to settle down and get his breathing regulated, despite the putrid atmosphere. Neither of them offer to clean up the regurgitated mess off of the floor.

Vincent speaks in a more appropriate tone.

"I think I did hear a woman though. She sounded like something was going to hurt her."

"Did you speak to her?"

"No, but it was strange because she called out my name. Is that bad?"

Hery stops for a moment and ponders over which question to ask next.

"What did she look like, Vincent?"

"I don't know. Everything was black. I couldn't see much. I saw a couple of construction workers but I couldn't see her. I just heard her footsteps. I think she was running away from something, something really big because I heard its footsteps too."

Hery stays silent for a while, pondering on this new information. This gives Vincent a chance to fully take in where he is exactly. Unlike in his dream, there are no other people present in the disheveled room besides himself and Hery. Production must be at a halt at this moment, but something seems off.

"Hey, where did everyone go?"

This question broke Hery of his concentration.

"Come again, Vincent?"

"All the workers! They were all over the building. Where did they go?"

"No one is present here, Vincent. I didn't see anyone when I came to find you."

A peculiar thought crosses Vincent's mind.

"Wait a minute, if I disappeared from you, then how did you find me Hery?"

Hery fumbles around in his pocket for a while and pulls out the Blood Stone necklace. He is extremely careful in avoiding the sharp pricks on the gold chain, but then Hery decides to let the entire thing fall from his hands and dance about on the floor. It rattles for a while and then settles onto a bent floor board.

"It told me. I heard your voice through it. Then it started glowing like a beacon once more, increasing in velocity whenever I got closer to you."

The poisonous red glow maliciously starts flirting with Vincent once again, but he has had enough. He kicks the jewel aside with as much energy as he can muster and watches it scuttle across the wood. Hery goes to pick it up by its end piece, like a snake, and then sets it down on one of the benches that the construction workers must have brought with them. He turns and faces Vincent once more.

"It is true that you disappeared from my sight, Vincent. You took one step forward and then your body diluted into thin air. I could only catch glimpses of a light outline of your body, but then again, my eyes are far more experienced than most."

"What? But how is any of that even possible?"

"It must be one of your abilities Vincent. When our people reach maturity and discover themselves, oftentimes they discover some sort of natural talent that they possess, something completely unique to the individual."

Vincent starts to become restless and annoyed with all of this gibberish. His head still aches from all of that terrible static and a horrid taste still lingers in his mouth from the mess he made.

"So what? I can turn invisible now or something? When do I get my cape?"

Hery is quick to anger over Vincent's disrespect.

"There is no need for such behavior! These affairs should be taken seriously Vincent!"

"How in the world am I supposed to take any of this seriously? I've lost my home, my nanny, my mother, my old house, everything! You're just lucky that I'm being a smartass and not hurling myself through that window over there!"

Vincent haunches over and hides his face from Hery. He shakes a little and a few tears come out despite his best efforts to appear composed. Hery gets down lower and crouches down to Vincent's level. They make eye contact.

"I'm sorry that you feel this way Vincent, but you are not alone. This is what happens to us, to our people. You see, our abilities, our world, we never said any of this is a blessing. In fact, it behaves a lot more like a curse. We are a cursed breed, and will continue to live this way if you and I don't put these sorrows behind us. It is our fate Vincent. This is your fate. You may carry more curses than the average person, but this only means that your fate will be the greatest."

Hery grabs Vincent's shoulders firmly but affectionately. Vincent sniffles a bit, but then is able to keep himself together long enough for Hery to continue on with his explanation.

"No, I do not think invisibility is your ability, at least not exactly. Even if you were invisible I should have been able to sense you, or your body heat, but I could feel absolutely nothing. It is a type of teleportation, perhaps. The problem is, though, most people need to tear themselves apart and completely rearrange their atomic structure in two different places in order to achieve this. This makes this ability extremely difficult."

He pauses and then continues.

"However, what's interesting is that you must have been completely conscious of what was going on around you. This is probably why your body took such physical damage. To think, not only did you have the energy to pull off shattering your atomic structure and then rearranging it perfectly, you've managed to maintain your essence in this dimensional plane instead of getting lost.... But how...?"

"How on earth am I supposed to know that? All I know is that I never want to do it again!"

"That is how everyone feels when they first discover their ability, Vincent. Trust me, it does not come easy."

Hery pulls up his sleeve and reveals a whole collection of scars and torn flesh. It is impossible to distinguish old wounds from recent ones at this point, and it didn't help that his skin is so aged anyway.

"When I was younger, I pushed myself to see how fast I could go. I got close to breaking the sound barrier, but my human body couldn't keep up with my supernatural desire. I've never matched that speed again, although sometimes, as you can see, I am extremely tempted to try."

He rolls his sleeve back down and stands back up.

"I can train you if you wish, Vincent. We can figure out how you can properly use whatever your talent is and try to make it as painless as possible."

Vincent thinks for a moment, but eventually responds.

"Did you train my father too, Hery? Do you remember what his initial talent was?"

There's a pause before Vincent carries on.

"I probably shouldn't ask. I just want to know."

The atmosphere of the room warms slightly with the mention of Vincent's father. Both Hery and Vincent's spirits are lifted a tad.

"Honestly, Vincent, I do not know the answer to that. You see, I met your father later on in his life. I could not be there for the initial stages, but he had a certain favoritism when it came to electricity and playing around with magnetic fields."

Hery chuckles to himself.

"It would explain why his hair always stood on end whenever you would shake his hand!"

He laughs some more.

"Your father always had the best sort of party tricks."

Hearing someone's laughter now proves to be extremely refreshing for Vincent at this time. He's euphoric because this is the first time in his entire life that anyone has ever discussed a memory of his father. Vincent has grown accustomed to finding information about his father in newspaper clippings and through some of his research papers, most of which tended to put Vincent asleep like a silent lullaby. During his lifetime, his father wrote many papers on anthropology and the cultural history of various indigenous tribes around thc world. His most entertaining pieces are all centered on obscure folk tales from isolated locations of the world. It was the closest thing to a bedtime story Vincent has ever had.

Vincent returns from his nostalgic thoughts and begins to intently listen to Hery finish a story about his father.

"And your mother absolutely hated birds. She thought they were pests. So one day your father somehow managed to throw off the flight pattern of all these sparrows and sent them all to your house just to pick on your mother for April Fool's day! It was priceless! She would have been more upset, but all of those birds made a mess all over your father's car and they didn't even consider touching any of her things. She was a big believer in karma."

Vincent's heart fills with an overwhelming sense of joy. At last his parents seem like actual emotive human beings instead of distant unknown titles. He can now tangibly imagine what a life with them would have been like, and all of the laughter that would have resounded like a symphony off of the glass walls.

Vincent implores for more information.

"What else could he do, Hery? Tell me everything!"

Hery realizes that he had gone off on a tangent with Vincent and that his action was inappropriate. He becomes more reserved now, withdrawing the intense admiration he has for Vincent's father.

"I know you appreciate these stories Vincent, so do I, but we must not lose focus. If you must know, when I left your father on Madagascar, he was trying to understand the effects lightning had on earth and how he could incorporate that into his abilities. You see, the soil there is extremely eroded and your father wanted to help the farmers add more nutrients to their fields."

Hery catches himself rambling once again.

"Anyway, without guidance from your mother, I'm afraid that your father's training progress is slowed. Even though she is not of our descent, her knowledge of the physical world around us outmatched any other human being. Now that she is gone, we have lost a vital asset to your development, but her journals might still be able to aid you and your father."

Vincent pauses for a bit to process all of this new information. He is slightly disappointed that Hery refuses to talk more about his father, but he understands that this might not be the best place in the world for that right now. Besides, finding his mother's journals might provide him with some sort of closure as well.

"So we need to find them then, huh?"

"Exactly, Vincent. Now we need to figure out where exactly those vicious people are located. Then we must infiltrate their Intel and find a list of places that seem unordinary. After that we can search one by one -"

Vincent interrupts him.

"I think they're here."

Chapter 10

Baffled, Hery goes on to question Vincent.

"What? How would you know that? Why would they be here?"

"Well, why would I want to be here?"

They both pause for a moment, waiting in shock to see what the other has to say. A time passes without a response, so Vincent chimes in again.

"I'm just saying that I don't think I would have come back here this soon after what happened to mom… and Rosa."

A still silence comes over the two of them and lingers uncomfortably for quite some time. It's Hery who caves in first.

"I suppose your logic is sound."

Hery takes another moment to think to himself. He personally finds it contradictory that sound logic can come from emotional assumptions, but he knows that this is the course the two of them need to follow. This is what Lalaina would have wanted the two of them to do.

"Is there some place that you suggest we should begin?"

Vincent scans the room and tries to look past all of the rubble and debris, but he eventually realizes that these efforts are useless.

"Well right now we are in my room. I never really kept any clutter around here before, so all of my belongings were always in sight. You would think that I would've noticed extra notebooks by now. I don't think they would be in this room exactly, but maybe they are on my mom's floor!"

"Wait, your mother had her own loft, Vincent?"

"Yes! Well at least… that's what everyone always told me. I just wouldn't go there because all of my caretakers told me that I'd bother her. She was always working… supposedly."

Vincent's mind begins to drift off. Suddenly he can feel all the lies that he has been told throughout his life sink in all at once. The idea of his mother living just below him, even if he could never see her, still acted as a safety net underneath his glass palace. If anything were to shatter, Vincent still wholeheartedly believed that his mother would come through to rescue him, but now that the truth has revealed itself, his mind began to prepare for a free fall.

Hery senses that Vincent is drifting off deep into thought and breaks him of this spell.

"Vincent, even if she wasn't there, that space still existed, yes?"

"I mean, I guess so. I saw workers go in there to bring her things occasionally."

"Then that is all we need. It would be an ideal spot to start searching."

Upon this agreement, Vincent and Hery walk towards the elevator, get in, and press on the button with the floor number directly under Vincent's. However, instead of being greeted by the familiar elevator ding, an automatic voice message rings out from the speaker.

"Passcode verification."

Hery turns to Vincent.

"Has it done this before?"

A small black box with an array of numbers pokes out underneath the normal elevator buttons.

"No! Well, ... Hery I have to be honest with you. I've never even tried to visit my mom's room before. I don't have any clue what it's talking about, but we could try her birthday. My birthday was always used by the staff to access my flat."

Vincent presses the corresponding numbers with his mother's birthday, but is immediately greeted with an error message.

The machine asks once more.

"Passcode verification!"

"I see..."

Hery sighs deeply.

"This is going to be exciting."

Hery pulls the same strange lighter that he used at the shanty house from his pocket and twirls it in his fingers for a few seconds. In his hand, the golden contraption seems to shine even brighter than before.

"Vincent, pay attention. This will be your first lesson into other skills that you can develop, but keep in mind, the more tasks you need to accomplish, the more energy is needed to carry out these abilities."

A small flame emerges from the lighter once again, but this time Vincent notices something slightly different about the trinket. It glows at a pulsating pace as if it is receiving slight waves of energy. Vincent glances at Hery's arm and sees miniscule moments of Hery flexing his biceps in the same exact rhythm as the glow from his device. With each flex the flame grows bigger and brighter until Hery believes it is strong enough to tackle the elevator door.

"Hery? Are you doing this? Are you feeding that flame yourself?"

Hery ignores Vincent's question and takes one more single breath in. He manages to utter one more order.

"Now watch, Vincent."

This time Hery takes his other hand and grips the lighter even tighter. The flame instantly flares and contracts itself into a single solid beam of heat. Hery attempts to attack the door with a single horizontal slash. The elevator metal is extremely heated, but instead of melting at the seams and splitting away, the door immediately began to cool and rearrange itself back to its original form. This catches Hery extremely off guard and in a moment of panic, Hery extinguishes the beam from his contraption.

The automated voicemail becomes angry and changes into a much more distorted voice. Sirens fire off from every direction and all the light in the elevator disappears. In the darkness Vincent and Hery hear a distinctive threat.

"Unauthorized activity. Intruders detained. Continue with extermination."

Vincent panics.

"What the hell did that thing say? We have to get out of here Hery!"

"Give me your hand Vincent!"

"What? What for?"

"That's an order!"

Hery aggressively grabs Vincent's wrist and pulls him towards the buttons of the elevator. Underneath, Hery feels around for a hatch. Once discovered, Hery forcefully presses Vincent's hand against it.

"I need you to break into the control box now Vincent."

"What? But Hery it's so dark! And I don't know how to –

"Your ability Vincent! We need to stop this electronic defense system before it's too late."

"But I'm not an electrician!"

"You're your father's son. You'll figure it out. But you need to try! Or else."

Hery clasps on tighter to Vincent's wrist, to the point where Vincent hears tiny pops and cracks. All of this added pressure pushes Vincent to his breaking point. The only way he can escape Hery's grip is to make his body fade away like last time, but that instance was almost as unbearable as this one. Vincent loses all feeling in his hand before he finally makes his decision.

He becomes extremely dizzy and begins losing consciousness once more. However, this time these side effects and the added on blurred vision, aren't nearly as frightening as before, due to the pitch black darkness of the tiny elevator. This time Vincent only feels a deep tranquility and airiness. It is as if his body now behaves as water ripples on a still lake once rain begins to fall.

Vincent hears Hery's cries, but now they have become muffled messages that can't quite reach Vincent's new state. The only true audible noises now are his own heavy drum-like heartbeat and the sound of wiry snaps and cracks.

His entity gravitates towards the snapping and cracking sound until he encounters an overwhelming stream of power. Despite his intuition, Vincent feels his new membrane of a self, and travels closer and closer towards this energy. His extreme attraction forces himself to embrace this current of streaming power, but once he accomplishes this, Vincent begins to feel a strange painful sensation. Every microscopic fragment of himself becomes super charged through a surge of electrons passing through him. The power becomes too much for Vincent and his being is forced to expand even further. However, in this confined space, there is no more room for Vincent to expand. In an extreme aversive response, Vincent's essence contracts.

The newfound power condenses his mass to ten times his normal size. With this density and rapid growth, his solid body tears through the boundaries of the space with ease. The stream of energy no longer has use for his corporeal body and releases its bond with Vincent. It escapes through the newly made tear and its magnetic characteristics pull Vincent along with it. The momentum increases as Vincent's filtered body begins to reassemble itself, and is only stopped when Vincent makes contact with the elevator's wall.

Vincent once again feels extremely nauseous and can barely maintain his equilibrium when he comes to. Bright, threatening bolts of electricity scatter themselves across the inside of the elevator, nearly striking Hery on multiple instances. All of the previous alarm systems go awry and eventually crash. Hery dodges every flash with a masculine grace until he finally has an opening to break through the elevator door. Using the same pulsating energy technique from before, Hery charges his body with enough energy to break completely through the giant metal doors. Before entirely clearing the area, he grabs onto Vincent's arm once more and flings him through the opening along with him.

They slam onto thc ground and roll onto the floor of the flat. Hery recovers in an instant, but Vincent remains hunched over in the fetal position. Even though the shock of this experience isn't nearly as harmful as the previous one, it has still taken a great physical toll on Vincent.

After a moment, Vincent is able to sit up and face the elevator door. The bolts of lightning continue to fire off and chase each other through the giant metal space. Vincent hears a loud distinctive snap. The chords couldn't handle the commotion inside the elevator and it suddenly goes crashing down the shoot with an unmatched speed. The impact slightly shakes the floor enough to where Vincent is knocked back down onto the ground.

"Ugh…my head hurts again Hery!"

"It is fine, Vincent. You performed your duty excellently. You may have a moment to rest since I doubt anyone will be able to reach us now."

Vincent tries to get back on his feet, but this takes a tad longer than usual.

"Well then thanks Hery, but… what exactly did I do?"

"You manipulated your particles and converted yourself from matter into energy. Once you became energy, you were able to find the main electric current controlling the elevator and make it go haywire, all without any instructions. Very impressive."

Hery's casual tone coupled with this unnatural feat truly frightened Vincent.

"But wait, wouldn't I have to catch on fire or something in order to release my chemical bonds and turn into energy? I'd have to lose some mass too!!"

Initially, Vincent's proud of himself for retaining this information from chemistry class, but this emotion is fleeting. With this thought, Vincent searches frantically around himself, counts all of his fingers and toes, feels for his nose, and runs his fingers through his hair in order to make sure everything important is still intact.

"Well, essentially yes. You didn't exactly burn to a crisp. There is no need to worry! You are naturally very discreet when you dematerialize. But you're correct, Vincent. All of our actions come at a price. Your physical illness is just one price for your actions, but if it is missing mass that you are concerned about, I am unable to detect any significant damage."

Hery decides to tease him a bit.

"At most you might have lost a pound or two."

This does not strike the right tone with Vincent.

Hery continues on and talks to him as if Vincent is in a simple doctor's appointment or sports checkup instead of having a proper conversation about Vincent becoming his very own chemical reaction. This makes his skin crawl. Vincent does his very best to ignore all of Hery's ramblings. He searches around the room to find some sort of temporary distraction, and unfortunately, he finds it.

Chapter 11

A doll. A giant, rotten, ragged, monstrosity of a doll towers in the corner directly behind Hery and perhaps due to the lighting of the room, it appears to loom over his shoulder. Vincent can't help himself but to peer into its damaged glass eyes. Nothing else exists besides her cracked porcelain face, her smirk, and those menacing opaque eyes. Vincent stares long enough that he can begin to distinguish a tiny reflection of himself, but once he can make eye contact with it, the glass instantaneously shatters into billions of dangerous bits. Vincent flings himself backwards in a moment of panic in order to avoid getting cut, but Hery behaves as if he didn't notice her at all.

"Vincent, what is the matter?"

"h...h...her!"

Vincent points out towards Hery's shoulder. Hery quickly turns around, bracing himself for what could lurk in the shadows, but relaxes after a minute, despite staring at the doll directly in its vacant face. Hery moves about in all directions to locate the threat, but cannot find her anywhere. In all his commotion, she stands perfectly still, never breaking her gaze with Vincent. He starts sweating profusely and backs himself into a corner. In a fraction of a second, she lunges towards Vincent and appears centimeters away from his face, her lace ruffles still flowing from her burst of momentum. Her jaw slowly begins to drop gradually, exposing more and more of a concealed dark abyss within her. Terrified, but observant, Vincent sees various tiny lights within her mouth eerily resembling a small spiral galaxy.

As her mouth widens to its completion, she leans in closer and Vincent feels a small but powerful force pulling him in. Vincent tries to resist, but before she can fully devour her prey, Hery turns on the light switch and she evaporates into a dark cloud of smog. Hery finally sees her vapor and springs into action. He clenches his hands together in a forceful prayer. Energy pulsates from the core of his body, down his arms, and into his hand which are already glowing a fierce white. He slowly pulls his hands apart with a great strength and wraps his fingers around her oozing mist.

Hery compresses her gaseous form into a tiny ball in his hands. Once she is completely withdrawn from the atmosphere, Hery takes that white light and converts it into a bold blue and white flame. She becomes absorbed into the fire and once added, tiny wisps spring forth from the original blaze. Unlike their previous states, these wisps have an airy whimsical gesture about them as they float up and phase through the ceiling. The threatening atmosphere in the room completely disappears and Vincent is finally able to relax.

Vincent takes a moment to catch his breath.

"What took you so long?! I was almost a goner!"

"I'm terribly sorry, Vincent. Someone must have put a trap, some type of dark magic in this room. I didn't see it, well, because it must have sensed that you were a bigger threat than I am!"

Hery laughs at this but Vincent hardly finds this amusing. He's still dusting himself off from the aftermath of the attack.

"Thanks for the compliment, but seriously? A creepy doll? What horror movie did they pluck that from?"

Hery pauses and collects himself.

"I know this ritual very well, Vincent. I have seen it used before. The magic condenses itself into some sort of object that can blend into the environment. Take a look around and you might understand why this doll fits in well."

Now that the lights are on, Vincent can see everything properly and listens to Hery's suggestion. They stumble into some poor gaudy attempt at a Victorian parlor that contains more fills and doilies than should ever be allowed outside of a nursing home embroidery club. The colors of the room seemingly consist of muted tones of green and pink, but they fuse into each other so often that they become a muddy mess. It is as though some poor woman is trying to overcompensate for the dollhouse that she never received as a child. Vincent can hardly take it anymore.

"Ugh, you're telling me that my mother lived here?"

"Not quite Vincent, take a look."

Hery points over to a small wooden shelf, painted an off white color. On the shelf stands numerous picture frames, pressed flowers, and small porcelain puppy figurines. The picture that Hery references contains a large familiar woman in an inappropriate business attire, exposing more skin than the occasion called for, and smiling with a gaggle of drone-like businessmen.

"Rosa?"

Vincent thinks to himself.

"Go figure."

"Trust me, this décor…"

Hery ponders over a polite way to phrase it.

"Would have never matched your mother's taste."

He smiles to himself in pride for using such forgiving language. Vincent initially felt the same way, but still held onto the idea that his mother lived beneath him until Hery disproved it once and for all.

"Well, your mother's journals must be here then, Vincent. The trap confirms it. Let's take a look around before something else unfortunate happens."

Vincent is quick to get as far away from the husk of the doll as possible.

"You don't have to tell me twice."

Chapter 12

The two of them take a turn about the elongated flat, Hery with a brisk step and Vincent with a more cautious shuffle, careful to not knock over any of the other trinkets scattered across the apartment. A few items become casualties in their search: an old golden spittoon, a bust of a young cherub, and various chandeliers that are scattered not only on the ceiling, but also lay in different nooks and crannies along the floor. It becomes obvious to Vincent that Hery has no concern for the person who lives here or for any of their belongings.

They walk into the bedroom which would be spacious to say the least, if it didn't have hoarded clutter carpeting the floor and working its way up the corners of the room. It's a miracle that they even managed to open the door in the first place. Hery pokes his head in first while Vincent observes behind him.

"Yes. I know they must be in here."

"How can you even tell, Hery? There's papers and junk everywhere! I can't even see some of the furniture."

"Do you sense anything, Vincent?"

Vincent takes a deep breath and contracts all the muscles he possibly can. He puffs his chest out and tries desperately to concentrate as much as he can on whatever slight changes in the atmosphere there might be. After what feels like a century passes, Vincent finally exhales and shrugs his shoulders in defeat.

"Sorry, I got nothing."

Hery shakes his head, slightly disappointed, not in Vincent's inability, but in his failure to take this threat seriously after what had just happened a few minutes ago.

"Here, let me show you."

Hery puts his hands up, as a gesture to Vincent to stay put. He remains in the doorway, but crouches down onto his knees and takes out a small concealed knife from his sleeve.

"How long has that - ?"

Hery barks at him.

"Quiet, Vincent!"

He then makes a small incision into the center of the palm of his hand. A couple of delayed drops of blood trickle down his hand and onto his wrist. Hery drops the knife down onto the floor and uses his healthy hand to reach into his pocket and grab his golden lighter once more. This time once exposed, the lighter vibrates rapidly like it's trying to flee from something. Hery grasps it firmly with not only his free hand, but with his injured one as well. As soon as the lighter makes contact with Hery's cut it stops moving abruptly. After a few moments of absolute silence an eerie creak fills the room.

The rounded bottom of the lighter surprisingly drops open, suspended on a tiny camouflaged gold hinge and an oozing ruby red substance leaks from the newly created opening. Hery draws a small circle around the discarded knife with the dense red waxy mixture and then draws an even larger circle about six inches away from the circumference of the small circle. Once this is completed, Hery draws several random jagged lines connecting the two circles. After this is done, the unused liquid retracts back into the lighter and Hery puts it away once more. Hery slams his injured hand feverishly onto the wooden floor with enough force to make thick shrouds of dust appear from nowhere. Satisfied, Hery shows Vincent his palm one last time. It looks as though the cut never even existed.

Hery motions Vincent over towards his brand new creation.

"Now stand here and don't move a single hair out of place, no matter what!"

"But…"

Hery pushes him into the circle before Vincent could finish his thought. Once Vincent is placed, Hery takes a leap back into the door frame. This makes Vincent nervous and he decides to quickly turn around and face whatever sort of monstrosity that is about to ensue, but he sees nothing.

Vincent stands there for a second, completely confused. He tries to locate Hery to determine what's going on, but Hery is no longer behind him. Hery begins lurking around the perimeter, palms pressed against the walls, with intricate and calculated steps every few dangling moments. He ducks and leans back every now and then, avoiding some sort of invisible force with extreme intensity. Hery's wiry hair and clothes also flee from some sort of overwhelming gust that Vincent cannot feel. He becomes frustrated.

"Hery! What's going on?"

He behaves as though he cannot hear Vincent and continues on. This concerns Vincent, so he tries again, this time leaning forward and taking one small step towards Hery.

"Hery! Can you hear me?"

As soon as Vincent's foot reaches the ground, a small tremor can be felt throughout the bedroom. Hery snaps his head around furiously.

"I said stay put!!"

Vincent looks down and sees that his foot moved an inch out of the circle that Hery drew. He looks up once more and jumps back in fright. Now that he is standing back in the door frame instead of in the protected area, he can see everything that Hery has been trying to avoid the entire time.

A dark tornado of manuscripts, plus-size dresses, perfume bottles, mirrors, and furniture whirls around the enclosed bedroom, flinging whatever it possibly could find straight at Hery with an unbeatable strength. Additionally, this elemental force chucks objects every now and then at the spot where Vincent had been standing, but a vertical ring of green energy encloses the circle safely from all attempts at harm. Now that he is an observer in the corner of the room, instead of the treasure safe within its chest, Vincent is exposed to the full capability of this whirling circus.

It seems to notice that Vincent is out of his cove, and now the insidious disaster places its full attention on him instead of Hery. It moves forward, tearing a line through the floorboards, pointed directly at Vincent.

He drops down to the floor and hears a shrilling smash against the wall. The tornado fired a fat ceramic feline with a bright pink ribbon at what would have been his head. Its attacks begin to increase in frequency and velocity and Vincent panics.

"Hery, help!"

But Vincent's cries are ignored.

Hery then lunges towards the middle of the room, but whilst midair he disappears completely out of sight. Vincent is left alone to fend for himself. He tries to make a dive back towards Hery's circle, but with Hery's disappearance, the circle vanishes as well. Vincent falls to the ground and smears Hery's drawing into one giant waxy blob.

"Oh shit!"

The whirling entity moves even closer towards Vincent. He panics and tries to chip away some of the wax in order to restore it back to its evenly round shape. Once the remedial curves have been restored, Vincent jumps inside and cuts his hand on the exposed wood on the floor, trying to emulate Hery. Instead, he would immolate himself to the powerful, dark tornado.

Chapter 13

Vincent's poor imitation of a spell does not go according to plan at all. After his own blood touches the waxy surface, the power of the enemy increases tenfold. It develops a crazed bloodlust and thrashes about the room for a few moments in order to release its rage. It then turns back towards Vincent and enters his enclosure. Once they make contact, Vincent's vision blurs once again and he enters into blankets of darkness. He can barely even feel his own breath anymore.

The only thing Vincent can feel is the gust that split his entity apart. Various microscopic parts of himself separate and are thrown about every which way. His soul stares helplessly, until he feels the tremor of those exotic rhythms once again, shaking his core.

He feels her as well.

Although Lalaina's golden glow could not be seen, he could feel her warmth radiating and moving slowly towards him. However, something is different. Another cooler temperature swirls around her in an attempt to block her comforting warmth. Little bursts of heat flash towards Vincent every now and then. He assumes that it is Lalaina trying to push past whatever force is trying to contain her.

She breathes out his name.

"Vincent!"

It sounds exactly like a silver chime dancing in the last little bit of summer wind. He searches for her and tries to move closer, but the other parts of him are still moving about in this space. He can't do anything to help her.

Hery's voice appears somewhere out in a distant corner. It is very faint but just as equally demanding as ever.

"Lalaina, don't!"

A sudden surge of intense heat whips Vincent and blasts him to his core. It now feels as though a small star has gone supernova within the confines of the tornado. The atmosphere begins to distort itself as the heat manipulates every single particle present.

Lalaina is even bright enough to see without opening his eyes. Her dark, earthy skin not only takes in her newfound sunlight, but radiates the entire surrounding area. Her small frame demands all of the power found throughout this mysterious realm. He can finally see her delicate face, her plump lips, and her gorgeous high cheekbones. She is an embodiment of all of God's sovereign power. The brightest light comes from her chalky red braids. They behave as though they are the source of all of this energy. However, her eyes lose any detection of human qualities. The amber color Vincent has seen before completely consumes her vision, covering her eyes in a sort of flammable syrup. Little wisps of fire act as her eyelashes. It was the most beautiful, but terrifying experience Vincent could ever imagine.

"Vincent, where are you?"

She pauses to allow him to give some sort of response. He is so baffled by her appearance that he loses the ability to speak.

"I'm… he…he…here!"

"I believe that you've separated again, but you cannot find your way back. Let me help you."

She leans in closer into Vincent. Although his physical face has disappeared off to some other place, he can still feel Lalaina cupping it in her wonderful, powerful, tender hands. She pulls him in closer to her face, so close that he feels an intense but delightful burn from her energy. Her thumb grazes over various places that would have been on his face, like his temples, forehead, cheeks, and his chin. She then whispers something so softly that Vincent couldn't hear even from his distance. The insidious winds that have been blowing and separating Vincent from himself become calm. Once her chant is complete, she brings her lips to where his forehead would have been.

"Nooooooooo!!!"

Vincent can feel Hery moving towards them, but he knows that Hery will never reach.

Vincent's various tiny parts become drawn back to their energy, and stick appropriately back onto Vincent. The more put together he becomes, the less he can see of Lalaina and her beauty. The background reverts back to bookshelves and the gaudy wallpaper, and he is gently brought down onto the stained carpet. Lalaina is still in front of him, but she is rapidly dimming and losing her energy. Before Vincent could even think to reach out to her, she extinguishes.

Without her light, Vincent wilts and slouches down on the floor. He feels a tremendous ache in his chest, but this isn't the normal pain that goes along with one of his splitting spells. In fact, his normal nausea is nowhere to be found. Instead a tremendous heart ache fills his cavity. It's as if he intuitively understands that he will probably never witness another sight as magnificent as the one that just ensued.

Hery gets closer to Vincent without him noticing. Vincent's daze protects him from seeing Hery's pure rage, but this only makes matters worse. Convicted and angered by Vincent's apparent ineptitude to fully understand the situation, Hery begins shouting, swearing, and breaking everything in his path inside the already destroyed bedroom.

"She's gone!!! Don't you understand that?! She's lost now!!"

This last phrase breaks Vincent from his current mental state and brings him back into reality. His speech is still slowed but at least he can communicate.

"What are you talking about?"

"Lalaina is gone! She was consumed! All thanks to you! And your blatant disregard for my orders!"

There is loneliness in the air, unique to this current situation. Even when coming to, Vincent felt it. A happiness and courageousness that normally subconsciously uplifts them despite being under constant attack is gone, removed from their intricate equation. The true fortitude of these two characters is gone and instead of unifying to retrieve it, their fear only makes matters worse.

"Hery I was trying to save you! You needed my help! That huge tornado thing had you pressed against the wall!"

"Did it really? Vincent, you were not thinking rationally! It had most of its forceful attacks used against you! Why do you think I created that shield in the first place? You were the distraction!!"

This makes Vincent stumble a bit, but he regathers his thoughts.

"What do you mean? Why would it go after me and not you? You're stronger!"

Hery coils his arm back and snatches Vincent's wrist like a snake. He then forcefully raises the hand with Vincent's self-inflicted wound as close to his own face as possible. All Vincent could smell is the pungent odor of blood and dirt.

"This may be true, but you have more potential. You have more vitality. You are fresh, raw, and your blood is more malleable than mine."

He lets go of Vincent's wrists and lets it fall lifeless at his side. Hery attempts to calm himself slightly. His anger still dwells within him, but lays dormant in order to be used at a more appropriate time.

"You would have been the desirable target and thus the creature was to focus on you whilst I retrieved your mother's diaries. It wasn't conscious enough to understand that I had used my magic to protect you and you would have worn down its stamina. After that I was going to get rid of it without you getting harmed."

"Okay, but Hery don't you think telling me all of this would have been just a little more helpful than leaving me in the dark?"

"We had a limited amount of time and I thought that by now you would trust me enough to not disobey my orders. Apparently, I was misled."

Vincent doesn't quite know how to respond to these statements. Noticing that Vincent has nothing to say on his behalf, Hery continues with a deep sigh.

"You panicked. Did you really think that gust of wind had enough power to tear you apart? No. It was designed to make a constant mess and deter us from finding what we needed. You were so concerned about yourself that your body went to immediate self-defense. Normally this wouldn't be a problem, except you foolishly wasted energy on a spell that you didn't even know how to complete. You gave the monster enough strength to keep you from realigning yourself. You would have been stuck like that permanently if she hadn't saved you!!"

The more Hery thinks about Vincent's deeds, the more hostile he becomes. Vincent notices this change in demeanor and attempts to scoot away without Hery noticing. While Vincent is in mid-motion, Hery continues.

"Because of your inability to control yourself, rationalize your actions, or even strategize at all, she is now lost. She used all of the energy keeping her connected to this realm in order to make sure you didn't suffer the same way she did."

Hery pauses as his face contorts into an emotion of guilt and sorrow for a split second. He recovers and continues lecturing Vincent.

"Misused and interrupted rituals are the most dangerous and disastrous things that could happen to someone, even people like us. If you do not die, you will suffer restlessly in manners and places that we are not meant to understand."

Hery takes another sigh and whispers under his breath.

"We need her."

"Hery, I'm sorry. I didn't know any of this!"

Before Vincent can finish graveling, Hery pulls out a collection of black leather books bound together with gold thread and drops them down in front of Vincent as if they had lost all of their usefulness. Vincent counts seven of them, but they have no title or indication about their content anywhere on the cover.

"Here. Educate yourself."

With that, Hery takes large powerful strides out of the room, not even glancing back towards Vincent. Scared of being alone, Vincent gathers together the black books and scurries along behind Hery like a disciplined dog trying to regain its master's favor. They leave not only the room, but also the flat and the entire building this way. The only time there is contact between the two is when Hery climbs down the elevator shaft with Vincent connected to him at the waist by a regular piece of rope. Vincent just dangles, careful to not drop a single book, while Hery lowers the both of them down to the bottom floor. They do this in silence, and when it comes time for the two of them to separate, they continue on in silence. Silence through the lobby, and silence on the streets. On this day, Vincent makes a quiet vow to never see Hery with that same fraction of expression of guilt. The anger he can tolerate, but seeing Hery with sorrow is something that he never wanted to experience twice.

Chapter 14

For the next couple of days, Hery is very distant and refuses to talk to Vincent under any circumstances. They shack up in alternating hotels for a while, all made possible with Vincent's built up inheritance. However, all transactions need to be made in cash. They are unsure of the forces they disturbed.

Currently, they are residing in an emerald green motel room just off of the interstate. Jumping around this frequently is very uncommon for Vincent, coming from a glass cage before hitting the ground hard. He had never been given the ability to go out on his own, so now he is forced to trudge along with Hery, who won't even make eye contact with him. Despite these shortcomings, Vincent is able to find sanctuary in some of the tiny black journals that used to belong to his mother, even though most of her writings equate to some sort of chicken scratch and jargon.

The only true digestible part of her first couple of journals is the intro. Like in any proper lab report, Vincent's mother outlines and summarizes all of her well-kept research and her purpose in all of her endeavors. However, the prior portion reads more emotionally than any love letter from any romance he's ever seen on tv. This is the part that Vincent reads to himself every night routinely. He becomes hypnotized by her words so much that he cannot bring himself to move forward to the following pages.

"To my dearest, where ever you might be, and in whatever form you may take,

I pray that some of this research can bring you back to this world and maybe even closer to mine. I do not fully understand the forces that took you away from me, but I do understand you. I always have. Even before we recognized your gifts, you were always special to me. Your spirit ignited and engulfed my soul the minute I heard your voice. It is only fitting that such a simple wildflower would be taken in by such a fantastic whirlwind of a man. Now I am stuck in the lull after the tempest, but I will never stop searching for a way to return to your, what I wish to be, our chaotic life. These pages are filled with my heart, my love, in its most basic form. I cannot be the romantic that you are my darling, but I know you will be able to decode the ciphers of my affections. My darling Victor, I am and always yours. I will forever linger on your tailwinds until I can be with you once again.

Your bed of roses, Adrianna"

On this particular night, Hery finally walks in on Vincent reading his mother's passage in his hotel bedroom, with yet another singular tear dancing across his bottom eyelid. Vincent looks up, embarrassed, and Hery returns the sentiment with an uncomfortable scoff.

"You know, it's impractical to just read that one part."

Vincent isn't surprised at all by Hery's bitterness, but there seemed to be an undertone of an unspoken apology mixed in. After all, this had been the first time Hery has directly spoken to him since they have been on the run.

Vincent replies lightheartedly.

"No offense Hery, but I don't think that anything I have seen lately has proven to be very practical either."

Hery laughs at Vincent's unwavering spunk.

"Come this way."

Hery leads Vincent into their joint, cramped bathroom. The mint green tiles covering the walls lose their appeal with the darker rusted chocolate flaking off of the edges and in between the vanilla cracks. The lightbulb clumsily hangs onto an aged wire, connecting it to the ceiling and flashes in a secret morse code, desperate for someone to bring it stability. The tainted bathtub below behaves more as a suspicious cavern for the light bulb rather than a potential safety net.

Hery turns Vincent toward the miniscule vanity mirror over the sink. It's manufactured in such a ridiculous way that a compound make up mirror would be more useful to use for morning routines, but this wasn't the only problem with it. It now resembled an inanimate burn victim, with pieces of glass slowly flaking and peeling off of the outer surface like burnt parchment. Vincent and Hery stare at it long enough to observe one of these unnatural flakes take an eternity to dance through the air and transform into a small silver liquid pool onto the floor, collecting itself with the other flakes that had landed before it and staining the cheap shower curtain.

Vincent is the first to speak.

"Well, I don't really remember seeing that while I was brushing my teeth…"

"Don't worry. It wasn't there earlier today. Sometimes, I make mistakes when I'm trying something for the first time."

Vincent whips his head around in shock as soon as Hery says this. It is unusual for Hery to be in such a joking mood at any time, let alone when dealing with something that could have fractured the laws of physics.

"What the hell did you do, Hery?"

"Oh there is no need to be afraid. I learned from my mistakes, Vincent. I just need you to help me with the rest of this process. You should be well versed in these sorts of things by now, since you've been reading your mother's journals."

Naturally a deep cold sinking feeling of panic takes over Vincent's inner core. Hery knows very well that Vincent never got past the first page of the first little black book. Heck, his family's picture poking out of the first page could hardly be called a bookmark at this point. He knows that he hasn't been contributing to this endeavor as much as he could have been, but is this really the best way for Hery to call him out on it, by throwing him into another life or death situation without any sort of warning?

"Hery! I... I..."

Vincent can't bring himself to finish his own thoughts. Hery removes not only his coat, but all layers of protection covering his torso, exposing himself for the first time. Vincent is taken back at how resilient Hery's skin appears despite his age. Scars decorate Hery's arms in a pattern like constellations. Their frequency is so grand that it is impossible to detect any original flesh. They should cross onto his chest or his back, but they cease to exist in a surprisingly clean line. His chest is bare, while his entire back is covered in letters burned into his skin, forming strange complicated words too long and intricate to belong to any language that Vincent understands.

Hery bends over and dips his hand into the small silver pool at the base of the shower curtain. He attempts to scoop the liquid into his palm, but as soon as his skin makes contact with what once was glass, small drops gather together and form tiny beads that fling themselves as far away from Hery as they can. Once they accomplish a safe distance, they return to their liquid shape.

"This is why I need you, Vincent. Go ahead. Take them and draw the symbol on page 30, the one at the end of your mother's summoning chapter."

Midway through this Hery places his fist over the middle of his chest in order to indicate the canvas for Vincent. Vincent panics for a moment.

"Come again?"

Hery's body tightens and his biceps flex for a moment. A brief silence occurs, but then Hery bursts out in a hollow, deep, suspicious laugh.

"Oh you are such a character, Vincent!"

He then releases all of the energy in his contracted muscles to playfully nudge Vincent hard enough that he falls back into the bathtub and cracks it. Vincent gets the message. Hery means business.

Beyond frightened, Vincent tries to look past Hery into the bedroom, where some of his mother's books lay sprawled out on the hotel bed. Vincent spends a few moments desperately attempting to calculate ways where he can get past Hery and his monstrous body, but in this moment of intense concentration, Vincent feels his hand go numb. He glances down at it out of the corner of his eye but notices it has completely vanished.

Vincent quickly tucks the area that would have been his hand back behind his back and prays that Hery didn't notice any of this. A rapid second of eye contact confirms that Hery is still unaware, or at least wants Vincent to believe that he is unaware. Either way, Vincent is convinced not to do or say anything relatively stupid for a while to provoke Hery, at least not until he can figure out a way to get to his mother's journals.

He looks back towards the bedroom once more, but sees something impossible occurring; his disembodied hand is shuffling through one of the books on the bed. The majority of the hand is solidified, but the tail end at the wrist gives off some sort of unnatural pixelation of skin cells. This reassures Vincent that there is still some connection between his left hand and the rest of his body. He concentrates even harder to try and find the specific symbol Hery asked for, as if he could somehow read without seeing.

However, he still needs more time to actually find the appropriate page, so he has to risk saying something stupid again so soon.

"But Hery, how am I supposed to use those if you can't use them?"

Vincent points down at the transformed beads that have rejoined their melted motherland. He desperately hopes that Hery would go on yet another mystical rant about forces that still have yet to make sense to Vincent in order to buy some more time, but unfortunately this fails.

"Vincent, surely you remember the incident with the Blood Stone as well."

Hery pauses for a microsecond and pulls out the object mentioned from his trouser pocket. The red-black ink continues to swirl within the glass protected by rusted spikes. However, once put in close proximity with Vincent, gradual bits of color become more intense and frantic like a shark frenzy in the middle of a dark ocean.

"This is a similar concept! No need to be shy. Use that gifted lineage of yours!"

Hery brings the relic closer to Vincent's face, but stops the process as soon as he notices the peculiarity at play. Instead of the bright bits of color trying to reach out to Vincent's body, they face the opposite direction, back towards the bedroom. Vincent realizes that the Blood Stone must be lusting after his disembodied hand and tries to soak up as much information as he can before Hery turns around.

Vincent panics. He grabs the book he has been scanning for the past few minutes and manages to reel in his left hand before Hery notices anything. Once it is reattached, Vincent moves as fast as he can to open the book, scoop up some of the liquid glass, and place a thick hand print of it in the middle of Hery's chest. He then takes the remainder of the substance and makes a circle of silver dots with his knuckles.

Hery's big brassy arms lock onto Vincent's wrist in an attempt to stop what is happening, but they are too late. Vincent finishes the image and now has only to recite the proper words. However, in all the excitement, an extra ingredient is added to the spell. From Hery's grasp the Blood Stone withers and flings itself about in a desperate attempt to be free. It glows erratically with pulsations too irregular to be any sort of heartbeat. The Blood Stone can't control itself, being this close to Vincent's flesh, and leaps forward to be reunited with him. It pierces Vincent's skin and suckles at his veins.

Vincent screams in pain for a brief moment, but focuses on what he feels needs to be done. He shouts, "Hiverina!" without knowing what would happen next.

Chapter 15

Hery throws his hands back, breaking the rusted chains between him, Vincent, and the Blood Stone. The Blood Stone drops to the floor and rattles against the tiles in protest of being separated from its favorite host. However, Hery and Vincent ignore its outbursts due to the vibrant streams of gold light breaking through the newly developed cracks in Hery's chest.

Vincent's spell causes a rupture in not only Hery's physical body, but it seems to be having an effect on his entire being as a whole. Hery shouts in pain, but his voice is extremely distorted, operating not only in tones of extreme highs and lows, but in pitches that Vincent's human ears can't even register. Each variation in voice comes about at the same time a new painful gold crevice breaks apart his skin.

All of the fractures originate from the initial image drawn by Vincent, and continue to spread out over Hery's body. His skin flakes off like scales and glimmers as they become their own entities of light. A shimmering hand reaches through Vincent's own imprint and catches the glittering flakes in its palm.

Vincent takes a few steps back to distance himself from the emerging entity. With this added space, another extremity pushes itself out of Hery's chest. The two semi-transparent arms grab onto Hery's torso and propel the rest of its body from the portal. The golden figure collapses down on the tile and makes similar movements to the Blood Stone, throwing itself about in its disturbing rhythm.

Hery falls back and goes limp. He hits his head on the bathroom sink and his eyes shut. Once his body makes contact with the ground, the glowing figure leaps up and straightens itself up to make room for the floor's new guest.

Vincent realizes now that the figure is shapely like a woman, but her slenderness is still her most prominent feature. As she stands, her entity becomes stronger and more powerful even though her stature has not changed. Her hands move toward her head and run themselves through her voluminous hair. She shakes her head back and forth to cleanse herself and let her spirit free.

Her eyes open.

The same burning embers that have imprinted themselves forever in Vincent's mind have finally returned.

"Lalaina?"

She snaps her head towards him.

"Vincent?"

With this recognition, slight facial features begin to reform. Her plump lips, high cheekbones, and tiny flared nose all rise from the previously flat, gold surface that was her face. The unnatural golden color dims and reveals her beautiful dark skin and a perfectly effortless wild red natural style. Her previous braids have loosened, corresponding with her new freedom. However, she still remains covered in a tiny veil of light and the fires in her eyes are yet to be quenched.

"Where am I? How did you find me? Where is Hery?"

She turns to locate her friend, and once she finds him faint on the floor, she throws herself at him. However, her efforts are useless because as soon as their bodies make contact, she phases right through him. She quickly collects herself and turns to Vincent.

"What are you doing? Get some water for him! He could be hurt!"

Vincent turns toward the sink, now realizing that it has been completely destroyed by Hery's cranium. He hesitantly turns on the faucet wondering how in the world they are going to explain all of this to the hotel manager.

"Hurry!"

Vincent scoops up water in his hands and flings it over Hery's body. After a couple of tries, Vincent hits Hery's face. Hery flinches slightly, giving him and Lalaina a sign of life.

Lalaina is overjoyed and calls out Hery's name, but he never responds to her. She becomes upset and looks over towards Vincent for help. Vincent obediently lays a hand on Hery's shoulder and calls out to him.

"Hery! Can you hear me? Hey, Hery! Are you okay?"

It takes a moment for Hery's eyes to adjust, but once he pulls himself together and recognizes what happened, he gets pissed. Vincent ducks into the bathtub for safety, but Lalaina stands right in front of Hery and tries to talk him down.

"Hery, no! Ajanony io! Ampy izay! No more!"

When she notices that her words have no effect on Hery, Lalaina tries a different tactic. She spontaneously combusts and emits golden flames throughout the entire bathroom. The tiny golden flames collect themselves into a stream of fire and force their way into the circuits of the overhead light fixture, causing the bulb to burst directly above Hery. Hot pieces of glass fall upon him as gently as snow, giving him a very loving but stern warning against his actions.

Hery winces at the pain. He brushes the bits of glass off of him and relaxes his disposition. He looks around the room.

"Lalaina?"

He still can't see her.

Lalaina is back to her normal form, huddled close to the edge of the bathtub where Vincent is hiding. She is exhausted from her latest powerful display and is struggling to breathe. She keeps her eyes closed to conserve energy, but manages to whisper to Vincent.

"Tell…him…I'm okay."

Vincent pops up from the sanctuary of the tub while Hery is still busy looking around.

"Ummmm… Hery?"

Hery turns his head towards Vincent, looking sad and confused.

"Hery, Lalaina's here."

Vincent points down towards the floor.

"She's kinda beat up, but I think she is going to be okay."

Hery's eyes go directly to where Vincent indicated and stay fixated there for some time. A small tear comes to his eye.

"I need you to prove it!"

Vincent looks down at Lalaina too, not knowing exactly what he is supposed to do. She mumbles something Vincent can barely understand. He does his best to try to pronounce everything correctly.

"Namana, tia arnao aho."

Hery drops to his knees and a few more tears find their way down his face. He hasn't broken eye contact with the tiles on the floor.

Hery thinks out loud without a filter.

"It wasn't supposed to be like this."

He reaches his hand out into the empty space. Only Vincent can witness Lalaina's tired hand meeting Hery's and resting on top of it.

"I was merely the vessel for this ritual, not a participant. You weren't supposed to state the enchantment. I just needed your energy for the symbol. I was supposed to speak the language. My mother language. I inherited those words. I am the one who serves her. I am meant to protect her, and now she is separated from me!"

Even though they cannot physically see each other, Hery and Lalaina look at each other as if this is the last time they will ever meet. Vincent is overcome with guilt that he can't even explain. He tries to articulate his apologies to Hery, but ends up delivering a very different message.

"Look Hery… I'm sorry for whatever I did. I don't quite understand what I did, but don't you think that's a huge problem? Like, you're asking me to do all these really freaky magical things that I didn't even think were possible a few days ago without giving me any sort of directions and then blowing up at me when I don't do it right! You could have told me that I wasn't supposed to say anything on my own! But no! You just threaten me and smash stuff to scare the shit out of me! You two need to start telling me what the fuck is really going on or I'm walking for good!"

Hery and Lalaina turn their heads in an unrehearsed unison towards Vincent and rise up off the floor.

Hery begins.

"I see your point, Vincent. We have been unfair to you. We treat you as though you have been a part of this world already, like how we treated your father when it was his time."

Vincent lessens his anger at the mention of his father. Lalaina flutters over to Vincent's side and grabs his wrist gently. He looks into her eyes while she asks him for permission to intervene.

"May I do something so that he knows I am here? I want to help both of you."

Vincent nods his head. Not letting go of him, she releases a small painless glow into his forearm. It spreads all the way up to Vincent's lips and he feels them go tenderly numb. Using his body as a beloved puppet, she addresses Hery.

"Inty aho!"

Hery looks overjoyed, relieved, and weepy all at once at the sound of Lalaina's voice coming out of Vincent's mouth. However, he gathers the strength to compose himself and continue on with the explanation.

"These abilities and all of these occurrences are not new Vincent, although they are new to you. The magic you have been experiencing lately, and that you will continue to experience whether you desire it or not, has been inherited for generations by those belonging to our people. It is a gift that's in our blood, going too far back for any mortal to count."

Vincent stammers.

"Wait, mortal?"

Hery picks up where he left off.

"Vincent, what you are being exposed to, what we have to face, requires a battle that can't be contained within the boundaries of this world and its laws. We must adapt ourselves to meet the demands required to keep this world safe."

Lalaina giggles and then replies with Vincent's own lips.

"Trust me Vincent, you do not want to know how old we are!"

Vincent looks over at Lalaina astonished. She responds to him with a devious laugh, the kind every young woman does when she reveals her deepest secret to her unsuspecting prey.

Hery also smiles to himself, not so much at what was said, but in an appreciation of Lalaina's newfound happiness.

"These sorts of adaptations begin to come naturally, Vincent, once one accepts their initial abilities. You're already developing and adapting far beyond someone of your age, but of course this is expected with our crash course method of teaching."

Lalaina doesn't let that comment slide.

"Leave him alone, Hery. He has earned the right to be informed by now, don't you think so?"

"I suppose you are right."

Hery takes a breath and then continues.

"Vincent, you, your father, Lalaina, and I are all descendants of a powerful legacy, lost to the rest of this world, but essential for the survival of others. Our ancestors made contact with a powerful force, living inside the cracks of our reality. They were desperate for an exchange, eager for a trade that would eventually lead to destruction. One of our past leaders gave into their temptations, and now…"

Hery begins to trail off, but Lalaina finishes what Hery started.

"Now, Vincent, we have to rectify what he caused, and repay those who have sacrificed themselves for these efforts. But it's even more dangerous now. Someone is trying to contact these creatures once more, and the past is bound to repeat itself. That is why we are desperate for your help, Vincent. We need all the allies we can get, but I'm afraid you won't be much help unless we take you back to the islands for extensive training."

"Islands? What are you guys talking about? Where do we have to go?"

Hery answers.

"The place on this earth that was never settled by mortals. A land so rich in magic, that it contorts the environment and gives it the most unique landscape on this planet. A place where mortals from every corner of the world inadvertently send their prayers when their institutions fail them."

Lalaina places the answer on Vincent's tongue.

"The Arivesto Archipelago!"

Chapter 16

The next morning Vincent and Hery gather all of their necessary belongings into a couple of duffle bags and make their way to the nearest airport. They leave an entire bag dedicated to his mother's journals and place that one directly underneath them once on the plane. Hery is gracious enough to allow Vincent to have the window seat, although it is apparent that Hery couldn't stomach the idea of flying through the clouds due to his constant mumblings about how humans were never meant to take to the sky. Vincent is also scared, but mostly excited because he had never traveled this far from home, but the more he thinks about this new adventure, the more puzzled he becomes.

"Hery, how come the woman at the desk never asked to look at our passports? I've never been out of the country before, but I do know that they are supposed to check for stuff like that."

Hery replies in a very hushed tone, implying that Vincent should do the same.

"It is because we are people that can be overlooked, Vincent."

Lalaina's voice dances along Vincent's ear.

"Or I might have had something to do with it! Don't tell Hery that I told you. I don't think it's fair when he doesn't include you in the plans."

Vincent cannot see her, but he can feel her hair against his shoulder and a warm sensation against his side. It is comforting to know that he does not have to deal with Hery's eccentrics on his own anymore.

She grabs his hand in hers.

"He is still angry that we cannot communicate directly anymore. Please don't take anything too personally."

Vincent is relieved that Hery is testing Lalaina instead of himself for once, but he can still recognize what's going on. He understands that if concealing their identity is necessary, then they must be being followed by someone, or something. There is absolutely nothing that he himself can do, and must put his safety in Lalaina's hands. Vincent trusts that Lalaina will do the same trick she did with the other security members in order to put Hery and Vincent on the next flight to Madagascar and is once again thankful that Lalaina is here with them. There is no way that he could have made it this far without her.

They land in the capital city without any complications. They are both fortunate enough to have Lalaina, who is amazing with people these days.

Vincent steps out of the airport and is immediately greeted by the commotion of the streets and the sound of staggering lives piling over one another just to get by. Colorful square buildings decorate the sides of roads, being used as marketplaces. The ones that stick out most to Vincent are the ones with a rustic orange hue. Off in the distance, he can see a sign with the city's name fashioned in the same exact style as the one in Hollywood. With this display, and more European looking buildings, Vincent could feel the Western influences surrounding this place and muting the hymns of its original culture. All of its nativity is condensed to the people in the street selling fruits, fabrics, and other sorts of wares.

Vincent becomes enticed by all the excitement and makes his way towards an older woman with layers of fabric resting on her lap, and others hidden under lids of woven baskets. She is placed next to a boisterous fruit salesman, who obviously is taking away most of the eager customers. Despite this, Vincent is more fascinated by her quiet demeanor in such a traditionally extroverted profession.

He stands before her and remains silent.

It did not occur to him previously that they would not be able to actually communicate because Vincent does not know any French or Malagasy, but now the realization of this made him blush profusely. He feels so rude and ashamed of his impulsiveness that could have scared this old woman half to death. However, she seems to understand the situation immediately and exchanges his embarrassment for a gentle smile.

She motions him over to her. Vincent obeys and she grabs his wrist with papyrus hands. Then she nods towards the woven basket next to her and pulls Vincent's hand on top of it. He removes the lid for her and she seems pleased. She encourages him to explore the basket and his fingers fondle a piece of bright red velvet.

Before he can process what is going on, the piece of velvet makes its way up Vincent's and coils itself around his wrist like a snake. It then ties itself together, latching it to him permanently. Vincent looks towards the woman for an explanation. She is giggling to herself and moving back and forth very slowly.

"Vincent, come this way!"

Vincent shouts back towards Hery, filled with fear. He continues to tug against the fabric, but it refuses to let him go. It isn't until the woman spots Hery off in the distance that she releases Vincent from her trap. Without hesitation, Vincent takes off in an all-out sprint in the opposite direction, following Hery's voice. While running towards Hery, he looks back towards the stand, but the woman is no longer there. Her basket is empty, rolling past more unsuspecting customers looking for a bargain.

Because all of the evidence of this transgression disappeared into thin air, Vincent decides to keep this story to himself, but remains cautious throughout the rest of their journey.

Chapter 17

Hery leads him in the exact opposite direction, away from the bustle of the afternoon, towards a road that would eventually lead them to a very large heart shaped lake within the city, a popular tourist site. There is a large bridge that connects the shore to a large island in the middle of the lake, and in the middle of that island is a large gold sculpture of an angel who traditionally watches over those who have fallen. However, it now mostly watches over the birds that rest in the waters.

Hery ushers his first command.

"We need to get to the island. It may not look like it now, but this lake used to be part of the swamps where our ancestors lived. The Rano have always settled near and utilized the power of the water."

Vincent nods and makes his way amongst the tourists to the bridge until he runs into something unexpected. The blockade in his path knocks him down onto the ground.

Lalaina manifests with her arms crossed. She is obviously annoyed, but she also appears to be drained of energy. She muffles little puffs of air under her words.

"Vincent, we are in hiding. Do you really think we can walk among the civilians?"

"Well then, where are we supposed to go?"

She motions over towards Hery, who is hidden amongst purple jacaranda trees. He is trying to negotiate a ride from a man with a paddle boat.

"Of course, we flew halfway around the world so that Hery and I could have a romantic ride around a lake."

She tries not to smile at Vincent's joke but it slips out anyway. She giggles and fades away.

As Vincent walks towards Hery and the paddle boat, little purple flower petals flutter about and fixate themselves onto his arms. He tries to brush them off, but they remain in place.

He laughs.

"Okay Lalaina, you can be a third wheel."

He finally makes it over to Hery and his gaudy yellow plastic boat. The stranger still stands besides Hery, but once he sees Vincent and his flower petals, he becomes frightened and runs away.

"What did you do?"

Ignoring the man's reaction, Hery replies.

"I paid the man and now we have a boat."

Vincent scoffs at him.

"But that's… not... whatever, let's just go."

Vincent crawls into the seat on the right and Hery plants himself on the left. Hery then twists around and places both of his hands firmly onto the soil. Before Vincent could process his movements, Hery pushes off against the shore and the two of them are propelled across the lake. They land with a giant splash and the waves sprinkle the nearby tourists.

"Hery! Lalaina said that we aren't supposed to draw any attention to ourselves. You shouldn't use your strength or any super enhanced abilities for the time being."

Hery seems frustrated by these limitations, especially coming from Vincent as a mouthpiece, but he has a clear reason to follow orders. As Vincent speaks, more and more flower petals stick to his face and skin. Concerned, Hery complies with Vincent's wishes.

"Okay Vincent, I will keep a steady pace with you."

This proves to be easier said than done. With every movement of Hery's massive legs, the boat jumps at least 10 feet, even with taking all of the necessary precautions. As a result, Vincent is forced to pedal for the both of them, in order to remain inconspicuous.

Vincent attempts to speak in between his exhausted pants.

"Are we almost there yet?"

Hery, fully rested, directs Vincent on the best course of action.

"We just have to go around directly behind the statue. There should be a marker somewhere on the - "

Tremors on the water prevent Hery from finishing his sentence. At first, they behave like normal waves, but as the frequency increases, the water behaves strangely. Small droplets begin to rise as if they were being pulled by a magnet, hanging in midair like they are suspended in time. More and more rise to be part of the collection until they finally have enough for their creation. They gather directly above the paddle boat and arrange themselves into a giant golden coelacanth. The creature still maintains the transparency of water, but is distinguished by its golden sheen. Vincent stares at it in awe until it crashes back down into the lake, falling without making a splash.

Frightened, Vincent shouts.

"Hery! What was that?!"

Once again, Hery does not have the time to answer. Coming to Vincent's defence, hundreds of flower petals spiral around Vincent's body and coat him in their embrace, creating another skin. When his flesh is completely covered, the purple petals harden and become an armor for Vincent.

A look of panic passes over Hery's face for a brief moment, but he recomposes himself.

"Relax Vincent, this is the Guardian of the Rano, the people of the water. It means no harm."

Vincent tries, but can't completely distract himself from what's unfolding around him. Along with the petals and the water, Vincent notices something wrong with Hery's pocket. A familiar bloodthirsty glow shines through his pants and becomes stronger with each solidifying petal. He focuses on the light and can see a swirling cyclone within the jewel that mimics the motion of the petals.

He finally realizes that Lalaina hasn't been with him since the bridge.

Vincent quickly becomes enveloped in his cocoon. This new cast prevents him from moving his arms and legs. He tries shouting for help, but the petals on his lips trap the sound and send it back at him. Vincent's vision blurs as Hery frantically throws punch after punch against the petals in order to break the spell.

Roots dig into his skin deeper and deeper with every crack Hery puts in the armor. Hery finally grabs onto the mouthpiece and rips it completely off, but as he achieves this, the roots penetrate the back of Vincent's skull.

"OUCH!! Hery stop it!!!"

Hery throws the torn bits up into the air and to everyone's surprise, the giant coelacanth reconfigures itself and consumes them. They can observe the petals dissipating within the fish until there is nothing left. Hery makes eye contact with Vincent and Vincent realizes Hery's plan.

"No no no no no no no no!"

But it's too late.

Hery grabs Vincent and chucks him up into the air so high that Vincent can no longer see the boat below. He hangs there for what seems like minutes, waiting for the creature to come, until finally he sees the ripples once more. The giant coelacanth jumps out of the lake with open jaws for Vincent. He holds his breath and the monster swallows him.

It's just like being underwater.

Even while inside the fish, Vincent can see right through his skin and observe the undisturbed tourists on the bridge, growing larger and larger as the coelacanth comes closer to earth. The petals and roots slowly erode away within its stomach, giving Vincent mobility once again.

However, once the plants were taken care of, the monster's body began to come after him. Vincent sees his hair and fingertips beginning to decompose and become part of the fish. At first he panics, but then the sight of Hery down below inspires him to take action. He understands that the only way to escape this situation is to embrace his own magic.

Vincent concentrates on the movement of the water within the coelacanth's body. He embraces the fluidity of the creature and he himself becomes like water, spreading himself throughout its body without completely letting go of all of his own essence. He travels to the creature's head and attempts to see through its eyes. At this moment, they are one. Vincent is able to coax the fish into banking right in order to avoid Hery and the boat.

They hit the water once again without disrupting the lake. Once they are deep underwater, Vincent sees a hidden cavern underneath the rocks through the fish's sight. The stone above it is covered in a script similar to the words that are on Hery's chest. Vincent realizes that this is the door they have been looking for, and decides to separate himself from the Coelacanth. He slowly reassembles himself bit by bit as he swims towards the surface to fetch Hery.

Vincent pops his head out of the water before the rest of his body is fully formed.

"I found it! This way!"

He then combines himself with some of the water within the lake to form a larger, stronger transparent arm and grabs Hery before he has time to respond. Vincent creates a whirlpool within the lake and throws Hery into it, knowing that it will take him directly to the underwater entrance of the cave. While Hery is enjoying his ride, Vincent swims alongside him and focuses on rebuilding the rest of his body until they reach their destination.

The funnel carries Hery through the opening and spits him out on the first patch of dry land it finds. Vincent follows close behind, sickering at Hery gasping for air while he is forming the fingers on his still watery hand.

Once Hery finally catches his breath, he lets out a bellowing laugh that shakes his entire body so hard, the water jumps right off of him.

"Yes! That is the spirit! That is how our people grow stronger!"

Hery punches his chest as an action of pride. Vincent is very glad to see Hery react this way instead of his usual disapproval.

"Now you understand how to react and use your abilities without being told. Come, let us find a place where I can finally tell you everything you need to know about our family."

Vincent lets out a sigh of relief.

"Finally! Who knew I would have to be swallowed by a giant fish before we would see eye to eye?"

Hery and Vincent walk side by side up the underground beach until they reach a group of sharp red boulders. These boulders framed the entrance to an ancestral tunnel. Vincent stares down the long dim corridor. All he could make out is red painted walls and a path of golden bricks decorating the floor.

"Vincent, before we enter, sit here. I need to elaborate on some things before we enter the domain of the people."

Vincent obeys and chooses to sit on a rock that would give him enough height to be on equal footing with Hery.

"First of all Vincent, you must always remember, some of your worst enemies appear to be friendly in order to convince you to let down your guard. I bet you believed those flowers to be Lalaina, didn't you?"

Vincent looks down, a little embarrassed, but says nothing.

Hery continues.

"I admit that I did too. But once we were on the boat I realized that something pushed her away from us, hopefully just for a little while, and that something was this."

He pulls out the Blood Stone from his pocket. Its light is feeble for now. It needs to rest from the spectacle it just performed.

"Vincent, listen to me very carefully. This amulet, and all that it contains, preys on you. It will try to attack you every chance it gets and it doesn't even need to be in direct contact with you. It has tasted your blood and now it can find you. It can manipulate others to do its will, to come after you."

This scares Vincent terribly. He starts swatting at the Blood Stone, desperate to knock it out of Hery's hands. However, this would prove to be futile, given Hery's advanced agility and dexterity.

Vincent shouts at Hery.

"Then why the hell are you still carrying it around?!"

"Because Vincent, your father needs it. It's the strongest, darkest relic we have. With its great power, it will help us understand the greater forces at bay and those who continue to attack our people. It is our cross to bear. I will do my best to keep you safe, but as you can see, I am limited."

Vincent ceases his attacks on the Blood Stone, but still interrogates Hery.

"Well then, why doesn't it attack you? Why does it want me so badly?"

"It is because of your abilities, Vincent. Your adaptability. Someone could use you, your blood, and your energy to amplify spells and rituals that are already catastrophic on their own. You are a natural catalyst. The epitome of our evolution."

Vincent speaks much more softly as he is trying to contemplate all of this new information.

"I don't think I understand what you mean, Hery."

Hery matches Vincent's tone out of courtesy.

"You and I come from a long line of powerful beings. The people, regardless of their domain, share the same ancestor, the one who brought the magic. Because of this, we are of both worlds, which is why we can see, hear, and do things that the others can not. You just happen to be the youngest and newest member of the bloodline, which means you have more potential than those who stood before you."

Hery pauses to gauge Vincent's reaction. There is a moment of silence before Hery begins again.

"I want you to try something, Vincent. Relive what you felt and thought while you were in the water. Try to transform yourself once more, but this time just in your arm."

Vincent does as he is told. At first it is difficult, but once he closes his eyes, he is able to reconnect with what he felt while he was with the fish. He concentrates the fluidity in his arm. His fingers disappear and merge into one bulky entity. Once he notices this difference, Vincent opens his eyes and looks down. His arm has transformed into a large transparent fin, just like the coelacanth's.

Hery shouts in celebration.

"Yes! That's it!"

Vincent shoots a questioning look back at Hery. He shakes his arm back and forth until it merges back into a normal arm.

"Vincent, when you merged with the Guardian and then reassembled yourself, you took a part of it with you. You may have separated your bodies, but the connection you felt and the ritual you made with it cannot be undone."

Vincent looks down at his arm and whispers to himself, unable to fully focus on Hery's lecture.

"The Guardian?"

Hery tries to bring Vincent's attention back to the matter at hand.

"Yes. The creature you saw guards the entrance to this ruin. It is a pure entity placed there by the Great King of the past. There are Guardians at every entrance of every ruin on the islands. The majority of them are connected through underground tunnels like these, but there will be times where we have to encounter other creatures and Guardians. But Vincent, I warn you, it may not be wise to fuse with the other creatures so freely the same way you did with the Guardian of the lake. If the Blood Stone could fuse with the surrounding environment, I'm sure that as it gets stronger, it could fuse with stronger creatures as well."

"What do you mean Hery?"

"Those flowers wanted to fuse with you and it hurt you. It is because they were under the influence of dark magic from the Blood Stone. It is essential that you stay away from the influence of this amulet in any way, shape, or form. This means if you encounter a Guardian or monster under the influence of the Blood Stone, you can not fuse with it. Your blood must not mix with it. As with most rituals, both parties need to consent to the fusion, but the Blood Stone can surpass this. It can rob from others like a leech. It will never stop until you are completely void of energy and it absorbs the rest of your remains. Once this happens with you Vincent, I'm afraid that it will finally have the power to do whatever it wants with this world."

Vincent is scared to ask his next question, but does so anyway.

"And what exactly does it want with this world?"

"To subdue it."

Chapter 18

Hery and Vincent decide to spend the night on the beach before heading into the mysterious tunnel. Vincent had used up quite a bit of energy from the encounter with the first Guardian, and even though he didn't feel it then, he is quite sore and exhausted. He lays in the sand while Hery works on protective ritual circles for both of them. Vincent is mesmerized by Hery's monotone circular movements and is eventually lulled to sleep.

The dark backside of his eyes slowly fade into a pure white. As the color lightens, so does his spirit. Vincent feels weightless, almost as if he is floating. He is formless until he feels a sharp pang. Strong unseen fingers swirl his essence around and manipulate him into being.

Through the white facade, Vincent begins to make out some large faces. The fingers pull him in even closer, until he is inches away from a pair of giant lips the size of mountains. A cold gust of wind passes through Vincent and he finds himself choking on air. He continues gasping until the hands drop him into a golden tank of water. Once he is able to fully breathe again, the rest of his senses come too.

Vincent is now able to see two people standing over the tank, watching their new creation swim about. The hands from before belong to a tall, dark, regal man with chalky red locks. He is covered in gold jewelry and a more organized form of Hery's scarring. He has a strange text embedded into his skin, but unlike Hery, this added to his beauty. However, the true source of his radiance came from his glowing smile. Finished with his work, the man turned to his side and began to clean up a plethora of bowls with ingredients that Vincent has never seen before. While he's fading away, the second figure gets even closer to the tank.

She is a toddler with the same chalky red hair as her father, but instead of locks, she proudly wears her hair in a little afro. She imitates her father's smile and his authoritative stance while he has his back turned, but this cannot be realized because she is still pulling at her golden frock like a child. She waddles over to the tank and hits the glass with a loud thud. The man turns back around to make sure she is alright, and once the two of them are reassured, he scoops her up in his big brassy arms and leans her over the tank for a closer look. She giggles at the creature and pokes her baby finger in the water. Her skin is a blank page in comparison to her father, but Vincent can see that she has one minute word written on her finger, andriambavy.

The tank is filled with a glowing warmth as soon as her flesh touches the water. It is as if Vincent is feeling happiness in its purest form.

"Lalaina?"

But this moment is quickly tarnished. In an instant, a flash of violent purple light breaks out between Vincent and the pair. It flashes on and off as quickly as a strobe light and scares away the warmth from the scene. The man's face contorts into a sinister smirk and his eyes are engulfed in a pool of murky green until it completely drowns his soul. Vincent quickly shifts his focus to the young girl to see if she is okay, but she is even worse.

Her eyes shift from a flirtatious amber to a ferocious fire and then extinguish until they are as black as coal. The skin around her eye sockets becomes grey and flakes off like ash. The ash spreads to the rest of her face and neck, disintegrating everything in its path until it can no longer sustain itself. The body of the toddler crumples into a pile of dust on the floor.

Vincent jolts himself awake out of shock.

It takes a minute for Vincent to realize he isn't dreaming anymore because he still feels sopping wet. He finds himself in a pool of his own sweat and another dark liquid. He panics, jumps up, and examines himself. Vincent has remnants of charcoal drawings all over his arms and legs. He must have sweated all the symbols off during his nightmare.

"Hery!"

He shouts.

"What is all of this?"

Upon further examination, Vincent discovers that a ritual circle was also drawn around him while he was asleep and that the markings on his limbs completed the circular patterns on the ground. It was as if someone considered him as part of the terrain.

"Hery! Did you literally cast a spell on me?"

Hery lays in a similar circle, but lacks the same charcoal drawings on his body. He sleepily rolls over enough to glance at Vincent and respond.

"You fell asleep while I was doing the protective rituals. You weren't there to enter the spell, so I made you part of the spell."

Satisfied with his own answer, Hery rolls back and tries to fall back asleep.

This isn't enough for Vincent.

"Well it didn't work at all!"

Hery is obviously concerned and sits upright to listen.

"What are you talking about, Vincent? Did something attack you?"

Vincent doubts his own anger and initially becomes sheepish in his response.

"Well… not me, exactly. It was a nightmare, but I've never had one like this. I don't know who I was but all I remember were these people who turned into monsters! And I knew I was next. I know it sounds weird, but it didn't just seem real. It was real!"

At this, Hery keeps a straight face and presses Vincent for more information.

"Think Vincent. Was there any hint or indication of who you could have been?"

Vincent pauses for a moment.

"I was in a fish tank..."

Hery becomes more confident.

"There you are! This is natural Vincent. You were seeing the memories of the Coelacanth, the Guardian of the Rano. Because you absorbed part of it, you are more than yourself now. It's a logical side effect. Now go back to sleep."

Hery rolls over in a huff, which irks Vincent.

"Yeah, that's perfectly logical…"

Vincent trails off. He is talking to himself at this point.

"But that doesn't explain all the horrible stuff that happened…"

All he can think about is Lalaina.

Hery returns to his previous position to address Vincent and puts his mind at ease.

"You can't trust a memory, Vincent. Memories are just interpretations, not facts. It is natural to exaggerate if one is scared or frightened."

Vincent still presses the issue.

"I guess, but there was a girl -"

Hery winces as soon as Vincent mentions a girl, but tries to play it off as if he is calm.

"I'm sure that the Guardian has seen so many atrocities since its creation. Afterall, it is almost as old as the royal bloodline itself, but it's best not to let this cloud our focus on the task at hand. There is a long road ahead of us before we can find your father. Try to get some more rest."

With that, Hery rolls over once more. His loud snores indicate that he's fallen asleep before finishing their conversation. Knowing that he won't get any more information out of Hery tonight, Vincent obeys and goes back to sleep.

Chapter 19

The next morning, Vincent opens his eyes and turns to his side to find that Hery is no longer there. This startles Vincent to the point where his body reacts defensively, and his arm dissipates into the ground, throwing him off of his balance and forcing him to hit his head on the boulder he had been using as a pillow.

"OUCH! Son of a -"

"Now Vincent, we will have to do something about your choice of words!"

Hery laughs in Vincent's direction. He is busy gathering up their things in order to progress even further underneath the island.

Vincent sits up with an attitude, pulls his arm out of the ground, and shakes off whatever dust is left on it.

"A 'good morning' would have been nice, Hery."

"And a companion that gets up at a reasonable hour would also be nice. Now hurry up, we have a lot of ground to cover if we are to find your father!"

Vincent complies with some mumbling and makes his way toward the tunnel's entrance, even though he is still disturbed by the nightmare he had last night. He knows that if Lalaina was involved, it should be taken more seriously, especially by Hery. However, Hery seems pretty determined to reach his destination quickly in order to help both him and Lalaina, so Vincent decides not to divulge the details of the dream right now. Besides, what are nightmares compared to the giant ancient Guardians that they are going to be facing?

Vincent bends down and starts washing his arms in the water, scrubbing even harder to get all of the charcoal symbols off of his body. After he scoops up the last bit of water he would need to be completely clean, it rearranges itself into a tiny goldfish, flopping around and gasping for oxygen. Vincent quickly puts it back in the water without much thought. The fish gratefully swims around Vincent's hands and in between his fingers before dwindling off into the deeper water, leaving gold sparkles in the behind it. Vincent leans in to get a better look, but Hery interrupts his investigation.

"Vincent, we must get going. Come on, this way!"

By the time Vincent looks back, the water returns to its normal state. He decides to get up and follow Hery, still pondering on his dream and the little friend he just left behind.

Hery leads Vincent further into the small tunnel about a mile away from their campsite. The tunnel clearly had been carved out from the initial bedrock, but is now paved with crimson bricks and stones, from floor to wall to ceiling. The larger stones are covered in geometric designs and various pictographs while the bricks supporting these murals are engraved with lines upon lines of text. There are no blank spaces to be seen anywhere. The juxtaposition is striking and Vincent is afraid to even step foot in the tunnel in fear of ruining all of this work.

They stand at the entrance while Hery searches his pockets for his lighter. He draws it and extends his arm a little further into the passageway, energy pulsing through his arm, all the while feeding the flames. Hery's eyes start to water, but Vincent is unsure exactly why. Perhaps it is nostalgia for a familiar place, or the recognition of something unbelievably beautiful. Either way, Vincent feels that it is best to not let the silence go on for too long.

"It's incredible, Hery."

Hery breaks away from his own thoughts.

"This is our true first step on this journey, Vincent. The people agreed to build these tunnels to connect each other no matter where they were in the archipelago. This is what keeps us tied together even when others no longer identify themselves with their origin. These pictures tell the story of our voyage, our conquest, and… our downfall."

Vincent's curiosity peaks.

"Downfall?"

Hery answers.

"We have dwindled and been replaced, yes, but we have not lost."

He pauses and smiles.

"You are here Vincent... You are proof that we continue."

An overwhelming sense of pride comes over Vincent. This is the first time he has ever been connected to something bigger than himself, let alone connected to anyone else by blood. The mere promise of a family excites him: people like him, who are out there, waiting for him, just like his father. Sure he's had friends, been in clubs, and worked together on sports teams at school, but this feeling is completely different. He wouldn't have to prove his worth to belong. He inherently does. Vincent smiles to himself at the thought of others who would embrace him the same way as Lalaina and Hery.

"So, where are we heading now? Do you think my dad was down here too, Hery?"

"Your father first came to Madagascar in order to find the entrance to our tunnels and learn more about our history and his lineage. We exist beyond the reality of mortals, but those of the bloodline can enter here and return to their homeland. As I understand, he visited the other islands for information first. I know he spoke with Ahitra, the current ruler of the Nofon, the people of the soil. I think she led him to another site on a different island, so it is best to ask her before continuing too far into the labyrinth."

Vincent's ears perk up when he mentions her name.

"So then, she's like us, right? She can use magic too?"

"Yes Vincent, she can, and so can all of her people, but they are not nearly as powerful as her. Be careful. She is of our blood, yes, but she is of her own people. Just keep that in mind when discussing the mission with her."

Hery's warning does little to nothing to dissuade Vincent from being excited about meeting this strong, enigmatic woman.

"Don't worry Hery, I might be new to magic, but people I can handle. Not gonna lie, I was pretty popular with the ladies back home too!"

Hery scoffs and replies.

"Trust me, you've never met a young woman like her."

Chapter 20

They reach a fork in the road after a couple of hours of travel in the submerged tunnels and decide to take the path that would lead them further east. During this time, a new sense of motivation comes over Vincent and he decides to read even more of his mother's journals. He is completely engrossed in her notes; notes describing the changing geography of the islands, unique flora and fauna, descriptions of others she met with abilities similar to Hery, and even direct English translations of powerful spells. Vincent is so preoccupied that he fails to notice the light coming from Hery's lighter slowly beginning to dim as they continue on inside the tunnel.

"Don't worry Vincent, we are almost to our destination."

Vincent notices that Hery takes uneven breaths between his words.

"Oh hey, Hery, are you getting tired or something? Do you want me to hold your lighter for a while?"

"Lighter?"

Hery responds.

"No, no. This is not a toy or a simple flame. This is a precious relic given to me by the future Queen of our people! It is not something to be handed over to one who cannot fully control their own magic yet. Besides, it made a blood oath with me when I received this gift. You could not wield it even if you tried."

Vincent rolls his eyes while Hery finishes his story.

"Okay, okay! I was just trying to help you know."

Hery lets the conversation drop, but the situation does not improve. The flame continues to dwindle. After a few minutes, Vincent decides he should step in whether Hery wants him to or not.

"You know; Mom wrote a little something in here about these tunnels I think..."

Vincent begins flipping through the pages feverishly, as if he needs to prove a point.

Hery is dubious in his response.

"Oh, did she now? It is amazing that she was able to get information on this place without ever coming here herself."

Vincent continues to turn through the pages while speaking, keeping his eyes on his mother's notes the whole time.

"How do you know that she never came here? It seems like she knew a lot about this place -"

Hery cuts Vincent off before he could finish.

"Because the tunnels only respond to those who are part of the bloodline. She is an outsider, and therefore, it would be impossible for her to enter."

"They respond to the bloodline, huh?"

Vincent trails off after finding the paragraph he was looking for.

"There it is! She has a spell that can help us!"

"Very interesting, Vincent, but I am afraid that we don't have any time to set up a ritual or draw the proper enchantments."

"This one doesn't need any of that!"

"What?"

Hery sounds genuinely surprised.

"But all spells require exchange, sacrifice. Simple words aren't strong enough -"

This time Vincent interrupts Hery.

"Fahazavana!"

Suddenly, both Hery and Vincent feel a rumbling underneath their feet. The words engraved on all of the red stones rearrange themselves like a rubik's cube until they find their appropriate match. Once the words begin to pair up with other unexpected letters, they lock into place and give off a soft amber glow. The warm light against the red brick reminds Vincent of a young Lalaina playing in the water.

Hery grips against the tunnel walls, clinging on for stability. He is taken aback at the events that just transpired.

"I see that these old chambers still have secrets to share."

He hesitantly closes his relic and puts it away into his coat pocket, eyes traveling around every corner of the space as he does so. Hery stands up straight and dusts off his clothes.

"Let us continue, Vincent."

Vincent smiles to himself and continues to linger behind Hery. He gets back to reading his mother's journals by the light of the tunnel until they eventually reach the exit.

Chapter 21

It isn't long until they spot a bright square light in the distance. A new sense of vigor fills the two of them as they climb towards the exit.

"We have arrived!"

Hery declares as they both emerge into the fresh open air.

They arrive on the side of a large hill covered in wild grasses. The two of them are high enough on the hill that they can see a small farming community down below. The town consists of red and white mud - brick buildings, with one main dirt road leading in and out of the area. Other hills surround this little valley town on every side, but the locals have obviously learned how to utilize the landscape. Along the sides of the hills are carved terraces for rice fields, something Vincent would have expected to see in an East Asian country. The scene is especially charming for him, as he grew up in a giant city all of his life.

As Vincent is taking in the view, he feels small trembles in the earth coming from behind. He turns around to see small rocks rolling themselves in front of the tunnel's entrance. Once they situate themselves, vines and grasses would embrace the rocks from the surrounding wall and hold them in place. There was no way for them to go back.

"Hery, look!"

Hery is already looking at the tunnel by the time Vincent speaks, but he seems completely unbothered by what is occurring.

"The tunnels are hiding themselves. That must mean someone else is coming."

Almost as if they were summoned, a pair of young men emerge from the base of the hill. They seem pretty inconspicuous, like local high school students in their jeans and t-shirts. They are close to Vincent's age, so he relaxes a bit.

Hery is the first to speak.

"Salama! Mpandeha mila fitsaharana isika."

They nod their heads out of respect for Hery, but they quickly turn their attention towards Vincent.

"What are you doing here?"

Vincent is surprised both to hear the boys speaking in English and choosing to address him instead of Hery.

"Who, me?"

Vincent pauses for an affirmation and then continues.

"You guys speak English?"

They look at each other and laugh.

"Miss Ahitra told us you were coming, city boy. Come on, we will take you to her place."

Vincent can't help but smile to himself, but Hery is less enthusiastic. He rolls his eyes at their informality, but follows them to Ahitra anyway.

They all head down through the rice patties into town, where the other locals seem almost clueless to their presence. Their attitudes remind Vincent of the drones of pedestrians back home, although this town is miniscule in comparison. He assumed that people living in the countryside would be friendlier, or at least would meet his gaze. Vincent finds himself disappointed, but keeps this to himself.

"Don't look so glum, city boy. These people aren't supposed to notice you. You are hidden from them."

"Wait, what? What are you guys talking about? How did you know -"

The taller of the two boys decides to respond.

"Ahitra made it this way. Just until she knows that you two won't be causing any trouble. Relax, if you behave, it is only temporary. Then you can go ahead and be a tourist, city boy."

Vincent looks to Hery to see how he reacts to this news. He had been looking down this whole time in grave frustration, and this didn't seem to make things better. Vincent knew that he would have to be the one playing diplomat in this situation.

"Don't worry you guys! I don't mean any harm. Just wanted to ask this Ahitra lady a few questions and then we'll be on our way. You won't have to be babysitting us for too long."

The boys look at each other as if they knew Vincent and Hery would be there a while. The shorter boy turns around and starts walking backwards with his hands behind his head.

"We are in no rush, so you shouldn't be either. Take your time and just relax. You look like you need a breather anyway."

"Well, I can't argue with you there."

Vincent responds more to himself than to his young guide. Satisfied, the boy turns back around, keeping his hands where they are, and continues to lead them to Ahitra's house.

Chapter 22

They finally arrive at the largest building in town. It is a white, two story mud house that happened to be as wide as four or five homes put together. Despite how wide it is, it didn't have any other major decorative details that would have made it stand out from the other homes in the area. The house was also situated on the easternmost side in town, placing it as far away as possible from the tunnel's entrance. However, despite the distance, the building definitely faced the tunnel as if to keep a watchful eye on it.

The taller boy knocked on the door three times without a distinct answer. Rather than being deterred from this, he turned around and smiled at both Hery and Vincent.

"You two may enter when you are ready. Miss Ahitra is just a little preoccupied in the parlor, but you can still go speak to her."

The two boys then step to either side of the door frame and wait for them to enter. Vincent looks up towards Hery, but he is still pouting for some reason in his own way. It is up to Vincent yet again to take the initiative.

He pushes the door open and steps inside. The interior of the home seems to magically expand as soon as he enters. It no longer seems like they are in a farmhouse, but rather a jewel toned French palace. Rich velvet curtains cascade down in every corner of the many rooms. Large mirrors and paintings clothe the walls and striking gold details highlight every feature of each room. To contrast all of the color on the walls, the floor is a marbled white, like something you would see in a contemporary museum.

Vincent looks toward the left after hearing a bunch of older women making a fuss. In the separate parlor room, Vincent sees a young woman in her early 20s slouching in an oversized gold chair, completely uninterested in the fuss surrounding her. The older women are applying various products to her hair. In the corner, a small group of women are pulverizing mushrooms into a vibrant red powder, while another group is tasked with turning that powder into a creamy hair dye. The third and final group of women are busy applying this red dye to the ends of her long hair, creating an ombre effect. While all the women are busy at work, she is scrolling on her cell phone and chewing some bubblegum.

No one looks up when he enters the room.

Vincent can feel Hery hovering over his shoulder and is determined to not make a fool of himself in front of him. Although he has some strong resentments about his upbringing, at least it prepared him for situations like these, where he needs to become the perfect prince, or at least someone who knows how to command and control the attention in a room. This is the perfect arena for him to demonstrate these skills in front of Hery.

He coughs at first to try and get their attention, but this fails. After a second attempt at a discrete cough, Vincent decides to speak up.

"Miss Ahitra, I presume. You're looking absolutely lovely today. My name is Vincent and this is my associate, Hery. Thank you so much for inviting us into your home on such short notice -"

Vincent stops himself when he hears the sound of a camera click coming from Ahitra's cell phone. She turned her phone towards him, took a picture, and is now swiping through and carefully choosing a filter to put over it.

Vincent stammers.

"Ummmmm… Miss Ahitra?"

Just then, a ring goes off in the pockets of the two door boys. They each grab their phones to check their notifications and giggle at the screen.

"Way to go Casanova!"

The shorter boy turns his phone towards Vincent after shouting at him so he could see the image. Ahitra took a photo of him mid gesture and edited it to where Vincent is covered in anime sparkles and wearing a cartoon crown. She shares the caption: "Really? This is my Prince Charming?" and adds a GIF that would indicate that she would swipe left on his profile. Although this was definitely not what Hery and Vincent came here for, his ego is still a little bruised. He's never received such a humiliating public rejection before, but for some reason, he is more amused than upset. She is the first woman, or person for that matter, that didn't want anything to do with him. Vincent was so used to being pulled in each direction by people who wanted something from him, or being fawned over by people who wanted to be with him, that he never knew how seductive indifference can be. Hery was right about Ahitra, she wasn't like anyone he's met before.

Vincent reacts completely on impulse when responding to Ahitra's post. He runs his hands through his hair and laughs softly under his breath.

"You know, if you wanted me to look cute for one of your stories, all you had to do was ask."

After hearing this, all of the women who were busy working on her hair come to an abrupt halt. They stare at Vincent in complete shock. Even the two door boys behind him fall quiet and nudge each other's arms, waiting for Ahitra to respond. Hery is now on high alert, with one of his hands in his coat pocket, grabbing his relic just in case.

Ahitra finally looks up from her phone and meets Vincent's eyes. She has a vivacious smile on her face and playfully laughs while she responds.

"Cut that corny shit, city boy."

She then addresses her ladies.

"That will be all for today, thank you."

The women grab all of their tools and scurry off through different doorways like garden ants. Ahitra turns her attention back onto her guests.

"You two may come with me. I'm sure we have plenty of things to discuss. Come on, let me give you the tour!"

She grabs Vincent by the arm and they head into the opposite direction with Hery close behind, muttering something underneath his breath.

She leads them back to the center of the house where they ascend a grand spiral staircase. Vincent looks back and sees all of the women standing in the grand foyer staring up at them, expressionless. They look as though they would remain there until Ahitra gave them another command. A chill goes down Vincent's spine, but nevertheless, he follows Ahitra to what he would assume to be her personal chambers.

They enter a large room with vaulted ceilings that are painted dark like the night sky. This gives the room the same sophisticated edge that is found throughout the rest of the home, proving that Ahitra is well versed on modern trends as well as stylish enough to be ahead of the curve. While Vincent previously lived in a glass house, this woman was able to create her own fortress.

As soon as they enter, a small baby cow with a slight hump in its back leaps off of the bed and dashes affectionately towards Ahitra. It runs in and around her legs playfully.

"Shhhh…. shhhhh….Milamina hatrany ry namako. We have guests!"

Ahitra looks back towards Vincent.

"You can pet him if you'd like. He is very friendly."

Vincent crouches down to meet the calf at its own level. This excites the little cow and it leaps into Vincent's lap, nudging its face against his. When Vincent strokes his back, the tiny black spots on the cow begin to shimmer with the same gold flakes at the Coelacanth from before.

Hery sees this and finally breaks his silence.

"What?! What is this madness?! You've turned the Mighty Guardian of the Isle of Tendrom, the protector of the Nofon, into a … a … pet?!"

Ahitra seems to get pleasure from seeing Hery so agitated.

"His name is Spot!"

Hery absolutely loses it.

"How dare you, woman? It should be up in the mountains watching over the Nofon! Do you have no concern for their lives?"

Spot seems very upset at Hery for screaming at his mistress and tries to force itself out of Vincent's arms. Vincent desperately holds on to the little animal out of concern for Hery, but it is becoming too much for him. Ahitra notices this, and scoups up the calf into her arms effortlessly, calming it as if it were an infant.

She responds to Hery.

"You know very well that we are protected here. Our Guardian is our last defense, as it is designed to be. Would you rather I send Spot to stomp you to death when you arrived here? Didn't my messengers treat you well?"

Ahitra pauses for a second to give Hery a chance to respond, but does not wait long enough for him to come up with an intelligible answer. She continues.

"Besides, I know you let him bond with the Water Guardian, and he is a foreigner! Imagine what Lalaina would think if she found out you let him turn her protector into a tiny goldfish! Hypocrisy, Hery."

Hery finally screams at Ahitra before storming out of the room, slamming the door behind him.

"I am her protector!!"

Vincent is still trying to process everything that was said. He's never seen Hery turn his back on someone before, no matter how angry he might be.

Ahitra speaks up.

"Don't worry, one of the chamber maids will show him to his room. You're more than welcome to join him if you'd like, but personally, I would give him some time to cool off."

"What was all of that? I hope I'm not out of line, but both of you seemed like you were ready to pounce on each other."

Ahitra exhales while tickling Spot's stomach, almost as if it's their calming ritual. His noises and movements drive her to smile once again. Ahitra looks up to meet Vincent's eyes.

"Yes, I guess I should apologize for all of that."

With that, Ahitra moves towards the corner of the room where a small table and two chairs are waiting for them. She sits down and pats on the other chair cushion, encouraging him to sit by her side. He follows.

She continues.

"After all, you haven't been around long enough to know the history between us… between Hery and I that is."

Vincent sees the perfect opportunity to lighten the mood.

"History, hmmmm? What kind of history are we talking about here?"

She laughs and slaps him on his arm.

"Get your mind out of the gutter! You think I would ever fall for an old geezer like that?"

She sighs and then continues.

"No, we can't stand each other. I'm afraid that Hery can't bear to even be near me..."

She drifts off into her own thoughts for a moment.

Vincent responds, trying once more to cheer her up.

"Now that probably isn't true, it seems like everyone loves you."

Spot lays down and rests his head in Ahitra's lap, reaffirming what Vincent just said.

"You don't know half of it, city boy…"

She trickles off into pensiveness, but Vincent is determined to break down her walls.

"What could he be so mad about anyway?"

This seems to perk her up. Ahitra chuckles a bit to herself and pulls out her cellphone. She opens up an instagram account and shows it to Vincent.

"This is why."

The instagram account is full of scenic pictures from the surrounding landscape and local people smiling while they are completing everyday tasks. Some of the best pictures are taken from difficult angles in the rice fields at sunrise and sunset. The captions are full of encouraging messages inviting the reader to come and visit this beautiful area. It is very clearly a travel page dedicated to bringing in tourists to the countryside.

"Woah, this is really impressive, Miss Ahitra. You almost have a million followers on this account!"

"Thank you Vincent, I'm glad someone around here appreciates my hard work."

"But I don't understand. Why would Hery be upset at something like this?"

Ahitra takes back her phone and tucks it into her pocket.

"Well, Hery believes in old fashioned ideals. Those of royal blood made a pact years ago to not interfere in the lives of mortals anymore, but how can I stand by any longer in an age where I can reach them within an instant? So I like to take pictures of my beautiful home and other places on their island in order to bring more visitors to Madagascar. However, Hery thinks that my traveling and more tourism would bring in people who could discover us and our abilities or try to use them maliciously."

Admittingly, this logic makes a lot of sense to Vincent, but if this is the case, then why is he, as a foreigner, allowed to be a part of their world?

Is it simply because he is a descendant or part of some bloodline? Ahitra interrupts his thoughts.

"But Vincent, you must understand, this exposure and tourism could bring in a lot of additional revenue and business to their island. It could provide great opportunities for these people, opportunities that thrive because of tourism in other parts of the mortal world. You saw the capital city for yourself didn't you? The Water Guardian itself lived in the heart of the city for years and none of the outsiders noticed!"

She grabs his wrist for emphasis.

"They cannot see anything that we don't want them to."

"What do you mean by that?"

"That is the power of the ones descended from the true kings, Vincent. Myself, Vatosoa - the Princess of the Reef of Haran and Lalaina... as the rightful heir of the Rano. We may choose to give our champions powers and our guardians are strong enough to protect us, but everything comes from us three."

Vincent finally feels the need to speak up.

"Miss Ahitra, if that's true, then how come I could see it? I mean I am an outsider aren't I? How come I have powers if I've never met the three of you before? I know I am connected to all of this somehow, but it doesn't make much sense."

"Ah, yes. Your concerns are valid! Shame on Hery for not explaining this to you as he should."

She stops and asks.

"Are you like us, Vincent? What can you do?"

Vincent decides to reveal himself to her. He breathes deeply and closes his eyes to concentrate. He makes his wrist tingle slightly at first, but then this feeling grows even stronger to the point where he can no longer feel Ahitra's grip. Vincent opens one of his eyes to check on his progress and is impressed with what he finds. Just like back in the old motel room, Vincent detaches his hand from his wrist and moves it around the room. A single pixelated thread keeps the adventurous hand from getting lost altogether. Spot sees this and runs into the corner of the bedroom to hide. Rather than being frightened, Ahitra smiles from ear to ear and traces her index finger along Vincent's thread.

"Ah, so you are special, aren't you?"

Vincent reels in his hand and continues the conversation.

"Miss Ahitra, I would love to show you more of what I can do at a later time, but honestly, I came here because I'm looking for my father. I know you and Hery have some sort of beef or whatever, but he told me that you were the last person to see him before he went missing. Do you have any idea where he went?"

She rests her hands on the arms of her chair and leans back, trying to relax, but showing concern in her face.

"Yes, there was another foreigner here a while ago actually. He was a very nice man who was eager to talk to the locals, just like you, city boy. He wielded lightning."

"That's him, Miss Ahitra! Did he say anything to you? About why he came here -"

"Vincent, I don't want you to get the wrong idea. Your father said he came to my village to help us out during a drought. You see, sometimes the soil doesn't give enough nutrients for a good harvest, so your father used his lightning to bring nitrogen back to the ground. It was his actions that helped us expand our village in the first place, especially since we no longer get offerings from the mortal realm. It was a prime example of how we should be using our abilities to help the people around us -"

Vincent interjects.

"But, Hery said that he came to Madagascar to learn more about our heritage, our bloodline."

Ahitra looks towards Spot in the corner. He is no longer shaking from fear, but he is still looking over with plenty of intensity, as if he is on high alert.

"Well, I did repay him for all of his help. I gave him the exact information he asked for, a secret that has remained silent for thousands of years."

Vincent leans in and grabs her hand.

"Please, Ahitra, tell me what you told him -"

"Vincent, I can't. I've already shared so much with you. There are things about us that I need to protect, people outside of us that I need to protect."

"He's the only family I have left. Please."

She stops and motions Spot to come closer. He obeys but watches Vincent with each step he takes. When he gets close enough, Ahitra picks him up and puts him in her lap, gently stroking the back of his neck.

"Your father wanted to know more about the origin of our power, not just what we can do, but what makes us different from everyone else on earth. I told him that path would only lead him to great sadness, but he persisted anyway."

She pauses, moves her hand away, and then continues.

"Vincent, I'm telling you this as a friend. Sometimes it's best to leave things in the past and focus instead on what needs to be done for the future. Don't let Hery walk you into something you do not understand."

She stands up with Spot in her arms. This forces Vincent back into his own seat, but he eventually stands as well, unsure of what to expect. She turns towards her own bed and lays Spot down on top of the comforter. Without looking back at Vincent, she continues.

"I think it's best if you get some rest now. One of my maids is standing outside the door to take you to your room. I'll be ready to greet you in the morning. Thank you."

Vincent looks at her with obvious disappointment, but adheres to her request. It's best not to push too much right now. Afterall, both he and Hery are determined to stay as long as they must in order to get the information they need.

Chapter 23

Vincent opens the door and is immediately greeted by a small older woman standing right at the entrance's edge, staring up at him with blank eyes. He nearly steps on her before realizing her presence. Vincent fumbles about for a moment before he acknowledges her.

"Hello? Nice to meet you Ma'am -"

She turns around rapidly and begins walking away, moving very quickly with short strides. Without saying a word, she makes it apparent that Vincent is meant to follow. He does his best to keep up, but this woman buzzes about like an insect. Her steps may reverberate, but she never utters a sound.

The maid leads Vincent through a seemingly never ending hallway towards the opposite end of the house. Vincent can see a grand white door in the distance, slowly growing in size until it reveals itself to be at least three times his height. Once they arrive at their destination, the old maid sharply turns around and walks forward, as if Vincent wasn't even there. He hurries and moves out of her path just in the nick of time.

"Uh, thanks I guess?"

Vincent looks to see if she notices his politeness, but she remains unfazed and continues on with the next task at hand.

Vincent turns around and pushes the white door open with all of his might. He somehow manages to nudge it halfway open and slips inside. The room is covered floor to ceiling in dark walnut bookcases with two queen sized beds perched up in a loft on the left side of the room. Underneath the staircase to the loft, Hery sits in a green velvet chair reading a book on gardening that he found from one of the many shelves behind him. He does not look up when Vincent enters the room, but when the giant door slams shut on its own, it causes both of them to stir.

Hery excitedly stands up from his chair and pretends like he is trying to find a spot to return his book.

He mumbles underneath his breath.

"That wretched girl just can't help herself…"

Vincent walks over towards the ladder, climbs a few steps, and then sits down out of exhaustion. He may be tired from the conversation with Ahitra, but he knew he would have to have some sort of reconciliation with Hery if he wanted to get any sleep tonight.

"You know Hery, I think you should give her a little break every once and a while. I know you two have some long standing rivalry about ideologies or whatever, but it seems like she has a lot on her plate and -"

Hery cuts Vincent off with a sarcastic laugh and some more grumbles, but then he pauses and becomes more vocal as if he's had a sudden epiphany.

"Be careful young man. Ahitra is a dangerous person to give your heart to… and to do so quickly? I thought you were stronger than that, Vincent."

"Oh come on, you know it's not like that! It's just…"

Vincent trickles off.

"There's a lot of things about her and her life, where I can, you know, relate..."

Vincent dares not say this outloud, but he thinks to himself.

"I know what it's like to constantly be surrounded by people while feeling like you are all alone."

Hery sees that it's best not to tease any further. Therefore, he changes the subject. He comes out from behind the reading nook and looks at Vincent directly.

"Did Ahitra say anything else to you? About your father?"

Vincent meets Hery's eyes. Something about Ahitra's warning doesn't sit right with him, but he decides to be honest anyway.

"Actually, yeah. She said he was here helping her out with the soil and the farms, but he wanted something else from her. A secret that she really didn't want to share."

Hery leans in a bit closer.

"A secret? About what, exactly Vincent?"

"Well, Ahitra says that my dad wanted to know about the origin of our powers, or what made the people with our bloodline have these magical capabilities. I guess she really didn't want to let him know, but she felt like she owed him something somehow."

Hery turns back around and faces the wall. After hearing this news, he balls one of his hands into a fist and hits it against a bookcase. His head sinks down, but after a moment, he picks it back up mid-way and tilts his chin towards Vincent.

"I can't believe she did this…"

"Hery?"

Hery straightens up once more and remembers his surroundings. He then addresses Vincent.

"I know where your father went, Vincent."

Vincent stands back up and braces himself on the railing.

"What??"

"On the northernmost tip of the archipelago, there is a sacred site to the descendants of our people. The Nosy Zona is the origin point of our people, where the initial contract was made. However, we do not visit this island anymore, out of respect for those who have fallen to the curse."

Hery begins pacing as he talks.

"It is also impossible for foreigners to step foot on the island. Only people of the royal bloodline can escape the death that follows anyone who visits the area. Why would your father even attempt a venture like this one? There is no way you could chase after him Vincent… unless…"

Vincent chimes in while Hery gathers his thoughts.

"Hery, my dad was a scholar who was heavily invested in this place. He must have known about these dangers and found a way around them!"

Hery looks around the room for a bit before answering Vincent. His hands glide over all of the shelves as if they were looking for a hidden wire. Once Hery is satisfied that no one is listening, he gets closer to Vincent, puts his hands on his shoulders, and whispers.

"The only way an outsider could survive Nosy Zona, is if they were able to embody the powers connected to the royal bloodline. The only other figures, outside of the royal family, that have done this though are the Guardians of our people. That means you need a power equal to theirs to survive."

Vincent pulls away from Hery, physically rejecting his proposal.

"But there's no way I can be as strong as the Guardians here! I mean, sure Spot doesn't look like much, but the Coelacanth just smacked me around for fun!"

Hery remains calm and takes a step towards Vincent.

"Ah, but you forget so soon, Vincent. You did defeat her didn't you?"

Vincent pauses for a moment to try to understand. He looks down at his fingers and watches them shift on their own to translucent liquid with gold flakes while maintaining their shape. They gradually change back one Vincent realizes the answer.

"You mean like how I bonded with the Water Guardian?"

"Exactly, Vincent! It is as if this is your destiny…"

Hery climbs over Vincent and sits down on one of the beds, still lost in thought. Vincent feels the need to chase after him. He sits down on the other bed and faces Hery.

"What do you mean, my destiny?"

"You are the Catalyst, Vincent. An eternal bond. Only someone with your exact power would be able to pull something like this off. If you could convince all of the other Guardians to lend you a fraction of their powers, then you might be able to survive the curse of Nosy Zona and rescue your father."

Vincent grows more concerned as Hery elaborates on the situation at hand.

"Do you really think he is in that much trouble?"

Hery finally looks up at Vincent and meets his eyes.

"I am certain of it."

Vincent feels overwhelmed with this news and surrenders into his bed. He falls backwards onto the mattress and lets the back of his head collapse onto the pillow. He tries his best to just feel the smooth satin pillowcase in an attempt to ground himself, but the weight of this new responsibility is too much for him. The distress refuses to submit to simple coping techniques. Once he realizes that his efforts are futile, he rolls over to his side and addresses Hery.

"Well, what's the plan now, sarge?

"We must stay here until you find a way to convince the Guardian of the Nofon to lend you its power."

Hery shudders internally at the thought of spending one more moment this near to Ahitra, but he quickly continues.

"Then we must travel to the Westernmost point of the archipelago, the Reef of Haran, and meet with Princess Vatosoa. She may not be as open with you as Ahitra, but I am sure that she would be more sympathetic to our cause. Only after we have the trust of the last two Guardians, can we even think of heading north towards Nosy Zona."

Vincent laughs unexpectedly, treating this difficult situation with the same level of defensive sarcasm that he has grown accustomed to.

"So you want me to wine and dine some other mystical princess? Geez Hery, I'm not some gigolo, you know."

"Vincent, show some respect -"

Vincent cuts Hery off in a softer voice.

"Relax. I'm only joking. Trust me, nothing matters to me more than this."

Vincent rolls over on his side and faces the wall.

"Goodnight."

Hery responds, a little concerned by the tone of Vincent's voice.

"Alright, get some rest. Goodnight."

They both finally get somewhat comfortable and drift off into sleep.

Vincent gets to dream once more. Again, he is floating around in a large tank, and a little girl's fingers dance along the water's edge. She couldn't be more than six years old. He is compelled to swim up towards her, and feel her warmth. Her tiny fingernails scratch at his scales and he is in complete bliss.

However, they are interrupted once more when another little girl around the same size barges into the room with a swaddled baby in her arms. The baby is nearly the same size as the little girl, throwing her off her balance every now and then as she walks. The second girl runs up to the tank and shows her friend the swaddled infant. Vincent sees a peculiar flat ear dangle outside the cloth and swims back a bit in surprise.

The new girl unwraps the cloth and reveals the face of her baby. A young calf flops its head out of the wrap and turns toward the fish tank. It squints to get a better look at Vincent, but strains itself too much and then lets out an explosive sneeze. The entire front of the glass is covered in the projectile goo from the calf and Vincent can no longer see the others in the room. He can only hear their laughter as he wakes.

Chapter 24

Vincent opens his eyes to the sight of Hery using a mirror to inspect his ears. At first, Vincent thinks Hery is just trying to do some personal grooming, but then Hery whips out a knife and starts carving a small circle into the tragus of his left ear. Of course, Vincent thinks to himself, Hery would pick now of all times to give himself an ear piercing.

"Jesus Christ..."

He mutters to himself and rolls over to bury his face in his pillow.

Not too much longer, they are both startled by the sound of the gigantic bedroom door opening. A small old woman pokes her head out from behind the barricade.

"Good sirs, Princess Ahitra invites you down to breakfast. She will be expecting you soon."

With that, the maid somehow has the strength to shut the door all on her own, even if it rattles most of the large bookshelves in the bedroom. The tremors also manage to shake a new form of optimism within Hery.

"Wake up, Vincent. This is our chance to win over the Guardian! Be sure to look presentable!"

Vincent gets out of bed and shuffles about.

"Yeah, Hery, I'm pretty sure that the cow is going to be very picky about what I wear to our date this morning."

Hery colds Vincent.

"Just watch your manners around the Guardian. It may not resemble it now, but it is a truly powerful spirit."

Vincent scoffs.

"Okay, I'll be extra polite to Spot if you behave yourself in front of Ahitra, deal?"

Hery rubs on his ear for a while but then eventually answers Vincent.

"Alright Vincent, that sounds fair. I will do my best."

After they finish getting ready, Vincent and Hery head back downstairs to the main hall for breakfast. This time, the room is completely swallowed by a large white dining room table with gold accents on all of its edges. Ahitra is obviously at the far end of the table in an equally regal chair with purple velvet cushioning. She stands up once she sees them enter the room, although her eyes are mostly focused on Vincent.

"Welcome! Please sit and enjoy all of the spoils that the Isle of Tendrom has to offer!"

Vincent bows slightly.

"Thank you, Miss Ahitra."

Hery remains standing, so Vincent nudges at his side discreetly. Hery then dips his head low in Ahitra's direction as a form of gratitude.

Ahitra looks surprised, but pleased at Hery's response. She motions for Vincent to take his seat at the right hand side of her table. Hery sits directly across from Vincent on Ahitra's left. Spot stands guard in the corner behind Hery, sleeping with his ear raised to the sky. Ahitra sits down and stirs some sugar into her tea.

"Did you gentlemen sleep well?"

Vincent is the first to respond to her question.

"Like a log! How about you Hery?"

Hery looks up from his coffee directly at Vincent. He understands that this is his cue to carry on the conversation, but does not seem very eager to partake.

"Like the dead."

Ahitra laughs at Hery, like she would be surprised to hear anything else come from his mouth.

"My, how morbid. Perhaps it was all the black decor in your room that's brought on this mood? If you'd like, I could prepare another space for you. Although I'd have to admit it is one of the more masculine rooms in the house and I spent a lot of time collecting items that I thought would suit both of your tastes."

Vincent speaks up on behalf of Hery.

"Oh no, don't feel like you have to do that! We're flattered that you've put that much thought into making us comfortable while we're here. That's very generous of you, right Hery?"

Another cue.

Hery speaks to the group from behind his tea cup.

"Yes, very generous. Thank you, Princess Ahitra."

Vincent seems to choke on his breakfast while hearing Hery call Ahitra by her official title. Both Vincent and Ahitra look up at him in surprise at his uncharacteristic cordiality. Spot decides to get up with a little stretch, sticking his rear up in the air, and walks closer to Ahitra. She bends down slightly to scratch his ear.

"Well, well. You are both quite welcome! And please, don't hesitate to reach out to myself or one of my maids if you need anything at all."

She smiles and motions to the two older women and the gentlemen standing back in the doorway. She continues the conversation while mostly looking at Vincent.

"Now, do you boys have any plans for today? There is a fantastic hiking trail up in the hills that has the most amazing views of the area. It's also where I take the majority of my pictures for my Instagram account -"

Hery slams his knife down onto the table and speaks up before Vincent has a chance to apologize for his sudden change in character.

"I do not think it is wise for Vincent or I to entertain or encourage this social media craze of yours -"

"Hery, it's not like she's asking us to take photos for her. I'm sure it's a really nice place."

Ahitra chimes in.

"No, Vincent. Let him speak. Despite what he believes, he may speak freely here in my presence. I am not the one who keeps secrets in this house."

She arches an eyebrow and waits for Hery to continue. Vincent's stare travels between Hery and Ahitra. It's almost as if they are having their own silent conversation.

Ahitra is the first to speak up.

"Where is Lalaina, Hery? I have not felt her presence once since the two of you arrived. She is tied to him, yes? Was that your doing?"

Vincent isn't sure how exactly Ahitra got this information, but he definitely knows what she intends to do with it. She's provoking Hery for snapping at her earlier, but she struck a serious chord within this desperate old man. The veins in his arms and neck throb as if he is trying to power his lighter once more. Spot notices this and lowers his head toward Hery, as if he is getting ready to charge. The hairs on his back are standing on edge. Ahitra continues, unbothered by their reactions.

"Vincent hasn't been able to see her either. Why are you keeping both of them in the dark? She's my friend, Hery! I have a right to see her too -"

Hery finally responds to her accusations.

"Have you told the boy about your true power? I would say that qualifies as a secret, does it not?"

Ahitra grows quiet and speaks as if only to herself.

"No…but I don't see how that concerns either of you!"

"I will give you the answers that you are owed, but only if you reveal your true self to Vincent. You can no longer have any control over him!"

"How dare you?! I have done nothing, Hery! Besides, you know damn well he is not like the others! It wouldn't work even if I tried."

"Prove it!"

Ahitra looks over towards Vincent with concern on her face.

"Do it!"

"Alright!"

She pauses.

"Let me explain it to him."

She then returns her attention to Vincent and addresses him with the same solemn expression she had when she was retelling her encounter with his father.

"Vincent, I am the Princess of the Isle of Tendrom, and because of this, I embody all of the growth and prosperity that this land has to offer."

Ahitra opens one of her hands and a small flower begins to sprout from her palm.

"However, my abilities can encompass more than just the elements tied to the earth."

Just as soon as it came, that small flower wilted away to nothing. After it's death, Vincent looks up once more to meet Ahitra in her eyes, but they've changed. They've been completely filled with a brilliant swirling gold liquid. Her eyelashes flicker with a similar glimmer. Vincent panics, but can't help himself but to be taken in with her beauty.

"I've learned how to cultivate the things that you cannot see."

She takes hypnotic pauses in between each of these words.

"Connections."

While she speaks, a sparkling, golden mist escapes her mouth and makes its way toward the servants at the door.

"Information."

It swirls around the tallest doorman and brings him closer to the dinner table.

"Thoughts."

It envelops his mouth and enters his system.

"Movements."

He raises his own hands and brings them to his throat.

"In reality…"

The man's grip tightens and Vincent can hear him gasping for air.

"No matter where I put it…"

Vincent can hear a crunching noise behind him, but is too afraid to turn around.

"If I plant a seed, it will grow."

At this last word, Vincent hears a loud thud. The doorman collapses to the floor, immobile.

Chapter 25

Vincent jumps out of his seat without a second thought and leaps towards the doorman. He grabs the wrist of the corpse, frantically looking for a pulse. Flashbacks of the old man who worked in Vincent's building and his granddaughter playing in the lobby appear inside his head. He becomes overwhelmed with a sense of urgency to save this man's life.

Vincent shakes the body and addresses it.

"Hey, Mr! You gotta get up! Are you okay? Hey!"

He then turns his attention to the other servants in the doorway.

"What are you guys doing?! He needs help!"

None of them move. They stand completely still with a blank expression on their faces, never taking their eyes off of Ahitra.

Vincent notices this and turns to her as well. Her eyes are shifting between gold and her natural eye color.

"What the fuck is wrong with you?!"

"What -"

"Why would you do this?!"

Ahitra stammers and struggles with a response. She seems to be surprised by Vincent's reaction. Vincent gives up on getting anywhere with her and turns his attention back to the body.

"I promise. It's going to be okay."

He lays his hand gently on top of the man's chest, unsure of exactly what to do next. Vincent takes a deep breath and surrenders himself to the mercy of whoever will listen. Suddenly, he feels a familiar warmth come from behind and lay itself on his shoulders. He feels a small hand rest against his back and another on top of his right hand. He looks to his side and sees Lalaina guiding his arm over the man.

She smiles back at him once he meets her gaze.

"So you've met my Guardian, huh?"

She dances her finger over Vincent's hand and it instantly turns to water. He looks down in surprise over his lack of control. Instead of having golden flakes like the water normally does, there are pixelated particles that resemble Vincent's own natural abilities scattered throughout the transparent hand. It is almost as if Lalaina fused both his essence and the essence of the Water Guardian for this specific purpose.

She then grabs it and plunges Vincent's fingers into the man's chest.

"Don't be afraid, okay?"

Vincent nods in response to Lalaina's direction.

A sacred fire comes over Lalaina's shoulder and makes its way down to her fingertips. It then spreads to Vincent's transparent hand and covers it in tiny white flames that are cool to the touch. Vincent, having complete trust in Laiana, does not flinch at the sight of the flames. However, the same cannot be said of the others in the room.

Hery seems to recognize these little flames almost immediately and stands up in excitement.

"Miss Lalaina?!"

Ahitra hears this and snaps back to reality.

"What? Where is she?!"

Ahitra looks around the room until she discovers the white flames on Vincent's hand. She remains transfixed on them until she receives some sort of confirmation that Lailaina is truly with them.

"Now Vincent, listen to me very carefully."

Vincent looks back at Lalaina and hangs onto her every word.

"I need you to go a little bit deeper in his chest. Once you're in there, you need to spread out and reach his throat. I can handle the rest from there."

Vincent obeys as if he is following the directions of a top surgeon. He plunges the rest of his hand deep into the man's chest cavity until he permeates the lungs. Then he shoots his hand up through the windpipe like a mighty stream, water droplets and tiny flames dancing around each other until they reach the broken windpipe.

Once they reach their destination, Lalaina takes a deep breath and concentrates. The fire dances along the surface of the water inside of the man's trachea. The flames reverberate off the walls of the throat and make a hushed humming noise. They grow louder and push the man's head back, opening his mouth in order to escape. Once they flee, he is able to breathe again. The small white flames scatter around the room like confetti.

Ahitra is overcome by the sight and lets out a small tear.

"Lalaina?"

She whispers.

"At last."

Ahitra brushes her hand across her face and realizes her mistake. She turns around and screams.

"Spot!! No!!"

It is too late. A giant hoof smashes its way through the opulent dining room table and rattles the ground. Its impact instantaneously fills the room with mosses that swallow all of the walls and decor. Spot continues to rapidly grow in size until the hump on his back crashes through the ceiling of Ahitra's mansion, causing large chunks of rubble to fall on the unsuspecting people below.

Hery quickly springs into action and grabs Ahitra before a large chunk of marble lands on her. He carries her into the street and away from Spot's wrath. The servants finally snap out of it and run away from the scene. Vincent gives the injured man to one of the workers to take to safety before he faces the true form of Spot, the Guardian of the Nofon.

To his surprise, Lalaina is still standing there in the doorway right beside Vincent. She's staring directly up at the beast with the utmost concentration. Her flames rest on the newly created jungles of the mansion without burning them.

"Lalaina, what's happening?!"

Without taking her eyes off Spot, she answers.

"The Guardian saw Ahitra cry. She never loses control of her emotions like that. It must have thought something hurt her. That's why it's coming after us -!"

They both dodge a swing from Spot's colossal horns. Unfortunately, Ahitra's home isn't as lucky and even more rooms crumble in the aftermath of Spot's anger.

"Us? But no one else can see you!"

"Guess again!"

Spot swings his head once more to try and attack both Vincent and Lalaina. Vincent is able to jump out of the way, but Lalaina is hit by his horns. It takes all that she has to get a solid grip on them. She climbs up, wraps her legs around the edge of the horn and lets it carry her into the upswing.

Once she reaches the highest point, she loosens her hold on the horns and steadies her footing. Lalaina then finds her balance and sprints down the curvature of the horn until she reaches the top of Spot's head. She then jumps onto his neck and grabs on tightly to his hide.

Even in this position, Lalaina somehow finds the strength to give Vincent commands.

"Vincent, get up here!"

Spot is no longer swinging his horns at Vincent. Instead, he is focusing all of his energy into bucking Lalaina off of him. His back legs are reaching beyond Ahitra's mansion and are now destroying the surrounding homes. Although Vincent's instincts are telling him to get the hell out of there, he must help Lalaina in order to keep the other villagers safe.

Spot's front hooves slam to the ground once more as he lowers his head, preparing to buck. Vegetation sprouts from every area of impact, with vines wrapping up the bull's legs like veins. Vincent sees this and gets an idea.

Vincent turns his hands into water once more, and condenses them into solid streams of liquid rope. He spins his arms above his head and whips his watery lasso around each of Spots horns, trying to keep him from thrashing about.

"Lalaina, I can't keep him still for too much longer. Jump off and run!"

Lalaina refuses to move and keeps herself planted onto Spot's neck.

"No! He has to calm down! I'm the only one he might recognize, but I can't get through to him like this!"

Before Vincent could retort, he hears a large thud and sees Spot fall to his knees. Vincent peers past Spot's legs to see that Hery had pinned his tail down onto the ground on top of a large summoning circle, painted with blood. Hery's arms are covered with similar self-inflicted wounds in order to give him the strength to keep Spot in this position.

He looks toward Vincent and shouts.

"Listen to her, if you know what's good for you!"

Trusting in Hery's capabilities, Vincent obeys. He takes a few steps back to prepare himself, and then releases the tension in his arms, in order to slingshot himself up into the air directly above Spot's head. He twists his body around in midair. Vincent then fires the same watery lassos once more around the ends of Spot's horns, pulling back the Guardian's giant neck right before he lands on the apex of his hump.

Spot's front knees buckle and bring him completely to the ground.

Lalaina still seems worried.

"This isn't good. He needs to cool down before he hurts himself."

She takes a deep breath and places her hand on the Guardian's neck. Little droplets of white fire drip down her arms and onto the bull, but once they reach his skin, they extinguish themselves, as if they can not permeate the surface.

Lalaina presses her face against the hide and whispers.

"Spot, it's me. Don't you remember?"

The bull grunts and shakes his head around profusely.

"Lalaina, we don't have much time left! He's going to break out at any minute!"

"Vincent, I need you to let go of him."

"What?! Are you crazy?!"

"I need your help getting through to him. You have to bond with him instead! You're the only one that can do this!"

Spot whips his head around with all of this might. Vincent struggles to regain control.

Lalaina continues.

"Spot should recognize the powers of another Guardian. It's the only way!"

Against his own judgement, Vincent decides to put his trust in Lalaina and release Spot from the lassos. Spot rises to his feet once more and lets out a bellow of rage. Anticipating more thrashes, Vincent sprints down the curvature of Spot's hump. Once he reaches the base, Vincent leaps in the air to join Lalaina at the neck. He lands, but manages to slip on the hide. Lalaina grabs his arm and manages to save him from falling off of the giant beast.

"Hurry, Vincent. Place your hand here!"

Vincent lays his hand on Spot's back, but the Guardian reacts negatively to his touch. Spot thrashes about and does all that he can to prevent Vincent from making contact.

Suddenly, Ahitra stumbles and emerges from the rubble. She calls out to the Guardian.

"It's okay, Spot. I'm alright. There is no need to worry. You can trust him. Vincent is one of us."

The Guardian seems surprised to hear his master's voice. He pauses for a moment, searching for her presence. Vincent and Lalaina make use of this brief window of opportunity.

"Now!"

Vincent slams his hand down onto the back of Spot's hide. Instead of making a loud thud on contact, Vincent's hand phases through Spot's body without him realizing it. Vincent accidentally plunges about shoulder deep into the Guardian before becoming aware of the situation. He uses his other arm to brace himself from getting absorbed even further.

"Lalaina, is this supposed to happen?!"

Lalaina pushes against his back and forces him further into the Guardian.

"Don't worry Vincent, I will be with you, okay?"

"But -"

Before he could fully respond to Lalaina, Vincent completely submerges into the Guardian of the Nofon.

Chapter 26

His particles spread throughout the Guardian's body and filter through its stream of consciousness. At first, Vincent feels a peaceful sense of nothingness. His own identity becomes disintegrated into the masses. Gradually, varying shades of grey begin to layer on top of each other until everything is swallowed by an inky black. This black takes on textures until it manifests into a thick cloth. Vincent finally regains sight and peers beyond the curtain.

The thuds coming from above indicate a small child jumping up and down on her bed. Her giggles fill the room and give her the feeling of confidence she needs to jump off of the bed and land forcibly on the ground. Vincent can see her little feet dance around in between the cracks of the bedskirt.

All of the sudden, the bedroom door slams open and a large man barges into the room. The girl fumbles a bit and falls against the dresser behind her.

The man calls out to his subordinates.

"Grab her!"

Four more soldiers crash through the door and surround the girl. She begins screaming and kicking profusely, but the men begin to overpower her.

In a final act of desperation, the girl slams her palm down on the ground and wild grasses shoot out at the soldiers. They wrap around their muscular legs and render the soldiers immobile.

The original man seems to be unaffected by the natural magic and powers through the grass, swooping up the girl in his extremely scarred arms. This triggers something in Vincent's being and forces him to act. He darts out from under the bed and rams into the shins of her captor.

The man barely flinches from this attack and instead, forcibly kicks Vincent in the stomach. The impact is so strong that it launches Vincent through the wall and into the next room. Rubble crashes down on top of Vincent and keeps him from moving. All he can do now is helplessly watch the events that are about to happen through the hole in the wall.

Vincent hears the screams coming from the other room. The man has the little girl in a headlock while he's busy making a large cut in his thigh with an oversized knife. He then uses the same knife to vertically cut the bottom of the small girl's foot. Tiny drops of blood soil the grass that she cultivated in self defense.

The man drops the knife on the ground and uses his free hand to pull out the Blood Stone. Its iron thorny chains shake about like tentacles, looking for its next prey. It naturally gravitates towards the young girl, which obviously upsets the strange man. He slams the Blood Stone down onto his own thigh and wraps the coils around himself. The spikes dig into his leg and suck on his tainted blood.

A surge of energy runs through the man's body and gives him a primordial fury. He lifts the girl high into the air and lets her blood drip into his mouth. He drinks as much as he can before he throws her down onto the ground.

She scours back in an attempt to escape, but the man slams his foot down and encircles them in a brilliant fire. He then picks up the blood stained grass and forces her to eat it. She bites at him in protest, but he forces his fingers deep into her throat.

Once she swallows the bloody grass, a bright yellow glow begins to form in the base of her throat. It consumes her neck and makes its way up to her mouth. Her entire face shines and her eyes fill themselves with a thick golden liquid. Once her transformation is complete, the man relinquishes his fire and takes a step back. She stands back up with a blank expression and he stares at her with a look of admiration.

Vincent's vision blurs after this scene. He feels a tight grip around his ankles. The force pulls him away from the little girl and the strange man. They fade further and further away until Vincent returns to the nothingness. This nothingness brings him peace once more. Vincent is desperate to stay in this place, but a voice calls out to him.

"Vincent? Where are you?"

There's a brief pause. The voice grows more and more faint, as it is drowned out by menacing snarls and swirling black clouds. He hears lightning crack somewhere behind the smoke and it startles him. He looks around in the direction where the voice came from.

"Please, come back to us. We need you!"

Vincent hangs onto every word and they eventually reel him back into reality.

He blinks a couple of times, but is able to finally see his rescuer. Vincent wakes up with his head in Lalaina's lap. Although she's offered up her thighs as a pillow, nobody else can see her presence besides himself, so it just looks like his head is cocked up in the air at an awkward angle. Vincent doesn't seem too concerned though. He just stares up at Lalaina's comforting face, while she's busy stroking his cheeks with her hands.

"Thank God, I thought we lost you there for a second."

Vincent snickers to himself.

"Yeah, I'm sure Hery was balling like a baby about it."

She gives him a playful little slap on the cheek.

"Oh stop it!"

He laughs to himself and turns his head to the side.

Vincent sees Spot laying in a bed of moss, exhausted. He gradually shrinks down to his normal size in phases, which takes about seven minutes in total. As Spot grows smaller, Vincent can see more and more details of the person behind him. Ahitra is busy soothing Spot's wounds and rubbing his back as he finishes his transition. She's clearly been crying.

Vincent immediately jumps to his feet once he sees Ahitra. He instinctively walks over to her and stares at her for a while without saying anything. Vincent realizes this may come off as extremely weird, but honestly, he couldn't figure out the right thing to say to her, especially after what he saw.

She addresses him first.

"Spot told you, didn't he?"

She doesn't look up at him at all and continues to attend to her Guardian.

"Ahitra, I'm really sorry -"

"Why? I'm not."

Her response throws Vincent off a little, but she quickly explains herself.

"I've come to terms with it, but he hasn't."

She motions down to Spot, who is still resting in her lap. She strokes the top of his head gently as she talks.

"I know that what happened, my curse, made me stronger in a way. I don't mind using it if I'm in control and I know that something good will come out of it…"

Although Vincent wants to be supportive of her, he can't help but flashback to the face of the poor man that Ahitra made to strangle himself. In what way could any good possibly come out of that situation?

"It is when I'm not in control that things get scary. It frightens a lot of people; it scares Spot, and honestly, it terrifies me too. It reminds Spot of the day that he couldn't protect me and sometimes he overcompensates. It is not his fault."

Vincent hears the sounds of people emerging from the damaged buildings. They are careful to avoid the rubble and other sharp objects involved in the aftermath of Spot's rampage. Once they get over these hurdles, the villagers cautiously walk towards Ahitra and circle around her. They watch her to see what she will do next.

Hery also emerges from the crowd. He stands tall right in front of Ahitra without saying a word and makes it a point to look down at her. Of course she notices this and it upsets her.

"Well, you got what you came for, didn't you?"

Hery doesn't respond. Ahitra never takes her eyes off of Hery.

Vincent is clearly bothered by the silence and tries to understand what is going on.

"What do you mean?"

Ahitra responds to Vincent not out of anger, but with a little frustration.

"Look at your hand, city boy."

He looks down and notices what should have been his hand transformed into a mossy hoof with a crack down the middle. The moss continues to grow up his arm until he vigorously shakes it off, much like the fin he received after wrestling the Coelacanth. This could only happen if he truly did bond with the Guardian.

Their mission was a success, but something didn't sit right with Vincent.

"Now, if you have everything you need, I think it is best that the two of you be on your way."

Ahitra tilts her chin up towards the hill where Hery and Vincent first arrived. Even from the village square, they can hear the creaks and moans of the large boulder moving aside for them.

She continues.

"I assume you'll be visiting Vatosoa next, but be careful. She knows what happened here."

Hery accepts this warning and turns around to head back toward the hill. Vincent doesn't want to leave on such negative terms. He can't leave Ahitra this way, just not yet.

"Ahitra, we can help you fix things up around here first. It's the least we can do, considering everything that went down."

She doesn't answer him. Instead, she continues concentrating on Spot and petting his head. Her eyes begin to glow once more, but not nearly as intense as they were when they put the doorman under their spell. Once her eyes change, the villagers stand at attention and start to get to work cleaning up the rubble. They seem perfectly organized, despite not uttering a sound to each other. During this commotion, Spot opens his eyes slowly and licks her hand. Ahitra's face returns to normal at his touch and she smiles at him.

Hery grabs Vincent's shoulder and whispers in his ear.

"She doesn't need us, Vincent."

Hery tugs on Vincent's shoulder a bit, but he refuses to budge. He lets go and starts walking away from the scene. In one last attempt, Hery calls Vincent over his shoulder.

"There's nothing more we can do here. Come."

Vincent realizes that there is no point in staying if Ahitra does not want him here. The best thing he could do to help everyone in this situation is to seek out Vatosa for help. Not only could she help Vincent find his father, but maybe she could also help Ahitra either with rebuilding her village, or helping with her long term goals of building up the town. This thought makes Vincent feel a little less guilty about his choice.

Vincent turns around and joins Hery at his side. The two of them make their way back up the hill and enter back into the mouth of the underground tunnels.

Chapter 27

Hery and Vincent venture into the tunnel in complete silence while Hery's lighter illuminates the way. Vincent is still filled with so much remorse over Ahitra and Spot that he doesn't even have the energy to verbalize his mother's spells to light the tunnel. Hery attempts to break Vincent away from his own thoughts.

"Vincent, are you still thinking about what transpired on Tendrom?"

Vincent doesn't respond. Hery continues anyway.

"You should know that Princess Ahitra and her Guardian are immortal beings. It is impossible to really harm them. They hold an immense amount of power…"

It's still no good.

Vincent is still having a hard time concentrating on anything tangible. However, in this state Vincent can hear disembodied voices and mysterious whispers calling out to him like an enchanting song. He turns his head in small ticks to try to locate the sounds, but this proves to be difficult in this lighting.

He finally locates an ominous light source coming from Hery's coat pocket. A threatening red glow waxes and wanes with Vincent's breath. The light swirls around the room until it completely floods the space, engulfing Vincent until Hery's voice breaks the spell.

"Vincent, are you listening?!"

"Hmmmm? What?"

The light coils back into the orb, looking for another opportunity to strike. Hery has scared it off, for now.

"There's something strange happening in these ancient tunnels."

Vincent mumbles under his breath,

"You can say that again -"

"Are you noticing anything peculiar occurring, Vincent?"

Vincent hesitates to tell Hery about the light coming from his pocket. It seems like its presence didn't phase Hery at all, which means either it is completely normal given the circumstances, or that he can't see it himself. If this is the case, would Hery even believe Vincent? Would he downplay Vincent's concerns like he normally does?

Vincent decides to listen to what's bothering Hery before saying anything.

"What are you talking about, Hery?"

"This is just a suspicion, but I need more light to be sure. Will you cast your mother's spell again for us, so that I can see the exact texts on the walls?"

"Alright."

Vincent brings out his mother's journal from his bag once more and repeats the spell.

"Fahazavana!"

The carvings on the wall lit up once more, but this time, there is something strange about them. Instead of being distinct characters embedded in stone, the symbols glitch out as if they are being infected by a virus. These glitches ultimately cause enough changes in the individual characters that whole new words and sentences appear on the wall.

"It's just as I thought!"

"What's going on, Hery?"

"Something is affecting the tunnels. It isn't just the text that is changing. The walls are rewriting themselves!"

"Wait, rewriting themselves? You don't mean…"

"Yes, Vincent. They are also changing. We have been walking in circles for hours!"

"But... How could this happen?"

"There must be another dark force at work, one that is as old as the tunnels themselves -"

Just like that, Vincent's attention snaps back to the content of Hery's pocket. The Blood Stone jitters at the same frequency as the inscriptions on the walls. However, once the two are aware of its presence, the movement of both the writing and the amulet grows exponentially faster. Hery's concerns himself with what transpires on the walls, whereas Vincent remains fixated on the Blood Stone.

"Hery! It's that thing!"

Vincent points towards Hery's pocket, but Hery acts as if he can't feel a thing.

"What are you talking about, Vincent?!"

Vincent responds, clearly desperate and annoyed.

"Are you kidding me?!"

Vincent lunges towards Hery's coat and makes a grab at the Blood Stone. Hery trics to pivot away from Vincent's reach, but the Blood Stone acts on its own. It jumps out of the coat and towards Vincent's outstretched hand. Luckily, Vincent moves out of the way fast enough before the Blood Stone can latch on, but one of its thorns still grazes his wrist. It falls beside him with a crashing sound.

Now that there is enough distance between the two of them and Hery, the unthinkable happens. For the first time, disembodied text begins to move at a ninety degree angle and form a transparent barrier between Hery and Vincent. Once the characters combine and create intricate words and completed sentences, red clay solidifies behind it. Both Hery and Vincent run up to the barrier and try to break it, but it's no use.

Hery takes this opportunity to speak to Vincent before the wall fully forms.

"Vincent, Vincent! Listen to me! You need to get to the Reef of Haran! Just keep heading West and you will find her Kingdom!"

"But how will I know when I get there? What's going to happen to you?"

Clay continues to form and fall into place.

"Find the rocks! The rocks will lead you to the palace and I will meet you there! Now hurry, before it is too late!"

"But, Hery!"

"That is an order! Now MOVE!"

The last clay block falls between them with a loud thud. Vincent shuffles back in shock, from both the clay slab and Hery's last command.

"Hery? Hello?!"

There is no response.

He pounds on the walls with his fists, but it doesn't budge. Out of desperation, he places his palm directly on the text and tries to phase through it.

His particles are able to spread throughout the surface, but they can not penetrate it. As soon as they try, Vincent is met with an incredibly painful burning sensation both on the surface and in his soul. Vincent stops what he's doing, reforms, and falls back in pain. He turns his head slightly and sees the Blood Stone lying there next to him, mocking him with its swirling red ink.

Chapter 28

After a while, Vincent finds himself frantically pacing within the cave and speaking to himself.

"Okay, good going genius. You got yourself trapped with the one thing that's been wanting to eat you since day one."

Vincent stops and looks down at the Blood Stone. It is silent and motionless, but the red ink inside its jewel continues to stir rhythmically. He remains suspicious of this unnatural amulet.

He knocks over the amulet carefully with the tip of his foot and then jumps back in anticipation. To his surprise, the amulet remains silent, even when provoked by the blood it so desperately craves.

Vincent takes this moment to ponder over his options. If Vincent is going to survive the rest of this journey, then it is in his best interest to abandon the Blood Stone in the cave. However, if what Hery says is true, then he has to keep the amulet in order to find his father. Or is it to help save his father? Admittingly, Vincent is still a little fuzzy on the details. Either way, Vincent is going to need this cursed object in order to find the only family he has ever known.

Vincent reluctantly picks up the Blood Stone from the tip of the chain. He holds it away from himself at arm's length, just in case it decides to lunge at him again. Once more, it remains still.

As soon as the amulet reaches eye level with Vincent, an eerie ambiance takes over the tunnel. The white inscriptions on the wall glimmer and shake once more. However, this time, an ominous red liquid fills the script from the floor and gradually makes its way to the ceiling, creating an ombre effect until Vincent drowns in its light.

Nevertheless, he doesn't let this deter him. Vincent tucks the Blood Stone into his backpack, using his mother's journals to offer a barrier of protection between the amulet and himself. He swings the bag over his shoulder and makes his way through the tunnel.

He walks for what seems like hours, but barely makes any progress. The lights never return to their natural color. Originally, he is forced to head back the way they came, but the tunnels take it upon themselves to make some unfamiliar twists and turns in order to disorient Vincent. He isn't sure what direction he is facing anymore.

Vincent keeps walking until he reaches a dead end. The clay path itself may come to an end, but the tunnel continues, hovering over a dark underground river. He can't tell how deep the water actually is because someone dyed it an artificial black. Water replaces solid ground underneath him for the rest of his journey.

Vincent feels the Blood Stone tremble in his backpack, but he can't tell whether it's trembling out of fear or excitement. Vincent puts the bag against the wall and crouches down to get a closer look at the water.

He stretches out his hand in preparation to stick his index finger into the water, when suddenly the droplets of water rise towards him in a similar fashion as his first encounter with the Coelacanth. Vincent initially takes this as a positive sign and decides to poke one of the droplets in midair. It bursts, but all of its particles latch onto Vincent and scald his finger.

He jumps back in pain and bumps into the backpack. After tasting Vincent, the droplets become more vigorous and form into a shadowy figure. Once formed, the figure lunges rapidly towards Vincent. He instinctively grabs the bag and puts it in front of him for protection. It continues to attack with full strength, but never reaches the backpack. The water droplets change their trajectory as if they were bouncing off of an invisible shield.

Vincent notices this and uses it to his advantage. He keeps the backpack close to his face and starts trudging forward, forcing the droplets to recede. They continue to attack with a mighty fury, but Vincent is able to push them back towards the water.

Once he reaches the edge of the path, Vincent notices another peculiar phenomenon. The peaceful still water also reacts to the presence of the Blood Stone. It scurries away and clings to the tunnel walls, revealing the bottom of the river about 5 feet below. He jumps down and lands with a loud thud. The peaceful water ventures even further away, while the agitated droplets continue their pointless cycle of attack. The Blood Stone is the only thing safeguarding him from both.

It becomes clear to Vincent that he will have to keep the Blood Stone close to his chest for the rest of the journey.

He takes a deep breath and steps forward. A strange gurgling sound takes place behind him. Vincent twists his head towards that direction and sees water returning to the edge of the river. However, he stays dry. The peaceful water still wraps around whatever invisible force trapped Vincent in its bubble, but doesn't dare penetrate it. The agitated water now attacks from all sides, but still cannot break through.

This pattern continues with every step Vincent takes, the Blood Stone glowing like a beacon all the while.

Chapter 29

This beacon is the only light source for the rest of the voyage. The previous inscriptions are nowhere to be found. This river must have always existed here, keeping the ancient people from treading this part of the tunnel. Vincent marches into new territory as the stone walls themselves begin to morph into a more natural limestone. The cave begins to reclaim the tunnels for itself. Any traces of spells are nowhere to be seen.

Vincent walks through the river for about another hour with a constant downpour above him. The droplets never ease up their attacks and Vincent drowns in their roaring noise. He can barely see beyond their presence and fears that he's growing more and more lost. He finally snaps.

"Oh Jesus Christ, will you give me a break?!"

And they stop.

But not out of courtesy.

Vincent regains his sight and finds himself at the mouth of a large underground lake. The lake itself acts as the perfect mirror for the thousands of stalactites up above. They behave like menacing fangs dripping from the outwardly stretched jaw of the cave, waiting to swallow any intruder whole.

The droplets are not permitted to enter.

Vincent isn't sure how to proceed with this newfound silence. He makes his way towards the shore, where he finds an awkwardly shaped rock that would make for an adequate stool. He sits and rests for a moment, dropping his backpack on the floor next to him out of exhaustion.

Vincent doesn't have it in him to get up and properly explore this place. Instead, he takes a quick glance around the space and concludes that there is no other exit in this cavern other than the tunnel he just came from. Vincent definitely isn't too excited about dealing with all of those possessed droplets again. He lets out a large sigh and tilts his head upward towards the roof of the cave.

Silence hangs in the air for the time being, while Vincent is trying to orchestrate a plan of action. He taps his foot unconsciously, trying to make sense of his predicament, but the more he thinks about the situation, the more fearful he becomes. The only thing easing him at the moment is the pure sound of his foot against the limestone. This tapping encourages his hands to join in and play a complimentary beat on his thighs. He becomes lost in thought and is carried by the music.

Vincent starts whistling the intro to "DNA" by BTS in order to make the space feel less imposing. The notes reverberate off of the limestone walls and create new voices, whistling in the dark. Together, they form harmonious rounds that echo vertically throughout the never-ending cavern. At first, Vincent is relieved because this makes him feel less alone. However, as they stretch further away, the sounds become more elongated and distorted, turning themselves into an eerie siren song.

The momentary comfort is gone. The contortion of his song puts the chill back into Vincent's spine. He closes his eyes in an attempt to focus inward, but he is interrupted by a tiny drop of water landing on his forehead.

Vincent wipes the water off of his face with the back of his hand.

He opens his eyes and stares straight up at its source. All of the stalactites in the cavern naturally drip mineral rich water into the lake, but the one directly above Vincent was different. He sees the water drip off of something resembling dark seaweed along the edge of the rock formation. The chalky rock seems to shiver once it's caught. He can't see much in the dark, but Vincent definitely notices something moving around the stalactite.

A grotesque, ghostly white hand emerges from the shadows and wraps itself around the edge of the stalactite. Its long, black nails chip away at the limestone. The shavings glaze Vincent's hair as if they are seasoning for a delicious meal.

He jumps up and screams.

Before he could even shake off the dust in his hair, Vincent panics, picks up his backpack, and runs back towards the mouth of the river. However, his path is blocked by another one of those ghastly creatures. It crawls down from the ceiling and tilts its head towards Vincent. A wet mess of hair covers the majority of its face, but Vincent is able to make out a giant mouth, full lips, and an array of razor sharp fangs.

"WHAT THE FU-"

The monster lets out an unnerving gurgle from its throat that builds into a drowning screech. This summons the rest of the hoard from the shadows. More of these aquatic demons scale down the sides of the cavern, the slime from their bodies catching onto the walls of the cavern and converting the space into a proper lair. With enemies approaching on all sides, Vincent must retreat inward towards the lake.

He rushes towards the water without a second thought. At first, he is able to run through the lake's shallow shoreline without getting anything wet besides the outsole of his sneakers. However, the monsters completely take over all of the stone space in the cavern and spread out along the lakeside. As they approach, Vincent treads deeper and deeper into the water until he is forced into a full out swim towards the center of the lake.

He stops for a moment to catch his breath and survey his surroundings. Vincent wrestles to keep control of the floating backpack, which seems to be drawn to their attackers. The creatures encircle themselves around Vincent, swimming forcibly enough to create a small whirlpool. They continue to swim around their prey and tighten the vortex with every rotation.

Vincent pulls the backpack tightly to his chest in order to protect the contents inside from the monsters, but unfortunately, this pulls the bag underwater and could potentially ruin the contents inside. However, the Blood Stone continues to glow even when submerged in water. Its light illuminates the entire lake and exposes a possible exit for Vincent: another entrance to a tunnel at the bottom of the lake.

Chapter 30

Another harsh shriek pierces the air. In response to Vincent's realization, more creatures drop from the stalactites right above his head. He swings the bag onto his back and dives into the lake to avoid them, swimming as quickly as he can. Vincent can hear the monsters break the surface of the water behind him. He's filled with fear because he knows that they have the advantage.

Vincent tries his best to move in the water, but alas, it's no use. That clunky backpack of his is only adding resistance in the water and slowing him down. He whips it off his back and swings it in his right hand with every stroke, but this proves to be difficult as well. The monsters easily gain on him.

The light from the Blood Stone flickers even faster as danger encroaches. One of the creatures is inches away from grabbing his heel.

Vincent panics and screams down at the backpack.

"Get me out of here!"

Vincent can hear a smug snarl answer his plea. He can feel the backpack vibrating as quickly as the light flickering. It gravitates closer to his chest and wastes no time shielding Vincent from the monsters that are about to strike.

The red glow from the Blood Stone gets even brighter and encircles Vincent completely. The monster on his heels strikes Vincent with its claws, but once it makes contact with the light of the Blood Stone, it is propelled like a torpedo back into the shadows. It cuts through the rest of the platoon and jostles them a bit, but they regain their focus and swim towards his direction once again.

The red particles of light now latch onto Vincent's skin and contort it cell by cell. His flesh elongates and twists itself briefly into unnatural shapes. His chest cavity bursts open into a plethora of tentacles that resemble antlers more than any other fluid appendage. They wrap around the bag and enclose it in a makeshift ribcage. Gills painfully tear across Vincent's throat. Finally, fins unfurl from his forearms and calves, ripping apart the clothes that kept them captive.

This transformation leaves Vincent disoriented, but he has no time to rest.

The vortex continues to tighten around Vincent while the second brigade chases him from behind. With his newfound mobility, he is able to swim fast enough to keep a safe distance away from the predators. However, some of the monsters maintaining the whirlpool notice this and react. They break away from the vortex and propel themselves at Vincent like missiles.

He manages to dodge all of their attacks with his uncanny swiftness and dexterity in the water. Vincent keeps moving towards the exit, but having to dodge these attacks did give the brigade a chance to catch up to him.

Vincent looks over his shoulder and sees the battalion gaining on him. He is several feet away from the entrance of the tunnel, but he can feel the whirlpool pulling him into the current. In a final attempt to break away, he kicks his legs with an unnatural amount of strength and thrusts himself straight down into the tunnel.

Once he plunges into the tunnel, all of the light from the cave above vanishes. Vincent would be completely blind if it wasn't for the presence of the Blood Stone. However, this is not enough light for Vincent to keep track of the predators pursuing him. He must rely on the sounds of jaws snapping and claws scraping against stone in order to track the movements of the creatures.

Vincent continues to swim at a supernatural speed, but this doesn't deter the monsters at all. If anything, this newfound challenge sent all of them into a frenzy, the blood lust causing them to even turn on each other if need be. They are no longer an organized unit. They are beasts that have completely given into their instincts. This tight tunnel forces the torrent of creatures to scramble over one another like a swarm of piranhas desperate for their last meal.

Their miserable cries follow Vincent for a short while longer until he spots a bright light in the distance, indicating the end of this hellish maze. The monsters behind him also realize that Vincent is nearing an escape. They increase their pace to the point where they could reach out and grab Vincent's back fins. One of them slashes the back of Vincent's calves, but he pushes through the pain and continues to swim towards the opening.

He finally reaches the mouth of the entrance, but something strange happens.

Once he stretches his hand through the opening, an intense burning sensation overwhelms Vincent. Small sections of his flesh recede as if someone had thrown acid on him, the fin on his forearm taking the most damage.

He should've been deterred from pressing forward, but with the creatures seconds away from tearing him apart, Vincent didn't have much of a choice. He'd have to continue swimming in hopes of finding a way out.

Vincent passes completely through the opening and feels this scorching sensation throughout his whole body. Pushing through the agony, he manages to open his eyes and take in his surroundings.

He finds himself painfully floating in the middle of a completely silent lake. Tiny rocks and other mineral deposits bring death to the lake floor and prevent any vegetation from growing. Vincent looks directly downward towards the tunnel to see if the creatures followed him here, but to his surprise, they are trapped. The agitated monsters continue to roll over one another, but they are unable to break whatever barrier is preventing them from entering the lake.

Vincent is quick to make use of this unexpected opening, and decides to swim upward towards the surface. However, the more he moves his body through the water, the larger the burns become. They now attack his new fins on each of his appendages as well as the gills on his throat, so much so that Vincent now chokes on the water entering his system. The suffering proves to be too great and Vincent faints from the pain.

His lifeless body continues to float upwards towards the surface. Despite being completely immobile, other agents in the lake water are quick to get to work. They continue to strip Vincent of his strange aquatic features until his body returns to its natural state. The makeshift ribcage is the last to be disassembled. The Blood Stone glows violently in protest, but they continue their work until each tentacle disintegrates into the watery abyss.

Without its cage, the backpack floats away from Vincent's chest and he is free from its spell. They continue to rise until they finally break the surface.

Vincent lets out a huge gasp for air. He fumbles around a bit in the water until he can get his bearings. He looks down at his hands to check for burn wounds, but there isn't a single scar to be found. Despite his body being in perfect condition, Vincent is still weary of what dangers could still lurk inside this lake.

He hurries to grab his backpack and swims to shore.

Chapter 31

Finally, after what seems like ages, Vincent reaches dry land. He starts off trudging through the water, step by aching step, until eventually the water no longer acts like deadweight. He throws his backpack onto the bank out of exhaustion. Once he can move freely, he uses whatever energy he has left to sprint onto a small arid beach and collapses onto the dry clay.

His crash landing manages to shake up the remaining water in his lungs and it rushes to his nose and mouth. This causes Vincent to jolt and sit back up. Vincent reactively spits out this mixture of leftover lake water and mucus all over the ground in front of him. He isn't sure if he is more repulsed by the mess he made or the salty taste that it left in his throat.

Vincent whispers to himself.

"That's disgusting."

He tries to wipe his mouth with his shirt sleeve, but it too is sopping wet and now covered in clay. Up until this point, Vincent never realized how waterlogged he was. He panics and scrambles over to his backpack to check on his mother's journals.

In a haste, Vincent dumps all of the contents of his bag onto the ground without a second thought. The Blood Stone tumbles into the clay rocks with a clanging sound, but Vincent is deaf to it. It scurries away from the soaking wet books, but he doesn't notice. Vincent is too focused on combing through each one of his mother's journals to make sure they aren't ruined.

While on his hands and knees, He fans out each book and inspects every page. For the most part, it seems like all of his mother's notes are on the verge of being destroyed. Vincent has to act quickly in order to save them.

Taking a deep breath, he tries to calm himself by focusing on the feeling of the book in his hand. Vincent drags his finger down its spine and watches the water droplets on the surface follow his fingertip like a magnet. Once he notices this strange phenomenon, Vincent amplifies his energy to try to pull the rest of the water from the heart of his mother's journal.

Vincent's hand begins to pixelate once more, but this time there is an addition to this spell. Gold glitters appear alongside the pixels and behave like the scales of the Coelacanth. The glitters swim down Vincent's hand and attach themselves to the cover of the book. They burrow deep into the journal, looking for water damage as Vincent carefully turns every page for them. Each scale carries water on top of it and they eventually conglomerate like a swarm of carpenter ants gathering water for their queen. The scales continue to forage and combine droplets of water until they eventually create a large sphere of water hovering over Vincent's pixelated hand.

Once they are finished, Vincent places the dried book next to the others and continues on with this process. He grabs the next journal in sequence and uses these scales to remove the water gently. The ball of water continues to expand exponentially as they move from one journal to the next.

Vincent finally dries the last journal in his mother's collection and places it with the others. The scales return to him obediently, wrapping around his hand like a golden glove until they sink back into his natural skin. Vincent uses his last bit of energy to chuck the water over towards the clay rocks. He collapses once again onto the beach, falling asleep in his own muddy clothes. Vincent may be an absolute mess, but he ensures that his mother's legacy is safe.

Something strange stirs Vincent from his sleep. He wakes up in the middle of the night to hear eerie sounds coming from the arid forest behind him. There is a rattling in the sparse shrubbery covering the ground. Vincent cautiously gathers his things, careful not to make a sound. He starts tiptoeing away from the forest, but this wouldn't be enough to keep him from being detected.

As Vincent starts walking away from the noise, a couple of small, grey, mouse-like lemurs emerge from the plants. They are equally as cautious: sticking their wet noses in the air, looking for his scent. Once they spot Vincent, they immediately scurry back towards the foliage, emitting high pitched squeaking noises all the while. They run past the safety of the previous bushes and with an almost supernatural-like strength, these tiny creatures leap into the giant baobab trees in the distance.

The moment they are no longer in sight, the rest of the forest erupts. Every single plant rattles back and forth at an extremely high frequency, creating its own humming sound. Vincent sees endless pairs of large, yellow, ghostly eyes appear from the darkest crevices of the forest. It becomes clear to Vincent that he is outnumbered nearly a thousand to one.

These eyes rapidly blink at one another in strange patterns, almost as if they are communicating in an unknown form of morse code. They get their message across in a matter of seconds and let out a disturbing battle cry. Vincent's thoughts drown in a crescendo of three sinister clicks, followed by a chilling, alien-like gurgling.

This summons a symphony of threatening yaps, squawks, and roars that signal an attack. Before Vincent could react, countless flocks of large lemurs leap from the trees. They form a waterfall of black, white, and brown fur and mob him.

Vincent tries to fight them off.

He hollers at them.

"Get off of me!"

But it's no use.

The group pins him down onto the ground and waits for a special troop of ring tailed lemurs to secure him. They approach him on all fours and surround him. Once they assume their positions, they all squat down while keeping their backs perfectly straight. They stretch out their arms as if they are saluting the absent sun.

After basking in each other's presence, the ring tailed lemurs unravel yards upon yards of thick green vines from the black glands on their wrists. They fling these vines across Vincent's body to one another, tightening their web.

Their little hands are busy at work, wrapping Vincent in a cocoon of creepers. He tries to break free from them, but it's as if they are using some supernatural force to keep him still. Once they completely envelop him, some larger brown and white dancing lemurs grab the excess vines and pull him along the ground, dragging him by his feet. The other lemur species act as a spotter, following Vincent from behind.

Vincent bangs his head on the forest floor with every little leap that the sifaka lemurs take. Their long legs keep them from running on all fours, so they have to shuffle about in order to drag Vincent. He mumbles to himself with every smack.

"Damn it…"

Another thud.

"Shit…"

This goes on for a little while before Vincent finally speaks up.

"Can you guys just chill for a minute?! You're killing me here!"

The Sifaka lemurs courteously stop and regroup. Vincent can hear wailing trumpet noises coming from his captors, but they are not speaking to each other. They seem to be calling out to someone much further away, as if they were asking for permission.

They remain still in silence, waiting for their leader to respond.

Vincent can feel the ground tremble before the order even arrives. A long deathly moan cuts its way through the mighty baobab trees and other ancient vegetation in the forest. Its cry mirrors that of the Sifaka lemurs, but barely. It is much deeper and sounds as though it's been draining in the back of the creature's throat for quite some time.

The lemurs don't waste a single second. The Sifakas obediently take the excess vines and tie them tightly around their own waists. The other lemurs pull on the makeshift ropes for inspection. Once they are satisfied that the knots are secure, they take to the trees.

The Sifakas continue forward, leaping elegantly and harmoniously from tree to tree. They are far more agile in the air than they are on the ground. The other lemurs struggle to keep up, but some hover below Vincent's head on the ground to make sure he is safe. With all of these vines behaving as extra appendages, Vincent's suspended body acts like the torso of some giant horrid arachnid, grappling through the forest at an extreme speed.

They continue this way until sunrise.

Chapter 32

As they approach dawn, they finally reach their destination: a sea of colossal jagged rocks positioned to kill should the need arise. Despite the overwhelmingly threatening aura of the environment, Vincent notices various leafy green trees taking shelter within the crevices of the sharp limestone. It is as if the gigantic shards are protecting them.

The lemurs pause a moment at the border of the forest, but the dancing lemurs begin to loosen the harnesses around their waists once they see the next wave of reinforcements. Immaculately white lemurs of a similar size contrast perfectly against the grey stone below. These new recruits leap from the stone and join their superiors in the forest.

The hand off is executed smoothly and precisely.

The dancing lemurs wrap the vines around the new carriers while the lemurs on the forest floor make sure that Vincent is still tightly sealed in his cocoon. His backpack and belongings are also passed along to the smaller lemurs in this new brigade. Once everything is secure, the white lemurs make their way back towards the rocks at a far slower pace than their agile cousins.

Vincent looks back towards the forest and notices that no one else follows. He will have to rely solely on his new guardian angels from here on out.

The first to step out onto the stone forest is the youngest among them. The child braces himself and then leaps onto one of the many sharp limestone peaks as if it were yet another tree. She lands gracefully without a single flinch. Her rubber-like paws are impenetrable even to the fiercest edge in this forest. After realizing her feat, she waves her arms in the air to celebrate and her family returns the gesture.

After this, the rest of the group leaps onto the limestone, some landing on the rough sides of the jagged pillars, while others land on the pointed tops. Although they all move with the same grace as the child, they leave behind a series of clanking noises behind them as they scratch the rocky surface with their claws.

One of the smaller lemurs stumbles a bit on one of the ledges. This creates a chain of movements that knock Vincent slightly off of his course so that he scrapes his cheek against one of the rocks.

The cut hurts a lot more than it should. Blood trickles down his face.

"Hey! Be careful you guys!"

A member of the senior lemurs hears Vincent and immediately scolds the rookie for his mistake. As a punishment, the clumsy lemur is no longer allowed to act as an appendage with the rest of the group. He leaps onto Vincent's body and stays there for the rest of the ride, snuggling up against his neck as if he is apologizing for the accident.

Although Vincent is still frustrated with this whole predicament, he can't help but find this gesture endearing.

They finally reach their destination in the middle of this rocky jungle.

All of the snow lemurs occupy the border of a grand circular opening, causing Vincent to hover above a hidden oasis of lush green trees and running waterfalls. The waterfalls seem extremely out of place, considering Vincent never saw any sign of a running river before reaching this point. Additionally, the vegetation is so overgrown that it is impossible to see the forest floor from above. However, this doesn't stop the lemurs from gradually scaling down the limestone, lowering Vincent further and further into the dark abyss.

Other than the occasional branch or two, his descent into the forest is a relatively smoother ride than the rest of the journey so far. Despite this, Vincent still remains uneasy. It becomes so dark that Vincent can no longer see in front of his face. He must rely solely on his hearing and whatever brushes against his face to determine what's going on around him.

Vincent tries his best to catch his bearings, but the lemurs decide his next steps for him.

He stops moving.

Vincent assumes that he and the lemurs reached the forest floor, but he isn't exactly sure. He is still suspended in mid air. If they did reach the bottom, wouldn't they set him down on the ground like they did before?

Now Vincent hears a bunch of scurrying and feels something cold, wet, and hard against his back. The initial contact was made in between his shoulder blades, but the lemurs wrap their vines against this giant boulder and now he can feel it from the back of his head to the edge of his heels. They continue to tighten the ropes until it is clear that Vincent wouldn't be able to break free.

The rookie grazed his tail across Vincent's chin as if to say goodbye.

He leaps from his chest and joins the others in their retreat.

Vincent calls out to them.

"Hey! Come back! You guys are just going to leave me here?"

He doesn't receive a response.

Vincent squirms about a bit to try to escape, but his efforts are cut short by the arrival of the General.

Vincent sees a bright yellow light approaching from a distance.

"Who's there?"

The light grows larger and separates into two as it approaches.

"I'm warning you, you better get me out of here!"

A cold stern voice replies.

"Is that a threat?"

Vincent is able to make out a charcoal black foot with elongated toes covered in wispy white fur. A peculiar thumb hinges on the side, distinguishing it from anything remotely human. That and the fact that the creature is approximately seven feet tall.

His eyes travel up the creature. Vincent can make out even more features now that the figure is near. It has extremely long white legs just like the lemurs who brought him here, but the fur changes color as it reaches the torso. The creature is now covered in a greyish brown fur with distinguishing black stripes on its arms. Its shoulders are dusted with celebratory gold highlights that make their way up into a collar. The creature leans in closer to properly address Vincent.

"I think you have gravely underestimated your predicament, child."

Vincent is finally able to make out a face even in the dark. An elongated snout with a disturbingly wet nose makes contact with the side of his face in order to reach his ear.

"We know that you travel with the Cursed One."

The creature pulls away and addresses Vincent directly. The glowing light from before originates from the creature's round hollow eyes. The white fur appears again covering the creature's head while unruly black hair dances on the ends of its oversized ears.

"Look man, I have no clue what you're talking about! I was literally walking around by myself in those old ass tunnels until these crazy fish things started chasing me… I popped up in some lake when I escaped and then all your little monkey buddies brought me here!"

The creature whips its long striped tail across Vincent's mouth without even blinking.

"You will not disrespect my troop in such a manner."

Vincent spits out little tufts of fur from his mouth.

"Your forefathers would be ashamed. In all their wisdom, they regarded us as their protective ancestors, watching over them and the rest of the forest with our ghostly eyes. You will soon know the power of the Spirit of the Haran!"

On command, the stripes on the creature's tail glow with the same color as his eyes and pulsate at a rapid rate. However, this intimidation is cut short by a delicate voice coming from behind the rock.

"Anka, what are you doing out here? Come inside and help me prepare for our…"

The creature quickly snaps his head around in the direction of the voice. Thanks to the creature's light, he can make out a young woman around his age wearing light denim overalls and a white t-shirt, with a bun full of chalky red braids that is almost as large as her head. The creature's light is reflected right back at him in her large rounded glasses.

Vincent takes advantage of the creature's shock and calls out to her.

"Hey, Miss! I could use a little help…"

Vincent is finally becoming fatigued from all of the blood rushing to his head.

"Do you think you could get me down from here?"

She recognizes Vincent instantly and becomes flustered.

"Oh my God! What are you doing?! How long has he been upside down like this?!"

Vincent mumbles under his breath.

"You have no idea, lady."

The general comes back to reality and hits Vincent once more with the end of his tail.

"You will not speak to the Princess of the Haran so informally -"

"Anka, you have to let him down! He is an expected guest!"

He looks back at her in disbelief.

She responds with her version of a command.

"I mean it!!"

The creature begrudgingly grabs Vincent by the chest in one hand and rips him off of the rock in one solid sweep. Vincent can hear all the vines that bound him fall to the forest floor.

"Now bring him here and put him down!"

Anka takes a few giant steps, the forest trembling beneath him with every stride. He towers above this girl, but he's powerless against her.

"Drop him, Anka!"

He opens his hand and releases Vincent. Vincent hits the ground with a large thud. He stumbles about, but has a very difficult time finding his balance after being suspended upside down in midair for so long. It's obvious that he can't overcome this vertigo on his own.

The Princess of the Haran runs over towards Vincent without hesitation. She gives him a quick look over to make sure he didn't need any immediate emergency aid. He fainted, but is relatively unharmed. When she confirms that he is okay, she pulls him up herself and lets him lean on her for support.

Anka's negative attitude immediately changes when he sees her struggling to physically support Vincent.

"Princess Vatosoa, please allow me to assist you!"

He reaches out his hand to cover both of their shoulders, but she shrugs it off.

"No, it's fine. You've done enough for today."

She determinedly moves forward through a hidden path between the rock pillars, making sure to be ahead of her guardian at all times. Anka trails behind, respecting her wishes, but cautiously monitors all of her movements. His bright eyes continue to light up the path for her in the dark.

Chapter 33

Vincent wakes up in an unfamiliar place. It is a tiny library within a limestone cave, but its owner uses every possible inch of the space. Endless stacks of books travel around the curvature of the limestone, so much so that the only exposed rock is that of the perfectly polished floor. This floor acts as a mirror, making one feel as though they are suspended in a tunnel of tomes.

This optical illusion doesn't help Vincent's vertigo at all, so he falls back and collapses into the giant cream fuzzy bean bag he had been sleeping on for several hours. His eyes remain transfixed on the ceiling, so he is completely oblivious to the young woman reading next to him. That is, until he hears her turn the page.

Vincent rolls over in surprise, but she remains perfectly still, completely unbothered. She looks up towards him, but keeps the book over her mouth.

"Hey, I've been waiting for you to wake up."

Her eyes return to her book.

Vincent continues to stare at her, trying to get a read on the face behind her spectacles.

"Who are you? And how the hell did I get here?!"

She makes eye contact with him once more, sighs, and closes her book inches from her face. Then she places the book in her lap and pivots towards him a bit, giving Vincent her full attention.

"Yeah, sorry about that. I'm Vatosoa."

She reaches out to give him an awkward obligatory handshake.

Vincent looks a bit surprised, but he accepts her hand. He knows that Vatosoa is the person he and Hery have been looking for, but she's nothing like he imagined. Ahitra always carries herself with authority and surrounds herself with her royal servants, while Vatosoa is just… there, alone, all by herself.

He asks for some clarification.

"You mean the Princess of the Haran Reef?"

Vatosoa instinctively winces a bit at hearing that title. She retreats her hand and breaks eye contact. Nervously, she looks around the room until she finds an excuse to walk away from the conversation.

She gets up to return the book back to one of the many piles, turning her back towards Vincent.

"I'm afraid that my guards got a little too carried away with themselves when they were bringing you here, but I promise it will never happen again! They just get too protective of me sometimes..."

Vincent scoffs.

"Protective, huh? I think that's putting it a little too lightly."

She whips her neck and looks at Vincent over her shoulder.

"Excuse me?"

Vincent responds.

"You're joking right? All of those crazy lemurs jumped me for no damn reason!"

Vatosoa turns around to defend her soldiers.

"Oh come on now, they aren't all bad -"

Vatosoa gestures over to the corner behind Vincent.

"He's been watching over you this whole time."

Vincent turns around to find a small white lemur curled up sleeping atop a stack of old books. Its tail twitches every now and then as a response to its dream. Apparently, the rookie still felt the need to atone for its mistake before.

Vincent sighs a bit.

"Well, I can't argue with that logic, now can I?"

Vatosoa smiles at his response, but feels an overwhelming internal sense of relief. She would think that Vincent would be more upset over everything he's been through recently, but she doesn't question it. Anything to avoid a confrontation with the mysterious stranger she has heard so much about. He interrupts her thoughts.

"Just so you know, I insist on walking everywhere myself from now on."

She claps her hands together enthusiastically.

"That can be arranged!"

The vibrations from her clap travel down her body and plunge into the floor. The mirrored limestone shakes forcibly as if an earthquake is passing through. This is enough to make a still recovering Vincent fall to the ground. The baby lemur in the corner remains undisturbed as the world trembles around him.

The vibrations are strong enough to change the stone's state of matter. A large lake of molten stone appears next to Vatosoa. Its presence melts the stone beneath it until it sinks into the ground, transforming slab by slab into a solid staircase to the darkness down below.

Once the new path is finished, Vatosoa drops her hands to her side. There is absolutely no indication of her being tired from using her powers.

She notices that Vincent had fallen during the metamorphosis and panics a bit.

She stomps her foot down in a haste and a giant limestone pillar shoots up from the ground. It catches on the back of Vincent's shirt and hoists him up in the air.

He kicks his feet about to try and break free.

"Hey! Vatosoa! Put me down!"

Her eyes widen and she covers her mouth with her hands.

"Oh my goodness! Sorry!"

She taps her foot on the ground. The pillar gradually recedes back into the floor, letting Vincent back down gently. He finally is back on his feet.

"Is that better, Vincent?"

He smiles to himself. Vincent isn't sure what he finds more amusing, the anxious look on her face, or the fact that Vatosoa thinks she can hurt him. It's nice to have someone worry about him, to see him as something so fragile and worth protecting.

He dusts off his shoulders and answers her question.

"Look Princess, if giant creatures, aquatic vampires, and magical lemurs couldn't get me, I don't think getting snagged on some rock will do me in. Don't worry about it."

Vatosoa is reassured, but not completely convinced. Despite her reservations, she brightens her mood to keep Vincent comfortable. The best way to do this is by involving his latest companion.

Vatosoa addresses the small lemur in the corner and points towards the direction of the stairs.

"Lead the way, good sir!"

He takes a minute to get up from his nap, but once he shakes off his grogginess, he eagerly does what he is told. The rookie jumps off the stack of books and lands on all fours, but then he quickly transitions to hopping sideways on two feet. He leaps down into the darkness without much of a second thought.

Vatosoa laughs and chases him into the dark.

"Wait for me, little one!"

Vincent watches her frolic into void until he could no longer see her.

After a moment, he hears Vatosoa call out to him.

"Hey, are you coming Vincent?"

He feels rushed and takes a few hurried steps down the staircase.

Vincent shouts out to Vatosoa.

"I would, if I could see where I was going!"

He waits for a response.

Nothing.

She must have continued ahead with the lemur, assuming that Vincent was close behind. He can't afford getting lost in another potential subterranean labyrinth, but is it really safe for him to follow her so blindly in the dark? Vincent cautiously takes another step, but something calls out from inside him.

A brass bell rings from inside his chest. It isn't light or fragile, but it's constant and strong, like the bells that announce the arrival of cattle. It starts off faint, but quickly amplifies itself after every ding, even more so after Vincent takes notice of it. He looks down and finds that his chest is glowing.

Upon his gaze, small petals of light emerge from his torso and float down the hallway, as if they were caught up in a gentle breeze. Their light is faint, but collectively they light the path for Vincent to follow.

He takes another step and a few more petals flutter from his chest. Vincent takes a few more steps and the pattern continues the same.

Vincent pauses briefly and whispers to himself.

"Thanks, Spot. I owe you one."

He hears the bell gleefully jump inside his chest and then continues on, practically running down the long flight of stairs ahead of him.

Vincent finally catches up to Vatosoa at the base of the stairs. She and her tiny lemur companion stand in front of a large ornate door with detailed figures carved into the metal bindings. Columns surround the entry on every side, but right now the small lemur is using one of them as another resting spot. Vatosoa is playing with some of the gold jewelry in her hair before she notices Vincent's arrival.

"There you are!"

She reaches out her hand and a small petal dances on her fingertip.

"Oh wow. This is so beautiful! I didn't know you had such charming, delicate magic, Vincent!"

Vatosoa meant to say this as a compliment, but Vincent's manhood took this as a bit of an insult. He responds in a manner that is almost like a pout.

"Well, I wouldn't have to use it if you didn't lead me down such a dark tunnel…"

Vincent fiddles with some of the light petals that are getting caught in his hair. Vatosoa would've offered to help, but she seems very confused.

"Dark…?"

Vincent finally yanks some of the last petals from his hair.

"Yeah. Didn't you notice it's like pitch black down here?"

Vatosoa looks down, a little embarrassed.

"No... I guess not. Our little friend here is nocturnal so he's used to it, and I guess, in a way, I am too."

She takes a second to herself, but then looks up and looks Vincent straight in the eye.

"I'm really sorry to inconvenience you like that, especially after all that you've already been through."

She slams her palm on the limestone wall next to her and the hallway begins to shake once more. This time, little skylights form above their heads, allowing the light from what he assumes to be the library to flood in. This light renders the petals useless, so they dissipate in thin air. The glowing from Vincent's chest also immediately stops.

"I'll go ahead and let everyone else know about your lighting preferences. You'll never have to worry about that again!"

Vincent can now see her give him an apologetic smile.

Before he can respond with something polite and reassuring, she continues.

"Now, this will be your room! I hope you don't mind sharing it…"

Somehow, Vatosoa is able to pull open this large door with only her right hand. However, her achievement would be overshadowed by the very contents of this room.

Vincent steps inside and is immediately transported back into his old apartment back home. Everything is an exact replica, from the modern decor and minimalist design, to the tiny regrettable stain he made on the couch from one of Rosa's many grilled cheese sandwiches. Everything is just as it was. Perfectly preserved, as if these recent life altering events never happened.

This is the first time Vincent stops and realizes how much his life changed in such a short amount of time. Before he was content with his loneliness, but now it is an endless chase; a cycle of searching for people who understand him, maybe even love him, and either hurting or being hurt by those very same special people. Not to mention, a malevolence that's constantly hunting him down through all sorts of means. What he wouldn't give to be home again. To be able to be lulled asleep by the absolute silence that waited for him every night.

Vincent starts sobbing at the thought. All of the exhaustion he had been forced to suppress rises to the surface. He almost forgets that he isn't the only one in the room.

Vincent turns back around, but finds it extremely difficult to muster up any words at all.

"... How…?"

Vatosoa lingers in the doorway, speaking very softly.

"This is my favorite room of the whole house. I built it eons ago because I found myself needing some extra comfort."

She walks up to Vincent and wipes away one of his tears.

"Nostalgia will do that to you, sometimes."

She removes her hand and takes a peek around the room, as if she's never seen it this way before.

"Huh, why did I think there would be My Chemical Romance posters everywhere?"

Vincent laughs and shrugs off the rest of his tears

"You're way off on that one!"

Vatosoa returns a smile and then turns around back towards the door.

"You stay here and get some rest. Your body probably still needs it after your rough journey. I'll send someone to come get you soon."

She shuts the door behind her.

Once Vincent gauges that she is gone, he goes over towards his old bubbled window, lays down and watches the clouds of smog roll in and out of sight. Occasionally, a star or two may appear through the pollution, but their light is almost drowned out by all of the activity in the city below. He finally falls asleep, suspended in the sky while simultaneously buried under limestone.

Chapter 34

After a couple of hours, Vincent gently wakes from his sleep. He's relieved when he opens his eyes and sees the pollution swirling above him like a toxic mobile. However, while this area remains the same, Vincent quickly notices some dramatic changes in the opposite end of the room.

He looks over and finds Hery with his back turned to Vincent, his shoulder lying against a golden column in the center of the left half of the room. It is surrounded by several other ornate pillars, all of them dusted in a brilliant gold. They connect a dark oceanic smooth floor to a gold leafed ceiling. Although this space is beautiful, Vincent is upset that someone else infringed on his sanctuary.

Vincent calls out to him.

"Hey, Hery!"

Hery doesn't give a direct response, but rather, answers with a loud snore.

Vincent is surprised that Hery could even fall asleep in a position like that.

"Hery!"

Still no answer.

Vincent begrudgingly climbs out of the dome shaped window and crosses the rest of his apartment to get to Hery's hallway. He swings around the large pillar to get a good look at Hery's face, but something peculiar happens. As soon as Vincent faces Hery head on, a mirage of phantom armor drapes itself over Hery like a translucent blanket. A gold shimmering helmet covers his forehead and cascades down the bridge of his nose.

Hery remains fast asleep during this whole process.

Vincent shakes his hand up and down in front of Hery, but it's no use. Vincent is met with a loud snore from the man who's on guard even when he is asleep.

"You knew that wouldn't work, didn't you?"

A familiar voice chimes in from behind. Vincent turns around to see a beautiful young woman trapped inside an oversized mirror with a bright gold frame.

"Lalaina?"

He isn't exactly sure when or how this mirror appeared in front of him, but he is sure glad that it did. Vincent is taken aback by the sight of Lalaina in a long, floor length cream gown with a shimmering gold cape that acts as an elaborate train. She wears matching gold bracelets, necklaces, and trinkets in her hair, all of which contain tiny red stones in peculiar patterns. They almost radiate as brightly as the red color in her voluminous hair.

"Who else would it be?"

Her elegance subconsciously makes Vincent do get down on his knees before her, but when he realizes what he is doing, he changes his stance and sits down with his legs crossed. He makes a joke to make himself feel less awkward in this situation.

"Well, with my luck lately, you would've been something with gills, horns, or a tail."

She laughs and plops right down in front of Vincent, sitting with her legs crossed despite the grandeur nature of her dress. Lalaina fans out the extra fabric so that it looks like she is surrounded in a sea of cream blankets.

"I'm not sure about the tail thing, but I promise that I'm relatively harmless."

She gives him a wink and Vincent feels more at ease.

He decides to open up more with her, a companion that's always been around, but he could never see.

"You know, we haven't gotten to talk in a while, just you and me."

He pauses for just a second.

"It's kinda nice."

Lalaina plays with a couple of strands of her hair.

"Well… that's because you only call me when you need me, Vincent."

He's thrown off by her remark.

"Wait? What? This whole time I thought you were only showing up to come to my rescue or something like that!"

She tosses her hair back and smiles.

"Oh I was! Trust me, you needed it too! But I only came because you were afraid. Your fear was strong enough to pull me into those situations -"

Vincent interjects.

"Ummmm you sure about that one? Because I think I could've handled some of -"

She leans back and challenges him on that.

"Really?"

He responds.

"I mean you can ask those fish fuckers if you want to."

Lalaina's smile recedes a little. She leans forward, slouching a bit, and puts her hands on the back of her neck.

"There was something keeping me away that day. I'm sorry."

A vision of the Blood Stone immediately enters Vincent's mind. He can still hear its menacing snarling even when it is out of sight.

He realizes that he took it too far with Lalaina. She obviously has limitations to her powers and that amulet doesn't help at all. Besides, she's constantly proven herself to be Vincent's savior in multiple dangerous scenarios already. He doesn't need to give her such a hard time for failing in one instance, even if it was absolutely terrifying.

Vincent is used to pushing people away until it's too late, but he can't do that with her.

"Hey, um, don't worry about it, okay? For real. I know you're here for this big lug anyway!"

Vincent points his thumb towards Hery, who's still leaning up against the wall, but his head slumps so unnaturally far down that his nose is practically buried in his chest.

Lalaina perks up a bit at seeing Hery in such a ridiculous position, but there is something more.

"He did constantly complain about neck pains after he would guard my room at night, and now I know why!"

She sighs to herself and then continues.

"But still, it is sweet that he still dreams in his royal garb."

Vincent looks at Hery and then back at Lalaina, then back at Hery and back at Lalaina. Then Vincent takes the time to look over his entire surroundings once more before coming to an important realization.

"Wait, okay so I kinda figured you were a princess too Lalaina, but I never thought Hery was one of your servants -"

Lalaina is quick to correct him.

"No, no, no! That's not it at all! I would never treat him that way!"

She pauses for a brief second.

"My father had servants… not me."

For some reason, Vincent thought back to all of the people who worked for him at his mother's building. He thought about Rosa, the nervous woman in the elevator, and the doorman he would see everyday. Vincent finds this strange, because he never really considered them to be servants before, but this instinctive association would say otherwise. Should he feel guilty about this, as Lalaina would? Does it make him a bad person if he doesn't? It was just part of a routine for him, something he never questioned.

Vincent decided to shake off this feeling and focus on Lalaina instead.

He continues.

"But, Hery always bosses you around and gives you commands. If he is just your guard, why do you let him talk to you that way?"

Lalaina looks up at Hery's sleeping face.

"Please don't judge him too harshly. He's always made my safety his absolute priority, even when he was just a young cadet. He may have gotten mouthier in his age, but people have done far worse out of fear than that…"

Her voice trails off at the end of that sentence. Lalaina's eyes begin to fill with tears. She looks back down and meets Vincent's eyes directly, unashamed to cry in front of him.

"This is why I need to talk to you now Vincent, while we are alone."

Vincent can tell that Lalaina is truly afraid of something and this deeply bothers him. This whole time she kept a calm, comforting face during every dangerous scenario they've faced together. If something is making her this upset, then that means whatever it is would render them absolutely powerless.

He lets her continue.

"I'm worried about all of them. Hery, Vatosoa, Ahitra… and most of all you."

"Wait, what? Why?! Lalaina, what's going on?"

A dark purple smoke appears, swirling like a vortex, in every corner of the mirror accompanied by an ominous drumbeat. They extend back towards Lalaina, hovering around her ankles and wrists. They snap tightly and shackle her where she stands. She tugs against the vapor, but it's no use.

Vincent panics and runs up to the glass.

"Lalaina, no!"

He presses his hands against the mirror and preps himself to try and phase into it, but Lalaina stops him.

"Vincent, no, don't!"

She lets out a giant ball of fire from her hands towards the mirror. Once it makes contact with the glass, it burns Vincent's hands with a great intensity. He recoils from the pain, which gives the smoke a prime opportunity to attack.

The beat quickens its pace and at this point, the smoke almost completely fills the mirror. It is now that the vapor goes in for the final blow. It wraps itself around Lalaina's neck, but she is able to utter one final phrase.

"Please! Leave me! You all need to forget about me!"

Vincent shouts back at smoke in the mirror.

"Stop it!"

His voice shakes Hery from his sleep. It isn't long before Hery surveys the environment and jumps to Lalaina's defense. He propels himself from the pillar and lunges towards the mirror. At this point, the smoke covers all of Lalaina's face but her eyes. Tears flood her eyes, not from the suffocation, but from the sight of her devoted protector springing into action. Once she sees Hery, Lalaina musters up the strength to lift her arm from her shackles and releases a river of hellish blue fire onto the mirror.

The heat shatters the mirror before Hery can reach it.

Hery doesn't bother stopping himself and lets the momentum carry him into the solid wall. His body bounces off the stone and crashes down onto the broken glass. The glass penetrates his body, leaving large, bleeding cuts and deep wounds. However, the supernatural flames also caused the glass to become so hot that some of the wounds included extreme burns and in some cases, an immediate seal of the cut with melted flesh.

Hery cries out, but not because of the physical pain.

"Why… why… why can't he just let her go?!!"

He slams his palm down onto the floor in between every word. His anger shook the entire room and summoned the help he needed.

Chapter 35

Suddenly, the wall that had been supporting the mirror solidified into a dark granite and slid back into the earth, taking some free glass along with it. It exposes another long dark tunnel without any solid steps. Shortly after, Vincent sees the rookie jumping from wall to wall with General Anka traveling close behind. Although the tunnel is definitely wide enough for both of them to leap as a form of movement, General Anka is significantly larger than the rookie, creating small cracks in the stone with every landing motion.

They both stop abruptly at the entrance to the room, as if something was preventing them from entering.

Vatosoa's head unexpectedly pops up from behind General Anka.

"Vincent, what's wrong?"

Before he can give her a response, she rushes and dismounts from her piggyback ride. She notices the glass and carefully creates more small stone pillars to catch every step she takes until she notices Hery's injuries. She halts her own magic and shouts to her companions.

"Anka, he needs immediate medical attention! Please take him to the infirmary as quickly as possible!"

General Anka scoops up Hery in one of his arms and cradles him carefully like an infant. Anka shows obvious disdain for Hery, but still cares for him as Vatosoa ordered. In a different scenario, Vincent would have found this sight amusing, but in reality, any small jerk or rough movement could cause Hery's wounds to deepen even further.

"As you wish, Princess."

He turns around and makes his way back up the newly created tunnel, this time marching instead of leaping. Vatosoa stops her foot and makes a few more stepping stone pillars to help Vincent avoid the glass left on the floor. She then turns to him and reaches out her hand.

“C’mon Vincent, this way.”

Vincent is still gripping the wrist of his burnt hand when Vatosoa makes this gesture. After seeing that he too is also hurt, she reacts by covering her mouth with both of her hands so quickly that it rattles her glasses a bit.

“Oh my God, I’m so sorry!”

She stops her foot on her tiny pillar once more, but it’s enough to create two giant stone hands on either side of Vincent. They act in unison and grab Vincent around his waist and torso. Each of the fingers wrap around his body and interlock into one giant mass. They lift him up into the air, and with another small step, Vatosoa sends them to follow General Anka into the dark burrow.

Vincent struggles to breathe as new air is constantly being rushed into his lungs by the pure speed of the rocks. Of course, all of this is absolutely necessary to keep up with General Anka, even at his normal marching pace. The stone hands move quickly, but the Princess of the Haran is even faster. Vatosoa uses the rocks beneath her to glide at a supernatural momentum as if she is on magical roller skates. She catches up to them and yells out to Anka.

“We need to hurry. He won’t make it at this rate!”

Anka comes up with a new strategy.

“I cannot afford to leap with this man in critical condition, Princess. If he is jostled any further, it might shift the glass that’s already in his system. He can’t take any more! In order to save him, you might have to use your -”

Vatosoa’s character completely changes. She comes to an abrupt stop and screams.

"No! Never!"

She crouches down and slams her fist into the solid ground. Vatosoa's hands penetrate deep into the stones and leave cracks within the structure of the tunnel. In the same instance, her hands glow with an intense light. The energy is so strong, that it blows back into her face and jostles all of her braids out of their bun.

She propels this energy deep into the ground, instantaneously turning the solid stone beneath them into swirling sands. This conversion spreads even further, gradually climbing from the base of the walls to the ceiling. More and more sand falls on top of Vincent, Hery, the Rookie, Anka, and Vatosoa, the latter being the only one not to take notice.

Vincent struggles to break free from the stony grip. All the while, a stream of sand pours down on Vincent's curls and sinks into his mouth. General Anka takes notice of Vincent's loud spitting noises and turns his attention back to the princess.

"Vatosoa! Stop this!"

Hearing General Anka address her so informally seemed to shock her out of her current state. Vatosoa quickly pulls her hands out of the ground and hurriedly stands back up, fumbling a bit to get her bearings. She pushes her glasses up a bit on her nose and gets a better glance at everyone.

She sees that Vincent's trapped in the stone and instinctively taps her foot on the ground to retract her creation. However, now that she has turned the stone beneath her into sand, her foot sinks down into the mess she made.

This catches her off guard, but Vatosoa is quick to react.

"Sorry, about this Vincent!"

She picks up a handful of sand and throws it in his direction.

He yells in protest.

"Hey! Hey! Hey!"

He closes his eyes to keep the sand out, but to Vincent's surprise, the sand gently caresses his face as if he was playing at the beach. The same can not be said of the rock supporting him. Vatosoa manages to convert that sand into razor sharp daggers that cut straight through the stone on impact. If any of them makes their way past the rock and moves towards Vincent's body, they soften and become gentle. It seems Vatosoa regained complete control.

Once his supports are destroyed, Vincent falls and lands onto the sand with a tender thud. He goes to place his hand over his lower back, but there isn't enough time for him to inspect his aches and pains.

Vatosoa observes the sand continuing to pour onto them from all sides. At the same time, Hery's injuries are getting worse with every passing minute. She needs to act fast so that they can reach the infirmary in time.

"Everybody hold on tight… Maybe hold your breath too."

This last comment throws Vincent off.

"Wait, what?!"

Vatosoa picks up her foot and traces the tip of her toe in the sand, making the same circular motion over and over again. The sand eventually catches onto her command, and forms a small whirlpool at her feet. As the whirlpool expands, she sticks her foot even deeper into the center, all the while swinging her arms in the same circular pattern. Once she is waist deep into the sand, Vatosoa calls for the others.

"C'mon, this way!"

General Anka obeys without question, taking steps, or rather, gigantic strides towards the whirlpool, sinking deeper and deeper after each movement. He carefully covers Hery's face with his own hand before completely submerging into the sand.

Vincent is not on board with this, at all.

"You know Vatosoa, I really do feel fine. Maybe I should go back and -"

The rookie leaps from somewhere behind Vincent and lands on the back of his head. This pushes Vincent off balance and sends him and the small lemur tumbling face first into the whirlpool.

Vincent holds his breath and keeps his eyes shut the entire time, but he can feel the rookie pulling at his hair, almost as if he is controlling the direction of their movements this way. They are caught up in this swirling motion, but every time a larger part of debris comes their way, the small lemur tugs at Vincent and pulls him away from the object, of course, all of this is without Vincent's knowledge. Without his sight, Vincent has to rely on the movement of the tiny grains of sand to determine which way is up and which way is down. However, with the rookie manipulating him, he constantly has to rediscover his bearings in this vortex. It becomes something beyond vertigo. Vincent grows more and more nauseous by the second.

The unlikely pair eventually reaches the tip of the vortex and trickles down from the ceiling into a brand new room. General Anka stands under the stream of sand, more than prepared to catch them when they fall into the infirmary. The rookie is the first to make it through the small opening and leaps onto General Anka's shoulders.

Vincent emerges shortly after. Surprised by this new straightforward gravity, Vincent flails about as he falls until he makes contact with General Anka's burly arms. Even though they are covered in soft fur, they are almost as hard as the stone walls surrounding them. On impact, Vincent gets the wind knocked out of him, or more aptly, the sand knocked out of him.

He rolls over to the side while still in Anka's arms and throws up on the floor. Absolutely disgusted, Anka stretches out his arms to keep Vincent at a distance and walks away from his mess. He takes Vincent to the otherside of the room and lays him down gently on top of a giant round powder blue crystal. It is apparent that the crystal had been carefully smoothed down over the years to become cool and comfortable to the touch.

The minute Vincent makes physical contact with the mineral, a cold breeze enters his lungs and fills his spirit. It calms him and gives him permission to relax. He places his palms down onto the stone and they become frozen in place. Instead of feeling weary, Vincent finds this sensation delightful and lets this newfound snow lull him to sleep.

Chapter 36

A peaceful darkness surrounds Vincent as he lays on the crystal he brought with him to his dream. However, he isn't the only one resting on it anymore. A woman sits and runs her perfectly manicured nails through his hair, tracing his curls as he rests his head in her lap. Her dark curly hair cascades down over her eyes and tickles Vincent's nose as she bends over to smile at him.

He can't see her face, but she feels so familiar. Vincent thinks back to the picture of himself in that sailor suit with his parents. This woman would be a dead ringer for his mother, that is, if she didn't have the same mannerisms as Lalaina. No one else ever touched him this way, with so much care. No one else let him lay in their lap like this, not even his own mother. However, Vincent was so overjoyed to be in this moment, that he didn't care who she was. All he wanted to do is look up and stare at her, at the face that could never look back at him.

She moves her lips as if she was talking to him, but Vincent is unable to make out a single word. Up until this point, the two of them remain transfixed atop of the celestial stone and fail to notice that they are indeed floating in the center of a large still lake. It is now that Vincent picks up on the fact that they are not completely alone. Thousands of frogs drown out the woman's voice with their own midnight symphony. Their croaks and cackles only add to Vincent's relaxation. He loses himself in their song and is no longer concerned with the woman's secrets. Vincent chooses to stay this way until it is time to wake.

Vincent wakes up gently, slowly, focusing on one micro movement at a time. Once he brings himself to sit up, each one of his senses comes back to him, one after another. At first, Vincent only notices the new soft fabric that's brushing against his skin. Someone must have changed him into this fleecy robe while he was asleep. Normally this invasion of privacy would bother him, but after the rest he just had, Vincent didn't have a care in the world.

Vincent takes his time to come back to reality. The next sense follows. He detects a salty aftertaste in his mouth, some lingering grains of sand maybe? Or is it something else? It seems reminiscent of the lake that protected him against those fish creatures earlier. Vincent smacks his lips together until the taste goes away.

With the salt cleared, Vincent is able to move on and discover all sorts of scents within the room. Despite being called an infirmary, it smells nothing like a traditional hospital. Vincent can make out several different floral aromas as well as a wet earthiness that comes with standing in the middle of a jungle.

He opens his eyes to take in whatever vegetation he might find. To his surprise, there isn't a grain of sand in sight. Vincent sees nothing but dark rocks making up every surface in this room. The only exception would be the small drops of water falling from the more jagged rocks in the corners. Vincent turns his head around, but the only plants he could find were the ones coming from the mysterious lemurs he met back in the forest.

A cluster of them form a circle around Hery's body. Hery is laying on the same type of crystal as Vincent, but he quickly realizes that Hery's injuries are far more severe than his own. The lemurs carry glowing vines between each other, connecting them as if they were holding hands. Whatever prayers they were chanting among themselves seemed to keep Hery stable, at least for the moment.

Finally, Vincent is able to make out his last sense as he hears Vatosoa sniffle gently. He sees her at the foot of Hery's stone, making a line on the ground with a bright crimson powder. Her eyes are almost as red as the substance in her hands. It is apparent that she had been crying for quite some time.

Vincent calls out to her, but his words are broken. He is still getting reacquainted with his own voice.

"Hey… Vatosoa… Where are we?"

Vatosoa jumps up at the sound of his voice. Vincent genuinely is unable to tell whether she is happily surprised or terribly shocked to see him awake. She drops the red power and gets it all over herself. Instead of cleaning it up, Vatosoa runs over towards him and gives him the most intense bear hug he's ever had. Her grip releases and tightens as she moves her hands around his body, double checking to make sure it's really him. Of course, by doing this, she's getting the powder everywhere. The most notable mess had to be the crimson handprint wrapped around the back of his head.

Vincent pats her on her back in order to comfort her. It's clear that she's been frantic like this for a while.

"It's okay… I'm fine. There's no need to worry."

Vatosoa pulls away from Vincent after realizing how forward she was with her affection. She looks downward out of embarrassment and scolds herself.

"I'm so sorry, Vincent. It's just.. you both have been like this for a couple of days now… and it's all my fault!!"

More tears fall down onto her thighs. Vincent scooches over and puts his arm around her.

"You don't need to beat yourself up like that. We're going to be okay! I'm sure it was an accident anyw-"

Vatosoa clenches her fists and cuts him off.

"This proves it! I'm way too dangerous! Cutting off my curse was a given, but I never thought I would still hurt people with my natural magic too!! I can never make things right!"

Vincent knows that she is speaking more to herself than she is to him, but still tries to talk her out of this spell.

"That's not true! What about this?"

Vincent knocks on the crystal beneath them.

"If it wasn't for this, I wouldn't be here right now. You did that! You healed me!"

Vatosoa looks back up at him, whipping one of her tears off of her cheek.

"I can't take credit for what was already on the island. I just listened to what was already there."

She looks ahead towards Hery and continues.

"Lalaina was the healer. It was her gift. Well, technically it was a curse too, but hers was always much more of a gift than mine or Ahitra's. Our magic obviously can't compare to hers."

She motions over to the lemurs who are still concentrating on the task at hand.

Vincent recognizes the glow from the vines.

"You mean they're using Ahitra's magic too?"

A new, surly voice inserts itself into the conversation.

"In a way, yes."

General Anka makes his way into the room, ducking down so he could fit through the doorway. The rookie pops up from behind and scampers over to Vatosoa and Vincent. He jumps into Vincent's lap and nuzzles at his chest, while General Anka carries a collection of warm, wet towels in one hand and several outfits in his other. The clothes mostly consist of oversized sweater dresses and bicycle shorts. However, there was one outfit reserved for Vincent: a pair of jeans and a bright pink hoodie.

Anka handed over the towels to Vatosoa and in turn, she gave a few to Vincent. The two of them began cleaning themselves while Anka continued his explanation.

"Years ago when the Princess of the Nofon expressed a greater interest in mortal affairs and a need to practice her secret cultivation ability, the archipelago's natural ecosystems started to suffer. Without her maintenance, some of the ancient landscapes became lost to time. In the interest of conservation, Princess Vatosoa and Princess Ahitra came to an agreement where this special troop of lemurs would take over the duties of Princess Ahitra on the western islands while she works on her personal projects. Of course, they only have a small fraction of her power, so we mostly focus on the upkeep of the trees and plants around the Reef and the surrounding area. Gratefully, foliage like the baobab trees are pretty self-reliant."

Once the two of them get all of the red dye off of their skin, Anka turns his attention away from Vatosoa and back towards his diligent soldiers.

"They are over exerting themselves with this task. They are meant to sustain the life of a plant, not a full grown man."

General Anka pauses.

"If you can even still call him that -"

Vatosoa reprimands him for his comments.

"General Anka! You will not disrespect him this way, not after everything he's done for us-"

General Anka uncharacteristically speaks out against his mistress.

"Your majesty."

This introduction is already enough to annoy Vatosoa, but he goes even further.

"I fail to see the logic in relying on a volatile human, a former servant with his own self-inflicted curses, for protection against threats that are far above his capabilities. Especially when you have a power such as yours at your disposal -"

Vatosoa hops off of the rock without a word. This motion is enough to put General Anka on his guard. She takes a few slow steps until she is standing directly under his snout. He looks down at her, miniscule in comparison to his size, but remains transfixed on her dead set eyes.

She never breaks eye contact when she addresses him.

"Thank you for your services General Anka. That's all for today. You may retire to your quarters after you set the clothes in each of our rooms. Good day."

Anka takes a step back and bows to her before leaving the room, his tail twitching back and forth before it disappears into the darkness.

Chapter 37

Vincent can feel an oppressive tension even after Anka exits the room. It keeps Vatosoa's shoulders rigid in place. Vincent decides to do what Vincent does best and relieves this stress with a poorly timed joke.

"Wow… you really put Donkey Kong in timeout, huh??"

She looks over at him and chuckles in response, but still seems focused on the events that just occurred. Trying to put on a brave face, she returns back to the rock and sits down next to Vincent, putting her hand on his knee. This surprises both Vincent and the Rookie that now has to shift his position onto Vincent's lap. After seeing their faces, she retreats and keeps her hands in her own lap.

"You don't need to worry about him, Vincent. Even the strongest of us are bound to our true nature."

Vincent tries to keep her from speaking only to herself again.

"What do you mean, Vatosoa?"

She turns and faces him with a forced smile.

"Lemurs are matriarchal. Anka in particular is obsessed with rank as well. As my Guardian, he wouldn't dare defy anything I say, even if I decided to never use my powers again and let him run wild."

She lets out a deep breath that she's kept in for far too long and whispers to herself.

"I can't say I haven't considered that option."

Vincent's heart skips a beat and panics a bit at the thought of a completely unhinged giant lemur with an obvious prejudice against humans tearing through the forest.

"Well it's a great thing you didn't!"

She stares at Vincent with blatant confusion on her face. He even admits to himself that his outburst was a little unwarranted, but it needs to be said. Vincent goes on to explain himself.

"Well, even if you do mess up every now and then, at least you feel guilty about what you've done. And I'm sure you learned not to do it again! I mean it would be another thing if you continuously did bad things over and over again right?"

Vatosoa groggily uses her index finger to point at Hery.

"This is what happens when we have guests at the Reef of Haran."

She pauses and lets her hand drop into her lap. Vatosoa's head lowers with it, continuing the conversation while suppressing tears.

"This is why I sent the rest of my people away a long time ago."

Vincent awkwardly puts his hand on her shoulder. She ignores him and still looks inward. Vincent tries to give her little love pats to break her concentration, but it's no use. It's like he isn't even there anymore. He lets his hand drop down behind her, distant, but still willing to support her weight if she needs him to.

The Rookie crawls across Vincent's lap and makes his way to Vatosoa. Once he gets comfortable in her lap, he looks up at Vatosoa and rests his nose against hers. This gesture grounds her and pulls her back to reality. Vatosoa lets out a big sigh, followed by a sweet smile. She affectionately pets the Rookie behind his ear as a way to say thank you. Now that she has returned, Vincent feels more comfortable continuing their conversation.

Vincent glances over at Hery and resumes.

"Look, all I'm saying is that not everyone can afford to be cautious all the time. Some of us can only get by if we dive in head first without looking back. If we don't, if we think about the situation for too long, we'll freeze. That can be even worse sometimes."

He returns his gaze back to Vatosoa.

"You know what that feels like, don't you?"

She carries on petting the white lemur, pondering over what Vincent just said.

Vatosoa whispers to herself.

"Now you're starting to sound like her too, huh?"

Vincent can't make out what she's saying.

"What…?"

This time Vatosoa speaks up, but it is difficult for her.

"It's nothing, Vincent… I just wanted to say thanks… for being patient with me."

Vincent moves his hand out from behind Vatosoa and places it on the back of his neck. He adopts a cheery disposition to lighten the mood.

"Don't worry about it, V! Really! We're cool."

He places his arm around her shoulder playfully, squeezing tightly this time so that she knows he isn't going anywhere.

"That's the one thing you won't have to worry about, okay?"

This comforts her. Although she may not show it, Vatosoa is delighted with her new nickname, so much so that she blushes a little when she hears Vincent say it.

Vincent doesn't notice any change in her right away, but Vatosoa still feels the need to change the subject quickly before he catches onto her.

"Can I ask you a question?"

"Of course, what's up?"

Vatosoa looks back at Hery.

"Is it true that you're bonded to Lalaina? Was that his doing?"

Vincent follows Vatosoa's gaze, but instead of concentrating on Hery lying on the holistic hospital bed, Vincent's mind travels back to that day in the motel bathroom. The look of disappointment and desperation on Hery's face haunts him until this day. He doesn't regret what happened, because he got to know Lalaina so much better this way, but he knows that this gift was never meant for him.

"Well, yes and no."

Vatosoa looks at him with some confusion.

Vincent goes on to explain the situation.

"Hery did ask me to help him with a ritual a while ago, but I messed it up somehow. I think he wanted to be attached to Lalaina so he could bring her back or something, but instead she got attached to me. I can see her now sometimes and she's always there to help me when I need it. But now he can't talk to her anymore…"

Vincent pauses and thinks about Ahitra as well.

"I don't think anyone else can."

Vatosoa listens intently.

"Have you seen her recently, Vincent? Could she be here with us?"

"Actually, she's the one that caused that."

Vincent nudges over in Hery's direction.

Vatosoa gasps in shock.

"No! But she would nev -"

Vincent interjects.

"To be fair, Hery's the one who decided to leap head first into a molten hot mirror, but he was trying to save her from someone... or something. It was trying to take her away from us, but instead of being afraid for herself, she was thinking about us. Lalaina didn't want us to follow her, so she attached the mirror with this blue fire and I think that's what hurt Hery."

It takes Vatosoa a while to respond after taking in all of this information.

"Are you sure it was fire and not water?"

Vincent uses his free hand to conjure up a small marble of water and rolls it over and in between his own fingers.

"Trust me, V. I know what water looks like."

Vatosoa watches his little magic trick, but doesn't give Vincent the reaction he was expecting. Instead of being charmed, Vatosoa is more concerned with Lalaina's choice of attack. She puts her fist in front of her mouth and concentrates.

"That's troublesome… but we have to take things one step at a time now in order to help Lalaina."

She slams her fist down on top of her other palm as if she's giving her own plan a stamp of approval. However, once her hands make contact, Vincent can feel little tremors underneath his feet. He's happy that Vatosoa has finally regained her strength.

"Vincent, it's up to you to save Hery!"

Vincent drops his water marble and it splashes all over his lap.

"Come again?"

Vatosoa continues.

"If you've bonded with the Coelacanth, and you're as connected to her as you say you are, you might be able to access her curse as well. That means you would be able to use her power to heal Hery!"

Vincent stands up to address Vatosoa.

"Look V, I really want to help, but I'm not sure if I can actually manage to do all that. I mean sure I can do some cool tricks now, and I get pretty lucky with my powers when I'm in a pinch, but I don't have the control over them like you do! Imagine if I tried to tap into a crazy powerful curse like Ahitra's! I'd do some pretty serious damage to a lot of people if I didn't know what I was doing."

The Rookie hops off of Vatosoa's lap once it detects Vincent's distress. It climbs up his legs and wraps itself around his shoulder. The two of them stare at Vatosoa after Vincent's speech.

She stands up and meets their gaze, rising with an overwhelming sense of dignity that intimidates Vincent the same way it intimidates General Anka. Now Vincent feels guilty for picking on the poor guy so much.

"I wish the circumstances were different, but you're the only one that can do this. Hery's life depends on you."

Chapter 38

Vincent doesn't try to argue with Vatosoa. He lowers his head due to the immense weight of his newest responsibility. The Rookie leans forward and contorts his body to meet Vincent's gaze. Vincent chuckles a bit at his newfound friend, but it isn't enough to relieve him of this stress. Vincent lifts his hand and scratches the back of his neck. One would think with the amount of force he is using that it would lift some of the red dye out of his hair, but it remains firmly in place, maintaining the shape of Vatosoa's handprint.

Vatosoa reaches out her hand to grab his. She grazes her thumb over the back of his hand in order to comfort him.

"We'll start our training tomorrow, okay? I'll help you with your new elemental magic. Then we can move onto the curses when we are both ready."

The Rookie climbs to the top of Vincent's head and gives Vatosoa a look of sheer determination. She smiles at her little companion, but Vincent remains still. Vatosoa pulls all of them towards the door of the infirmary, but stops for a moment when Vincent gives her hand a tight squeeze.

"Alright, I trust you."

After this exchange, the three of them leave Hery in the care of white lemurs. They make their way through the dark tunnel ahead. Vincent may not be able to see three feet in front of him, but Vatosoa never hesitates. She keeps trudging ahead, manipulating the path in front of her with her free hand, while holding onto Vincent with the other. Vincent feels a sense of comfort in her presence, but something's off. He can't help but feel a little helpless in this situation, but he knows he can't do much about it now. They stay this way until he finally reaches his bedroom.

As Vincent and Vatosoa approach the giant engraved door, it towers over them, reminding them of their fragility. Vatosoa goes to reach for the handle, but decides to stop at the last minute. Both of her hands fall to her side.

She turns to Vincent to give him a proper farewell.

"I think I'll go ahead and leave you here. Please don't be concerned about any mess. I already sent someone to come clean it up for us."

Vatosoa turns around abruptly to leave, but stalls after hearing a soft coo from the Rookie. With this distraction, Vincent manages to get a word in before she leaves.

"Hey -"

This stops her in her tracks. She listens out of courtesy.

Vincent continues.

"Umm… thanks, V. And don't worry. We got this, right?"

Vatosoa keeps her back to him, but her shoulders drop a little bit as she lets out a heavy sigh.

"Right. I'll see you bright and early tomorrow, then."

She walks away and disappears into the darkness.

After Vatosoa's exit, Vincent's eyes stare directly upwards in search of the baby lemur on his head.

"Well, how do you think that went?"

A small smack on the forehead from a tiny black lemur paw gives him his answer. Vincent flinches on impact and laughs to himself.

"Yeah I thought so too."

He grabs the Rookie and lifts him over his head. Vincent suspends the lemur directly in front of his face so he can get a good look at him. The lemur's body droops down with the pull of gravity like a wad of taffy. The Rookie tilts his head to the side, questioning Vincent's intentions.

This only makes Vincent laugh even harder.

"You're such a goof, you know that?"

He affectionately pulls the lemur close to his chest. Vincent cradles him in one hand while he uses the other to try and push the massive door open. The Rookie hears Vincent huff and puff while he exhausts all of his strength in this one task. He secretly decides to step in and help Vincent by discreetly pushing against the door with the tip of his tail.

It creaks open slowly and Vincent is quick to celebrate.

"Finally!"

Vincent wipes the sweat off of his brow and they make their way inside. Unlike the last time, Vincent's isn't transported back into his old bedroom or any fond memory for that matter. Instead, the two of them are surrounded by four solid walls of granite, while the ceiling and the floor are made of the same powder blue crystal that healed Vincent in the infirmary.

Vincent mutters to himself while he takes the first step inside the new space.

"So this is how she did it, huh?"

The Rookie leaps from his arms and makes his way towards a pristine king sized bed in the middle of the room. He's quick to make a mess of the perfectly white crisp bedding, but stops when he sees the bright pink hoodie hanging on the edge of the bed. The lemur dives head first into the bottom of the sweatshirt and squirms around until the hoodie covers the front of his face.

Vincent sighs as he struggles to close the door behind him.

"You can keep that for now, I guess."

He eventually gives up on ensuring his privacy and leaves the door cracked open. His attention shifts towards the wall that previously held

Lalaina's mirror, but it seems perfectly fine. Likewise, whatever glass and debris had been on the floor surrounding it is completely gone now. The room is made to look like nothing ever happened.

Feeling a mixture of relief and disappointment, Vincent takes off his robe and gets into bed. He spends a few moments tossing and turning under the covers, trying to make himself feel more comfortable. Eventually, he drifts off to sleep with the Rookie resting diligently at his feet.

Swirling black clouds cover Vincent's vision as he closes his eyes and falls asleep. Almost immediately, Vincent returns to the dream that sheltered him during his time in Vatosoa's hospital. His head rests once more in this mysterious woman's lap. He still is unable to decipher anything about her character, other than the fact her long dark hair cascades down her face. She brushes his hair with her finger tips while a choir of chirping frogs serenades them in the background.

She whispers something to him, but Vincent is unable to make out exactly what it is. He strains to focus on her words, but the frogs and their song prevent this from being remotely possible.

Vincent tries to talk to her.

"I can't hear you… What are you trying to say?"

Instead of raising her voice, she continues to respond with the same lulls and smiles while stroking his hair. Vincent is a little disappointed, but this feeling quickly fades as this woman and the animals in the background work to create this soothing safe space for Vincent.

Chapter 39

A deafening rumbling stirs Vincent from his sleep. Tiny rocks crumble and land on his forehead. He brushes them off and looks up to find the crystal on the ceiling slithering away from the center of the roof. Instead, it descends down the neighboring walls like ivy, spreading and reconnecting with itself. The celestial crystal leaves room for a new long circular opening to a fresh blue sky.

One could easily be taken in with the beauty of this sight, but Vincent instinctively knew that this meant trouble. He braces himself for what is about to happen.

A giant crystal pillar shoots up from the ground and propels Vincent's bed through the new opening. It moves at such a rapid speed that Vincent can't help but choke on this rush of new air entering his body. He's stunned, while The Rookie moves around freely. The lemur rushes to Vincent's side to let him know that everything's going to be alright.

They come to an abrupt stop once they reach the very tip top of the Reef. The bed is tossed up into the air along with its passengers, but it isn't long before they all crash back down to earth. Vincent lands flat on his back, bounces around a bit, and then checks his neck for signs of whiplash. The Rookie also comes over to inspect Vincent, but Vincent reassures him that he's alright. Vincent is so preoccupied with this exchange that he fails to notice Vatosoa sitting on an oversized cushion and drinking her morning earl grey tea next to him.

"Good morning!"

Startled, Vincent grabs the comforter and covers himself.

"Geez Vatosoa, give a guy a break!"

She looks at him, once again with a confused expression.

"You didn't get enough rest last night? Was there something wrong with the bed?"

Vincent expresses his frustrations while grabbing the pink hoodie that was meant for him.

"Come on, you know exactly what I mean."

She waits for him to finish his sentence while he pulls the sweater over his head. Vincent goes to grab the jeans at the foot of the bed, but secretly gets embarrassed. He does his best to hide his blush.

"...Turn around."

Vatosoa quickly catches on and adverts her gaze to the horizon in front of her.

"I just thought it would be nice to bring you up to the canopy so we could watch the sunrise."

She takes another long sip of her tea.

Once Vincent finishes dressing himself, he makes his way over to her side. The Rookie follows and perches himself of a jagged rock directly behind the two of them, uncharacteristically alert. Vincent reaches them and leans against chalky limestone pillars while another set protects the two of them from the front like a guardrail. He peers over the tip of the jagged stone and takes in the scenery.

From this height, Vincent surveys the Kingdom of the Reef in its entirety. The dawn brings with it a myriad of pink and purple hues that descend from the sky and sprinkle themselves along the backs of the limestone peaks. Individual leaves from the protected forests stand at attention in hopes of catching a glimpse of the morning sunlight. Similarly, the sound of ocean waves from somewhere off in the distance wake a myriad of white lemurs as they make their way from shadowy crevices to greet the brand new day. It was incredibly refreshing to be outside in this moment after being buried in caves for so long.

Vincent lets out a long breath.

"It's beautiful."

Vatosoa smiles at him while he's still taking in the scenery.

"This is my favorite spot in the whole kingdom. It really helps clear your head, don't you think?"

Vincent nods his head in agreement.

"We should come up here more often."

She isn't sure why, but Vatosoa feels a slight pang of remorse and delicate guilt for herself and her guest after hearing Vincent say that. Her smile softens a little, but she continues on with the conversation.

"Come here."

She taps her hand on the cushion next to her. Obediently, Vincent sits down and crosses his legs in a more comfortable position.

Vatosoa hands over her mug to Vincent and offers him some of her tea. He thanks her and cautiously takes a sip on the dark bitter liquid.

"I realize that if we are going to be working together, I should be more transparent with you."

Vincent puts down the mug and gives her his full attention. She fidgets, but continues on with what she has to do.

"I've already caused you enough trouble by being so secretive, and my outburst the other day seriously put your life at risk as well as Hery's -"

Vincent tries to interject,

"Vatosoa, I'm fine! Really, I -"

but she won't let him.

"You need to know why. Especially if we are going to be working together and studying the ways of the past, including our curses. You need to know mine… in order for things to start making sense."

Vatosoa takes a deep breath in and lets it out slowly. Vincent allows her enough silence so that she can take all the time that she needs.

"A long time ago, when the three of us were still young, we all served under a great king who was thought to be the origin of all our people. He was wonderful, not only because he was a conduit for the magic of the island, but also because he acted as its benefactor. The king was always quick to give wonderful gifts to the people of the islands, without expecting anything else in return."

Vatosoa pauses and removes her glasses. She keeps her hands busy by using the end of her shirt to clean the glass while she continues with the rest of her story.

"But something happened to that man. It's hard to tell if it was a gradual change, or something that happened all at once. Some said that he grew worried about all the commotion in the mortal realm and the possibility that it would bring new visitors to the islands. All of these new people from faraway lands, it was hard at times to understand what their true intentions were, but I'm not sure it's that simple. Regardless, he felt the need to protect the Arivesto Archipelago. That's why he created these wonderful Guardians for myself, Ahitra, and Lalaina, each chosen specifically to best suit our personalities and abilities."

As she finishes her thought, General Anka emerges in front of them from somewhere behind the wall of limestone. Vincent jumps back at the sight of his giant inky black hand seemingly materializing from nowhere, but relaxes once Anka decides to reveal his face.

She carries on.

"I can't imagine where I would be without my Guardian. So despite everything that's happened since then, I'll always be grateful to the Dark King for you."

Anka smiles at Vatosoa with a tenderness in his eyes.

"And I for you, Princess."

He bows his head to her out of respect.

It may have been his imagination, but Vincent swears he can feel the Rookie roll his eyes behind him. The little lemur dismounts from the rocks and ventures back onto the bed, curling up for another nap. Everyone else continues on as if they did not notice.

"Do you need me to stay here and assist you?"

She shakes her head back and forth for a bit and then responds.

"No, I'll be alright for this next part. Thank you, Anka."

Anka looks back up at the two of them with concern in his face, but he doesn't dare go against her wishes.

"Alright then, Your Highness."

General Anka finally addresses Vincent before he leaves.

"I'll take that mug from you, now that you're finished."

Before Vincent could even utter anything to the contrary, General Anka swipes the mug out of his hands with about ten or so good sips left in it. He then scales down the limestone once more until he is completely out of sight.

Vincent turns to Vatosoa.

"What was that about?"

Vatosoa laughs nervously. She waves her arms around a little to reassure Vincent that everything is fine.

"Oh, you know how he gets! He's just worried about me, that's all!"

Vincent isn't convinced.

"I don't know, that seemed like more than just a dad checking on some kids at a sleepover to me…"

Vatosoa lowers her arms and drops her shoulders. She leans her head back against the rock and looks towards the horizon.

"I've been so emotional lately, well maybe volatile would be a better word for it…"

She stops and points to a grey limestone canyon off into the distance.

"Do you see that crevice there? Just beyond the forest to your right?"

Vincent cups his hands around the sides of his face to keep the sunlight from his eyes. He strains a bit, but then nods a bit once he notices the rupture.

"That's what happened the last time I had a difficult conversation with a stranger."

Vincent whips his head back towards her so quickly that he forgets to lower his hands from their current position.

"That's not going to happen this time right?!"

Vatosoa busts out laughing over the expression on Vincent's face. She grabs his hands and lowers them from his eyes.

"Relax, Vincent. You aren't a stranger to me anymore!"

She smiles at him to offer some comfort, but it doesn't work.

"Besides, I know that you would never try to hurt me."

Vincent unwinds a bit after she expresses her confidence in him, but in all honesty, he is still frightened of Vatosoa and her unstable power.

"Well I'm glad you feel that way, V, but there was no need to scare me like that."

A quiet seriousness comes over Vatosoa.

"Vincent, I promise you that I will no longer lose control of myself, especially while you and Hery are here. You have my word."

He can see true conviction across her face. It's obvious that she's determined to turn her word into reality and that nothing could shake her spirit.

Vincent lets out a small sigh and raises his pinky. Vatosoa stares at his finger in confusion. A minute of silence goes by before Vincent explains himself.

"It's something we do back home."

Vincent grabs her pinky finger with his and shakes it a few times.

"It makes a promise between two people become real."

Vatosoa seems absolutely delighted.

"That's such a charming little ritual! I'll have to remember this one for later."

She pulls her hand away and smiles at him.

"Thank you, Vincent."

He returns her grin before turning to the horizon once more. Vatosoa also turns her attention towards the scenery before continuing her tale.

"As I was saying, in the beginning, the man who would become the Dark King embodied all of the elemental magic of the islands. As the peoples divided and spread out, he realized that they would each need a protector, and so a daughter of each kingdom, including his own, would inherit one of the elements. As Princess of the Reef of Haran, I was given a connection to Earth. Ahitra of the Isle of Tendrom has her vegetation, and Lalaina kept to her water."

Vatosoa pauses for a moment.

"Even in geography, she connected us all."

Vincent breaks her focus with his next question.

"Aren't you missing one? I've seen Lalaina and Hery both work with fire before as well."

Vatosoa lets out a large sigh and puts her glasses back on.

"Yes, and that's what concerns me the most right now."

She pushes her glasses up onto the bridge of her nose and continues.

"The Dark King was insistent on retaining his fire. It's a powerful element with the ability to create, as well as destroy. If that's true, that Lalaina and Hery have both called upon the power of fire, that can only mean a couple of things. Lalaina either somehow inherited her father's power and passed some of it onto Hery, or she's spent far too long in that realm and it's starting to consume her."

Vincent's heart races as his mind transports him back to the moment where Lalaina struck the mirror with a bluish hell fire. He was initially impressed with Lalaina for having so much vitality in a moment of desperation, but that's exactly what it was: desperation. It was unnatural, especially for her.

Vincent jumps to his feet.

"We need to wake Hery up. He knows more about Lalaina and what's going on with her better than anyone. He'll know a way to help her and fix all of this!"

Vatosoa remains still.

"I'm not so sure about that."

Hearing that Hery too can manipulate the elements, even if it is on a miniature scale, worries Vatosoa. Her anxiety is painted all over her face, but instead of admitting her true concern to Vincent, she shares an equally likely issue that they would have to face.

"Even if he did know how to save her, don't you think he would have tried it by now? If that's the case, then he failed -"

Vincent reaches out his hand to her.

"I don't care."

Vatosoa is surprised by what just came out of Vincent's mouth. She grabs his hand out of curiosity and lets him lift her up.

Vincent continues.

"None of what happened in the past matters now, because he didn't have us. Even if he doesn't have a clue what he's doing, I'm going to be there to help him. Just like he helped me when I didn't know what to do with all of my power."

Vincent pauses and takes both of her hands in his.

"And I hope that you'll be there to help us too, V."

Vatosoa is touched by this gesture, but she also realizes what she must do. She squeezes Vincent's hands as a sort of confirmation, but is quick to let them go. Instead, she keeps her hands behind her back and adopts her royal diction once more.

"If that's the case, then I think I should prepare the library for our training. I'll go ahead and set up while you have something to eat with General Anka in the dining room. You must be famished!"

As if on cue, Vincent's stomach squawks loudly, begging for brunch. Vatosoa laughs and makes her way over to the bed. She pats on the comforter gently, summoning Vincent. He obeys without any protest.

"General Anka will be waiting for you in your bedroom, no worries. He'll also escort you through the Reef to your meal."

Vincent listens intently as he hops up onto the bed. The Rookie welcomes him back and goes over to sit on Vincent's lap. Once Vatosoa is convinced that they are both secure, she stops her foot once more.

"Have fun on your brunch date!"

The bed goes crashing downward at an exuberant speed as the crystal pillar supporting the bed recedes into the crystal bedroom. The bed lands in its original spot with a monumental thud that sends Vincent and the Rookie flying upward. They make eye contact as they are suspended in midair and Vincent instinctively pulls the tiny lemur into his chest. Vincent cradles him as they land once more, taking the full effect of the springs. He bounces off of the bed and lands on the solid blue floor.

Vincent looks up and finds Anka standing there, heavy in the doorway with his arms uncharacteristically crossed. The Rookie leaps from Vincent's arms and scurries over to greet his superior. He stands perfectly straight and looks up at Anka like he is the rising sun.

Anka readjusts his posture to reciprocate the Rookie's salute. He professionally tucks his hands behind his back and barks orders to the Rookie in a series of snorts and growls inaudible to Vincent. After their conversation, the Rookie nods his hand in understanding, and leaps away into the dark tunnel without even a single glance back at Vincent.

He isn't sure why, but he feels a little hurt by this. However, General Anka doesn't give him much time to process his grief.

"I believe the Princess has given you an order, young man."

Vincent stumbles about but eventually stands back up. He brushes himself off, confused by Anka's statement. Rather than resort to aggravating Anka merely by asking stupid questions, Vincent takes this opportunity to directly mess with him instead.

"You mean the brunch date, lover boy?"

It takes everything in General Anka's power to keep a composed face and not retaliate.

"You are fortunate that I too am under the same command. Come, this way."

He turns around abruptly and marches off into the same dark tunnel. After the first step, Vincent reacts quickly so that he can manage to follow General Anka, as one slow stride from this creature feels like a sprint to Vincent.

General Anka is fully aware of this.

"Please, do keep up."

Vincent knows that Anka is getting some sort of pleasure from this. However, he is unable to tell if this is a punishment for his sarcasm earlier, or a true test of skill. Either way, Vincent's pride would never let him concede to such a crotchety old man.

Chapter 40

They twist and wind through different paths, some consisting of solid smooth limestone, while others are composed of dirt and gravel, with giant dark grey pillars towering over them and doing their best to block out the sunlight. An occasional tree branch makes its way past the stone, acting more like a friendly neighbor than any true intrusion. The two of them weave between the indoors and outdoors without much rhyme or reason until finally, after about 30 minutes of Vincent playing the world's most aggressive game of 'follow the leader' with a giant lemur, General Anka, leads him to the dining hall.

They enter into a gargantuan room covered entirely in smooth dark grey stone from floor to vaulted ceiling. There are absolutely no windows or any exterior light source of any kind. Instead, the brightest light in the room comes from the giant gemstone thrones that are acting as dining chairs. Their edges give off a murky brownish blackish hue, but their true beauty seeps through from within. Beyond the black streaks on the surface, a variety of rich blue hues radiate intensely from the gemstone. Occasionally, a few pools of green and amber tones will appear amongst oceanic luminescence, but rather than detract from the charm of the gemstone, it creates a sort of rainbow effect that dances along the walls.

Vincent is so taken aback by this enchantment that he hesitates to reach for his seat. General Anka breaks his daze by walking through the rainbow projection and assuming his position at the head of the table on the other side of the room. Vincent does his best to nonchalantly sit in the glowing chair across from his monstrous guide.

Vincent fidgets about in his oversized seat trying to get comfortable, but ceases his movements immediately when he hears a frightening moan come from the back of General Anka's throat.

As summoned, a small troop of lemurs arrive from somewhere in the shadows behind Anka's massive chair bearing fruits and all sorts of midday treats. They place an enormous tray of tropical fruits in front of General Anka along with a jar of his favorite seasoning, granulated cane sugar.

"Got a sweet tooth, don't ya?"

General Anka twitches his ears a little, but generally ignores Vincent's comment. He instead continues on sprinkling his sugar over his sliced mangos.

Another pair of lemurs clumsily make their way over to Vincent with their tray. As they leap, a little bit of the contents on the platter splatter all over the floor. They finally manage to jump onto the slate table and present Vincent his breakfast: a large bowl of rice pudding with a hint of vanilla and cinnamon, topped with apples and a bottle of coke on the side.

Vincent reaches for his spoon in order to take his first bite. The minute he tastes his breakfast, a sudden burst of energy travels from the tip of his lips to the tip of his tailbone and back up again. It's so strong that it makes his curls stand on end.

Vincent's surprise is apparent as he frantically examines his utensils and searches his chair for the source of this sensation. General Anka catches him acting in this strange way.

"Is everything in order, young man?"

Vincent is quick to straighten up once he's called out.

"Did you feel that too?!"

General Anka sighs and taps on the arms of his chair.

"Everything in the Haran is purposeful, child. Even this dining set is part of our training regimen. The princess insists that the labradorite brings forth inner strength. As such, she crafted this furniture herself, in an attempt to nourish our mind and spirit while we also nourish our bodies with meals."

General Anka returns to his food, but Vincent's determined to keep the conversation going.

"I don't know if a bottle of coke is really that nourishing, but I'm not complaining!"

Vincent grabs his beverage and takes too long of a swig. The bubbles rush up his nose, forcing him to make an unsavory facial expression. Anka can't help himself but laugh underneath his breath.

"We felt that it would be more in line with your American tastes."

This attempt at hospitality is a far cry from how they initially met, a violent interrogation in the middle of the rock forest. It throws Vincent off for a second.

"Thank you… sir."

Now it was Anka's turn to be pleasantly surprised by Vincent's manners. He nods his head in response and continues to peel the rest of his fruit. They continue with their meals in cordial silence, but it wouldn't last long.

After a few more bites of his rice pudding, Vincent speaks up once again.

"So, why did Princess Vatosoa want us to eat together?"

General Anka stops what he's doing and gives Vincent his full attention.

"The Princess did not submit this request, I did."

Vincent chokes a little on his food out of disbelief.

"What? But why?"

"There is something of dire importance that we need to discuss."

As he is speaking, General Anka dismounts from his throne and starts walking about the room, hands fixed behind his back and his chest on full display. Vincent didn't dare move from his spot.

"I know why you are here. I know that you intend to make a pact with me the same way you did with that playful little creature from Tendrom. The Princess knows this as well. She may not be opposed to it at the moment, and quite truthfully, if she ordered me to bond with you, I would obey, but…"

He finally stops in front of the elongated wall to Vincent's right.

"I cannot trust anyone, anyone who travels with that!"

General Anka slams his fist against the wall, sending a powerful tremor throughout the stone. This tremor causes the slab that had been covering the entire surface to crumble to the floor. A brand new chamber is revealed, with pillars of crystals guarding its entrance. Vincent recognizes the towers of labradorite accompanied by equally massive powdery blue crystals. This must have been where Vatosoa got the gemstones she needed to keep himself and Hery alive in the hospital wing.

However, in this instance, the crystals are meant to do more than just heal. The pointed towers act like rows of sharp teeth, keeping whatever's inside trapped within its jaws. Vincent can hear harsh rattling from inside the cage.

He works up the courage to go inspect the noise for himself. Once he arrives at the pillars, Vincent peers over the apex of the crystal nearest to him. The sharp clanging appears to be The Blood Stone twisting and contorting in pain, scraping its thorn like arms against the gems and limestone. It is desperate to get as far away as possible from the rainbows projected onto the stone. The colorful lights come from the light inside the crystals and it's obvious that whatever magic is at work is in direct violation with one another.

General Anka interrupts Vincent's inspection.

"What business do you have with the Cursed One?"

Vincent looks back at Anka while pointing at the amulet.

"Is that what you've been talking about this whole time? Hery told me it's called the Blood Stone -"

General Anka's tail twitches uncontrollably. Vincent can't tell if his host is angry with him, or nervous to be around him. Anka buckles down on his interrogation.

"Why do you carry this abomination? No one has seen it since the fall of the Dark King."

Vincent is clearly getting more upset.

"Look, I don't know what you're talking about! Honestly, I don't care about anyone's king! I need this thing to find my dad! It was the only thing keeping my mom alive…"

Vincent catches himself on his own words.

"... after what happened to her."

He looks away from Anka and focuses on the jittering amulet, keen to make sure that The General doesn't see him cry. General Anka notices a shift in Vincent's tone and adjusts his own communication accordingly.

"Vincent…"

Despite his best efforts to hide, Vincent turns his face towards General Anka after hearing him call him by his name. It was the first time he ever did so.

General Anka continues.

"I am unfamiliar with your family's situation, but I must tell you, no type of healing in any capacity could come from this relic."

Vincent has a hard time processing this information. Would this mean that Hery lied to him when they initially met? No, it couldn't be.

Vincent lashes out at General Anka.

"No! You're lying! I mean sure, I know it's dangerous, but it helped me just as much as it hurt me if you really think about it!!"

Anka takes a step towards Vincent with his giant arms outstretched. It is meant to be comforting, but with his stature, it could easily be misinterpreted as a threat.

"Vincent, you must listen to me. This amulet has a long history of destruction. It is not like the magic that you possess. It has no place here."

Anka takes another step, but his gesture seems to have the opposite effect. Vincent feels like he is backed into a corner and lashes out in order to escape.

"No shit! I knew that from the beginning! But if you ask me, a giant talking lemur doesn't feel like it belongs here either!"

General Anka drops his arms to the side in defeat.

"You're correct."

He looks down, trying to cover up his shame, and makes his way back over to the dining room table.

Vincent is so surprised that he isn't sure what to say. He stands there in silence while Anka heals his wounds in the labradorite throne.

Once he regains his composure, General Anka continues.

"I am an unnatural being, as are the other Guardians on this island. We may take on natural forms, best suited for our princesses and our environment, but at our core, we are the same as that wretched thing."

"What do you mean?"

Vincent takes a step towards General Anka, his first attempt at an apology, but keeps a keen eye out to track the movements of the Blood Stone.

"Princess Vatosoa began her report this morning I'm sure. She told you that we were gifts from a generous, magical king, who wanted the multiple kingdoms of this archipelago to be able to protect themselves should a powerful threat arise."

Vincent nods his head in conformation. He lets down his guard in order to listen to Anka's tale. Vincent leans against one of the protective crystal canines, confident in its ability to protect him from unwanted threats.

After a long sigh, General Anka continues.

"Yes, it is true that this island and all of its inhabitants uniquely retained natural magic from its original formation. However, the king also felt the need to dabble in a magic that had never been part of our world before."

General Anka motions Vincent to come over to the table, but Vincent stays put. Disappointed, Anka carries on.

"It began with a whisper. Simultaneously, coming from a faraway place, while tickling the insides of your ear. Those whispers converted themselves into the thoughts of anyone who was desperate enough to hear them. These thoughts manifested into poems and drawings, and eventually, became incantations and rituals. They became so ingrained into the budding society, that the people had long forgotten the secrets they were meant to keep behind their songs. However, without the proper intention, these phrases became absolutely harmless, that is until contracts started being made."

General Anka's attention now turns over to the Blood Stone shaking behind the crystal barrier. Instead of anger or fear in his voice, there's a shame that could only be felt by betraying a close friend.

"The Dark King was the first to make a contract. For what purpose or gain, no one is exactly sure. However, it brought him the power that he needed, but at a price. It tempted him to its terms. That's what we all do"

Vincent interrupts.

"We?"

"Yes, Myself, the Coelacanth, and the Calf. We are just a few of the many who place the whispers in your head from the shadows."

Mindlessly, Vincent makes his way back towards his seat at the table. He thinks back to all the prophetic dreams and messages that he's received from each of the guardians so far. Vincent assumed that their connection was due to his actions, his powers and the physical bond he now shares with both of them. If they could freely communicate with him before, why didn't they? And if that's the case, who else could be influencing him now?

Vincent brings these concerns to Anka's attention.

"So you mean to tell me that this whole 'bonding with the Three Guardians' thing has been bullshit this whole time?"

Vincent slouches into his chair until he relinquishes his entire body weight in one loud thud.

"Well…"

Anka thinks about his answer carefully.

"I can't fathom what you would accomplish by bonding with all three of us, but I promise you Vincent, we are not meant to collaborate with anyone who wasn't explicitly marked by us."

Vincent brings his coke bottle close to his lips, both to help him concentrate while also providing him with some sort of subconscious comfort.

"Marked?"

"Yes, as I explained, we were called upon from our realm for each specific princess. They were each marked in their youth shortly after we came into this world, tying us to them for all of eternity."

General Anka twitches his tail once more, wincing at the memories.

"It is a truly painful process, Vincent. One that shouldn't be taken lightly. That being said, after this transformation, each party becomes unimaginably more powerful. They give us the natural magic and physical form that we so desperately crave, and in return we give them their curses."

Vincent can't help but recall the scene Spot shared with him back in the Isle of Tendrom. Picturing Ahitra in so much pain as a little girl had a tremendous effect on him, not only because of the injustice of the situation, but because he was seeing it through Spot's eyes. The Guardian of the Nofon clearly empathized with his tiny friend, so much so that he felt helpless in his inaction, as well as immense guilt after her curse was forced upon her. His emotions cling to Vincent in the form of second hand memories.

Vincent tosses the coke bottle aside to shake off those memories. The clattering of the glass shattering against the stone transports him back into the moment. When he comes to, Vincent stands and pounds his fists against the table.

"Did you know? I mean, did you and the other Guardians know that they were going to hurt Ahitra that way? Is that what happened to Lalaina? What did you do to Vatosoa?!"

General Anka isn't fazed at all by Vincent's outburst and decides to be direct with him, giving Vincent the right to process the situation how he sees fit. There is no hesitation in his voice.

"Yes, someone always suffers when one of us is born. It is the cost of transferring us over to this world. This universe and the many like it operate on a system of equivalent exchange. However, the three of us never expected this much cruelty. It is true that the greater the sacrifice, the greater the power one can conjure from our realm. I'm afraid that the rulers of these islands fully intended to draw out as much forbidden magic out of our realm as possible, and they succeeded."

Vincent still remains transfixed in his spot. He stares down at the table, not once glancing over in Anka's direction the entire time he was speaking. General Anka continues his story, hoping to provide Vincent with some relief.

"Those girls were always exceptionally talented, not only when it came to conjuring the natural magic of this island, but also in their emotional strength and their vitality. They were chosen by their elders based on the very attributes that made them so incredible."

General Anka pauses before sharing something that he's been feeling for centuries.

"Even after what happened, not a single one of them blamed us. In the past, I told myself that it was because they were not fully aware of their situation, but I know this to be false. They just had the kindness to forgive, or at least, the capacity to forgive us for being born into their world… It's been a complete privilege to protect and serve them."

Vincent trembles while suppressing his anger. Clearly, General Anka and Spot love Vatosoa and Ahitra, respectively. They've proven this to Vincent within the short amount of time that he's been around them. Regardless of their inception, it is clear that their relationship with these women are real. However, once again, Lalaina is unable to experience this.

Vincent snaps his head up and looks General Anka directly in his moonlike eyes.

"What about Lalaina?! Why couldn't the Coelacanth protect her?!"

General Anka stares back at Vincent. He replies, this time more softly with a heaviness in his heart. Vincent fails to detect it, but it's still there.

"There are things in this world that even I don't know, but let me tell you what I do know, my child."

This last pet name really throws Vincent off. He does not completely forget his anger, but becomes a lot tamer after hearing General Anka treat him with the same patience he gives to Vatosoa.

"Each of our relationships is vastly different, Vincent. For example, the Calf remains a calf because Princess Ahitra has made the decision to fully embrace her infernal magic, draining it constantly from her Guardian. As such, it can never fully materialize and only has the strength for short bursts of power. With this strategy in mind, the calf choses to store their natural magic in its body whenever it can, saving it for when its shackles are released. As for myself, Princess Vatosoa rejects her curse altogether, which forces her to rely solely on the magic of the earth. Luckily, with all of her time and dedication, she's mastered all of her natural abilities and uses them without exhaustion. Likewise, I've kept up my full physical form, including my ability to communicate with other living creatures, for pretty much my entire new existence. However, the essential component in each dynamic is some form of balance. It has to work for both parties."

General Anka takes this opportunity to leave the comfort of his chair and marches slowly over towards Vincent, careful that the sound of his gargantuan footsteps don't spook the boy any further.

"Regarding the poor Coelacanth… without her master, she's completely lost her sense of self. Princess Lalaina is caught somewhere between our world and yours. You see, she cannot die, and because of this, the Coelacanth suffers as well. She's succumbed to the ferocity of wielding both natural and infernal magic at all times. Without the princess to anchor her, I'm afraid she will always be lost."

General Anka carefully takes Vincent by the hand. His entire palm wraps around not only Vincent's hand, but his entire forearm as well. It's no question that he could crush Vincent in one swift motion if he wanted to, but Vincent felt no danger at this moment.

"I understand that you must train with Princess Vatosoa to save your friend, but please, if you can, try to rescue mine."

Before Vincent can respond to Anka's request, the two of them hear a loud creaking coming from the wall opposite of the Blood Stone's cage. Within a matter of seconds, the black stone parts like the Red Sea. Vatosoa appears, catching the two of them in a surprisingly intimate moment.

A delightful shock splatters across her face when she sees them holding hands.

"Am I interrupting something?"

Vincent and Anka give each other a brief look, and in unison they let go of each other and try to assume a more formal disposition. They struggle to compose themselves and respond at the same time.

"No, no!"

Vatosoa folds her hands together and rests them against her cheek while tilting her head slightly.

"Aaawwwwwww were you guys talking about your feelings?"

The two of them respond at the exact same time with opposing answers.

"No!"

"Yes, Princess."

General Anka salutes Vatosoa after his reply. Vincent shakes his head at General Anka, but is hardly surprised that he would be unable to lie to his superior officer.

Vatosoa giggles and smiles at the two of them, but then turns her attention to Vincent.

"Vincent, I thought we could do some studying in the library, if you're ready. I'm sure there's something there that could help us with our predicament. Will you come with me?"

Vincent is quick to nod at Vatosoa's request, but lingers to say goodbye to General Anka. He turns and bows his head slightly to the general, surprising everyone in the room.

"Thank you for the meal, Anka. I really enjoyed our conversation."

Vincent pauses and looks up at the Guardian before continuing.

"You've given me a lot to think about."

General Anka stands up straight with his shoulders back in an attempt to reaffirm his rank while also showing Vincent the respect he deserves.

"Likewise."

Vatosoa breaks their spell by grabbing Vincent by the wrist.

"C'mon, we have a lot of work to do! Anka, you better get some rest for Vincent's combat training tomorrow-"

Vincent interjects, trying to pull away from Vatosoa without much luck.

"Wait. Combat training?!"

"Oh don't worry, tomorrow is ages away. Right now, we better get back to the library!"

She pulls him towards the freshly made tunnel without much effort while Vincent flounders about behind her.

"Hey, V! Slow it down will ya?"

"No time, Vincent…."

Their voices fade the further they enter into the burrow, leaving General Anka standing frozen into place. His joy travels with them, leaving his body once they are gone. Instead, it is replaced by a highly regarded solemness, something that can keep him going, at least until the next morning.

Chapter 41

Vatosoa and Vincent re-enter into the room where they first met. Well, technically when they met, Vincent was dangling upside down on a giant boulder, but this is a memory that the both of them would love to forget. This library was where they had their first cordial conversation, which makes for such a much better introduction than an interrogation.

Vatosoa twirls around on the mirrored floor upon entering the space. Amused, Vincent crosses his arms and watches her at the entrance.

"You really like this place, huh?"

She stops dancing but still retains her smile.

"I think under normal circumstances, I would have made a terrific librarian."

She stomps once more, conjuring another stone pillar from underneath a stack of old books and sending it gliding across the room to her side. She picks out the second book in the stack, starts examining it, and once she's made her selection, she taps on the stone with the back of her heel. This causes the pillar to crumble instantaneously, allowing the tiny rock fragments to intermix with the books on the ground.

Vincent lunges forward and gathers the remaining books, dusting them off to make sure they aren't damaged. To his surprise, they were still in great condition. He was about to lecture her for her neglect, but didn't have the materials to back it up.

"To be honest, you kind of give me more eccentric professor vibes -"

Vatosoa snaps her book shut and tosses it over in Vincent's direction. He manages to catch it on top of the already impressive stack of books in his arms.

"Well, if that's the case, you better be a good student and get to reading! If we're going to help Hery with your abilities, we have to be sure to understand them fully first. After watching you and talking with Ahitra, I think I have a better understanding of what exactly -"

Vincent pokes his head out from behind the books.

"Hold up. You talked to Ahitra about me?"

He drops the stack of books on the floor and tries to play it cool. Vincent tucks one hand into his pocket while using the other one to rub the back of his neck.

"What did she say?"

Vatosoa looks really annoyed.

"Really?"

Vincent shrugs his shoulders and laughs out of embarrassment. She doesn't change her facial expression.

"Don't flatter yourself, Vincent."

He relaxes and continues to act goofy until he gets her to smile.

"Hey, a guy can dream can't he?"

It clearly didn't work. She crosses her arms in defiance, but Vincent puts his arms around her to try to break down her wall.

"Okay, V. You got me. Tell me what you learned about my superpowers."

She sighs heavily, but puts up with him and gets back to work.

"As I was saying, I learned a lot, but I still have some questions for you. How exactly did your powers manifest themselves naturally? I mean, before you came to the island and started bonding with the Guardians."

Vincent takes his arm off of Vatosoa and instead, lifts both of them behind his head. He takes some strides over towards the white bean bag chairs on the far side of the room, answering her questions before he plops down onto the cushion.

"Well, the first thing I did was teleport, I think. Hery said I disappeared, but I sorta remember walking through a crowd of people in order to get back home. Then there was the whole thing of me merging with an electric current -"

Vatosoa interjects.

"I am aware that you can tear your body apart and rearrange it on a subatomic level. Your natural ability may be unconventional, but it isn't impossible to understand. What I'm asking is how it presented itself to you. What happened before you used your power for the first time?"

Vincent pauses for a moment to fold his hands in his lap. He stares down at his thumbs and his playful demeanor changes.

"Why do you want to know?"

"Well, in our cases, we were trained to embrace our natural abilities from childhood. We have special games and lessons to help us harness our powers, even when we are emotionally volatile. Although, I have to admit, I still struggle with this too sometimes."

Although Vincent is normally patient with Vatosoa and her ramblings, being forced to relive the trauma of his early adventure is keeping him on edge.

"And your point is?"

Vatosoa gets the hint and gets to the point.

"You didn't have this training when you were younger, so I wonder, did you have any indication of this ability, or did it come to you all at once one day -?"

"My mom died."

Vatosoa stays silent after hearing this, so Vincent continues.

"I mean, I guess I never really knew who she was. I hadn't spoken to her in years, because I thought she was always working and didn't have time, but that obviously wasn't the case."

Vincent rubs his eyes with the palms of his hands while he continues.

"It turns out she was…"

He hesitates to tell Vatosoa the truth about his mother. In all fairness, he still struggles himself with what really happened to her. Vincent subconsciously feels like if he admits it outloud, then he would be speaking this nightmare into reality. So, he chooses to avoid it at all costs.

"...really sick. I finally got the chance to see her again, but she was barely hanging in there. No one else was around to help her. Everyone had forgotten about her. So I had to make a choice."

His head grows heavy and tilts forward, hiding his eyes from Vatosoa. She quickly makes her way over to him and crouches down in front of the bean bag.

Vatosoa grabs his hands tightly in order to reassure him.

"Vincent, I am so sorry that you had to endure that. So much responsibility was thrusted upon you for things that are way beyond your control. I'm sure seeing her that way was painful enough, let alone having to -"

"That's why I'm here, V. That's why I came all the way here with Hery and agreed to all this magical crap. I need to find my father. My mom loved him more than anything else in the world, and he doesn't even know what happened to her."

"Good!"

Vatosoa shouts in Vincent's face and throws him completely off guard. He looks up at her without thinking, and she makes prolonged eye contact with him. She has a stern determination in her eye.

"Hold onto this feeling, Vincent. Keep this resolve no matter what!"

She nods her head and releases Vincent's hands from her grip. Vatosoa turns away from him and makes her way towards one of the bookshelves to her right, searching through piles and piles to find the exact book she needs.

"All magic runs on powerful emotions, Vincent. You are going to need to feel these sorts of things during your training to better understand your true power. However, it is important not to give into these negative emotions, or allow them to be any part of your magic, no matter how tempting it may be."

Her thumb rests on a book with a black velvet spine.

"Weaponizing suffering of any kind, even your own, will always lead to destruction."

She grabs the book and returns to Vincent on the bean bag. She sits adjacent to him in her own fluffy white bean bag.

"But if I'm being completely honest, I'm a bit of a hypocrite."

Vatosoa leans in closer to Vincent. She grabs the fabric of his chair and spins him around playfully to face her.

"My anxiety makes it really hard for me to control my powers at times. When I panic, I feel like I lose control and all hell breaks loose. But, we are going to learn how to manage our difficult emotions and negative reactions together!"

She drops the book in his lap and it lands with a loud thud. Despite its tiny stature, it weighs a lot more than Vincent would've imagined. It takes some effort for him to open even the front cover.

"I guess we all have some pretty heavy baggage, huh?"

Vatosoa smiles after seeing Vincent return to making his usual poorly timed jokes.

"This is a present for you. Since you were brave enough to share your story with me, I feel that it is best that I share this with you."

Vincent takes another look at this book and is in complete shock after reading the author's name at the bottom of the cover. In gold cursive lettering, he traces his father's name with his finger tips.

Vatosoa waits for him to comment on her gift, but Vincent is at a loss for words.

"Do you like it?"

"...How?"

"Your father came to me after visiting Ahitra because he was working on something he called 'The Testimonial of Living History: Seen and Unseen'. He asked me to do a series of interviews with him about my life, how I was raised, and the history of the Reef of Haran. At first, General Anka was completely against the idea, but just like you, your father won him over, eventually."

Vatosoa grins at him once more, but Vincent's attention remains fully focused on this book.

"Why didn't you tell me before?"

She immediately becomes apologetic.

"I'm sorry, Vincent! I wanted to give this to you sooner, but I wanted to see what your true intentions were. I see now that you're really a good person and that all you want to do is help those who are close to you. Besides, the history of my people is sacred to me. I can't trust this information to just anyone."

Vatosoa pauses and turns over the first few pages for Vincent.

"But you have taught me that it is important to share history, to help people understand it, so that they won't make the same mistakes again."

The two of them arrive on a page with various pictures of three girls, all wearing brightly colored cloths wrapped around their waists with dark tank tops and a matching vibrant head wrap. Despite each picture being the same three subjects, each photo looks as if they were from completely different time periods, each exhibiting different levels of wear and tear.

Vatosoa is the first to speak up.

"These pictures always bring back such happy memories."

She takes her finger and identifies each of the girls in the photo.

"There's me, there's Ahitra, and there's Lalaina."

Vincent can't help but smile back at these cheerful women, laughing and enjoying each other's company.

"You guys really were together all the time, huh?"

"The three of us were meant to work in conjunction with one another and our Guardians to protect each of our peoples..."

Vincent turns the page and Vatosoa's attitude shifts once she sees the picture of a tall, powerful man with fierce eyes and chalky red hair. He wears clothing of a similar style to the girls, a bright red and white cloth around his waist, but he leaves the rest of his chest bare. Bare, that is, except for the glowing ruby with jagged gold chains dangling around his neck.

"But overtime, it became obvious that we were not powerful enough for the King. He was determined to change us, something that he saw as an improvement, but in the end, none of us really wanted it."

She pauses.

"I'm not sure when or how the others got theirs, but I was the first."

Vatosoa takes a deep breath and turns to the next page, desperate to put off this part of the story for just a little while longer. They now encounter photos of several different people, all carrying some combination of spears, shields, and guns while accompanying a young woman in a man-pulled chariot. Although the umbrella covered her red braids, there could be no mistaking Vatosoa's likeness.

"My family traditionally served as the king's military advisers, as we had a knack for defensive strategy and our kingdom produced the best soldiers in the whole archipelago. As the next heir, I'd been specially trained in security studies and practical combat, should the need arise."

She points down directly at herself in the photo.

"I was destined to lead his armies. However, a man like that wouldn't leave anything up to fate…"

Her finger trickles down the page until she finds the bottom right hand corner. Vatosoa grabs it with her fingernails and slowly turns the page. After laying it down gently, Vatosoa is quick to point out a very particular photo to Vincent. A massive wooden house on stilts takes up the entirety of the page. Several of its unique features stand out to Vincent. First and foremost, the entire house had been painted white, except for a few thick wooden pillars and the dark red roof. In addition, the roof of the main house was extremely slanted, with a high triangular point at the top of the roof. Likewise, at this peak, two sticks poke out in opposite directions, similarly to the horns of a mighty bull. Regarding the smaller buildings on either side of the main house, their roofs reflect a design more common in East Asia. Red tiles slide down the slopes of both roofs, with gold ornaments decorating the base and summit, reaching upwards towards the sky.

Her hand rests on top of the middle of the photo, unintentionally blocking it from Vincent's view.

"He called me into his war chamber one day to go over plans on how to maintain stability with the fracturing Kingdom of the Nofon. I had my parents come with me, because this would be my first time drafting policies of my own for the king, but when we entered, I was immediately ambushed. My own parents had put me in restraints and brought me to my knees."

Tears run down her cheeks and soil the pages beneath.

"No matter how badly I struggled, it was no use. Even if I managed to break away, more and more soldiers would just pile on top of me to force me into submission."

Her hand moves away from the page and towards her face. She uses the backside of her fingers to wipe away her tears before they ruin the album.

Vatosoa continues.

"They eventually pinned me down to the ground, lying face up and stretched out like a star. That's when he performed the ritual. The Dark King brought over a wooden bowl filled with molten rock, stood directly above me, and poured it into my eyes. I screamed for hours in pain, but it was clear that I wouldn't be moved until the rocks finally hardened."

She pauses, taking in a deep breath before turning the page. Instead of the usual photos, the pages were filled with wild notes and strange drawings. The drawings were categorized into different symbols and ruins, documenting different combinations that would indicate their uses could have multiple effects on the caster, just like spells and charms.

Vatosoa takes the time to trace a few of these ruins out of order with her fingertips.

"I could feel them carving strange shapes and symbols into rock. Eventually, they cut so deep that the knives reached my eyes as well, but by then, they were so damaged that I could no longer see or feel anything. When they were done, I felt a horrible energy surge through me and pool around where my eyes should have been. When it settled, light started coming back to me. I was elated, but something was terribly wrong."

She stops at the very last rune at the bottom of the page: a design that creates a hexagon with a single line. Vincent couldn't help but notice an eerie comparison between this drawing and the outline of the Blood Stone.

"I could see my captures in the room once more, but I saw more than that. I saw them in their entirety. I saw the moment they were born, I saw their childhoods, I saw their present, and I saw their futures…"

Vatosoa's voice trickles off as she finishes her tale.

"I even saw their deaths. The horrible fires, battles, and betrayals that would be their demise, but at the time I didn't care. I didn't say a word to them. Even if I really believed what I was seeing to be true, then they more than deserved it for what they had done to me. I didn't want to give them the satisfaction of knowing that their cruel experiment was a success. The only reason they knew that the curse had taken full effect... was because of my eyes."

Vatosoa slowly and cautiously removes her glasses from the bridge of her nose. As she pulls them away, her eyes shift from their usual brown to a golden glow just like Ahitra's. However, the longer Vincent stares at them, the more he notices a subtle shade in their color. Around the perimeter of her eyes, a ghostly blue pigment swirls about like a forbidden storm. It isn't long before the outlining hue spreads, turning her eyes into cloudy crystal balls.

Vatosoa is careful not to remove her glasses completely. They linger on the tip of her nose so that Vincent can take in the full view.

"Whatever I see will become set in stone. Of course, this isn't a big deal if one is only looking at the past. The past, you cannot really change, but it can be detrimental for someone's future."

She pushes her glasses back up the bridge of her nose, securing them into place. Once they are secure, the cloudiness of her eyes recedes and they return to their natural hue.

"Once I see someone's future, there's no way to change or even avoid it. People tend to be malleable, but they become rigid once I see them fully."

Vincent chimes in with a question.

"When I was leaving the Isle of Tendrom, Ahitra told me you already knew what happened here. Is that what she meant by that? That you could see my future and knew what I would do?"

Vatosoa shakes her head back and forth and laughs underneath her breath.

"Yes and no. Ahitra wanted to spook you out of spite, in all honesty. She probably figured I'd read you as soon as you got here and found out that you trashed her house. That's something that happened in the past, so I can see it pretty easily. But to tell you the truth, I've never read you until just now. Your guilt about that day popped out to the forefront pretty quickly, Vincent."

Vincent blushes a little and tries to change the subject.

"If you saw all that when you read me, then you probably saw my future too, right? Anything interesting? Like, which one of my kids is going to end up winning the world series?"

Vatosoa crosses her arms in a huff.

"Ahitra's right, you play too much!"

Vincent tugs at the edges of her bean bag and drags her closer towards him, so much so that their legs rest against each other's.

"C'mon V. I know what happened to you was absolutely horrible. I can't imagine how you felt and continue to feel about it to this day. I'm not downplaying your suffering at all. But back home, people pay thousands of dollars for crystals and tarot cards just for the chance to see a percentage of what I know you see. I'm sure you of all people could find a way to turn your curse into a real gift -"

"You don't understand."

Vatosoa interrupts Vincent before explaining herself further.

"I know the King gave this to me so that I could be the perfect military advisor, someone who could come up with a flawless strategy against any enemy known to man. I was more than willing to assist him at the time as well, but…"

Vatosoa lets out a deep breath once more.

"There's no way I could've known who his first target would be."

Vincent can plainly see that Vatosoa is once again undergoing some emotional distress. He reaches out and places both of his hands on her shoulders, squeezing them slightly to let her know of his presence. With this reassurance, Vatosoa keeps on going.

"One day the King dropped by the Reef of Haran for a royal visitation, something he did at least once a month, but on that day, he deviated from his normal schedule. We went up to the peak, the spot where you and I had breakfast this morning, and he asked me to gaze over the whole kingdom. I saw so many families out and about, foraging for fruits alongside the lemurs, children playing in the caves with one another. He asked me to use my curse on them, but I wasn't sure why."

Vatosoa avoids making eye contact with Vincent. She finally settles on looking downward towards the book in their laps.

"Then I saw it. I saw his plans. He was going to attack the people of the reef. The king finally strengthened his own armies and people to the point where he didn't need us for soldiers anymore. In fact, he was secretly worried that even with their enhancements, the Rano would fail. That's why he needed me. He needed me to seal my people's fate."

She takes off her glasses and rubs her face again, attempting to conceal the fact that she is crying once more.

"I couldn't contain myself at that moment. I couldn't hide myself away like I did while he was inflicting the curse. I released all my power at once. That canyon I created, I knew the rest of his men were there waiting for his return, so I killed them. I made sure to use every pebble available to suffocate any Rano within our borders. I slaughtered them without mercy.... I did this to protect my people... at least that is what I told myself."

She lets out an emotional sigh so that she can work up the strength to keep going.

"The King was outraged. He subdued me quickly and ordered my own guards to lock me away in some prison cell. It wasn't long before Anka came to rescue me, but the damage had been done."

Vatosoa grabs the corner of the page and turns it for one last time. Vincent looks down to find a large photo of what looks like a civil war. The only true visible difference between these opposing parties is the size of the mouth of the Rano, and their sharp, protruding teeth.

"After what I saw, I knew that I had to send them all away. In my vision, I saw the King and his forces invade through our own underground network. I thought if I could evacuate everyone through the canyon, then they would be safe. Unfortunately, that's when I learned just how powerful my curse actually is. Somehow that wretched man knew when and how we were traveling and met us at the base of the canyon. He was ready with an ambush just large enough to overpower us. Despite our training and reputation, my people were gone almost instantaneously... I was the only one left."

Vatosoa closes the book and lets it fall into Vincent's lap.

"Ever since that day, I vowed never to use my future sight ever again."

Vincent pauses to move the book out of Vatosoa's line of sight. He then turns to face her.

"Can I ask… why did General Anka want you to use your curse on Hery?"

Vatosoa looks up to meet Vincent's eyes, but she isn't as strong as she thinks she is. She becomes more and more emotional while answering Vincent's question.

"If I saw him surviving his injuries, then it would not matter what action we would have taken, he would have survived. We could have dropped him down on the floor right there, and he would have pulled through, eventually. General Anka was relying on this prediction, and trusted me to solidify it into reality, but I can't control it. That's not how it works."

She starts sobbing uncontrollably.

"If I would have seen his death…"

Her voice becomes muffled as Vincent pulls her into his chest. He wraps his arms around her shoulders, patting her on the back of her head gently. She allows herself to let down her guard and in return, Vincent lets her sit and cry, taking as much time as she needs. After a while, Vatosoa is finally able to pull herself together, but chooses to remain in Vincent's arms for the remainder of their conversation.

"I can't bring myself to use any sort of ritualistic magic, anything that could possibly be tied to the Dark King or the Cursed One. However, I do recognize that if we want to save Hery, and in turn Lalaina, then we are going to have to draw on the power of her curse. It's the only way."

She pulls away from Vincent just enough to be able to look up into his eyes.

"I know it's not fair of me to ask this. I wish I was strong enough on my own. But I need you to do this for me Vincent. I can't do this without you."

Vincent stares back at her, but he's distracted by his own reflection in her oversized glasses. His tiny figure seems powerless behind the wire frames, as if it is trapped behind iron bars. Whether or not it's her intention, Vincent feels as though Vatosoa had already trapped him behind her eyes, sealing his fate. There is no way he could possibly say no to her now.

Instead, he replies with:

"Don't worry, I'm here."

And pulls her back into his chest.

Chapter 42

After a while, Vatosoa manages to pull herself together and breaks away from Vincent. She then closes his father's book in front of them, and hands it back to him.

"Here, I think you should keep this. It is more of your birthright, after all."

Although Vincent desperately wants to snatch this book out of her hands, he hesitates to do so.

"Are you sure? I know this is my dad's work, but these are your memories, Vatosoa."

She smiles while she stands. Vatosoa grabs his arm and brings him up alongside her.

"I'm positive. Besides, I'm looking forward to building more, even happier memories with everyone once we get through this mess."

Vincent smiles at her while holding onto his father's book. He squeezes it tightly enough so that this last fragment of his father didn't have the option of letting him go.

Vatosoa chimes in and interrupts his grappling.

"Although, I do unfortunately have one more small favor to ask of you."

Vincent loosens his grip on the book and returns to the moment.

"Of course! What is it, V?"

Vatosoa takes a deep breath. She is somewhat scared to ask Vincent this next question.

"Do you mind if I take some time to study your mother's journals, Vincent?"

Vincent seems thrown off by her request.

"Huh? What for?"

Instead of responding right away, Vatosoa taps her foot onto the stone floor, once again revealing the path that would lead to Vincent's private bedroom. This time the tunnel contains additional skylights so that Vincent would not tumble in the dark. She takes a few steps towards the entrance and indicates for Vincent to follow. When he does not budge, she grows concerned.

Vincent indirectly forces her to explain herself.

"I really think the contents would be helpful in our training, Vincent. Perhaps your mother learned something as a scientist that could help with our current situation. Admittingly, I'm also really excited to see how far an outsider was able to decipher our magic, even if it is from a purely physical perspective."

Vincent takes some time to truly ponder over her request. His hesitation comes from the fact that he's never trusted another being with his mother's information before. Even when he wasn't reading the contents as he should have, he never passed any of the books over to Hery. They were his and his alone, a mother's last dying gift to her son.

However, he also feels that he owes Vatosoa in some way. She had just freely given over her memories to him after coveting them for so long. If she could offer her prized possession to Vincent for the greater good, shouldn't he do the same?

Vatosoa detects this inner conflict within Vincent and quells it.

"I promise to return her work to you once I'm finished. You have my word, Vincent."

Hearing this reassures him slightly. Vincent takes a few steps forward and meets her at the entrance. He smiles and nods at her before the two of them make their way towards his room.

They finally reach those foreboding doors once more. Vatosoa may have been the one to open the door for Vincent, but she allows him to be the first to enter. She smiles at him as he walks past her, but Vincent was unable to tell if this was because she was being polite, or because he was once again adhering to her requests.

Vincent makes his way over to the bed in the middle of the room, leaving her in the doorway. When he gets close enough to it, Vincent crouches down into a plank position so that he can get a better look at the contents underneath the bed. He sticks his arm into the darkness, shuffles it around, and pulls out what was lying underneath.

Vincent turns and sits upright with his backpack sitting in his lap.

Vatosoa can't help but give Vincent a look of confusion and he is quick to address it.

"What?"

Vatosoa quickly tries to rectify her offense. She sheepishly raises her hands once more, palms outwards, and shakes them back and forth.

"Oh, nothing! I'm just surprised that you kept something this precious to you in the dark… and on the floor."

"There isn't really any other place to put it, is there?"

He gestures around the room to emphasize the lack of storage space and decor.

"Besides, I had to keep them close to me."

Vatosoa lowers her hands and sighs as she takes a few steps towards him, thinking of her own personal stash of books in her library and how they all eventually gravitate in piles towards her bean bag.

"I guess you do have a point."

She plops down and sits with her legs crossed directly in front of him.Vincent begins pulling out the books one by one and gently setting them on the ground in between the two of them.

Vatosoa is unable to contain her excitement. She hurriedly grabs one of the first books that Vincent sets down and starts reading right away.

"Oh wow -"

"Hey, be careful with that!"

Vincent reaches for her book but she unconsciously pushes him away. She's too engrossed in the new information to see that she's overstepping boundaries.

"Mutated DNA? Blood samples taken from the royal families? A molecular breakdown of the powder we use to dye our hair? -"

She continues to hurriedly flip through pages when she's interrupted by a new presence in the room.

"That is quite enough, Princess."

General Anka towers in the doorway. Incredibly, he has to duck his head slightly to avoid contact with the top of the doorframe.

"The field has been prepped. It is time for Vincent's training."

Vatosoa still seems oblivious to his comment, but acknowledges him anyway.

"Anka, look! There's a whole section in this one about lemurs and their stink glands. Did you know they have stink fights where they -"

"Princess!"

In that moment, Princess Vatosoa made General Anka nearly shriek in embarrassment, his tail twitching back and forth erratically. It was this wrongdoing that brought her back down to earth.

"Oh, I'm sorry."

She regretfully closes the book in front of her and places it in her lap. Unlike previous incidents, she seems too far away in her own thoughts to give Anka the genuine apology he deserves. Instead, she adopts a somber tone, like she is dreading what is about to happen next.

"I guess I got a little too carried away. How rude of me."

This feeling would prove to be fleeting, as Vatosoa tries to cover up her reservation with her usual demeanor. Vatosoa starts stacking other books and places them all in her lap, preparing to carry them with her to the training field.

"We should get going. Besides, the quicker we strengthen Vincent's abilities, the faster he can attend to Hery's injuries and -"

Once Vincent realizes what she's doing, he reacts in a way that even surprises himself. He slams his hands down onto the books in her lap and the impact shakes Vatosoa to her core. She seems frightened, and Vincent is instantly filled with regret. However, he can't stop himself from saying what needs to be said.

Vincent nods his head and looks down at the books before making eye contact with Vatosoa.

"They stay here, okay?"

Silence hangs in the air for a while, but eventually Vatosoa's shock wears away and it is replaced by her defensive royal demeanor. However, this tone of voice mixed with hery ready obedience confuses and intimidates Vincent.

"Of course."

Vatosoa carefully slides the stack of books back underneath Vincent's bed. She tidies up the rest of the fringe journals and joins them with the others, giving Vincent some semblance of peace of mind.

Vatosoa straightens up and addresses Vincent more cordially than she had before. However, there is something new buried in her voice that Vincent can't quite decipher.

"I'll come back to read the rest at a later time. Until then, let's go ahead and start your new training!"

She grabs Vincent by the arm before giving him time to respond and leads him through the dark tunnel ahead. Anka follows along with his tail between his legs. This time, Vatosoa deliberately refuses to make skylights as they go along, forcing Vincent to rely on her all the while.

Chapter 43

The three of them finally emerge from the series of chasms that would have rendered any other person completely useless. Thankfully, they had Vatosoa to guide them through these tunnels, a fact that Vincent is forcibly made aware of once again. Light pours in from the skies above, which welcomes like a long last friend. He takes a few minutes to enjoy its presence before recognizing where they've returned to.

Vincent realizes that he's standing in the very same field where Vatosoa saved Vincent from General Anka's interrogation. Ironically, Vincent's intuition warns him that Vatosoa is more of a threat this time around.

She interrupts this warning.

"Do you remember this place, Vincent? I understand if you do not. You were in pretty bad shape when I found you after all."

Vatosoa looks up at General Anka with a scolding look on her face. His shame compounds itself after what previously occurred.

Vincent notices this and attempts to make Anka feel better.

"Don't worry about it. I understand that you were just carrying out your duty. Anyone would want to protect their home if they felt like it was in danger."

Anka nods his head as a form of gratitude. His overall demeanor becomes lighter, but Vatosoa's severity still dominates the mood. She is quick to turn Vincent's attention back to her.

"Yes, duty. That's something I need to discuss with you now."

She takes a step towards Vincent and he reflexively takes a step backwards as well. Vatosoa's face changes for a brief second from her royal scripted appearance to genuine distress over Vincent's mistrust. However, this moment is fast fleeting and she adopts her strict persona once again.

Vincent takes another step back in surprise when he sees this change in Vatosoa, but before his heel can touch the ground, Vincent runs into a cold solid stone.

Panic instantly sets in.

Vincent looks up and instantly recognizes the boulder that kept him captive. It still towers over him, casting a shadow over its returning victim.

Vatosoa continues.

"In many cases, duty involves a great deal of sacrifice."

Almost as if on command, lush vines wrap around his wrists and ankles in unison. They tighten before Vincent has time to process what is going on and bind him to the rock once more.

Vatosoa recommences her monologue while Vincent squirms about.

"After reading you, I got a better understanding of your abilities and your connection to Lalaina, but I also realized that we would have to make substantial changes in your training."

Vincent works up the courage to yell over her.

"What the hell are you talking about, V?!"

She remains unfazed and walks towards him.

"You see Vincent, elemental magic is traditionally reserved for the royal families and their descendants, where any physical magic, or magic that alters one's physical state, is given to select loyal foot soldiers. Although you can manipulate the elements at your discretion, you are operating on borrowed power."

Vatosoa slowly reaches into her pockets and pulls out a sharp dagger.

"Woah there, hang on a sec -"

"This is all necessary, Vincent. I promise."

She grazes the dagger across Vincent's forearm, cutting slightly below the surface.

"Lalaina's curse allowed her to heal herself and others because she was able to manipulate life and death itself."

Blood trickles down onto the ground below.

"If you are still connected to her, even after all of this mess, then you should be able to call upon her curse to heal the small wound on your arm. Meditate on her Guardian. Concentrate."

Vincent does his best to ignore the cut on his arm and closes his eyes. He takes a few deep breaths to quell his nerves, but the pressing nature of this situation still gets to him. Vincent prays to himself and hopes that the Coelacanth is feeling generous enough to answer, but this never comes to pass.

The wound on his arm only grows more severe as time goes on. Vincent understands that he must act quickly in order to heal himself, but he doubts that he can even manage that without Lalaina's presence. However, he must try.

Vincent notices the sound of a small babbling creek coming from somewhere behind the giant boulder. Its cry is muffled by all sorts of vegetation, but there isn't a doubt in Vincent's mind that it's there. He concentrates even further on the sound to the point where it drowns out even his own heartbeat.

He takes in another slow, deep breath, pulling the water from the stream along with it.

Droplets of water sway and flow towards his arm like tidal waves, crashing and curling over his arm. They combine and swirl around the wound, forming a translucent armband that moves in unison with Vincent's breathing. Vatosoa and General Anka look on with coded astonishment and a glimmer of hope.

Nevertheless, this feeling would be fleeting.

In the past, this would be the part where some semblance of Lalaina, her Guardian, or her restorative power would manifest in accordance with his own abilities. Previously, Lalaina saved a dying old man by using Vincent's presence as a vehicle for her fire. Likewise, the Coelacanth decided to help Vincent restore his mother's journals once they were soiled from that demonic encounter, using its leftover gold scales as magnets to pull out any residual runoff. This time, there is no such assistance at Vincent's disposal.

He is completely and utterly alone.

Vincent does not come to this realization right away. Instead he makes the mistake of letting the water infiltrate the wound, expecting Lalaina to handle the rest for him. Water continues to enter his bloodstream. What first felt like a gentle chill has now spread throughout his entire body at increasingly dangerous levels. Before Vincent succumbs to this icy embrace, he breaks the arm band, hoping to rescue himself before it's too late. The water dissipates and falls to the floor, much to Vatosoa's dismay.

"What are you doing? You can't give up now, you're so close!"

Thankfully, Vincent can feel the chill leaving his body, but he is still exhausted from both the wound on his arm and the drastic change in internal temperature. He responds to her in between breaths.

"It's no use… She's gone, V."

Vatosoa stammers at him.

"No, no… You just aren't trying hard enough!"

She unsheathes the dagger once more and slashes the other forearm as well. Her precision is that so the wounds are scarily identical both in shape and in depth. Vincent yells out in both pain and fear.

"Stop it! She's not coming back!! She left us -"

"NO!"

Vatosoa screams and slices Vincent once more across his chest, cutting through his clothes with ease.

"Lalaina wouldn't do that!"

She lifts the dagger high into the air and swings downward, thereby carving an "X" shaped gash into Vincent's body.

"You have to try harder!"

Vatosoa becomes overwhelmed with desperation. It is clear that this is no longer just a mission to heal Hery, but something much deeper and darker than Vincent could have imagined. Vatosoa will not stop until she gets her desired result, whatever that is. He realizes that in order to survive, he's going to have to figure out a way to heal himself on his own without Lalaina's influence.

In a seemingly obedient act, Vincent draws the water he released onto the rocks back to the wounds on his body as well as some additional water from the stream. Vatosoa is pleased by his concession, but Vincent isn't quite ready to give in just yet.

He notices that the water he dropped onto the ground became contaminated with all sorts of minerals from the soil and this gives him a brilliant idea. He previously read some passages in his mother's journals about the many minerals needed to repair red blood cells and skin damage, minerals that should be present in this muddy mixture in some shape or form. Risking infection and possibly worse, Vincent decides to save himself using his own power.

Vincent lets the muddy water enter his system once more, this time limiting it to only the areas of concern. This proves to be taxing for him, but this is only the first step. Next, Vincent uses the water and what remains of his own blood to sift through the dirt and find helpful minerals. They then rip them apart. Vincent is drained of energy at this point, but he must keep on going. He breaks the minerals down on a microscopic level, allowing his cells to make use of this new material at their discretion. His body graciously takes over from there, reproducing blood cells and skin tissue at an extremely accelerated rate.

It isn't long before the wounds completely heal themselves and the remaining water takes the leftover debris away. This mixture falls onto the ground once more, splattering over the tips of Vatosoa's shoes.

General Anka speaks up for the first time in an attempt to lift Vincent's spirit. He claps along to congratulate Vincent.

"You did it, young man!"

Vatosoa loosens her grip and drops the dagger onto the ground.

"You didn't use her power at all…"

General Anka uncharacteristically works as a diplomat to try to diffuse the tension between Vincent and Vatosoa.

"There is no shame in that! You still managed to learn how to heal yourself, Vincent, meaning that you can easily heal others as well. After all, Hery received his supernatural speed because Lalaina regarded him as one of her most trusted bodyguards -"

Vatosoa interrupts, her face covered in contempt.

"Clearly, you are also destined to serve."

Before anyone else can react, she conjures up a stone pillar from somewhere over her shoulder and lunges in right at Vincent, ramming it against his chest. At least half of his ribs break on impact. Vincent screams in pain, but his cries quickly contort into wheezing coughs. His lungs quickly cave into the pressure from the stone and the jagged broken bones.

Vatosoa holds him in place against the boulder.

"Do you still think you can do this on your own? Are you so arrogant to think that you can face these horrors without her or her magic?"

Vincent feels a sharp pang as another one of his ribs cracks, piercing his lung.

"I challenge you to even try to survive this single attack using your magic tricks."

Something stirs within Vincent. He isn't sure if it is his pride, his anger in this moment, or his instinctual need for survival that causes him to react. Regardless, the culmination of these factors gives him the strength to surpass even Vatosoa's expectations.

Vincent grits his teeth and pushes through the pain. A strange glow appears behind Vincent, framing him like some long lost deity. It catches Vatosoa off guard, but she looks on with more curiosity than any actual fear. She continues to study him as Vincent's back pixilates and opens itself up to the boulder against it.

Instead of manifesting themselves as threads like Vincent is used to doing when he detaches his hand, each pixel drifts about like dust, aimless until they land on the stone behind them. Once they attach themselves to microscopic fragments of the boulder, they return to Vincent, bringing with them building materials. The pixels gather stone around the edges of the broken bones, reinforcing and giving them added strength until they can be pulled together and put back in place once more. Some of the pixels look past the rock, seeking out the assistance of any nearby water or leaves for nutrients that the stone can't provide. However, once everything is gathered and put back in its place, Vincent can breathe again and the pixels return to their default state of rest.

By the time Vincent heals himself, there isn't very much left of the mighty boulder holding him captive. In fact, Vincent's body had consumed so much of it that it was reduced to a mere footstool. Without anything keeping him in place, Vincent drops down onto the ground, vines still wrapped around his wrists and ankles. However, they would not be there for very much longer. Vincent wiggles his feet loose and gets back up, using Vatosoa's pillar as an edge to cut himself free, glaring at her all the while.

She can't help but be amused by the spectacle that just occurred, even if she knows Vincent is angry with her for what she had done. Vatosoa is clearly proud of him, and reverts back to her normal self.

"You have such beautiful, delicate magic."

Once the perceived threat has been quelmed, Vincent feels all of his energy drain instantly. His body goes limp and he faints, falling back unto the earth. Both Princess Vatosoa and General Anka reflexively run to his aid, but Anka reaches Vincent first.

"Please Princess, allow me."

General Anka scoops Vincent up with one hand.

"You carried him last time."

She decides to concede and leads the way for the two of them through the tunnels once more. Anka cradles Vincent's limp body in his arms and they continue this way until they reach Vincent's bedroom, where Anka lays him gently to rest. Anka takes the time to cover him with the comforter and tucks him in like a napping child. Once she believes he is stable, Vatosoa and General Anka leave Vincent to recover.

Chapter 44

Vincent drifts off to sleep once more. As he relaxes further and further, moisture from a mysterious morning dew clings to his sheets and pulls him deeper into his dream.

He wakes up drowning in a mixture of his own sweat and lakewater. However, this isn't very surprising, considering that his bed is currently floating in the middle of the same pond from his previous dreams. This time, however, there were no celestial stones to be seen. Likewise, his mother was absent from his side. It became clear to Vincent that there would be no source of comfort protecting him this time.

Vincent flings the soaking sheets off of him and surveys the area.

"Hello? Anyone here?"

Silence returns his call.

After a few moments of searching, Vincent spots a figure in the distance facing bed. Its features are indistinguishable at this range, meaning Vincent is unable to discern whether it is a friend or a foe. He takes the risk and addresses it anyway.

"Hey! Did you hear me?"

Instead of responding, the figure takes small slow steps towards Vincent. Every time the figure dips its foot back into the water, Vincent can hear the croaking of frogs come from somewhere behind the mist. The crescendo grows as it comes near. This puts Vincent on edge.

"Who are you? What are you doing here?"

Once again, silence. Vincent scrambles to the edge of the bed, preparing himself to lunge at her, but when the moment comes for him to launch his attack, he freezes.

She is finally in a close enough range for Vincent to make out her face. As if the sopping wet curls didn't give her away, the scar across her face is an obvious tell.

Vincent grabs onto the bed sheets for dear life.

"Mom?"

This stops her in her tracks. Her face shifts from its current state to confusion, then to a subtle sadness, and then back to concentration for the task at hand. However, this shift did bring about a weakness hidden within her. His mother grabs onto one of the bed posts for support. Her long pointed nails scraping against the metal.

"Hey! Are you okay?"

Vincent instinctively reaches out to help her, but his mother puts her hands up in order to shoo him away. He's hurt by this, but honestly it is pretty keeping in her character. This isn't the first time she refused his help, even if she truly needed it.

"What are you doing here?"

Vincent's mother takes a deep breath before answering his question. Once she opens her mouth, a weeping reverb drips from her voice.

"I came to warn you, darling. You can't trust them."

"Wait, what are you talking about?"

She uses her free hand to brace herself against the rest of the bed frame.

"You gave them my journals."

Vincent becomes anxious at the very thought of upsetting her.

"Don't worry mom, Vatosoa is using them to help people. She's even going to help us find dad -"

"NO!!!"

She thrusts her head forward, wailing all the while. Her back and neck contort unnaturally, cracking with every small movement she makes during this strange possession.

Vincent is petrified from fear.

His mother looks back up at her soon with her shoulders still perched in their defensive position. She opens her mouth once more, but this time a stream of water continuously pours out as she speaks.

"You can't let them have my books."

Vincent finally finds the courage to speak.

"But we need it to save them! How else am I supposed to use Lalaina's curse to save Hery?"

A new, twisted voice comes from his mother's throat and laughs at the mere mention of Hery's name. He provides the answer to Vincent.

"You know exactly what you need to do, boy."

He uses his mother's finger to point directly at Vincent's chest. It lingers there eerily in midair until his mother takes control once more. She slams her hand back onto the bed post and shakes her head back and forth profusely in an attempt to release the demon's hold on her. Once she is satisfied that he left, she returns to her son, tears streaming down her face. The water returns to her mouth as well.

She still struggles to speak, gasping as if she is drowning.

"They mustn't rediscover the secrets."

Before Vincent can inquire for more information, his mother undergoes a grotesque transformation. Her nails grow and sharpen into blood red claws. She yells out in pain as the sides of her fingers tear themselves apart and reassemble themselves into a translucent webbing. This webbing travels up her arms and coats her skin in a slimy substance, giving her more of an amphibian-like appearance. Her curls become matted and take on an inky black pigment. The transformation moves up to her rosy lips and converts them into some oversized caricature of themselves. Finally, oversized fangs drip down from her canines, tools to recover the life that she had just lost.

Vincent takes action and reaches out to his mother.

"Mom, what's happening to you?!"

She finally removes her hands from the bed frame and uses them to block her face. However, Vincent peers past the gap in between her fingers and sees a pitch black darkness swirling around in the whites of her eyes.

She acts before it is too late.

"You have to go, now!!"

"But -"

Vincent's mother pushes him away from her with all of her might so that he might have the chance to escape. With her newly added supernatural strength, she is able to send Vincent flying through the air, crashing into the headboard of the bed.

Chapter 45

Shock wakes Vincent up from his dream. He finds himself back in his regular stone bedroom. His sheets are still dripping wet, but this is clearly due to his own perspiration instead of any paranormal bodies of water.

The Rookie is quick to jump into Vincent's lap and nuzzle him in an attempt to calm him down, but Vincent ignores him. He gently nudges the lemur to the side and makes his way to the side of the bed. Vincent hangs off the edge upside down, lifting up the bedskirt to explore underneath. He leans forward too far and tumbles head over feet over the bed and onto the ground. However, this crash isn't enough to deter him from his mission.

Vincent scrambles about and fully submerges himself underneath the bed. The Rookie takes notice of this, and joins him out of concern. They both ransack the area until Vincent is forced to accept the fact that his mother's journals are nowhere to be found.

An intense anger swells within Vincent until he can no longer keep control over it. It boils cover, converting itself into a physical form. He twists over so that his back lies flat against the stone floor, sending cold shivers down his spine. This only aggravates him further.

Vincent kicks the bottom of his bed with both of his legs, sending it flying vertically until the bed crashes into the crystal ceiling. Vincent attacks it with so much force that the bedposts actually pierce the mineral and become a permanent fixture in the ceiling. The rest of the bed has no choice but to resist the pull of gravity and remain in place until someone comes to rescue it. It was a far better option than running into Vincent once more.

Without even flinching over the mess he made, Vincent jumps back onto his feet and dusts himself off. He reaches out his hand to the Rookie and the small lemur climbs up his arm, eventually reaching his shoulders and gently draping his tail around his neck. Instead of being afraid, the Rookie seems eager to see what exactly Vincent will do next.

Vincent makes his way toward the exit. Once he reaches the door frame, he takes one of the large intricate doors and uses it as a battering ram, swinging it back and forth without much regard for the surrounding structures. He makes a point to slam his new toy upward towards the ceiling, creating massive skylights for himself.

Vincent continues to bash his way through the random assortment of tunnels until he reaches the entrance of the dining room, leaving nothing but rubble behind him. He pauses for a moment to survey the room until his eyes fall upon the amulet.

He zeros in and focuses on nothing else.

Vincent abruptly charges towards the crystal, cocking the wooden door back as if it was a baseball bat. Once he is within range, Vincent plants his feet and takes a full swing at the crystal teeth blocking the Cursed One.

The door completely shatters on impact.

Fragments of wood fly off in every direction, but Vincent remains unfazed. The Rookie comes out unscathed, protecting himself by squatting behind Vincent's head, but the same could not be said for Vincent himself. His hands are covered in splinters of various sizes, but he pays them no mind. Instead, Vincent grabs a crystal pillar with both of his hands stretched out wide and plunges the splinters even deeper into his skin.

He pushes through the pain and tightens his grip on the crystal. Vincent continues to squeeze until the splinters pierce through the backside of his hand and fall onto the floor, covered in blood. These tiny perforations in Vincent's hands become openings for his pixels to act. As Vincent bleeds onto the crystal, the tiny pixels move through his wounds and attach themselves to minerals present in the gems. They bring with them the same celestial glow, but this time, instead of integrating the crystal into Vincent's body, they rob the crystal of its own properties and change the structure of Vincent's skin.

The longer Vincent keeps his hands on the labradorite, the more his skin adopts the crystal's hues. It starts with his fingertips and gradually spreads upward until it reaches his shoulders. However, at this point Vincent's will push it back, forcing it to reinforce itself within his arms, hardening them like the crystal pillar they're mimicking. He continues absorbing the pillar's power in this cycle until it completely disappears altogether.

Vincent moves his fingers about, testing his dexterity, and smiles to himself when he discovers there are no limits to his mobility, despite the crystallization of his limbs. The Rookie stares at Vincent's hands, well more accurately, his own reflection in Vincent's hands, and this makes Vincent laugh. He pets the lemur gently before continuing on with his mission.

He takes a step into the prison of the Cursed One. Light bounces around the room, keeping the amulet rigid in fear. However, Vincent has no issue walking in and out of this gleaming maze and plows through to the prisoner. Normally, the amulet would literally leap at the chance to be this close to Vincent, but instead it cowers away from him. Vincent takes a moment to tower over it, before picking up the amulet with his bare hands.

The Cursed One lays silent as it is powerless to Vincent's newly borrowed magic.

Vincent carries the limp amulet with him out of the room and into the dark labyrinth of tunnels. Instead of smashing through the tunnels out of anger, Vincent understands the importance of stealth for the rest of his operation. Therefore, he travels in the dark, but this time, he is accompanied by a friend who can see clearly where he cannot.

Because of their unspoken connection, the Rookie has a complete understanding of Vincent's intentions. Therefore, whenever they come to a fork in the road or some sort of obstacle, all the Rookie has to do is turn Vincent's head slightly with his tail and Vincent follows suit. The two of them are harmonious in this system and it isn't long before they reach their next destination.

They finally arrive at the hospital wing where Hery is still being housed. Vincent looks over and sees a familiar sight: Hery lying flat on his back against the crystal bed while the lemurs assume their sun salutations and do their best to keep him alive with their vine circle. It is clear that they are exhausted.

One of the lemurs is about to fall backward and collapse, but Vincent runs over and catches it in his arms just in time.

"It's okay. You guys don't have to do this anymore. I'll take over from here, okay?"

The lemur he caught clearly appreciates the gesture, but the others are full of suspicion. Some cease their spell work and watch carefully from the sidelines, but others take this opportunity to run off and alert their superiors of this situation, their calls echoing off the tunnel walls like a siren.

The Rookie sees this and shouts at them, ready to spring into action. He jumps in order to pursue them before they get a chance to squeal. However, Vincent grabs him in midair and places him back onto his shoulder.

"Let them come. It's not like we were being very discreet before anyway."

Vincent then turns his attention back towards the lemur in his care.

"Will you be alright if I set you down now? I need to fix my friend."

The lemur nods and moves to the other side of the hospital bed. He wants to get some rest, but is careful to stay alert just in case his services may be needed.

Once he sees that the lemur is settled in, Vincent moves on to attend to Hery. He keeps a tight grip on the Blood Stone in one hand while using the other one to survey Hery's injuries. From what he can tell, Hery is covered in minor scrapes and bruises, but the internal damage is much worse. He clearly has a broken arm, but Vincent needs to see if there is anything else preventing Hery from waking up.

In order to fully understand his condition, Vincent releases his pixels from his back once more. He's shrouded in the same soft glow from before, but instead of floating aimlessly like dust, the pixels drift directly towards Hery, landing on him like soft butterflies. They gather around his more serious wounds, clustering in specific areas of his body. In this case, they nest around his arms and his head.

This indicates that Hery is currently suffering from a significant head injury in addition to his broken bones.

Vincent orders his pixels to permeate the skin. They phase into Hery and get to work, mending his bones by attaching themselves to the fracture. Once attached, the pixels harden and glue everything back in place, becoming a permanent part of Hery's frame. However, these methods would fail to heal Hery's head.

The leftover pixels return to Vincent, unable to penetrate Hery's skull. Vincent bends over to get a closer look, when suddenly, something resembling an inky black leech leaps out of Hery's tear duct and hurls itself towards Vincent. His reflexes allow him to catch the bloodsucker just an inch in front of his face. Although this is a close call, Vincent remains completely unperturbed, almost apathetic.

He notices that all of the creature's fight seems to disappear once it makes contact with his crystal hand. It becomes limp just like the Blood Stone. In order to test his theory, Vincent dangles the leech over the amulet. It hangs there a minute, but it isn't long before the leech is sucked into one of the thorns on the chain and completely disappears.

Vincent lets out a huge sigh.

"Of course you would have something to do with this…"

Vincent casually dangles the Cursed One a few inches above Hery's head like a fishing line, waiting for the rest of the parasites to take the bait.

Hery's head trembles, shaking back and forth rapidly, as if the creatures inside of him are signaling their refusal to come out. This only encourages Vincent to lower the Blood Stone closer and closer to Hery's face, to the point where the leeches can no longer avoid their fate.

The first couple of leeches are pulled from Hery's eyes, like tears made of tar. However, more and more parasites flow forcibly from all of the orifices in Hery's face: his eyes, ears, nose, and mouth, until their numbers reach the thousands. They flood the amulet like a powerful inverted waterfall. Despite their potency, Vincent still keeps his jaded attitude and treats these monsters as if they are merely another chore. They all quickly become absorbed into the Blood Stone.

Once Vincent is satisfied with the results of this unexpected exorcism, he reels in the amulet and holds it in its entirety in the palm of his hand.

"Gross…"

He takes one last look at Hery and smiles because he can tell that Hery's condition is already improving. Color returns to Hery's cheeks and his breath stabilizes. It won't be long until Hery wakes up, finally.

"C'mon, big guy."

Vincent carefully throws Hery over his unoccupied shoulder, making sure he doesn't hit the Rookie or come into contact with the amulet. After Vincent makes sure all of his passengers are secure, they leave the hospital bed and make their way towards the exit. None of the other resting lemurs follow.

Chapter 46

Vincent and the Rookie continue through the tunnels once more using their previously flawless method of communication. However, this unlikely trio now finds themselves in a part of the reef that they've never been to before. They reach a fork in the road and it gets to the point where the Rookie no longer brushes his tail against Vincent's chin, but rather, ticks it back and forth in confusion. He clearly feels guilty for getting them lost, and nuzzles his face against Vincent's cheek as a way of saying sorry.

Vincent exhales and tilts his head towards the Rookie, accepting his apology.

"No worries. Looks like it's back to Plan A, huh?"

He turns back towards the wall in front of them and punches it dead on with the hand that holds the Blood Stone. His newly reinforced crystal fist makes contact against the dark limestone and sends a deep crack shooting up towards the ceiling, splitting it completely in half. It opens up to the night sky and reveals an unexpected full moon.

Moonlight illuminates the three of them while they stand at this crossroad. Vincent looks back and forth between the path on the right and the path on the left. He does this over and over again until he comes to a sinking realization.

There is a reason why they have yet to encounter any trouble thus far. Vincent has yet to face any obstacle, because all of his actions have been permitted thus far. Even though the Rookie clearly knew the path to find Hery and the amulet, they ultimately reached their destination because Vatosoa allowed them to. Now that their objective is to find her, she must protect herself. She's manipulating the tunnels and the stone walls so that they will never be able to reach her. It doesn't matter if the Rookie knew exactly where her chambers were. Vatosoa would have them running around in circles all night.

Vincent punches the wall in front of him once more out of frustration, leaving a significant dent in the stone. After a few seconds, his suspicions are confirmed. The limestone rearranges itself and contorts back into its original form, without any noticeable damage.

He realizes what he has to do.

Vincent double checks to make sure that Hery and the lemur on his shoulder are both secure before acting. He addresses the Rookie directly.

"Hold on, buddy."

The lemur grabs his ear to let Vincent know that he's right there beside him and ready for whatever might happen next. Vincent smiles to himself before throwing another powerful punch into the Haran.

Before the rock has a chance to heal itself, Vincent strikes again, creating an even deeper crevice. He fires once more, this time an undercut that is strong enough to make room for his legs. Vincent takes a step into the stone while firing another punch, shattering more of the obstacle in his way.

This becomes an exhausting pattern of destruction and reconstruction, with Vincent slightly gaining the edge after every attack. As a result, the Reef becomes desperate. It throws its own punch in the form of a condensed stone pillar, aiming for Vincent's head. Unfortunately for the Reef, the Rookie stands in between it and Vincent.

All it takes is a flick of its tail for the Rookie to completely demolish the Reef's attack. The limestone pillar shatters on impact, but after a second or two of the Rookie merely waving his tail back and forth amongst the rubble, all of the contents of the pillar disintegrate into dust. It happens so quickly that Vincent is unable to detect any of it. The dust from that pillar simply blends in with all of the other debris from Vincent's attacks.

The Rookie glares at the wall, as if giving it a final warning.

No other stone pillars charge at the two of them for the rest of their journey.

Chapter 47

With one final blow, Vincent sends the wall in front of him tumbling down, revealing Vatosoa's bedroom beyond it. The room has the same curvature as a crescent moon with a rounded glass window connecting its peaks. Instead of being one rounded sheet, the window is composed of small glass triangles glued together by some dark cement, giving the light entering the room a kaleidoscopic effect. These rainbows contrast directly against the bedrock walls, floor, and ceiling, but gather onto Vatosoa and her velvet pink bedding on the opposite end of the room.

Hearing the adjacent wall crumble stirs Vatosoa from her sleep. She sits up in a panic, pulling her weighted blanket close to her chest.

"Vincent, what are you doing with -"

"Where are they?"

Vatosoa responds, still groggy from her sleep.

"What are you talking about?"

Vincent is impatient, he balls his fists in anger.

"Where are my mother's things?!"

His shouts bounce off the walls and eventually return back to him. In all of this confusion, he unknowingly summons a giant shadowy figure from the other side of Vatosoa's bed. It's mere presence is enough to block out all of the light from the window. Vatosoa's whimsical rainbows vanish.

"You will do well to remember that you are in the presence of royalty, young man."

This voice is unmistakable. It belongs to General Anka.

His eyes glow like yellow apparitions in the nightlight, a truly ghastly sight.

"Choose your next words carefully."

Vincent isn't deterred. He takes a step toward the two of them.

"I've come back for what's rightfully mine."

Vatosoa throws her blankets down and shuffles to the edge of her bed.

"Please Vincent, I just need some more time with them. I'm on the verge of a breakthrough-!"

"Why did you steal them?! All you had to do was ask!"

Vincent lets his anger get the best of him. He uses his free hand to smash a giant hole in the stone wall next to Vatosoa's headboard. This would prove to be a detrimental mistake.

General Anka leaps over Vatosoa's bed and pushes it back against the wall in the same movement. He uses his tail to gently nudge her back into bed and uses it to keep her in place. When he lands, General Anka's body is positioned in a way where Vatosoa is completely blocked from Vincent's view.

Anka is close enough to whisper to Vincent.

"Don't make me do this. It is my duty to protect my Princess."

He responds to Anka's request in a hushed tone.

"You have your people, and I have mine."

The look on Anka's face makes it clear that this was not the answer he wanted to hear.

Vincent then turns around and walks over to the curvature of the room. He sets Hery down gently and makes sure to move any loose objects away from him, knowing that things may escalate quickly. He ties the Blood Stone around his crystal wrist, ensuring that no one else comes into contact with it. In the same protective vein, Vincent lowers his arm down so that the Rookie can climb down, but the lemur refuses to budge.

"I need you to look after him now, buddy. Okay?"

The Rookie seems hesitant, but Vincent insists.

"I'll be fine."

The lemur obediently leaps to Hery's side, but once he lands, he never takes his eyes off of General Anka.

Anka notices this and addresses his rogue soldier.

"As for you, you will be punished for breaking rank -"

"Don't you dare touch him!"

Vincent shouts over his shoulder at General Anka, but he doesn't respond. Instead he takes a step towards their direction, which sets Vincent off.

Vincent rearranges himself and sharpens his crystal hands to a point.

"Do I look like I'm playing?"

Before either of them get the chance to make a move, a large, overwhelming stalagmite shoots out from the floor, separating the two of them in an instant.

Vatosoa shouts over General Anka's massive tail.

"That's enough!"

The two of them finally turn their attention to her. General Anka looks over his shoulder, but Vincent stares her down directly.

"I'm taking the books. Then Hery and I are getting the hell out of here."

She stands on her bed in order to get around General Anka's tail while also simultaneously allowing her to tower over Vincent.

"I can't let that happen. There's still so much work to be done."

Vincent is quick to question her.

"What? What do you mean by work?"

"You still need some training Vincent, especially with all that you have ahead of you -"

Vatosoa struggles to convince Vincent that her actions are justified in this situation. Instead of sympathizing with her, Vincent comes to discern her ulterior motives.

"You needed to keep us here…"

Tears form and run down his face, but instead of wiping them away, Vincent keeps his hands firmly at his side.

"You knew how to heal Hery from the very beginning, didn't you?"

She doesn't respond right away.

"How could you do that to your friend?!"

Her silence was more than enough to push him over the edge.

Vincent screams and bursts through the stalagmite, lunging forward without discrimination with his full might. Luckily for Vatosoa, General Anka succeeds in being her barrier. Rather than protect himself from Vincent's attacks, General Anka allows him to make contact, but uses his tail as a pivot and changes the direction of their momentum. They miraculously move at a complete right angle, avoiding Vatosoa altogether. General Anka smiles at her reassuringly while the two of them go crashing through her glass window.

Chapter 48

They freely fall downward along with the glass fragments, sharp jagged stones waiting for them down below. General Anka reacts quickly, pulling Vincent away from himself and throwing him further up into the air. He then lands gracefully onto the spearlike rocks with the balls of his feet, his skin immune to the environment around him. The rest of the glass shortly follows and rains down onto General Anka. It shatters the moment it makes contact with the Haran, leaving small cuts on the rocks and their Guardian.

Vincent gets the message.

Anka just bought him another few seconds before being impaled by the stones. He may have genetically adapted and evolved to the Reef over time, but Vincent did not. However, Vincent does have the uncanny ability to reshape himself at a moment's notice, which comes particularly handy when put into dangerous situations like these.

While still suspended in midair, Vincent moves some of the crystal from his arms downward to the soles of his feet, while keeping enough in his palms to protect his hands. He reinforces them so they can harden and be able to withstand the impact of the Haran.

He lands on a pillar of limestone a few feet away from General Anka, using his hands and feet to wrap around the stone like the more subordinate lemurs that he befriended during his time here. Vincent looks up to find General Anka standing straight up on the tip of rock with his hands behind his back. He maintains this authoritative pose, absolutely unfazed, despite the deep wound in his side from Vincent's previous attack.

He is the first to speak.

“It doesn’t have to be this way, Vincent.”

Vincent scoffs, but Anka continues.

“Let me offer you a trade... You must bond with me in order to find your father. Is that correct?”

Vincent’s frustrated silence is enough of an answer for General Anka.

“I will loan you my power on one condition: end this tantrum of yours. You are putting yourself and everyone else around you in danger, and for what? Sentiment?”

Vincent scoffs and straightens up.

“For someone who values loyalty, you sure are quick to screw over people who are just trying to help you.”

He then climbs up the stone spike and stands on the tip, mimicking and challenging General Anka. Anka tries once more to quell his defiance.

“There is more at stake here than that, Vincent! You have to look at the bigger picture! -”

Vincent is fed up with being lectured. He screams at General Anka.

“Look at me!”

Vincent slams his hand against one of the pillars of the reef, absorbing the attributes of the stone once more and letting it spread. This time he holds no reservations. He allows the stone to pass through his skin, hardening to the point where his human form is no longer recognizable. He speaks once more as the reef slithers up his neck.

“You see what I am capable of doing. What’s stopping me from taking it by force?”

A soft voice rings throughout the chaos.

“Because that’s not who you are.”

Vincent looks around and mutters to himself.

“Lalaina?”

While Vincent is still trying to locate the origin of her voice, Vatosoa emerges from the broken window and calls out to him.

"Where is she? You heard her too, right? Lalaina?"

Vincent feigns ignorance and pretends not to notice, but it's too late. She's already seen his face perk up after hearing her voice. Vatosoa knows he's trying to keep her away.

"Bring her back, now."

"No. Even if I could, she doesn't want that."

Vatosoa fights to hold back furious tears.

"I said, now!"

Vincent returns her glares. He refuses to give her the satisfaction of an argument. She won't paint herself to be a victim in this scenario.

Instead, she simply tilts her chin upward to give her Guardian his orders.

Before Vincent could have the time to turn his head towards Anka, the Guardian of the Haran dropkicks him and sends him flying through the air. Vincent crashes through several jagged limestone pillars prior to slamming into the solid stone wall on the opposite side of the canyon. General Anka hits him hard enough that his body actually presses itself deeply into the stone, rather than rebounding off of the cliff and tumbling to his death.

Vincent hangs back and relishes in the pain.

"You are way over your head, young man."

General Anka leaps in front of him and lands on one of the pillars Vincent somehow manages to miss. He shakes his head back and forth before continuing on with his warning.

"You will not survive for much longer at this rate."

Vincent starts pulling his arms out of the limestone and sits upright.

"What makes you so sure of that?"

"Even if you're using borrowed power, you're still mortal. You're feeble. You haven't dedicated enough time to hone your body. You're no match for the elements of the Haran."

Vincent spits out some blood and smiles at Anka.

"Good thing I've been reinforcing my bones and muscles with all the minerals I've been taking in lately. You won't have to pull your punches any longer."

Vincent jumps out from the side of the cliff and leaps towards General Anka, snagging a loose pillar while in motion. He winds it back and swings it like a club with all of his strength. Anka springs upward and evades Vincent's attack, but the rest of the Haran are not as lucky. Vincent uses one of its own to cut through the rest of the stone, completely flattening the landscape of the area.

Vincent chucks the remainder of his makeshift spear at Anka while he hovers in the air high above the scene. Without anything to ricochet off of, he is helpless to the pull of gravity, making the stone spear completely unavoidable. General Anka braces himself to endure this blow, but it still knocks him off of his course and sends him flying into the trees above the gorge.

General Anka continues to fall downward into the ravine, but spreads out his arms and legs in every direction in order to catch himself on the limestone columns. However, he doesn't catch himself quickly enough because the tip of his tail plunges into the shallow creek. He instantly winces in pain and instinctively jumps forward into the trees.

Vincent takes notice of this and reacts quickly. He pulls the water from the creek and has it follow General Anka into the stone forest, but this does not last for long. Anka's familiarity with the terrain allows him to escape Vincent's pursuit and hide among the shadows of the remaining rocks and leafy trees.

Regardless, Vincent finds a glimmer of hope within the contents of the water. During the stream's initial trailing, Vincent notices some reflective gold scales in the suspended stream. His heart races at the thought of

Lalaina or her Water Guardian being with him once again after everything that's happened. However, he knows that the Guardian would never be able to fully actualize itself without some sort of assistance.

He brings the water back towards himself and embraces it in his arms, cradling it like an infant. It swirls itself into a sphere and sparkles in response to his touch. Vincent notices and takes a deep breath before releasing pixels from his body once more. He uses them as a vehicle to share his own body's moisture with what would soon become the Coelacanth. They carry tiny water droplets on their backs and fuse them to the sphere, which causes it to gradually grow larger in size.

However, even after Vincent shares as much of his body's excess water as he possibly can, it still isn't enough for the creature to retain its shape. Vincent sees General Anka emerging from the shadows, assessing the situation before his next attack. This causes the pixels to act reflexively, drawing whatever liquid it can find. They retreat further inward and pull out some of Vincent's blood as an offering to the Water Guardian.

As soon as his blood comes into contact with the water, it adopts a similar saintly golden glow. The golden scales condense and burn brighter with every passing second. Along with this newfound color, all of the water in the sphere vibrates at a higher frequency. It expands in short bursts, forming fins along its sides as well as a powerful tail. Once actualized, the Coelacanth uses its powerful tail to push itself out of Vincent's arms and high into the air.

The Water Guardian hangs there in moonlight like a reflective disco ball, illuminating even the darkest corners of the reef. As it absorbs and propels more and more light, it grows to gargantuan proportions until its size rivals the moon itself.

Anka is frozen in place out of disbelief at the sight of the Coelacanth. It is impossible for him to discern between admiration for a long lost friend and the fear of facing a powerful rival.

She completes her transformation and crashes back down to Earth, bringing the power of the tides with her. When she makes contact with the stone forest below, she disintegrates into the sea, completely flooding the Haran and bringing out anyone who may be hiding beneath it.

General Anka scurries to the tree tops in order to avoid the rising water. Once he reaches the highest branch, he looks out to see the Coelacanth leaping out of the water once more, adorned with her golden scales. Her brightness rivals that of the stars.

He's completely dumbfounded as the Coelacanth falls back to earth, crashing into the waves right in front of him. Some water splashes on his face, but he pays it no mind, no matter how hard it stings. General Anka is elated to be in her presence, even if it's just for this split second.

"Vincent!!"

Anka calls out to him while leaping from surface to surface at full speed. Vincent doesn't even have the chance to track his presence before General Anka grabs him with his bare hand.

He squeezes Vincent just hard enough to ensure that he wouldn't be able to escape. Vincent squirms about anyway, but Anka tries to calm him down with a whisper.

"Listen, we don't have much time."

The palm of his hand glows with the same intensity as the Coelacanth.

"What's going on?! What are you doing to me -"

"I was blind before, but I see clearly now…"

Anka looks upward as the Water Guardian leaps over the two of them. She lands in an open space between them and Vatosoa's bedroom window, creating a giant wave that obstructs Vatosoa's view.

"She's shown me the truth. We need to bond so that you can complete your mission. Nothing else matters now."

After hearing this, Vincent ceases his fidgeting and grabs onto General Anka's finger with both of his hands, careful to not let the Cursed One come into contact with Anka's skin. He pixilates his palms once more, letting General Anka's light travel up his arms and quickly engulf his entire body. Once he lets the light reach the top of his head, Vincent shakes uncontrollably as he receives visions of the life of someone else.

He now finds himself in the middle of a lush jungle. Vincent is young and happy, leaping from tree to tree, chasing after his mother and the rest of his siblings until some unknown force grabs him from behind unexpectedly. He shouts out in fear, but instead of coming to his aid, his family freezes in terror once they see his captor.

A dark, shadowy hand reaches out and swats at his family. They leap backwards in order to avoid getting hit and retreat back into the forest, abandoning him without a second thought. Instead of the betrayal he should have been feeling, Vincent's heart instead floods with fear caused by the maniacal gravelly laughter of his captor. This laughter centers his new reality, so much so that any shred of his former life dissipates into the background.

Vincent's vision gradually fades into a pure white. He hangs there, free from whatever held him as a hostage, suspended in this nothingness, that is, until he hears Anka calling him back.

"Vincent!"

His eyes open slowly, one after the other. Once he comes too, he sees General Anka in an exhausted state. Dark, sinister handprints are now visibly grasping his arms, still restraining him even to this day.

"Anka, are you alright?"

The General looks down at his arms and tiredly chuckles at his scars.

"Don't fret. I've already come to terms with this. It may be too late for me, but you can still help the others."

He winces before finishing his plea.

"I know you're capable of saving us all."

With these last words, Anka faints and falls backwards into the makeshift sea, taking Vincent along with him. The splash they cause is so grandiose that it even reaches Vatosoa in her observation deck.

"Anka, no!!!"

Vatosoa screams from her stone balcony and slams her foot on the ground, causing such powerful vibrations that they crack the very foundation of the Reef. They penetrate even deeper, summoning fourth molten rock from somewhere beyond the planet's crust. It rises and meets Vincent's flood, cooling and hardening on sight. This interaction not only reduces the strength of the freshly formed lake, but it also allows pre-existing rocks to ascend to the surface.

In the same motion, Vatosoa sends a stone platform shooting up from underneath General Anka, saving him from his watery grave. Vincent takes this opportunity to roll over and free himself from Anka's limp grip while Vatosoa is distracted. He stands and dusts himself off, preparing to face her once and for all, when an unexpected ally springs into the scene.

Hery comes running at a supernatural speed across the remaining water in Vincent's direction, carrying a knapsack full of his mother's journals and the Rookie on his shoulder. He grabs Vincent in midair and throws him over his unoccupied shoulder while sprinting away from the scene. However, before the three of them could flee the Haran, Vincent catches a glimpse of Vatosoa in all of her fury. She is chasing after them by generating new stone pillars underneath her feet and having them glide around like skates in the water. Her eyes are gradually becoming completely clouded, indicating that she is about to use her curse on Vincent and his companions.

As soon as Vincent notices this, he sees something shoot out from behind the other side of Hery's head. An extremely long slimy tongue lashes out and strikes Vatosoa in the eye, causing her to cease her pursuit and bend over in pain. After its attack, it then retreats back towards its owner and is reeled back into the mouth of the Rookie.

Although Vincent finds this terribly strange and frightening, he does not have the time to question this anomaly at the moment. By the time the creature finishes its attack, Hery has already reached the boundary of the Haran, climbing over the last few grey stone pillars before taking off into the ocean's horizon.

Chapter 49

The three of them travel north for quite some time before Hery's legs eventually tire out. He finally sees a short shoreline and rushes to reach it, setting Vincent and the lemur down before collapsing into the red sand. Admittingly, Vincent also needs some time to collect his bearings after being a passenger to Hery's lightning fast speed. Once he settles himself down, Vincent is able to take in their new environment in its entirety.

Despite running quite far from the Haran, they find themselves surrounded by similar limestone formations, except this time the stone takes on a distinctive powdery red color. In addition, unlike Vatosoa's kingdom, the vegetation is darker and put on full display. Trees outline the desert area and dust the landscape around the main muddy river running through the basin. Vincent is thankful for their presence, because without them, this area would be reduced to a martian landscape.

Vincent looks to his right to see Hery inching closer and closer to the river.

"Hery, wait a sec. Let me help you with that!"

He runs over and scoops Hery's arm over his shoulder, letting Hery use him as a crutch.

"Relax, Vincent. I am simply overheated. There is no need for all of this. I just require some water in order to cool down and replenish my energy. Then I'll be alright."

Vincent goes ahead and sets Hery down on the riverbank. Hery scoops up some water in his hands and splashes it onto his face. He takes another handful of water and presses his hand against the back of his neck, letting it trickle down his spine.

Hery lets out a sigh of relief.

"Much better."

He slowly reaches over to Vincent's back pack and pulls it in closer, getting everything together for their next move.

"I think it is best if we set up camp here, even if it's only for tonight."

"Yeah, you're probably right -"

Vincent gets up to scout the area and find a more secluded area to sleep, but Hery interrupts him.

"Vincent?"

He stops in his tracks to turn around and answer Hery.

"Yes?"

"I just wanted to say thank you, for everything you did for me back there. I never would have imagined that Vatosoa would put either of us in harm's way, especially given our relationship with Lalaina."

Hery grows quiet and mutters to himself.

"All those years in isolation really changed her…"

Vincent attempts to get Hery out of his own head.

"Hey, don't beat yourself up over this."

He gives Hery a love tap on his shoulder, but Hery seems very thrown off by this. Hery initially misinterprets this as an act of aggression, and reflexively raises his hands in a defensive position. Vincent sighs and continues.

"There's no way you could've predicted anything that happened in the last couple of days. Even if you could, I'm not sure there's much we could've done to change anything anyway. The more you try to force things to go your way, the more likely they are to go awry. It's best to leave those sorts of things to the professional. Let her stress over it for a while."

"Yes… things have done nothing but go awry, haven't they?"

Hery's regret shifts into a cathartic laughter and he returns Vincent's love tap.

"You've grown so much in such a short amount of time. I'm sorry that I couldn't be there to help you through the worst of it, when you needed me the most."

Vincent gently brushes Hery's hand off of his shoulder.

"It's okay. I just wish I could've snagged my dad's book before we left, you know. It's a shame that it got left behind."

Hery grins to himself before revealing his big surprise.

"Don't be too sure of that, Vincent."

Hery reaches into the very bottom of the bag and pulls out Vincent's father's publication. Vincent grabs it out of his hands and starts inspecting it immediately to make sure that it really is his father's work. Despite the impoliteness of this gesture, Hery can't keep himself from smiling.

"You have this little one to thank for that."

He pats the Rookie's head affectionately before continuing.

"He must have found it somewhere in Princess Vatosoa's room as well and tucked it away in the bag before we took off. Such a clever creature!"

Hery is too busy petting the small lemur to notice the uneasiness in Vincent.

"Yeah… really clever."

Vincent stares at the Rookie with concern. He specifically remembers leaving his father's book in his own bedroom before setting out on his destructive mission. Additionally, the Rookie was with him nearly the entire time. If he was carrying the book with him during this time,

Vincent would have noticed. Of course, the Rookie could have gone back to retrieve it during his battle with Anka, but something tells Vincent that Vatosoa would not have let it escape her sight.

With all that being said, Vincent comes to the conclusion that something strange is going on with his little lemur friend.

"Hey, Hery. We should really be getting some rest soon. I'm still worried that you haven't fully recovered from your injuries just yet."

Hery stops what he's doing and gives Vincent his full attention.

"Yes, that's quite right. We both just spent a great deal of energy in battle just then and we need to be tentative of our bodies' needs. Let's go to sleep."

Hery reaches into his pockets and pulls out a sack of dark powder. He then uses it to draw two large circles onto the ground with perpendicular lines running through the middle of them. After creating a smaller circle in each of the larger ones, Hery fills the negative space with strange symbols from Vincent's mother's journals.

Once he completes his design, Hery searches his pockets again and grabs his enchanted lighter. He bends over to light the powder, but instead of the fire spreading like a gradual burn, both circles and the contents inside of them burst into flame the instant the lighter makes contact with the ground. They extinguish themselves in the same breath, leaving nothing but permanent ash behind.

Satisfied with his work, Hery lays down across the circle, moving about trying to get comfortable on the rocky surface. No matter how much he moved about, the ash would never stick to his person.

Once he gets into position, Hery looks over towards Vincent.

"I appreciate everything you've done for me, Vincent, but there is no need for you to worry any longer. You've grown into such a strong and capable young man."

Vincent walks over and sits in his designated circle. The lemur jumps from his rock and sits down in Vicnent's lap. Vincent remains suspicious of this creature, but doesn't let it show. He doesn't want to rattle Hery any further, at least not for a while. After seeing the Rookie's sweet gesture, Hery smiles and rolls over to his side.

"There's nothing that can get in our way."

Chapter 50

Some time passes and Vincent watches Hery drift off to sleep. His loud snores confirm that Hery won't be waking up any time soon. Vincent laughs to himself for a moment, happy to be able to hear those obnoxious sounds again, but then adopts a more solemn expression as he looks down to see that the Rookie fell asleep on his thighs.

"We need to talk, buddy."

Confident that Hery will be fully protected by his spells, Vincent carries out his plan without the guilt of leaving Hery alone again. Vincent grabs the lemur from his lap and carries him away in the dark. They walk for a few minutes before Vincent decides to duck down behind a wall of red desert stalagmites.

He sets the Rookie down onto the ground and it looks back up at him with confusion in his eyes.

"Okay, time to cut the crap. I saw what you did to Vatosoa's eye back there. I might not be a scientist, but I know that shit ain't normal."

The Rookie grabs his head and lets out a heavy sigh.

"Shit…"

Vincent jumps back a little in surprise, but then tries to play it off as an intentionally dramatic reaction.

"Ha! I knew it! -"

The Rookie interrupts Vincent's celebration.

"I hoped we wouldn't have to cross this bridge yet, kid."

The lemur jumps into the air and its body folds in on itself. It swallows more and more of its figure until it contorts into some horrific ball of flesh, but this is a temporary stage. In less than a minute, the creature adopts his new form.

Four stubby legs are the first feature to emerge, followed by a giant head, a wide set mouth, and a pair of beady black eyes. The bumpy skin and rugged features finish off the appearance of an oversized prehistoric frog.

Vincent does nothing to hold back his shock this time.

"What the hell?!"

"Shhh keep it down, will ya? You're gonna wake up the old man!"

Vincent takes some shallow breaths in order to calm himself down before continuing with his interrogation.

"What even are you? Where did you come from and what do you want from me?"

Instead of hopping closer, the frog walks over to Vincent on all fours. Somehow, it makes the whole atmosphere of this situation even creepier, causing Vincent to take another step back. This doesn't deter the frog from advancing towards Vincent in the slightest.

"Back in the old days, folks called me Beezlebufo, the Devil Frog, but you can call me whatever you want. Bufo's fine, but I have to admit, I really liked being your 'little buddy'."

He rubs his bony skull against Vincent's leg, imitating an affectionate house cat, but Vincent is not comforted by this gesture at all. He tenses up and keeps alert, something that Bufo finds utterly amusing.

He laughs and then takes a seat right at Vincent's feet.

"Relax! I'm harmless, to you at least."

Vincent crouches down to get at eye level with the Devil Frog.

"Wait, what do you mean by that?"

"I think we both know what I mean by that, Vincent."

Vincent tumbles backwards and lands on his tailbone. He scurries away from Bufo in fear of the truth.

"But ...how?"

Bufo rolls his eyes and tilts his head towards the amulet that's still wrapped around Vincent's wrist.

"That's why you shouldn't be asking demons for any favors. They always come around to bite you later."

Bufo snaps his oversized jaws for a more dramatic effect.

"But I've never asked for -"

Bufo interrupts Vincent before he gets lost in his own thoughts.

"Just think back a little bit kid, I'm sure you remember."

As soon as Bufo finishes, a rush of memories come back to Vincent, more specifically, memories of being chased by those vampiric fish creatures back in the ruins. He did scream at the amulet, but only for a moment. There's no way it could have actually listened to his commands, right?

Bufo stops Vincent and responds as if he could actually hear his thoughts.

"What do you mean, did they actually listen to you? You grew fins for crying out loud! What did you think that was? Puberty??!"

Vincent shakes his head back and forth in disbelief. There's no way Bufo could have known what was going on in his head.

"What was I supposed to do, drown? Get eaten by whatever the hell those things were?"

Vincent pauses for a moment, letting his inquisitiveness get the best of his anger.

"... what were they anyway?"

"Your guess is as good as mine, squirt. I was born right after you made your pact, so I didn't even get a good look at them myself, but man were they scary. Kinda like the pictures in Vatosoa's book."

Vincent realizes that the aquatic vampires and the people in the picture of the Rano are nearly identical, but he is still utterly confused by this situation.

"But aren't you a monster like they are -"

"First of all, ouch. Second of all, I'm about as much of a monster as you are."

At this point, Vincent starts huffing out of frustration.

"So what does that mean? Are you my Guardian? I thought that was something reserved for the princesses around here."

Bufo sighs and crawls into Vincent's lap, making himself more comfortable before answering his question.

"The way I see it, I'm just an extension of yourself, kid. I'm not some big bad magical beast that's going to come in and somehow make things all better for you. However, I am here because you need me to be. Vatosoa needs someone to give her structure, guidance, stability, and all that jazz. Ahitra needs someone she can be soft with behind closed doors, and well, you need someone who's going to give it to you straight, am I right?'

Vincent pauses to ponder this a moment, but Bufo cuts him off before he can get too reflective.

"Maybe there's something pulling the strings behind the scenes. I've got a feeling that we're meant to be working together, squirt. Like something big is coming and you're going to need my help."

He plants his webbed hands onto Vincent's chest to get his attention.

"And that's why you got me, Cinderella!"

He puffs out his chest in a display of pride, but this does little to improve his already small stature. Vincent cups his head in his hands.

"Yay, me..."

Bufo removes his hands from Vincent's chest, taking offense at Vincent's ungratefulness.

"Hey now, I know I'm not some cute little forest creature, but this is no time to start getting picky - !"

Vincent releases his head from his hands and drops them in his lap, looking Bufo straight in the eye.

"No, no, you don't understand! I'm sorry. I didn't mean that. I really do appreciate you keeping an eye on me all this time, but the thing is, Hery told me to never, ever interact with this thing under any circumstances and -"

He gestures at the amulet on his wrist without even thinking. After a moment, his hand freezes along with the rest of his body.

Vincent pauses for a moment. His eyes widen when he realizes what he just said.

"If Hery sees you, he's going to be pissed!"

Bufo picks up on Vincent's panic and comes up with a plan. He hops off of Vincent's lap and puts a decent distance between the two of them.

"Don't worry about the old man. Right now, he loves treating me like a fluffy little pet. I'm willing to use my camouflage and keep it that way if you are. That way I can stick with you guys and spring into action in case any trouble comes around again."

He jumps up and contorts his body in midair once more, this time transforming back into his lemur form at a greater speed than before. Vincent is thankful that he didn't break it down slowly for him this time. When he lands, Bufo gets to work picking out any excess dirt from his tail.

"Besides, everybody else has their own secrets around here. I don't see the harm in keeping this to ourselves -"

Vincent completes his sentence with him, speaking in unison together.

"- at least for now."

Vincent blankly stares at the disguised frog who is ecstatic about being so in sync with him.

"Fine, but no more tongue thing around Hery, got it?"

"No problem!"

After his response, Bufo immediately launches his tongue out to catch a fly moving around the air. He reels it in and munches on it casually while Vincent watches in frustration.

"What? I had to get it out of my system!"

"Fine, let's just get back to bed before he notices that we're gone."

The two of them walk around the corner to find Hery chipping away frantically at one of the limestone pillars. He scratches at the surface like a madman, collecting any of the leftover debris within his lighter. Once that completely fills up, Hery switches over to a cloth bag he had been carrying around with him. He continues on with his burrowing, scraping the surface so diligently that one of his fingernails falls into the pouch and becomes coated in the rest of the dust.

Vincent tries to interrupt this frantic spell.

"Uh Hery, are you okay?"

Hery seems surprised to hear another voice besides his own. He looks over and wipes off his bloody fingers onto his shirt nonchalantly, ignoring his wounds and focusing on Vincent instead.

"Ah, you've awakened, have you?"

Vincent responds to Hery and watches him cautiously. The Rookie mimics Vincent's behavior, climbing up Vincent's shoulder to get a view.

"What are you up to?"

"This? I'm collecting more materials for protection spells. One can never be too cautious, you know? Especially after what we've been through, isn't that right Vincent?"

Hery closes his lighter and pulls on the drawstring of his pouch, securing all of the powder that he gathered.

"Yeah, I guess so."

Vincent is still concerned over Hery's wounds, but he seems unphased. Hery earnestly changes the conversation.

"Now, let's go find your father!"

Hery reaches out and grabs the tip of the rouge rock he had been carving. He pulls it back like some sort of crank and the ground shakes beneath them. The tremors give way to reveal a concealed staircase leading down into the ancient tunnels below. Each one of the steps is coated with the same inscriptions as the tunnel walls.

Hery gestures towards the newly created pathway with excitement.

"Well, lead the way, Vincent."

However, Vincent is hesitant to return the enthusiasm. He grabs onto the Blood Stone with his free hand, covering it from the rest of the group.

"But Hery, if we go back down there, we might get separated again."

Hery walks over and grabs Vincent by the shoulders. This was meant to be a solely comforting gesture, but his strength also straightens Vincent's spine and inadvertently lifts his head up. In this position, Vincent can't help but project confidence.

"As long as you keep the amulet dormant with your crystal, it won't cause you any harm. We will be able to travel anywhere in the world without its influence. You're actively protecting all of us, Vincent."

This brings him some reassurance. Vincent smiles up at Hery, indicating that he's no longer scared of what may come to pass. Hery lets go of him and Vincent makes his way over to the tunnel, still keeping the amulet covered with his free hand. Hery follows loosely behind and they descend the stairs together, ready to face anything that comes their way.

Chapter 51

After a few hours of walking in the same underground tunnels, Vincent, Hery, and the Rookie finally reach their destination. They emerge onto an unfamiliar beach and straddle the shore, anxiously staring at the forbidden island ahead of them. Unlike its sisters, with their pearly white sands and exotic wildlife preserves, this one is barren. It has become a sullen mound in the middle of the cove, where even its most zealous admirers dare not visit. Without any boats or ferries in sight, Vincent wonders how exactly they will reach the peak of the Nosy Zona.

He looks over at Hery, but is surprised by what he sees.

Hery is standing quite a ways behind him, digging his heels into the sand. He is careful to not allow any part of his feet to come in contact with the waves of the bay. Although this behavior is strange in and of itself, Vincent is also confused by Hery's motivations. If there was something dangerous in the water, why didn't Hery warn him about it before he got so close to the shore?

Vincent back pedals a bit until he catches up with Hery again. He then mimics Hery and buries his feet in the sand.

The old man catches a deep breath and exhales.

"We've made it, Vincent. This is one of the holiest sites of our ancestors. I have no doubt that your father is somewhere on this island."

Vincent is clearly excited, but keeps a straight face. He doesn't want to let his emotions get the best of him before he understands fully what he is up against.

"Okay, so what's the plan? How do we get there?"

Hery takes his eyes off of the ocean for the first time during this whole conversation. He looks down at his own feet before looking over at Vincent.

"We have to prove ourselves worthy of the land, but this may prove to be difficult. Only those of royal blood are permitted to traverse this particular island."

"Well, we're screwed."

Hery is clearly thrown off by Vincent's brash comment.

"Come again, Vincent?"

"Look, when Vatosoa was testing me or whatever, she made it very clear that I didn't have the natural magic that all the other royals possessed. She said that my magic was closer to yours..."

Hery scoffs and shakes his head back and forth.

"For one who can see the future, the Princess of the Haran is blind to what is directly in front of her."

Vincent does not answer, so Hery takes the matter into his own hands.

"Come here."

Hery grabs Vincent's hand and leads him closer towards the sea.

"Your father is the man that wields lightning. His blood courses through your veins. Up until now, you've only been using magic that you understand. Magic that is innate to your environment. It makes sense for the son of a biologist, especially one who constantly felt the need to dissect the behavior and motives of others, to foster abilities like the ones you possess. However, you are more than that. You've shown that in the past couple of days that you can remold yourself and create something new. You are embracing the inherent creativity and persistence of life itself. What can be more natural than that?"

Hery pulls Vincent down to the water and has him rest his palm on top of the water's surface.

"Your mother may have made you into who you are, but your father's presence will always be within you."

Before Vincent has any time to respond, he feels tremors underneath his feet. He watches them travel from the beach to the sea, where these vibrations cause the water beneath his hand to move in very strange ways. It scurries around itself and eventually pulls away from Vincent's flesh, as if it is forbidden to even come into contact with him. They are so desperate to get away, that they eventually clear a small path to the ocean floor.

"That's it!"

Hery shouts in excitement. Vincent can't help but celebrate with a great big grin.

"Alright, now just take little steps into the bay."

Vincent obeys and walks into the open space. He notices that with every step closer he gets to the ocean, the more it recedes from him. Vincent takes one more large stride, leaving enough space for Hery to follow.

Hery cautiously plants one foot into the empty space and waits for something to happen. When he's pleased with the inactivity, he continues with his explanation.

"The island has permitted you to enter, so as long as I travel closely behind you, everything will be just fine."

Feeling uplifted from Hery's inspirational words, Vincent is prepared to tackle whatever obstacle may come their way. He smiles at the Rookie on his shoulder and then turns his attention towards Hery.

"Okay, hang on tight!"

He turns right back around and continues forward, trotting along at a brisk pace as if this was one of his morning jogging routes. Hery easily matches his stride and the three of them continue to tread through the bay for a while, that is, until Vincent catches a glimpse of something following them in the water.

"Hold on a minute."

Vincent stops dead in his tracks. Hery clumsily runs into him, but instead of pulling back, he remains close to Vincent, avoiding any contact with the water around them.

"Vincent, we cannot cease our movements. For the spell to work, we must show no change in our desire to approach the island."

"But -"

"We must keep going."

Vincent decides that it's best to listen to Hery, but still keeps an eye on the figure in the water. It moves rapidly, making it hard to follow, but every now and then, Vincent gets a glimpse of its inky black hair.

When they reach the halfway point in their path, the creature decides to reveal itself once more to Vincent. It rushes past him along the watery wall until it stops a few feet away, standing straight while suspended in the water, as if to challenge him. The creature opens his mouth wide, unveiling his vampiric fangs. There's no mistaking his intentions.

Vincent stops, braces himself, and stares down his aquatic adversary. Hery runs into Vincent again, but this time with Vincent's added strength, he ricochets backwards into the ocean.

The moment his skin comes into contact with the water, the monster screeches in order to summon others to help it catch its new prey. However, it is impatient, refusing to wait for backup. It charges Hery in the water at an incredible speed, but luckily, the Rookie is much faster.

He whips his head around and launches his tongue to catch Hery. The tongue wraps around Hery's waist and pulls him back towards the path. When Hery is close enough, the Rookie swings his tongue upwards, sending Hery flying over himself and Vincent. The Rookie strains himself, extending his tongue even further so that Hery lands on the island shore.

In the midst of this relocation process, the water retaliates over this breach of contract. It floods the two of them, but has a greater effect on Bufo. Once the water meets his fur, each strand of hair folds in on itself and turns back into one of the many bumps on his rough green skin.

Bufo reacts quickly to his own transformation and leaps into the air, knowing full well that his true form would crush Vincent if he remained on his shoulder for even a second longer. He grabs Vincent with his tongue while he is still in the air and throws Vincent onto the same beach with Hery.

The moment he sees that Vincent is safe, Bufo finally let's go of his restraint.

He stops fighting his metamorphosis. His body warps and bubbles over, causing Bufo to grow nearly as large as the island itself. His mouth alone could swallow the sea and anything else that inhabits it. The Devil Frog lands at last with a pronounced thud, causing the ground beneath him to rupture and creating tidal waves massive enough to push all the other monsters back towards the mainland.

Bufo shouts over his shoulder to Vincent, his voice booming and shaking the trees.

"Go now!"

Vincent jumps to his feet, cups his hands over his mouth, and calls out to Bufo.

"But what's going to happen to you?"

Bufo lets out a bellowing laugh that could be felt miles from shore.

"Don't worry about me, kid. I'll catch up later, okay?"

With that, Bufo faces the front once more, standing tall against an army of aquatic vampires. He scans through the crowd quickly until he finds the one that initially discovered the three of them. Once he locates it, Bufo attacks him with his tongue, launching it with enough force to completely pierce through the creature's body in one blow.

Seeing this immobilizes the rest of the brigade out of fear. Bufo takes this opportunity to swing his tongue back and forth indiscriminately, entangling more and more monsters in their sticky demise. It isn't long before Bufo's tongue becomes completely coated in these marine beasts, like flies stuck in a trap.

Bufo retracts his tongue and slurps down his latest meal. He smacks his lips together and burps so loudly that it becomes his battle cry.

Chapter 52

With full confidence in Bufo, Vincent gathers his things into his backpack and thrusts it onto his shoulders. He also tightens the chains on the amulet around his crystal wrist so that it can't escape during the madness. Once he is put together, he quickly dusts himself off and shouts over at a stabilizing Hery, who is still in shock over seeing the Devil Frog.

"C'mon! We can make a break for it if -"

A familiar voice rings out through the chaos.

"Stop right there!"

Vincent turns around and spots Ahitra standing a few feet away from them on the beach. She stands there alone. Spot is nowhere to be found.

Another woman calls out to Vincent from behind him.

"We can't let you go any further, Vincent."

Vincent turns his head to see Vatosoa standing to his right. Like Ahitra, her Guardian is nowhere to be found. She is clearly still tired and disheveled from their last encounter.

"What the hell is all of this?"

Ahitra is the first to answer his question.

"You can't go see your father, Vincent. It's too dangerous -"

Vincent screams at the two of them.

"Too dangerous? Really?! Nah, you guys are assholes! Why should I listen to either of you?"

The Devil Frog responds to his master's emotions without a second thought. Bufo, finished with one enemy and ready to face the next, turns around with one giant earth shattering footstep at a time. Once he is forward facing, he lets out a piercing screech so loud that everyone on the beach is forced to protect their ears with their hands.

Vatosoa screams in fear.

"What in the world is that?!!"

However, Ahitra lowers her hands and acts out of pure reflex. She shoots out powerful vines from her hands and wraps them around Bufo, pulling with all of her might in order to drag him down towards the ground. Bufo refuses to submit, and the two of them grapple back and forth before he shouts out to Vincent.

"I said move, squirt! I'll keep them busy for as long as I can!"

He launches his tongue at an unsuspecting Vatosoa, but Ahitra reacts quickly, catching it with her vines before it can even touch Vatosoa. She now has one hand on Bufo and another on his tongue, giving him the chance to shimmy out of her trap.

"Soa, a little help here?!!"

Vatosoa is forced to take her eyes off Vincent to come to Ahitra's rescue.

"Oh right, sorry!"

Vatosoa swipes her foot along the sand, sending a wall of it flying towards Bufo. Because his jaws are wide open, the majority of the sand gets in his mouth, causing him to reel in his tongue in order to spit it out.

Vincent chooses to take this opportunity to flee from the scene. He grabs Hery by the arm and tugs forcibly.

"We have to go, now!"

Hery still seems like he's far off in some sort of trance.

"But the princesses -"

"Hery!"

Vincent's eyes start to water as they plead with Hery to follow through with their mission. Against his better judgement, Hery picks up Vincent and carries him towards the center of the island at full speed. They run until the beach is no longer in sight.

They run over a collection of hills before they finally reach the base of the peak and are immediately greeted by a similar set of stairs as the ones they found back in the Rouge Desert. Vincent leaps from Hery's arms and takes his first step. The script on the base of the stairs illuminates in a brilliant gold light as soon as they meet Vincent's touch. It spreads up the staircase that seems to reach the heavens, beckoning Vincent to climb. They are ready to welcome him home.

Although Vincent feels like nothing else exists in this moment, the world around him feels the effects of the battle between Bufo and the other princesses. The mountain itself trembles, sending rocks tumbling down the stairs at Hery and Vincent. However, this does not deter Vincent. He gracefully swerves in between boulders, continuing his ascension until he sees some sort of entrance in the distance. There seems to be a hidden chamber carved into the mound midway up the summit.

Despite all of the shaking, Hery finds his footing and runs up the stairs past Vincent in order to turn himself into a barricade. Once he reaches the doorway, Hery spreads his arms out wide and plants his feet into the earth.

"Vincent, are you sure you want to go through with this?"

Vincent is taken aback by this gesture, but does not let it deter him or throw him off balance.

"Hery, after everything I've been through so far, why in the world would I change my mind?!"

A couple of large boulders fall once again, one on either side of them, and another landing directly behind Vincent, preventing him from turning back. Their impact makes the two of them wobble, but only one of them seems concerned.

Hery's face turns pale, but he continues on with his warning.

"I have never seen the Princess of the Nofon and the Princess of the Haran ever agree on a key issue, let alone leave their homes without their Guardians. Something's wrong. There's no way of knowing what is beyond those doors! Can't you see they were trying to warn us about -"

In the midst of the argument, a new husky voice interrupts Hery and pushes through the chaos.

"Vincent? Is that you?"

Upon hearing this, Vincent's eyes widen and begin to water. Time seems to stop for him and nothing else could possibly matter.

"Move!"

Vincent pushes Hery out of the way without much regard for his well being and sprints into the room. In spite of Vincent's rash behavior, Hery chases after him with the intention of protecting him against whatever would be waiting for them on the other side.

Chapter 53

Vincent runs into the chamber where he is immediately swallowed by a massive collection of wooden sculptures, all resembling men and women standing atop of intricately carved poles. The carvings consist of complex geometric patterns with purposeful holes that allow the viewer to peer through to the other side. However, the view of the base of the statues is what's really troubling Vincent.

The floor is completely covered in what appears to be a mixture of animal and human bones, most notably, the horns of various types of cattle and the ribs of human beings. A draft enters the room and causes a horrible musical effect, combining the scratching of bones along the floor with the riffs from the statues, transforming them into makeshift pan flutes.

The only thing keeping Vincent separated from the artwork and its aftermath is a vertical strip of elevated pathing that seemed to endlessly continue, that is, if it wasn't for the current obstruction in the way.

Off in the distance, Vincent sees a man with a long afro lying face down on the floor. He groans in pain for a bit, but afterwards remains completely still to the point where Vincent can only assume the worst.

"DAD!"

Vincent races over towards the man without hesitation. He wastes no time breaking, or rather, sliding next to the body on the floor. He places his fingers on the man's neck, desperately searching for a pulse when Hery breaks his concentration.

"Vincent, stay away from-"

"Hery, you've always been such a fool…"

A monstrous hand shoots out from beneath the man and strikes Vincent's throat with the grip of a viper. He plunges his nails deep into Vincent's neck until they draw blood before raising him up into the air with immeasurable strength. The man takes his time getting back on his feet while Vincent gasps for air. He lifts Vincent higher and higher, his feet desperately dangling to reconnect with the ground.

"To think that you've brought me a second sacrificial lamb, you really are my most loyal servant, aren't you?"

Tears stream down Vincent's cheeks and Hery can no longer take it.

"Let that boy go. NOW!"

A hoarse, gravelly laugh drips from the man's mouth and oozes onto the floor.

"I'd hardly think you would be the one to give orders in this situation, slave."

Hery charges towards the man at a breakneck speed, but is no match for the stranger. He summons a bolt of lightning down from the sky so quickly that it singes the tips of Hery's hair. Hery's tumbles back from the sheer force of the lightning strike, followed by the rubble that used to constitute the cave's ceiling.

Light pours in from above and illuminates the stranger's features. Despite his soft features, something menacing lurked deep beneath his gentle eyes.

"Tsk Tsk Tsk… but we had a deal, didn't we? You bring me the archeologist's son, and I return my daughter from her hiding place. Don't tell me you're abandoning your mistress in her time of need? "

Vincent sees Hery fall to the ground and somehow manages to find the courage to stammer in between breaths.

"Who… are… you?"

"My, my, a tenacious little thing aren't you? Hery, I must compliment you on your trial-by-error training methods. They always produce outstanding results."

The stranger tightens his grip around Vincent's neck, leaving Vincent gasping for air. He revels in this torture.

"Oh, he didn't tell you? Your father's been dead for nearly two decades. Yes, this is his vessel, but he's never been here. It was me, all along. Surveying the islands. Chatting with those vapid heiresses. Keeping tabs on you and your prying mother, that is, until the day she discovered the truth."

He interrupts his monologue once he spots Vincent's backpack. The corner of one of his mother's journals is sticking out from the bag, enraging the stranger to the point where he rips it off Vincent's back in one pull, leaving the straps resting on Vincent's shoulders.

"That vile woman noticed the changes in her husband after his first trip back from the island."

The man lets out another guttural laugh as he reminisces.

"I guess I must have scared her!"

He chucks the backpack and all of its contents away from himself and Vincent. Then, as it hangs in midair, he summons another lightning bolt to strike it down, sending it ablaze like a comet burning up in the atmosphere. Once it finally lands, it turns to ash once it makes contact with the pavement.

"The poor thing did everything she could to keep you away from me, and here you are, running into my arms. I wish she could've seen this, but alas, you've already gone ahead and finished her off for me. Thank you, Vincent!"

Vincent freezes out of anger and shock. He no longer fights to resist the grip of the stranger, but instead, uses all of his energy to throw a punch at the stranger's face. The stranger instantly blocks his attack with his free hand, wrapping the palm of his hand around Vincent's entire fist.

"Oh! And you've brought me a gift!"

The man pretending to be Vincent's father grabs the amulet from Vincent's wrist and tears it away from him. He then slaps the Blood Stone forcibly onto his chest. Although they've consistently hunted after Vincent throughout his journey, the thorns in the amulet's chain happily sink their teeth into their new host. The chains crawl up the man's chest until they attach themselves around his neck like a gruesome pendant.

He shouts in excitement.

"Finally!"

The ruby center of the Cursed One glows brighter than ever before. Its usual hypnotic swirl hastens to the point where it looks like a spiraling tornado. It spreads outward and covers the man in an eerie red light. The redness calls forth suppressed tattoos of the same pigment to coat his skin once more in all matters of complicated words and mysterious symbols. The permanent spell work also enhances his overall physique, enlarging his muscles to the point where they tear away at his clothes. The transformation is complete once the light reaches his hair, dying it a vibrant red that bursts around him like the setting sun.

He runs his fingers through his hair triumphantly, the true manifestation of his crown.

"I, King Njaka, have returned!"

A cascade of lightning rains down from the heavens and circles around Vincent and the Dark King. When it strikes the ground in various spots, the lightning bolts reveal a hidden summoning circle that had been drawn underneath their feet this whole time. The powder beneath ignites and comes alive with heavenly fire.

"And now that I have a powerful blood heir once again, I can rectify the ritual and achieve my destiny! My pesky daughter's curse prevents me from true resurrection, but now that I have you, little boy, I will continue to rule over all that is mundane, malicious and magical for eternity!"

Portals appear through the openings in the sculptures surrounding them, leading to a vast, unknown realm of shadows. The same mysterious fog that continuously shackles Lalaina trickles into the room from these openings and crawls towards Vincent. They wrap around his ankles and Vincent struggles to break free.

The Dark King begins his incantations, his voice weaving in and out of the portals until it slithers its way through every corner of the room.

"Oh, Essence of the Other, accept my son, a true descendant of my people, as an offering! He is the true culmination of our strength, from his inception, to his new relationship to the land and all that it provides! Feast on his soul, and in exchange, grant me the power to conquer this realm and all that inhabits it!"

The smoke creeps up Vincent's body until it engulfs his face. King Njaka loosens his hold on Vincent's neck just enough for him to reflexively gasp for a breath of air. Instead, he inhales the full brunt of the smog until it completely fills his lungs.

Hery panics and charges at the Dark King, arms opened wide to grab Vincent from his clutches. However, it is too late. The ritual has already been completed, with all of Vincent's vitality being absorbed by King Njaka. The Dark King releases his grasp on Vincent and drops him onto the floor. His lifeless body flops about like a rag doll. Instead of avenging Vincent out of anger, he uncharacteristically shifts from anger to pure sorrow over his fallen companion. Rather than follow through with his attack on King Njaka, Hery changes his trajectory, scooping Vincent's corpse off of the floor and cradling it in his arms.

Ahitra and Vatosoa finally arrive. Ahitra is the first to enter, with Vatosoa not too far behind, carefully carrying a limp regular sized Bufo in her arms. They sprint into the chamber, but stop dead in their tracks once they see the Dark King fully actualized in the flesh.

He cackles at their fear.

"Hello, girls. I've missed you so-"

However, once the Dark King sees Bufo lying in Vatosoa's arms, all the color leaves his face. Frustration consumes him. He does his face to disguise his concern, but ultimately decides to withdraw in order to gather his thoughts. King Njaka pulls down his last lightning bolt from the sky and lets it strike him to his core. It shatters him into pieces and carries him away to the heavens, a safe haven where no one else can follow.

A few seconds pass, but each of them drag on for an eternity. The gravity of the situation keeps everyone glued in place, looking for some divine intervention on how to recover from this scene.

Rain pours down triumphantly after his exit, leaving behind the last remnants of the Dark King. It pelts the ground below, causing raindrops to ricochet off the stone as well as the now crushed bones underneath. The residue forms a heavy mist, covering the entire room and concealing each of them from one another. However, one figure emerges from the mist, clear and distinct from the rest.

Ahitra is the first to break the silence.

"Lalaina?!"

She takes a few steps forward and now they can all clearly see her wild red hair from behind the clouds. Almost simultaneously, both Vatosoa and Ahitra run over to greet their long lost friend. They embrace her, squeezing her tightly both out of affection and also to make sure she isn't just a mirage.

Once they can confirm that she really has returned to them, the two of them fawn over her uncontrollably. However, even through their excited praise, Lalaina can only focus on one thing. She attentively takes Bufo from Vatosoa's arms and cradles him against her chest.

"Please, let me see my brother."

The two girls grow quiet and cease their celebration. They lead her back towards Hery, who hasn't taken his eyes off Vincent this entire time.

Lalaina weeps at the sight of her beloved protector watching over Vincent's corpse. She leaves the two princesses behind to attend to her sibling and her champion in their time of need. The girls inherently feel slighted, but this jealous feeling leaves both of them once they hear the pain in Lalaina's voice.

"He's gone…"

Ahitra speaks up, trying to comfort Lalaina in some way.

"But you can bring him back, can't you? You've done it before and you were able to keep yourself alive all this time."

Lalaina squats down and takes a hold of Vincent's hand, rubbing her thumb across the back of his hand subconsciously to give his icy skin some warmth.

"This isn't like the others. He didn't perish in some battle or die of natural causes. Vincent was sacrificed in a ritual. I was as well, but even with my regenerative powers, I could only sustain myself for so long before being cast back into the shadows. I can't conjure him back if someone else is already holding him hostage. Right now, it's feasting on his soul. The only way to tear him away from the Other is to distract it with someone else."

While the other princesses attentively listen to Lalaina's explanation, Hery is sobbing with Vincent's body in his arms. His head rests in Hery's lap while Hery's fingers gently comb through his hair. His touch may be gentle, but it is powerful enough to resonate with Vincent even in his current state. Vincent raises his hand even though his soul is captive among the shadows, feeling around for Hery's invisible hand.

Hery shouts without hesitation.

"Take me instead!"

Vatosoa's voice shrills out of panic.

"But your power isn't strong enough to withstand their influence! You'll be devoured right away, and once they notice that you're not what they bargained for, they'll be sure to come back and find who they were promised! You aren't strong enough to change his fate!"

"No, but he is."

Hery swallows his tears and tries his best to appeal to the other princesses.

"The creature in your arms is a testament to what he can do. Where you three needed your Guardians to be gifted to you, he engendered his own when he felt truly threatened. King Njaka recognizes this and is afraid… If there is a way to stop all of this madness, it begins and ends with Vincent."

Lalaina moves Vincent's hand and rests it on top of his chest. She then takes her free hand and lays it on Hery's shoulder.

"Are you sure this is what you want?"

Hery nods and then addresses the rest of the group.

"It's your job to protect him, all of you."

They all agree in silence and Lalaina gets to work, trying her best to suppress her emotions. She places Bufo above Vincent's head, his favorite lookout spot, while using her new free hand to reconnect with Vincent's. Hery notices her crying and whispers to her.

"This is my last gift to you, Princess. Please let me do this. I am sorry that I've caused you so much pain. That's a burden that I've carried my entire life, and I've made so many horrible mistakes trying to rectify what I've done. If this is the only way I can make things right, then this is what has to be. Let me make this up to you, to both of you."

Lalaina trembles.

"I'm not ready to lose you, either…"

"You won't, Princess. I'll always be here with you… But right now he needs you quite a bit more than you ever needed me..."

Hery smiles at her and cups her small hand in his.

"Trust me."

Her eyes swell with tears as they shift to a fiery golden hue.

"Farewell, Your Majesty."

Once the pigment completely engulfs her, she swipes her left hand over Vincent's body, pulling out the smoky chains that bound his lungs together. She then swirls the smoke over her head like a tempest, allowing it to spread throughout the room and swallow both herself and Hery. Along with Vincent's body, Lalaina transports the three of them to the Other, where Vincent's soul is currently on full display.

He hangs there, suspended in midair, while all sorts of intangible creatures strike from the shadows, taking small pieces of his soul with every bite. Lalaina takes a few steps forward, dragging Hery limply alongside her. She illuminates the scene with her mere presence, forcing the smoke to recede further and further into the night. When she is close enough, Lalaina pulls Vincent's soul off of its mount and leads Hery towards the stand. He attaches himself to the spoke emotionlessly, as if he's been induced into some hypnotic trance. While Hery's busy attaching himself to his own skewer, Lalaina turns around and carries Vincent's soul back to his body effortlessly, like it's weightless in this space.

Once she is far enough away, her light is no longer able to protect Hery from the monsters at bay. The darkness devours him and the creatures begin their attack once more. Lalaina can hear the snapping of jaws and the tearing of flesh as she lays Vincent's soul on top of his body. The noises become too much for her to bear.

Her eyes flutter and her vision blurs. She becomes dizzy and drops to her knees as her eyes return to their regular state. Lalaina can faintly hear Vatosoa and Ahitra call out to her in the distance before she falls backwards. Luckily, Vatosoa is there to catch her before she hits the stone.

"Lalaina, are you alright?!"

Before she can respond to Vatosoa, she hears Vincent cough and wheeze. Lalaina can see Ahitra watch over him carefully as his body is getting used to breathing again. This brings her some sense of comfort, but this moment is fleeting. She looks around the room and becomes saddened when she sees that Hery is nowhere to be found.

Bufo slowly crawls up to her and affectionately rubs his head against her leg, thanking her for everything she's done.

About The Author

Kassidy VanGundy was born and raised in South Bend, IN, a city juxtaposed between Chicago and a sea of cornfields. Built with a set of wings, she set out to see as many parts of the world as she could, from Athens to Sao Paulo. Although, she admits that heat lightning and driving on dirt roads occasionally tempts her to come back home. Right now, she's nesting on the East Coast with her beautiful husband, Douglas, who is constantly subjected to chapter reviews of her writing, especially during the development of her first book, Cursed Fate. In 2020, Kassidy VanGundy graduated from the Pardee School of Global Studies at Boston University with her Masters in International Affairs and a specialization in Diplomacy, where she also taught multiple courses on sustainable development within the earth and environment department. Prior to this experience, she graduated from Hanover College with her Bachelor's degree in International Relations and a minor in English. She incorporates everything she's learned from both her academic and personal experiences into her work.